D1520743

Taffy

Printed by CreateSpace, An Amazon.com Company.
Available from Amazon.com and other book stores.

Made in the United States of America

Cover Design: Sanura Jayshan of J-shan Art Studio*
Page Layout: Milmon F. Harrison of milmonDesign
Project Editor: Michelle Browning of Magpie Editing

Author's Photo: Derrick Pearson of One Way Photos
Make-up: Vadia Rhodes, M.U.A.; Makeupbyvadia@gmail.com

ISBN-10: 1523298251
ISBN-13: 978-1523298259

*While J-Shan Art Studio created the overall cover, special recognition is given to Dr. Milmon F. Harrison for the creation of Taffy's face

ALSO BY SUZETTE D. HARRISON

When Perfect Ain't Possible
Living on the Edge of Respectability

DEDICATION

To my paternal grandmother, Ms. Jeanetta Louise Gulley, whom I never had the pleasure of meeting: brief telephone calls were what we had. Still, I smiled through every one. I've asked God to bless me to meet you in heaven when my work on earth is done.
I love you, Grandmother.

ADVANCE PRAISE FOR TAFFY

"Suzette D. Harrison has written a masterpiece. In her novel, *Taffy*, she has written what most novelists aspire to and never do achieve. Reading it provides an experience most readers incessantly search for and rarely find. This book is beautifully written, rich, and deeply musical. Ms. Harrison has a great ear for dialogue and a gift for humor. Her sense of language is refreshing in its originality, her use of syntax inventive. But make no mistake about it, this is a deep book, which will take you to the heart of the human stain. It is a work for the heart as well as the mind. The irresistible urge to turn its pages stems from a sense of both celebration of the language and terror for its inhabitants. Centered around the small, southern Black town of Bledsoe, in 1935, *Taffy* takes us into a world and a time few of us still living have ever known, and includes a varied cast of deftly developed characters, but even given those who are despicable, diabolical, and even maniacal, this is a setting even fewer of us will want to leave. *Taffy* is a book to pass on to the generations. Thank you, Ms. Harrison."

–David Covin, Blue Nile Press

"Suzette Harrison has written a novel rich with Southern charm. *Taffy*, aptly titled after the protagonist, is a story that will appeal to [readers] ages 20-100. Set in the 1930s, [when visiting the town] where Taffy's family is from, *Taffy* unearths explosive truths about her husband and herself. At first glance, you might believe this is a story about a beautiful, young woman who lived a tough childhood only to marry an older, womanizing man. Oh, but it is so much more than that!

Layered with intricate plots and sub-plots, all of Ms. Harrison's characters are larger than life and leap off the page at you. However, you will easily identify one or more of your own family members. Another superb job by Ms. Harrison in blending the intricacies of personalities and family into characters we can't get enough of!"

–Anna Dennis, author of
"Who Will Hear My Screams"

Taffy

SUZETTE D. HARRISON

Up North

JUNE 1935

PROLOGUE

Blood has memory. And memory, power; revealing secrets to those who heed. Crying, vying for attention—perhaps affection—blood unfolds stories worth hearing.

His blood spoke in saturated tones. Stripped from his body, it hollered long before hers. The forebear's watered the ground, splashing seeds that would one day become his nation—beautifully black, powerful, tall like trees.

She fell from one, fresh fruit nearly devoured. But her roots went deep, nourishing and fortifying despite the bleak. She would flourish. Or die trying.

Try she did, to outpace Evil loping alongside her—relentless and unrestricted despite the light of day—feverishly praying the train would wait.

Fully focused on boarding train and saving self, she was singular in intent. But Evil was bold, unbeautiful, harassing spirit and clouding mind. Yet, she stayed the course, eyes fixed on the Colored car where insistent, brown hands waved from open windows, urging her, "Come!"

Luggage proved weighty anchors at her side. Choosing freedom over finery, she let luggage go and raced towards the red-capped porter powerfully straining towards her from aboard the departing train.

Bending low, the porter extended a strong arm, full lips moving, pouring vital speech sleep prevented her from interpreting. Yet, the hot cadence and smooth rhythm of his words were milk and honey in which to bask and bathe.

She reached. He received. Fingers met and power collided.

With a grip firm and familiar enough to invoke tears, her porter hoisted her upward.

That's when Evil leapt, snarling, refusing to let her future intercept her past.

Ripping, tearing with talons forged in fire, Evil wailed, meaning to feast and keep.

Bloody streams rolled down her back. Saturating. Reminding. Blood spoke of struggles past, and sorrows gone. Of forebears who'd battled and overcome. So she chose to fight, refused to die.

Turning, looking Evil in its eye, she waged a war with weapons of soul and mind. Power came, flowing from her back, a crimson flood that refused to forget.

Blood was memory. Blood was strength.

CHAPTER ONE

She bolted upright, riding the terror of red dreams. Sweat between her breasts, teeth clenched against a jagged scream, Taffy tossed bedcovers aside, struggling to breathe.

She needed to sit an eternal minute—head cradled in hands, calming a raging heartbeat, dissecting a blood-soaked dream and resituating herself in perfect peace. But Taffy Bledsoe Freeman had sense enough in her twenty-three-year-old self to know heaven had spoken, setting fire beneath her feet.

Snapping on the lamp, Taffy quickly consulted her timepiece atop the bedside table, gray eyes squinting. She could make the early train. Barely.

She sprang from bed, smoothing linens over loneliness until order was restored. Straightening, propping, Taffy rushed about her room taking great pains to ensure her true self wasn't left behind. Heart never invested in this, Alfredo's arctic abode, Taffy assessed her finished handiwork without sorrow or sentiment. Strategically, she'd planned her disappearance after the festival next week. But if the red dream was God speaking, then her day of salvation had come. Staying a moment longer would feed Taffy's seven-year battle against sluggish death. Leaving was life.

How will Mr. Al react? she wondered without truly caring.

Like the hellion he is. Certainly, Alfredo Freeman—an unwanted husband of seven years—would pull-the-fool when learning of her desertion. But his antics would stem from power's departure, not the loss of non-existent love.

Taffy nearly smiled, imagining Alfredo's destroying the door lock that prevented his taking what she wouldn't give. Storming his young wife's chambers, the fifty-year-old undertaker would find a façade of normalcy, much like their marriage. Upon closer inspection Alfredo would see value was absent. Clothing Taffy hadn't worn since entering their forced marriage and coming Up North when just sixteen, hung limp in her chifforobe. Possessions of importance had been covertly shipped, bit by bit, to Cousin Gracie in the Windy City where stolen freedom waited. Now, only near-empty perfume atomizers and worthless cosmetics lined Taffy's bureau. Ghostly props whispering of a broken past, the useless and unwanted remained.

Alfredo named her both. Worthless. Unwanted. Claimed the dead in his deep freeze held more warmth. Preferring their company, he charmed cold corpses wholly submitted to his control. Unlike the 'dry-hearted, iron-backed wife with ice between her thighs'. So he constantly spewed—perverse words landing like bricks against Taffy's back. But Taffy never broke. Alfredo's estimation didn't matter. Never had.

Still, he won't let me go.

Despite her alleged failures, Alfredo ignored repeated pleas, refused Taffy's leaving. God was perfect; matrimony need not be. As long as Alfredo breathed there'd be no terminating Taffy's mandated misery.

I ain't dissolving no marriage so you can lay up with some nigga somewhere! You ain't no use to me but I'm keeping you on account of holy vows.

"Alfredo wouldn't know holy from hell," Taffy quietly bristled, recalling this response to her most recent request for resolution. Seven years of begging hadn't appealed to his immoral senses. She'd stopped pleading and took to praying, planning.

Taffy snorted. "And nobody said nothing about 'laying up' somewhere." It was a constant accusation, Alfredo's falsely projecting his own unfaithfulness onto her.

Looseness wasn't in her. Taffy wasn't dumb or numb to a Colored man's charms. Most knew she was Freeman's wife. Knowledge didn't keep some from making lusty interests known. Just the same, Taffy kept her legs together and came home.

Pushing trouble aside and reaching for her robe, Taffy cocooned herself in silk. Fastening her robe belt at her waist, she unlocked her bedroom door. Quickly, she stuffed the key to self-preservation back into the valley of her full breasts where it dangled on a slim, silver chain. It was her nightly assertion—this locked portal—Taffy's way of resisting connubial bondage and keeping what she could.

Stealthily, Taffy slid suitcases into the cool, dark corridor where she was greeted by darkness before dawn. Struggling to secure bulky luggage beneath her arms, Taffy cautiously proceeded as if her cat-like eyes were truly feline.

She need only deposit the luggage downstairs and call for a cab before dressing quickly. But approaching the stairwell, Taffy paused outside the closed bathroom door, arrested by the sound of feminine humming within.

Obviously, Alfredo had kept company last night, and company hadn't quit. Taffy was unmoved by her husband's endless infidelities. *Better them than me,* was Taffy's philosophy. Still…Alfredo's dalliances were usually gone before the crick-crack of day. When had he become bold enough to allow such evidence to keep?

The commode flushed. Sink water flowed. The bathroom door opened, pouring a young woman into view. A symphony occurred as a piece of Taffy's luggage and the young woman's sheet plummeted simultaneously, noiseless and crashing. There was a responsive shuffling behind Alfredo's closed door as the young woman stood naked, mouth moving frantically yet wordless and empty. Naked and backlit by bathroom light, she was an eerie angel of interrupted innocence.

Taffy's heart lurched realizing the young woman was a mere child with breasts beyond her years. They eyed each other silently until Taffy—conscious of a frenetic haze of color bathing the child—spoke, her recognition dawning. "You're Miz Truly's girl…Janie?" Taffy's rich alto hummed softly.

"Y-y-es…but no, ma'am…I'm Jonnie Mae…Janie Rae's my 'lil sis…," Jonnie Mae stuttered, peering up at the chocolate-skinned woman known for her sunshine smile and ladylike ways, whose infamous eyes now glowed ghostly gray.

Retrieving the fallen sheet, Taffy smelled the girl's fear, born of rumors and this early morning encounter. Careful to keep her gift to herself since living Up North, Taffy had still been dubbed a 'witch.' Inhaling Jonnie Mae's panic, Taffy knew the girl itched for her mama, and was intentionally gentle when wrapping the fallen sheet about Jonnie Mae's trembling nudity. Taffy intended calming words, but a bedroom door flew open and the undertaker emerged, cursing the girl for making noise enough to wake his wife.

Indeed, there his wife stood.

Alfredo and Taffy locked eyes.

"Miz Freeman…" Struggling with pants tangled about his ankles,

Alfredo emitted lurid smells of liquor and lust. "Why y-y-ou up at this ungodly hour?"

"The hour's not the only ungodly thing here," Taffy shot, stormy eyes curious and shifting. She'd never seen her husband naked. Doing so now left her disinterested.

Yanking up and fastening pants about a swollen paunch of a belly, a cornered Alfredo turned on Jonnie Mae. "Told you, don't be stomping 'round like you scaring snakes in route to no outhouse! Learn yo'self to approach an indoor toilet quiet-like!"

The frightened girl stuttered useless apologies under Alfredo's menacing advance.

Taffy quickly planted herself between husband and lover, levying a look that could wither leaves. "Don't you touch her," Taffy warned, knowing Alfredo had already done more than. She turned to the girl. "Get dressed and come with me."

"No, thank you, ma'am," the girl timidly replied beneath Alfredo's volcanic objections.

"You can't stay here," Taffy insisted, trying to maneuver the child towards the stairs, but Jonnie Mae planted her young feet like a tree, stiff and unyielding.

Knowing firsthand the perplexities of living bound, Taffy delved the eyes of a child perched at maturity. Taffy saw familiar entrapment, the weight of undesired alliance, and the futility of pleading. Still, she did. "Jonnie Mae, *please...*"

The child quivered at the tenderness in Taffy's voice. Studying the hardwood floor, she shook her head, refusing aid and choosing to stay. "I'll be okay, Miz Freeman."

Sick of dwelling with death and deception, Taffy breathed into Jonnie Mae's ear a truth the child had yet to perceive. "God made you better than this." Unable to afford the luxury of time, Taffy grabbed her luggage and rushed downstairs, wondering who to call to remove a child from her husband's unholy house.

CHAPTER TWO

L ack-of-life was everywhere. An unwanted perfume. Bitterness on the tongue. It was more than Alfredo's profession. Death was his passion and purpose.
With *Freeman's Funeral Home* on the first floor, their living quarters above, death was Taffy's housemate, coating the skin, seeping, like seasoning, into the meals she made. Death even masqueraded itself as a companion worth conversation.

Alfredo readied bodies for internment, but Taffy heard the joy of those who'd lived well, the moaning of those who'd been cut down. NuNu—the paternal grandmother with whom Taffy shared a gift and a name—taught precious mysteries. Consequently, Taffy didn't fear hereafter or the transition required to arrive. She was, however, terrified of remaining with Alfredo, merely existing, forfeiting life.

Dropping suitcases in the vestibule, Taffy snatched up the telephone and impatiently waited for the operator to connect the call, praying a cab would come quickly though the sun had yet to rise. She ignored the sounds of Alfredo lumbering down the stairs before the connection was complete.

Intent on polishing appearances, his undertaker's voice dripped insincerity. "Miz Freeman, now...ain't no need getting bent outta shape. All this ain't meaning much..."

Finding Taffy on the phone, Alfredo abandoned dulcet tones best suited for the bereaved. "Ain't nobody up this time of morning 'cept farmers and fools so who the hell you calling?!" Stomping across the distance, he snatched the telephone, slamming it onto the foyer table. "And where the hell you going with all them damn bags at my front door?"

Taffy's tone was distant, cottony. "Home for Founders' Festival."

"Found-a-festival my ass! That foolishness ain't 'til next week," Alfredo snorted, belittling the celebration marking Bledsoe's sixtieth year of existence, a miraculous phenomenon for a town founded by freed slaves and bearing Taffy's family name.

Taffy wore defiance like a gown. "Next week came a little early."

"You in a rush 'cause of whatchu seen?" Alfredo's sudden laugh was weak, watery. "Jonnie Mae ain't nothing."

Taffy's eyes flashed fire. "She may be a toy to you, but that's *somebody's* child! I've never cared about you sneaking painted ladies up the backstairs, Mr. Al. Or about that Hughes Street brothel you pour your pennies into. But Lord knows," Taffy quietly seethed, "I care about a little girl in a grown man's bed—"

"That "girl's" more woman at fourteen than you'll ever be," Alfredo interrupted. "Crawl on up in my bed—that ain't even your dam business, by the way—and let her teach *you* something."

Certain hate wasn't a virtue, Taffy breathed deeply. "Take her home."

"Sure thing, Miz Freeman. Soon's you do your wifely duties. 'Til then my conjugal sins gonna sit at your feet."

Spirit flinching, Taffy marched into the kitchen. Yanking open a cupboard, Taffy extracted a hidden envelope. With near reverence, Taffy placed the envelope atop the table as Alfredo entered the room. "Sign them." Like an afterthought, Taffy managed, "Please."

Scowling, Alfredo withdrew forms and read. Smiling, he moved to the gas stove. Taffy couldn't cross the room fast enough to prevent Alfredo from holding the document above the lit stove with malicious glee.Papers dipped in fire, he faced her—fumes of burnt hope wafting aimlessly.

"How long you been holding these here papers, sitting up waiting for a right time?" Alfredo waved the incinerating document. Ashes floated on air. "Like I'm in some kinda compromised predicament! Done told you before, but I'mma tell you again. This here," he waved an arm indicating all he surveyed, "is *my* house bought by *your* grandmother to keep you out her life. You," Alfredo jabbed a finger towards Taffy, "ain't nothing but a female with no voice and no say." Tossing useless papers in the kitchen sink, Alfredo stepped towards his wife, emboldened by decimated dreams. "You ain't *never* quitting me." Voice relaxing, leering, Alfredo visually savored Taffy like she was little more than meat. "I own you, Miz Freeman, lessen *I* say otherwise."

Gaze fixed on papers shriveling, Taffy silently thought, *Or until one of us dies.*

CHAPTER THREE

She found no evidence of Jonnie Mae. Grateful, thinking the child had escaped down the backstairs, Taffy bathed swiftly without the luxury of NuNu's homemade ginger-and-honeysuckle bath salts. Taffy moved expeditiously. Home was beckoning. She needed its purity, wide open spaces and skies so blue only God could've colored them. Taffy would stay only long enough to collect her Angel Baby before re-boarding a train to that Windy City where vanishing came easy.

The Windy City was secondary. Harlem had her heart. But Taffy's plans had been altered when, three months ago, March, Harlem erupted in riots, leaving Taffy's hopes in flames. She'd wept at the radio's broadcast. Brown Harlemites had exploded, unleashing centuries of pent-up pain over a child's apparent demise.

He was somebody's sweet little pickpocket thieving from a local five-and-dime. Mishandled by management and brutalized by the law, an ambulance arrived, leaving when a hearse crept onto the scene. Hell flared and Harlem broke, supposing the child had died. New outrage met old and Colored folks waged war—aiming projectiles at police brutality, rent gauging, crippling inequities, and each other in a first-ever intra-race riot of its kind. Businesses were destroyed. Looting was widespread. When smoke cleared rumors were revealed. That precious pickpocket-of-a-child lived. Three others lay dead—murdered by mayhem—and Taffy's sleep grew wet, the blood of that 1935 spring day saturating dreams and mind.

God no longer waited for her in Harlem. Riot's fire destroying the very boardinghouse where Taffy arranged to rent a room was a clear sign. In the chaotic aftermath, the landlord and the six months' rent Taffy had mailed in advance vanished, leaving Taffy distressed and numb. Now, Cousin Gracie had offered a second chance.

"Lord, You sure it's my time?" Taffy dared to question, rubbing fragrant oil over damp skin. She couldn't try and fail again. This time had to be it. Had she properly planned?

Quickly, Taffy dabbed a powder puff down her chest, knowing from bitter experience the value of stealth and strategy. Her last attempt had been ill-conceived and disastrous, with Alfredo retaliating by bundling up her Angel Baby and dropping him downhome in Bledsoe like something unwanted. Taffy's separation from Angel was sealed by blackmail that proved immobilizing. Now, she dared to believe in deliverance?

Shimmying into her undergarments, Taffy finished dressing in record time. She prayed the red-soaked dream was the sign for which she'd patiently waited. *Has to be*, Taffy determined, sick of treading an ocean of mockery, misery, and stale living. But if heaven was on her side, why the bloody, snarling thing...?

Evil always announces its coming.

So, her NuNu claimed. But what was this foretelling: danger yet unseen? Finishing her morning ablutions, Taffy refused fear and uncertainty. The scales would balance. One way or the other, she'd break the chains of a bloodless marriage, and its lack-of-love siphoning off life like a fetid carcass in decay.

Taffy paused enough to consult the looking glass aback the bathroom door. Patting coiffed hair, smoothing fabric over form, she twisted this way then that, assuring her figure was behaving best it could. Tall, two inches shy of six feet, she was Bledsoe built: bountifully. Wasn't one for indecency, but Taffy preferred flowing without corseted constraints, naturally.

Flowery froth-of-a-sun-yellow-hat situated, gloves on, Taffy double-checked her brassiere, ensuring hard-earned money was pinned securely.

Ain't no woman lounging in my house not being a wife. You paying rent!

The Depression had devoured most jobs, left folks searching for sustenance as Coloreds were fired and whites hired in menial, domestic positions once beneath them. Taffy had minimal options. But when Alfredo lewdly suggested rent could be paid in carnal ways, Taffy fashioned herself a living, despite the depressed economy, and diligently labored for every earned cent.

"The good Lord always makes a way," Taffy exulted, lifting her robe from the door handle where—considering Alfredo's penchant for peeking—it hung blocking the keyhole and an errant view.

With newfound excitement, Taffy exited the bathroom only to pause. Removing the silver chain from her neck, Taffy scrutinized its dangling key before unceremoniously discarding it in the wastebasket. Today, she'd leave oppression behind. She'd go without fantasies of her future. Deliverance from Alfredo was sufficient. Freedom, sparkling warm like the sun, pulled Taffy forward so that her soul was already dancing down the road and gone.

The cab horn had barely sounded before Taffy was outdoors, forsaking Alfredo's dead abode without—unlike Lot's wife—a backward glance. Tipsy with exodus, Taffy stepped onto the front porch and ran into weeping.

"Jonnie Mae? Sweetheart, I thought you were gone!"

The girl sat huddled against the wall crying in undergarments not worth wearing. "He's mad, Miz Freeman, on account I got you involved."

Taffy knelt beside her. "Don't worry about—"

"Mr. Freeman won't gimme my clothes! My mama'll skin me dead if I come back without that dress. I ain't the only one what wears it. My sissies do, too."

Sighing, Taffy signaled the cabbie to wait before turning towards the house.

"He ain't there."

Taffy halted. "Then come on in and get your things."

The girl sniveled, swiped at fresh tears. "He took 'em with him, and I don't know where he went."

"Dear, Jesus," Taffy mumbled, snatching the blanket from the porch chair and securing it about Jonnie Mae before heading indoors. "Lord, I can't wait to be done with that man and his mess! Told Alfredo to take her out of here."

You take her.

The gentle command was inaudible to non-listening ears. But Taffy's gift enabled receptivity. Indeed, The Gift absorbed and became all sound.

The Gift had many names. Second sight. Clairvoyance. Sixth sense. Once when angry, Taffy had secretly, jokingly dubbed her 'nuisance' although she was named Knowing. Over the years, in what Taffy deemed her exile, Knowing had begun to do what she'd never done downhome. As if Taffy needed "extra" while Up North, she'd begun manifesting shape and form. Knowing was diaphanous, like hazy light across a distant shore. Still, she was. Vague but visible. An old, luminous legacy. The Gift sat on the parlor stairs, visage indecipherable, white floor-length skirt gently billowing.

Taffy greeted her ancestral treasure. "Good morning, Knowing."

Likewise, Miss Lady. You too busy to help that child?

Harnessing racing worries of an idling cab and a soon-departing train, Taffy replied contritely. "No, ma'am."

Good, 'cause you well know not to overlook a young girl's plight.

Taffy shivered, thinking Jonnie Mae only a few years younger than she when…

Only a few, Knowing echoed, sliding into Taffy's thoughts easy as wind through leaves. *Take her on out of here and don't neither of you return.*

"I dreamed rightly, then?" Taffy questioned, seeking sense in nightmares.

Ain't a matter of right or wrong. You dream what you dream. Dreams're God's way of letting wisdom walk at night. Flowing up from the stairs to approach the window, Knowing inhaled. *What a day our Lord has made!* The Gift sparkled with praise. *I'd like to stand here and let it love me, but those traveling shoes 'bout to burn your feet,* Knowing remarked with a laugh so pure Taffy felt clean. *Let's journey…that boy'll be happy seeing you.*

Taffy's pleasure glowed, thinking of seven-year-old Angel. Long months had passed since last she held him, and her arms ached for love. Taffy missed her Angel, her people. Poppy, NuNu, Chloe, Drew and the rest of her fertile clan—seventy-deep, five-generations wide. She missed her Daddy and what her mother once was, labored to love what Rachel had become. Now that Grandmother Lacy was dead and buried perhaps Rachel, her mother, would right old wrongs…

You're not to worry about any of that!

With a sigh, Taffy addressed The Gift. "Knowing, it's been wrong far too long."

I know that, Miss Lady, still, you let God control the reckoning.

⁓∘⁓

Taffy sat, troubled, in the back of the cab. How to return this child without grieving Ms. Truly with knowledge of her daughter's having been polluted? "Honey, I'll explain as best I can, but I can't lie—"

"No worries, Miz Freeman," the girl interrupted, riding royally, admiring newly bagged prosperity, stroking soft fabrics and bundled finery. Recipient of every languishing garment in Taffy's chifforobe, Jonnie Mae beamed as if Christmas had come. She spoke absent-mindedly. "My being at Mr. Al's ain't no mystery to Mama. She's the one what sends me."

CHAPTER FOUR

The Flats were aptly named. Inhabited by shrunken people with lean wallets and crushed dreams, flat-roofed shacks sloped drunkenly on a dust-ridden lane absent of growth or greenery. Even the air felt thin, shapeless, as Taffy followed Jonnie Mae down a littered walkway.

Giddy with bagged glory, Jonnie Mae hauled acquired clothing up unsteady porch stairs, kicking aside refuse and chattering that her sisters wouldn't believe her bounty.

"Be right back, Miz Freeman," the child sang, dragging bag indoors.

Taffy waited outdoors watching the neighborhood awaken.

Residents of The Flats moved without urgency towards dreaded destinations. Women dressed like domestics, men in sun-bleached coveralls and sweat-stained caps treaded dusty paths, faces pinched by poverty—the meanness of their lives, like shadows, tagging behind.

Hearing squeaky wheels, Taffy glanced across the dirt road to where a little browned-butter girl, hair neatly plaited, struggled with a laundry-loaded wagon. Dipping in an uneven part of the yard, its highest load pitched into the dirt. The child scrambled to lift the twine-bound bundle as big as she.

Taffy stepped forward, intending to help.

"Leave it!" an elderly woman snapped, materializing in the darkened doorway of a weather-worn shack. "She gotta learn to lift her load."

Chastised, Taffy watched the child struggle as the old woman issued orders.

"You best wipe ev'ra specka dirt offa them clothes 'fore you delivers 'em to Miss Katie. Don't dawdle getting back here. Mrs. Grayson's load'll be 'ret when you returns."

"Yes, Granny," the child grunted, heaving and sweating.

Sick of unjust burdens of the female and weak, Taffy descended the porch despite the grandmother's caution against interfering. But sliding Taffy a smile, the girl managed. The old woman slammed her door as a smell, like milk souring between sweaty folds of flesh, curdled the air.

Recognizing the pungent odor often caught in Alfredo's clothing, Taffy turned.

"Whatchu want?" Truly Earl's surly bark was all the greeting Taffy would get. She'd never given Truly cause to dislike her, still Truly did. Taffy stood beneath Truly's glare as the other woman leaned against a rickety doorjamb hard-pressed to support her contempt.

Alfredo's taste in women obviously varied. Mother of six, Truly Earl's prettiness had seen better days. A firm body had melted into slovenly excess. Disenchantment had gnawed tender edges away. A hulk of anger and neglect remained.

"Good morning, Miss Truly. Pardon the intrusion, but—"

"Your mister ain't here. Least not now. Jonnie Mae says you wanting to tell me what I already know?" Truly Earl nodded towards the cab waiting at the end of a dirt road too narrow to travel. "Gon' back where you come from. You wasting time and dimes."

"Ma'am, my husband…was…*with* your daughter—"

"That cheap-ass Al best've sent a full dollar to cover the two quarters owed last time," Truly snapped, shifting weight and crossing arms. "I'm business not charity."

The woman sold her child's flesh?

Something in Taffy curved. Fury warmed neck and tightened spine. Fingers itching for Truly's thick throat, Taffy was marching without thinking.

"Somebody bring my smokes!" Truly hollered, hiding fear and dismantling Taffy's intent. She wouldn't strike in front of a child?

Taffy froze when the cigarette-bearer appeared. A petite girl slightly older than Jonnie Mae handed over cigarettes before pushing past Truly and down the walk, head lowered, pulling a sweater tight about her midsection. Her sweater-wearing-in-summer was conspicuous, concealing the bulge-of-life beneath.

"Ask that white lady for your pay a day early! Need me some pork chops. Sick of grits," Truly mumbled, lips perched about a lit cigarette while eyeing the departing.

Taffy eyed Truly.

Truly Earl was a seasonal parishioner, Christmas and Easter. Their social circles didn't converge. Rumor said her six daughters had each their own father. Dream-depleted and sharp-tongued, Truly guzzled corn liquor and earned her keep by questionable means. Including selling her children?

"Don't send your daughter back to that house," Taffy gently implored. "There's nothing there for her good."

Truly shrugged. "Your place, my place? Don't matter." Nodding towards the daughter nearing lane's end, Truly rubbed a distended midsection that suddenly seemed more than a matter of an unchecked appetite. "Can't believe he got us both caught."

Reality hit like bricks. Alfredo's infidelities never hurt. This was pure pain. He'd impregnated mother, daughter, and been unleashed on Jonnie Mae?

Truly's chuckle was raspy. "Al's getting old, and I've had much better, but he craves coochie," Truly blew smoke in Taffy's face. "And he pays."

"Is your soul worth the price?"

Truly shot upright. "Heffa, I tend my soul better than you do your man! You and your female issues is the sorry reason he over here humping like a rabid dog in heat!" Truly's ensuing avalanche of insults drew an audience of neighbors outdoors. Truly's children assembled, unsuccessfully trying to calm her. "Standing up here talking 'bout my soul! You ain't sinless, bitch. You done forgot Al married you 'cause *you* let him put you in a family way?" Truly Earl hawked a wad of spit at Taffy's feet. "Take your prissy, high-city ass offa my porch and don't come back long's I'm doing what you can't!"

"*Mama*...shhhh..."

"Shut the hell up, Jonnie Mae, and bring me them damn bags you hauled up in here!"

Ripping, tossing, branding with cigarette burns, Truly made a mess of Taffy's bequeathed blessings. "Don't nobody want your castoffs! Every time your husband's 'tween these legs I provide for mine."

Gritting her teeth, Taffy sidestepped Truly's fusillade of profanity and focused on Jonnie Mae. Taffy spoke, inspired by the moment. "Come with me?"

Shivering with hope, Jonnie Mae tucked her head. "Gon' where you going, Miz Freeman. I'm okay."

"You're better," Taffy reminded, turning from Truly's hurricane of curses. Taffy was well beyond the wobbly gate when she heard her name.

Jonnie Mae, daring her mother's wrath, raced down the path to hug Taffy's waist. "Don't mind Mama. She dislikes you 'cause you sweet." Jonnie Mae backed away, shy again. "I 'preciates your kindness, Miss Taffy, and every night I'mma pray *real* hard God let me do something nice for you one day."

⁓

There were no intervening agencies. The city had "real" concerns and the law wouldn't bother with domestic matters in Colored quarters—had even mocked allegations of Colored girls' exploitation, knowing Colored females had no virtue to violate. Social institutions would merely deposit Truly Earl's children in a system where they'd fade into obscurity. Truly Earl wasn't a member on the ledgers; the church was limited in its reach. Likewise, Taffy was limited in her ability to rescue another child from sacrifice.

Frustration draped Taffy's mind. Lord knew The Depression made times tight.

But prostituting your child? Taffy irritably thought while watching porters bustle about their business. Taffy shuddered at Miss Truly's degeneracy, and the plight of her daughters, all six. Four were younger than Jonnie Mae, but Taffy believed only time stood between them and their mother's depravity.

Taffy shook herself, tried focusing on the joy of putting miles between her and Alfredo, of never returning to this place as long as he breathed. But Truly Earl's indifference poked at Taffy's own calcified scars, reminding Taffy of a mother's prospering off of her child's vulnerability.

Taffy boarded the train, imagining a flight north—her Angel Baby in one hand, Truly's girls in the other. But Taffy's path was a tightrope. Precarious. She had work enough to keep herself and Angel from plummeting.

Taffy chose a window seat where she could calm her thoughts once land and time began rolling by. She'd be required to move to the Colored car before crossing the Mason-Dixon Line. With most Colored folks fleeing the opposite direction, seating on a near-empty southbound car would come easy.

Comfortably seated, the morning's excitement and perplexity tumbled about Taffy's mind. Why the dream *and* Jonnie Mae? Taffy understood one; and despite stopping outside the station to phone Miss Adele, Taffy still felt helpless in the other. If anyone could mitigate Truly Earl's deplorable ways, Miss Adele—head of the Colored Women's Benevolent Society—could. Still, Taffy felt as if greater trouble lay in wait for Jonnie Mae.

I'mma pray real hard God let me do something nice for you one day.

Lord, help that baby, Taffy pleaded, feeling as if Jonnie Mae would somehow sync their futures in a macabre way. Shaking off the sensation, Taffy watched a bevy of porters bustling to aid those boarding. Focused on the porters' swift efficiency, neglected aspects of Taffy's dream swirled to the surface and claimed center stage. Those large, copper-penny-colored hands reaching. Indecipherable words, milk and honey, smooth.

Jolted by meaning, Taffy nervously scoured the station platform, eyeing each porter carefully. The man of her past was nowhere. It was merely the dream.

Taffy breathed deeply, prematurely as her freedom train began moving. Her breath caught, watching a man rushing to hop aboard the train, unexpectedly.

He traversed the aisle, reeking villainy. Unbuttoning his too tight suit jacket, he claimed the opposite seat, facing Taffy. With a smug expression, Alfredo leaned back, answering Taffy's unspoken question that roared a silent scream: *Why?* "Felt the need to see you get where you claim you going. Nowhere more than that dead-as-a-doornail, dustbowl you call home." Her husband smiled viciously. "And that, like you said, you going alone."

Down Home

CHAPTER FIVE

Tinsley's General Store was officially closed. Nonetheless, Imogene Tinsley swept 'round her own front door, dallying on the off-chance of a needy night customer wandering in, allowing her to squeeze one last dime out the day. But downtown traffic, despite boasting Bledsoe's one paved road, was slow-to-none.

Old Man Matlock's barber shop sat empty, shoeshine booth forlorn. The shades were drawn at Dr. Blue's clinic. Hunt's Hardware and Moody's BBQ were shadowed hubs in descending dusk. The town had shut down. Folks were finished and so was Imogene.

"What from hell?!" Clutching her broom as if she might need it, Imogene watched something saunter her way. Whatever, *who*ever it was, was art on earth. Imogene wobbled when recognition hit. *Must be aging badly to forget this heffa comes home this time of year.* "Heya, Taffy!" Imogene waved, deciding the younger woman was too much Hollywood and not enough housekeeper, dressed in sunshine yellow and Sunday best.

Shifting her valise, a travel-weary Taffy waved at her elder kinswoman whose stilted welcome was warm as melting ice. With bright-bright skin and haughty smirk so like Grandmother Lacy's, the once dazzling Cousin Imogene had been reduced to chaotic colors trapped in venom, ill-fitting dentures, a strawberry-blond wonder-of-a-wig, and heavy face powder failing to mask time.

"Rayford!" Whipping towards the store, Imogene's once high-and-mighty bosom, now sagging like defeated mules, whirled too. "Come see who done sashayed her happy ass home."

Taffy ignored the gibe along with Imogene's plastic grin that failed to hide less than charitable feelings, so opposite of Imogene's converse, kind reaction to the man staggering up the raised, wooden walk, stressed with overstuffed luggage.

"*Alfredo*? Lord, honey, ain't seen you in a month of Sundays! You struggling?"

"Some help would do," Alfredo huffed as Imogene patted his shoulder fondly. "Rayford around?"

"I done already called that fool. *Rayford*?! Nigglet, drag yo' molasses ass out here!"

Cringing at Imogene's disrespectful summons, Taffy smiled at Rayford's reply.

"Quit hollering like water's on fire. I'll get there when I do!"

Rayford Tinsley Senior limped from the store looking tired enough to bury. Where Imogene was pleasing as rusty nails in rancid moonshine, Rayford Tinsley was sweet milk mellowing the bitter taste his wife left behind. Seeing Taffy, his countenance lifted. "Little gal, get over here and hug me some! Sure is good seeing you."

Taffy returned a warm embrace. "Good seeing you, too, Cousin Tinsley."

He held her at arm's length. "When you moving back here and putting some pretty on this place?"

"You're all the fancy a town can take," Taffy playfully responded.

"Gon' way from here!" Cousin Tinsley chortled. "Al, how you?"

"Better than my customers," Alfredo preened, shaking Rayford's hand. "You?"

"Making it with the good Lord's help," Cousin Tinsley testified. "You staying?"

Alfredo snickered, derisively. "Bledsoe ain't got nothing I want! Plus, business is busy and dead folks are demanding. Even hired on another somebody." His assistant would carry on in his stead so the dearly departed wouldn't be delayed by this tedious trip to Bledsoe, Alfredo crowed, boasting that The Depression hadn't done *Freeman's Funeral Home* any harm. "Hard times or not, thank God, folks still die."

Thank God, I helped you survive, Taffy thought, remembering Alfredo's habit of turning grieving families away for their inability to pay. She'd convinced him to take partial payments, extend credit, and accept day laborers and their fresh-grown collards as currency on occasion. Taffy's humane touch helped ensure the Colored community's loyalty. Now, Alfredo had more than most.

"I'm out on the morning express," he concluded. "Just delivering the missus."

"Gotta hitch tail to Richland for it," Imogene needlessly reminded.

North of Bledsoe, Richland was wonderfully white, pickled and preserved in the vinegar of bigotry and supremacy. Confederate flags waved high. Old money ran deep. The wealthiest municipality in Progress County—a conglomerate of six towns, Bledsoe included—white Richland was black Bledsoe's polar opposite. Yet the towns had more in common than either cared to admit.

"Judge Thornton still raising sand?" Taffy inquired of Richland's king of courtroom and klavern.

"Too old and fat. His henchmen do his dirt now. Least they got the good sense to stay outta Bledsoe," Imogene trumpeted as if responsible for thwarting racist rebels. Lore had it Taffy's NuNu fixed Goldie Hale Thornton good. Richland's rebels need only encounter Judge Thornton's addle-brained, faded-beauty-of-a-wife to know Bledsoe was best left alone.

Disinterested in a conversation centered on white Richland's relation to Bledsoe's blackness, Taffy moved away, leaving Alfredo conversing with the Tinsleys.

Fanning warm evening air, Taffy stepped into *Tinsley's General* intent on purchasing a cool drink. Instead, movement in a far corner of the store caught her eye. Taffy's full mouth melted into a smile. "R.J.?"

Rayford Tinsley Junior, R.J. to all, sat on an overturned crate, gently stroking a calico kitten with meaty hands while rocking to the unsteady beat of drums unseen.

Some faulted Imogene for her son's "touched state," hinting she'd dropped him when little more than born. Others whispered R.J. was the product of a cursed womb. In her unorthodox days, Imogene had enjoyed other women's men. Rumor was a betrayed woman in Bledsoe or beyond worked roots on Imogene's seed so that forty-eight-year-old R.J. possessed an underdeveloped, child-like mind. Still, in Taffy's opinion, he was the best thing to come from Imogene.

Setting her valise on the ground, Taffy bent to pet the calico kitten. Wild distress bubbled from R.J.'s throat. His parents appeared instantly.

"Don't touch that cat!" Imogene shrilled. "He's crazy 'bout that thing."

Taffy withdrew her hand, quietly inquiring, "R.J., how're you?"

Registering her reality, the man-child stopped rocking and bared a toothy grin. "Taffy. Taffy. Taffy." His steady, metronomic movement resumed.

She laughed. "Yes, sweetie, it's me."

"Taffy home, home, home. Hallelujah, I like Taffy."

"I like you, too, R.J. How've you been?"

"Fine. Fine. Fine," he sang in a voice that, like his mind, hadn't matured fully.

"I'm travel-weary and need to go greet my people, but I'll see you soon. Okay?"

"Okay-kay-kay."

Smiling, Taffy turned to leave, but R.J. clutched her hand, positioning it atop his kitten's downy fur. "Taffy nice. Taffy sweet. Taffy touch Cocoa."

Imogene gasped in disbelief. "What the H-E-double-L?! He don't even let *me* touch that thing."

"Boy got better sense than you think," Tinsley Sr. observed, chuckling.

Imogene snorted, marching forward. "Come on, son, its suppertime."

Taffy stood aside, allowing R.J. to rise. Despite growing stout over the years, R.J. moved nimbly. Imogene—transformed from waspish woman to gentle mother, caring for a graceful giant of a feeble-minded son—held his hand all the while.

Imogene halted. "Y'all Freemans, supper ain't much, but you're welcome to it. Hocks and greens. Hot water cornbread. Simple, but any homecooking's likely better than what you getting."

"Imogene," Rayford warned, glancing apologetically at Taffy.

Imogene shrugged, feigning ignorance. "Most young girls're too busy playing independent for keeping a house…or a child."

"You best believe I make sure this one cooks! And first-class at that," Alfredo countered.

Taffy's mouth opened with a ready reply, but Imogene spoke first, rubbing Alfredo's rounded stomach for good measure. "You sure this blown-up-ball-of-a-belly's due to red beans and not booze?"

"Hush it up, Imogene!" Rayford Sr. urged, shamefaced before all.

Imogene whirled. "Who you shushing? I'm grown with gray hairs to prove it," Imogene snapped, patting the sin-of-a-wig concealing snowy plaits beneath.

"Best keep your dress down and drawers up," Rayford offhanded-ly droned. "That head ain't the only gray thing,"

Lord! Taffy silently implored, feigning a sudden interest in ful-ly-stocked shelves to avoid laughing at foolishness and folly. Her family was a sight! Particularly these women in her maternal line who hadn't patiently waited when the good Lord distributed sound minds.

Amused, Taffy moved about the store, examining wares, until reaching its front once again. She stood at the freshly cleaned win-dows, absorbing the last of a buttery sun and savoring the flavor of home as the Tinsleys squabbled in the rear.

She'd made her way Up North, eventually finding her fit in the city like a second skin. Yet, Taffy deeply treasured her returns to this sleepy place called home.

Not even nightfall, Bledsoe rested—shops vacant and shades drawn with *Sorry, We're Closed* signs indicating customers need return another day. It was a sight easily forgotten living Up North. No late night juke joints or houses of ill-repute. No street-corner win-os preaching politics and circular sermons only other winos could comprehend. Only darkened buildings whispered, *Welcome to Bledsoe, population: too-many-Colored-folks-for-white-folks'-good.*

Taffy's pride swelled, beholding this all-Black township steeped in tradition and seemingly slumbering as time tiptoed by. Signs of yesterday mixed with notions of today—fresh paint, new street lamps, an undefined building being constructed at the end of a road that was dust her last visit. Now hard-packed dirt had been overtaken by asphalt and advancement.

Pleased and proud, Taffy turned towards the Tinsleys, only to stall at a curious lack of sight. Still setting Rayford straight, Cousin Imo-gene's voice stripped air, but Imogene was lost from view. There was nothing save audible lashing and a green pool of frothing filth where Imogene should have been.

"Lord, what is this?" Taffy murmured softly, not comprehending.

See what you know and know what you see.

Taffy need not look for Knowing. She was present even if her form wasn't; an absent embodiment similar to Imogene's...

Taffy blinked slowly, and looked again only to find Imogene restored, the green pool of stagnation gone. Yet, a smell of dead flesh stung the air.

"Little gal, your people coming to collect you?" Rayford called, limping Taffy's way, escaping his wife's caterwauling.

Taffy flowed away from vision. "No, sir. Didn't tell them exactly when to expect me." An unannounced homecoming was her ritual. Didn't make sense to most, yet Taffy preferred a lack of fanfare. Her exodus had been miserable. Always needed a tranquil moment to make peace with her place of birth upon return. That was best done alone.

"I knew I didn't see nothing slide through here announcing you," Imogene—both store owner and postmaster—crowed. "'Night, y'all." Imogene pulled R.J. forward, suddenly anxious to reach the family house situated beyond the back of the store. Taffy Bledsoe Freeman was still juicy news.

"That phone line 'bout to work a hot while?" Taffy questioned.

Cousin Tinsley chortled. "Fresh meat don't keep 'round here." Cousin Tinsley nodded towards the door his wife and son had gone through. "She 'bout to burn my supper yakking it up telling folks you're here. Lemme close up and I'll cart y'all home."

"No need to—"

"There's plenty need," Alfredo overrode, tucking Taffy's luggage beneath his arms, mumbling, "And the quicker the better."

"Take your time, Cousin," Taffy softened her husband's rudeness—certain Alfredo's sudden haste to wipe Bledsoe from his feet involved returning north where willing women waited. "We don't mean to trouble you."

"Ain't no trouble." Locking the front door, Rayford flipped the *Closed* sign. "Was headed out to drop a package to Reverend and First Lady Ellis anyhow. That boy of theirs stays so long gone riding them rails, he ain't never here. But he always sending something or other for his parents." Rayford sucked what was left of his teeth. "Yeah, Lord, them Pullman porters making a nice chunk of change these days. Y'all best hurry if you wanna get to Taffy's people 'fore Imogene."

"We're ready," Taffy assured, ignoring a potpourri of warm spice, cool mint, and red ash showering her senses at the mention of the Ellises and "that boy of theirs" who was once hers...

Alfredo gripped her arm, gaze hot, as Cousin Tinsley exited the back of the store. "I let you sass me in front of Truly's gal this morning 'cause she don't matter, but don't you *ever* contradict me in front of other men!"

"No need to, Mr. Al, when you contradict yourself." Extracting her arm from her husband's grasp, Taffy descended the back steps, Alfredo's glare burning holes in her back. Situating herself in Cousin Tinsley's old truck, Taffy eyed Alfredo's stomping down the path to dump her luggage in the truck bed.

"Alfredo!"

Taffy's attention drifted to Imogene on the front porch of her home, foil-wrapped plate in hand, hailing Alfredo her way. Taffy watched her husband reluctantly comply with the older woman's beckoning. Handing over the foil-wrapped plate that was little more than a rouse, Imogene spoke urgently, quietly. Still her nervous conversation floated Taffy's way.

"There a reason you came with her this time? She here to stir up trouble?"

"Miss Imogene, you know well as me I got my wife under control."

"Best keep her that way 'cause if you don't, Lord knows I will."

Taffy watched Imogene pat Alfredo's keloid-scarred back—reminder enough that absolute control over Taffy's life was something Alfredo would never have.

❧

Tinsley took her as far as the fence marking Bledsoes' private property. Just another of her eccentricities, Alfredo complained of Taffy's need to walk her people's land. Something about reconnecting with, embracing the earth. Just more hoodoo mumbo jumbo learned from her bat-black grandmother. Tinsley thought otherwise.

After life with Imogene he understood needing serenity. Still, he wanted to cart her to her people proper-like, but Taffy insisted. Taking his cue from a disinterested Alfredo, Tinsley acquiesced, honoring Taffy's need to rediscover home alone. Solitary and bathed by a sinking sun, dress ruffled by the breeze, Tinsely left her on the periphery of Bledsoe land, looking like something growing lovely from God's good earth.

CHAPTER SIX

"Angel, you've gotten so big!"
"Yep, and I'mma keep growing 'til I'm taller than you."
"Oh, I don't know about that," Taffy teased, kissing his brow, holding him tightly.

"Papa said I got extra good Bledsoe genes, so you gonna be short one day."

Taffy laughed like life lived on her tongue. "You're something else." And he was, this Angel Baby boy.

He'd nearly knocked her over, jumping into her arms when meeting up the road. Painting kisses across his face, she'd twirled him around until dizzy. Now, her smile bloomed as Taffy caressed his cheeks, adoring the sweetness bottled up in a seven-year old bundle of boy.

Angel was pure gift, the only right resulting from an illicit wrong. But he was here downhome in Bledsoe in the bosom of familial affection. All because Alfredo alleged she'd raise him wrong.

Sin and a shame a grown man jealous of a child—deeming Taffy too much mother and not enough wife. In a fit stimulated by excess liquor, nonexistent intimacy, and Taffy's grand attempt to leave, Alfredo banished Angel without care. But in Taffy something collapsed, leaving a fractured heart behind.

His accusations rang wickedly when dumping a then three-year-old Angel back in Bledsoe. Claimed Taffy was wild Up North, not tending the boy's needs. But what could she do other than wail and rail? Alfredo was backed by unfathomable threats Grandmother Lacy's blood-soaked hands itched to fulfill.

And Rachel? Like a wooden doll, her mother let the devil's business be done.

But they were together now, Angel skipping beside her, savoring this moment when Taffy was his alone. Soon they'd be overtaken by family wanting their fill and the world would cease to revolve solely for them. So hands clasped, arms swinging, Taffy and Angel took their time despite the near-fall of night.

"You been alright since I saw you last?" Taffy questioned. Their telephone calls and letters were a regular affair, yet nothing compared to observing Angel's well-being firsthand. Taffy's natural concern mingled with the sting of memory, of Angel's first weeks of life when his existence galloped across gossiping lips...

Her daddy was missing. Thaddeus Bledsoe had ventured over to Mississippi only to disappear the winter of '27. Her mother followed every trace, desperate to ascertain her husband's whereabouts. Into the spring of 1928, Rachel remained vigilant, taking Taffy with her that April on an extended search that expanded the family.

They were gone three-months running, Taffy returning with babe in arms—body blossoming in places gently rounded before. Folks stood stupefied. Out-fishing, out-running, shoot-as-good-as-the-next, Tomboy Taffy? Hiding a pregnancy? Tomboy or no she had that woman thing between her thighs.

Wild, outspoken, too-free-Taffy came home subdued and dismayed, like the world was inside-out. But those cat eyes could still flash gray fire when that newborn's paternity was questioned.

In 1928 in Bledsoe, certain matters dominated the mind: legalizing liquor, could Charles Lindberg fly or was it more whitefolks' lies, and most importantly, who was Angel Bledsoe's pa?

Eyes focused on Roam Ellis—Taffy's intended—but he was as bewildered as the next by that unmarried gal's wicked ways. Still...she didn't make that baby by her lonesome. Folks watched and waited for the pa to appear, praying he wasn't connected to their own lives, come from their wombs, or asleep in the center of their marital beds.

Rumors ricocheted, deflecting attention and suspicion. That baby was for so-and-so over in nearby Trenton or Drexel or Winter Cove. Then the story twisted, painting Taffy so loose the father *couldn't* be known.

Didn't help that Angel's face wouldn't tell. Boy was so Bledsoe his paternal line was impossible to come by. But what did it matter? Fast-tail gals got what they deserved: nothing. No husband, just signifying of the sullied. Suddenly one of Bledsoe's chosen was a whore, ruint, defiled...called every name except her own.

Life changed. Childhood was packed away like dolls in a box on the attic floor. Taffy became bitterness in women's mouths, a thirst on the tongues of men. Their grunts were guttural, eyes roving her body, regret roiling in men's chests at failing to notice her budding beneath their noses and missing the opportunity of first taste when she was prime for the picking. Still, the newness of her womanhood made the thought of second sampling equally sweet.

But then that unknown Alfredo Freeman showed up a month after Angel's birth—hat in hand—assuming paternal responsibility. Mystery solved, Bledsoe exhaled as Freeman married the gal and herded them Up North, leaving that broken Ellis boy behind.

"I'm fine," Angel answered, drawing Taffy back to the present.

"You sure?"

"Yep. Watch this." Releasing Taffy's hand, Angel launched into a succession of cartwheels, culminating in a grand handstand.

"Now *that's* worthy of somebody's Olympics somewhere!"

"What mark would I get?" Angel demanded.

"Ten, perfect as you."

"You're just saying that 'cause you like me."

"I don't like you!" Taffy protested.

"Yeah-huh, you do," Angel giggled.

"Says who?"

"Me!"

"Hmph! Me don't know what Me's talking 'bout."

Angel could barely talk for laughing. "*I* don't know what *I'm* talking *a*bout," he corrected.

"See, told you!" Taffy tweaked his nose. "Wanna race?"

Angel shrugged, suddenly less exuberant about minimizing these moments when Taffy was his. He knew she'd come walking up the wide, dirt lane running the length of the family's land. And family knew enough to let Angel have this time. Racing would get them home too soon.

"I wouldn't want to race either," Taffy concluded at Angel's silence, "especially knowing I'd lose."

"Nuh-unh! I won't lose. You're old and slow."

"Oh, Jesus!" Taffy removed her pumps and tossed them aside. "Turn your head," Taffy instructed, reaching beneath dress to unsnap garter belts and unroll silky hosiery she tossed atop shoes. "I'mma show you old! Bet you whatever I brought you I'll win."

"Wait…what'd you bring me?"

"Doesn't matter seeing as how you're 'bout to lose it."

Angel pursed his lips and narrowed big eyes. "To the plum tree and back," he decided.

"No back, just the plum tree. On your mark..."

Angel bolted, leaving Taffy in his wake before she managed 'go'." Catching up proved a feat. Maybe she *was* getting old, or a thigh-hugging dress shortened her stride. Either way, Taffy lost and Angel hopped about like Jesus crowned him king.

"Cheater!" Winded, Taffy tackled Angel, tumbling them both onto the grass. They lay laughing at a soft, dusky sky.

"So I have a plan," Angel ventured, catching his breath. "I'mma get sick tomorrow with scolioitis. I'll miss school, we'll go fishing—"

"Angel Nathaniel! Up here preplanning illnesses. You oughta be ashamed."

"But I ain't."

"I'm not," Taffy corrected, suppressing a smile.

"Neither am I." Angel screeched when Taffy grabbed him, tickling.

"The only place for a sick child is in bed or with Dr. Blue," Taffy cautioned.

"Oh...yeah...I guess."

Taffy touched Angel's crestfallen face, understanding Angel's attempt to orchestrate time. In two days, there'd be no need to wish a world where they could steal away. They simply would, heading farther north than Alfredo knew. The tide had changed. Power was hers. Taffy was attaching wings to her prayers. But would Angel adjust to whatever life they designed when his normal was here, downhome?

Taffy knew firsthand how the selfish acts of others could alter a world. Yet, leaving was the only way to shed her farce-of-a-marriage, and she wouldn't go without her Angel.

"Angel Baby, don't look so poor-mouthed." Taffy was tempted to divulge her plan, but she didn't trust Angel to keep silent. "We'll be together—"

"Really?" Angel brightened. "When?"

"Soon. And there's no need faking conditions you can't rightly name." Angel's look was questioning. "It's scoliosis not scolioitis."

"Oh. What's that anyway?"

"Something you don't have." Taffy tugged Angel's ear. "Guess I'd best get up and go greet the people."

"Just a little longer…"

"Honey, it's getting dark. Plus, I can't be rude," Taffy gently intoned.

"Yes, you can. Papa's hunting with Poppy and the uncles and Boss, so he's not home to miss your coming no how. Everybody else'll wait."

Thoughts of Boss, her favorite canine way past prime, increased Taffy's smile. "Angel, now, Mama's probably—"

"M'Dear's okay. She's keeping Mr. Al company."

"Did you show your manners?"

"Yes, ma'am. I shook his hand. But we didn't hold no conversation. Mr. Al ain't one for wasting air on warm words. Come on, Taf, pretty please! Let's stay here and sky watch."

"Alright… Hold on! Where's my plum tree?" Taffy demanded, bolting upright.

"Root rot," Angel informed. "Papa and the uncles cut it down."

"Such a shame," Taffy muttered, eyeing the massive stump not far away. The old tree was a favorite. As a girl, she'd perch in its branches eating too much fruit and awaiting her father's return from the fields. Mouth purple, clothes stained, she'd drop a plum at his feet. Thaddeus always played along, scooping up fruit, declaring it manna from heaven as Taffy scampered down, jumping him from behind. Feigning surprise, Thaddeus would hoist her onto his shoulders and head home, Taffy prattling all the while.

The death of that plum tree moved her deeply, symbolic of her losses in life…and love. Cut down. Unfulfilled.

In the distance, Taffy made out the rambling, two-story brick house where she was raised. First to boast indoor plumbing *and* electricity, some considered it the stateliest home in Bledsoe. With its wraparound porch and plethora of blooming vines climbing its sides, it was certainly a striking edifice. But seeing sorrow draped about it, Taffy was in no hurry to intercept misery. She lay down, head nestled against Angel's. "Ten minutes and then we go in. Deal?"

"Fifteen minutes."

"Seven-and-a-half," Taffy countered.

"Ten's good," Angel accepted, content.

CHAPTER SEVEN

She heard their approach. Angel's chirping swirled sweetly beneath Taffy's rich alto rendering Rachel Bledsoe paralyzed. Rachel sat at the kitchen table inert, deaf to Alfredo's self-centered mutterings, hearing only Lacy Marchand.

You did this! You conjured up this hussy! Six months decomposing below ground, Rachel's mother still had too much to say. *You brought this to life! Touching yourself...*

Rachel violently shivered.

"You alright, Miss Rachel?"

Rachel's gray gaze shot Alfredo's way. "Just a little chill."

Stuffing cake in mouth, Alfredo resumed his pontificating, ignoring a woman's shivering in eighty-plus degree heat. *Must be that female "change-of-life" thing.*

Rachel sat, staring at the screen door, expecting Taffy's entrance, praying a change *would* come. Couldn't deny mourning her mother's passing, but Rachel longed for change, to live without Lacy's chokehold undiminished by death.

Jezebel!

Lacy's ghostly accusation popped hot like bacon grease against Rachel's ear. Springing from her seat, Rachel stood afraid of finding her mother, gray eyes aflame, suddenly alive again.

"Miss Rachel?"

Rachel Bledsoe offered a plausible excuse and tepid smile. "Every time my child comes home I get all jittery and excited." And fearful and uncertain. Never knew what she'd find in Taffy's gaze. Pity, contempt, or worse...nothing?

Like the dry nothingness overshadowing Rachel's life, her days, and especially her nights. Brittle, empty nights that left Rachel craving and crying for the lost place in her husband's heart, and the heat of Thaddeus Bledsoe's embrace. Shooing dismal thoughts into a decorated box in her mind, a box already crowded with ache-inducing memories, Rachel resumed her hostess duties.

"More coffee, Al?" Dutifully pouring a second cup to accompany Al's second slice of cake, Rachel mourned. She was deprived and denied, no longer owning her husband's hunger or his touch. No visitations or connubial exchange. Bruised love had sprang from sources unknown.

Honey-Love, what's wrong? What had she done to cancel joy?

Thaddeus never could say to Rachel's satisfaction. He remained the big-hearted man she'd loved since the day she hid, watching him swim in the lake naked as birth. But now a dry river ran through their marriage bed. Having shackled her daughter to a loveless life, Rachel decided this was her lot. But Rachel didn't have Taffy's fortitude.

How to restore lost bounty?

The solution required more sacrifice than Rachel could afford. So she swallowed fate and prayed miraculous resolution of the mess she'd helped make.

The ringing telephone ended Rachel's thoughts. She ignored the phone, and Al's puzzled stare. Taffy hadn't been home long enough to set foot in the door and already the contraption had taken to ringing incessantly.

Calls came from the Women's Willing Workers—Bledsoe's Christian auxiliary committee of which Rachel was president. Thirty strong, not more than a handful showed at most W.W.W. meetings. Rachel frowned knowing this weekend's gathering would prove standing room only. Not because of preparation for next week's Founders' Festival, but because women wanted to satisfy themselves with a piece of Taffy.

They would come to witness time's effect on the fallen. Clouds of talcum and perfume-laced air would congest Rachel's parlor. Everyday clothes would be exchanged for Sunday's best. Happened whenever Taffy returned. Grown women contending with a child, dolling up, hoping to hide country cute in the face of Up North niceties.

Already news of Taffy's return was spreading like wild fire in summer, a disease in winter. Rachel's child belonged to Bledsoe, but city-dwelling made her something more. Loose. Unpredictable. An untrustworthy predicament-in-the-making.

Women would worry.

They juggled enough as day-laborers, sitting roadside waiting on a summons to earn a wage; others working for pennies on a depressed dollar, sweating in fields and mills. Or in white women's kitchens, with foul children and fondling husbands, while pulling their own children from school to work the fields, praying F.D.R.'s New Deal made it 'round their way. They were Colored women hanging on. Now this. Taffy. Rachel would see it in their faces. Taffy's presence put flesh on the bones of their fears.

Could've spared themselves their pangs. Taffy wasn't one to pit herself against others. Rachel pitied jealous-hearted women whose pettiness made their value decrease not rise.

Hypocrite!

Hadn't she been repeatedly petty when maturity was preferred? If not petty, then certainly weak. Spineless. Letting Lacy dictate her household affairs. When she complained, Thaddeus reminded his wife the home front was hers to run. If she objected to Mother Lacy's interference then it was up to Rachel to set things straight. Rachel never did as was painfully obvious in the gross cruelty she'd permitted.

Offering Alfredo yet another hunk of butter cake, Rachel decided she'd done her best, loving her daughter, straining to give Taffy something different. Something more. If only a broader worldview. Determined her child would be armed with knowledge for life, no subject was off-limits, not even intimacy. Rachel persistently taught Taffy one husband, one wife—that in marriage fidelity and faithfulness were their own rewards. Unlike Lacy, Rachel deliberately conveyed a wife's right to the physical privilege and pleasure the marriage bed supplied.

Knowing Alfredo, most likely, my child has neither.

Rachel's stomach turned at the thought of Alfredo sinking himself into Taffy. Alfredo. Lascivious. Selfish. Rachel didn't trust the man, not now and certainly not back when. The sight of Taffy chained at his side was a boulder about Rachel's conscience. Still, she gave him her child…

Send her Up North and spare yourself daily seeing her misery.

Mother's advice seemed sound at the time. Now Rachel admitted it was self-serving. With Taffy Up North, perpetual guilt went, too.

Alfredo proved all too eager to head north and leave skeletons behind. Namely, a hapless fourteen-year-old over in Greenville found in a fix. Caught between the two, Alfredo chose Taffy and the lure of Lacy's wealth guaranteeing a fresh start Up North where he could recreate himself at will.

Now Lacy was dead. Alfredo dripped blood money. And Rachel drifted amid the flotsam and jetsam of ungodly schemes—guiltier than Lacy and Alfredo ever could be.

Taffy brought this on herself, Lacy hurled from across the room.

Ignoring her phantasmal mother, Rachel tried focusing on Alfredo, but her mind bolted rabbit-like down another path hoping to lose itself in merriment. The Founders' Festival! It was a mere week away, this decennial celebration of a town established by liberated slaves daring enough to claim their own corner of land and life. Perhaps it was time to free Taffy of oppressive yokes so she, too, could lay claim to abundant living.

You don't owe that girl anything! Lacy shrieked, wildly flailing. *She's strong. She'll survive. Alfredo's twenty-plus years her senior. He'll die soon enough and she'll have her time.*

"Mother, hush!"

"Ma'am?"

Rachel covered her outburst with the pouring of more coffee and mindless chatter. "Alfredo, you think my cake is good? You haven't tasted anything until you have one of Sister Esther's pies. She's bringing plenty to the festival."

"Ain't hardly staying, Miss Rachel. Gotta get back north," Alfredo mumbled around a mouthful.

"You'll miss something special," Rachel gently opined. With the Colored populace from the neighboring towns of Drexel and Winter Cove attending, Bledsoe's sixtieth Founders' Day Festival was sure to be their best yet. The Women's Willing Workers would be occupied all week preparing food. Rachel relished the thought of the demanding week ahead, leaving a mind too occupied, a body too tired to crave...

Rachel couldn't keep her mind from veering. Back to Thaddeus. Back to a year-long celibacy Rachel couldn't pray away.

Dissatisfied with solitude and celibacy, Rachel's hands anointed her own chest with lilac talcum and long, lost love last night. She'd patted lilac-scented powder between her cream-and-honey breasts like a memory keeper and reminder that she'd once been sweet. Her slender fingers gently powdered and prodded sensitive orbs that once oozed baby's milk, caramel-coated candy that hadn't fed her husband in too long for tears. Just last night Rachel's lonesome hands strayed to the dark forest between her legs, conjured up moans that shocked

Rachel to her knees where she prayed a sinner's prayer, clasping hands reeking of the damp entrance of her mystery. All because Thaddeus had stopped reaching for her a year ago, near about the time of his brother's demise.

Cold needles stabbed the backs of Rachel's gray eyes. Did Thaddeus...

Fool-fool woman! Lacy spewed dead disgust.

"Excuse me, Al." Rachel hurried out the backdoor leaving Alfredo to stuff himself with cake. Instead of solace, Rachel found majesty, chocolate-colored and shimmering, moving like willows in wind. Naturally. Not bound, like Rachel, with sorrow, girdle, or regret.

Rachel gripped a porch beam for stability, whispering contritely. "Taffy?"

Don't start that sniveling!

Regretting the passing of mother-daughter intimacy, Rachel's words tumbled like a prayer. "I want my daughter back."

Relations between mothers and daughters get tried. Lacy admonished. *Yours is no exception.*

Rachel seemed destined to replicate Lacy's living. Like Lacy, she was the only child of an only living child. Her passion-lit marriage was, like her parents', nearing brittle and reserved. Rachel prayed she wouldn't follow her forebears' paths completely.

Her maternal line was haunted by melancholy madness.

Grandmother had been a sad shadow of a woman prone to wild outbursts resolving in rivers of ragged tears. According to Lacy, Grandmother's moods were justified, having tragically lost her first born and husband in one day. Lacy became the byproduct of her mother's inconsolable self, eventually displaying her own penchant for moodiness. Brooding and retaliatory, Lacy was a lake, smooth on the surface, perpetually churning underneath.

When Lacy's mother remarried, Grandmother's sharecropper-of-a-husband could barely manage bread on the table, never mind the finery that had cushioned Lacy's younger days. Wasn't until Lacy married the man destined to become Progress County's first Colored school superintendent—supervising only Colored schools—that a standard of living was restored. Yet, brooding never abated. Now, plagued by her mother's restless phantom, Rachel feared she was next in line for mental deficiency.

Had you listened to me we wouldn't be in this situation, Rachel

Marie. I warned—

Swatting incendiary and insensitive words with a backward flick of her hand, Rachel descended the steps mustering courage for an unpredictable reunion.

Forced to a halt by fear, Rachel stood on the cobblestone walkway, watching Angel's happy bouncing. He'd raced from the house when Alfredo arrived, barely pausing to shake his father's hand, before tearing down the lane in search of Taffy. Now, Rachel watched the two, was taken by Taffy's radiating peace and pleasure. A flash of envy came, it went, and Rachel resituated herself in pregnant hope.

Taffy slowed at the sight of her.

Separation was an entity between. Festering. Mocking.

With the weight of the world in her limbs, Rachel offered a tentative wave. For the briefest moment Taffy's countenance hardened, before softening into a sad, tainted smile.

Rachel beamed, thankful her child still felt *something* towards her even if it was flavored like hate.

CHAPTER EIGHT

Asoft-skinned treasure freshly bathed, he snuggled in the crook of her arm, breathing sweet breath as she stroked his slumbering face. Strong cheekbones had commandeered chubby cheeks. Forehead was high, skin kissed by a darker god, head covered by a cap of thick, black curls.

"Just like my Daddy's," Taffy admired, smiling as Angel—always her solace—rolled onto his side.

He'd brightened her tarnished existence when Bledsoe became a blizzard in the aftermath of his birth. The Bledsoe name was enough to mitigate damage, but it didn't eradicate ostracism or shame. Plummeting from grace, a two-sided sin was planted solely at Taffy's young, unmarried feet. Bearing sin's consequences, she became threat and deterrent.

"Straighten up and fly right 'fore you wind up like that ruint Taffy!"

Those first weeks of his life were harsh. Taffy buried herself in Angel, holding head as high as she dared, until Alfredo showed up assuming his role.

"A role is all it was," Taffy uttered, taunted by resentment and bitter ruminating.

Whatsoever things are lovely and just, think on those things.

Taffy raised up slightly, looking for The Gift but Knowing remained concealed.

It'll work itself out in the end. For now, get up and get moving. NuNu's waiting.

Despite Taffy's ritual of arriving unannounced, her paternal grandmother never failed to be ready with a ritual of their own. Tonight, Taffy needed it, desperately.

Easing from atop the bed, Taffy kissed her sleeping Angel before turning off the bedside lamp and exiting his room.

They met in the hallway, her mother's arms loaded with fresh linens. All cream-and-honey complexion, corn silk hair, and doll-like features, forty-three-year-old Rachel was a stunning woman, despite the guilty haunting of dove-gray eyes.

"He's asleep?" Rachel stared into eyes like her own. Color was shared, but Taffy's reflected truths Rachel shunned.

"Soundly," Taffy answered. "Supper was good, Mama. Thank you."

Rachel beamed. "I didn't expect you, so I'll fix your favorites tomorrow—"

"I'll be at Chloe's."

"Oh…well…I have your bedlinens." Rachel indicated the stack in her arms.

"I'll take them."

"No…it's my pleasure…the least I can do…considering." Harbored, painful secrets writhed between them. Rachel's eyes lowered. "Sorry I can't give you your own room. Your Daddy…"

It made Taffy no never mind if her father knew she and Alfredo occupied separate quarters, but Rachel shifted side-to-side under the discomfiting weight of farce and lies.

"I'll go out and stay with NuNu since Poppy's hunting with Daddy."

Rachel nodded, saddened by her child's desire to be elsewhere. "Think you could use some shoes?"

Glancing at her bare feet, Taffy laughed. Since tossing pumps aside to run a race she didn't win, she'd gone without. "I'm fine. I'll be back in the morning to walk Angel to the bus. 'Night, Mama."

"'Night, sweetheart." Rachel watched her daughter descend the stairs, adding softly, "God bless you and spare us both."

She found Alfredo sprawled in her father's favorite chair, belly stuffed, and snoring. Taffy shook his shoulder until he sputtered awake. Rejoicing that he'd leave on the morning express, Taffy bid him safe travels and god speed. "You can go on up if you like. My mother's making the bed." Taffy tried not to be amused by the wanton hope igniting Alfredo's face. "You can have it since I won't be in it."

Wanton hope was replaced by the evil and ominous. Hate glowed apparent across Alfredo's face. It was hate thick with disgust and the hunger to do to Taffy what had already been done. To *her*. A young, missing woman-child? Faceless, nameless, she swam in the darkness of Alfredo's memory and mind, her obscure image warning loudly, *Careful he don't place you where you can't rise to haunt him no more like he did me.*

Taffy struggled to see the child clearly. Sound rose instead, filling Taffy's ears with a one-word revelation, a name with meaning. Repeating that name aloud, Taffy was stunned by the terror instantly dismantling Alfredo's face. Taffy backed away, taking her leave of Alfredo not just for now, but always.

Despite evening's descent the June air was warm, clean, filling Taffy's lungs with freshness untainted by Alfredo's sins. Her nostrils flared with scents of evening and earth. Earth pulsed in welcome beneath Taffy's bare feet as her spirit reconnected with roots tried by time.

She walked leisurely, disturbed by Alfredo's bloody secrets while wondering how to bring her parents around to her way of thinking. Their blessing wouldn't come easy, if at all. Angel had been theirs these past four years. They wouldn't release him readily. Ready or not, in two days Taffy and Angel were leaving.

"I can't return." She'd given too much to a dead thing. No more untruths like millstones about her neck, suffocating, killing. Bending and scooping cool, moist soil, Taffy let dirt fall between her fingers. Time for uprooting and replanting. It was time to breathe.

She could've walked the path eyes closed, guided by recall alone. So she did, laughing at self for traveling blind.

"Child, you're crazy," Taffy admitted, letting her senses lead, testing a memory that hadn't dimmed with city dwelling. Moving steadily but cautiously, Taffy honed in on night blooming jasmine, the aroma of a vegetable garden nearby. Cattle lowed in the stalls of her family's ranch as something nocturnal scurried across her path.

Taffy stumbled. Her eyes snapped open. She'd encountered something, yet nothing could be seen.

Perhaps something lay *beneath* the earth? The cash-filled cans her grandparents entrusted to the soil that had done them only good? "Bledsoe banking," Taffy laughed, deciding to pretend she had good sense and continue the journey eyes wide.

Rounding a bend in the road, Taffy saw *The Place*, a crude structure crafted by her grandfather's hands. The Place was where Bledsoes began. Five boys were raised there. A newborn girl breathed long enough to break her parents' hearts before slipping back to heaven in seraphs' hands. Refusing to abandon it for the cushy comforts their sons and wives offered, Taffy's grandparents remained in The Place lacking modern amenities and electricity, but radiating life five-generations-deep.

Mounting a creaking porch, Taffy called out while entering. "NuNu?"

Silence replied as Taffy entered a cozy sitting room, its mantle consumed by family photographs. Poppy and NuNu's overstuffed chairs—where NuNu embroidered and Poppy wove tall tales—sat like thrones. Wasn't much else to The Place besides her grandparents' private domain and NuNu's tiny, closed-off space behind the kitchen.

"NuNu's world of wonder," Taffy mused, finding it empty save jar-stocked shelves hosting a colorful plethora of earthen treasures above an enormous tin tub that purified and cleansed. They'd frolicked there—Taffy, her cousins—under NuNu's watchful gaze. "*My little brown nakeds*," NuNu called them, tickled by her young grandchildren's bathtub antics that splashed water across her clean, plank floor.

Now filled to the brim, the tub emitted tendrils of fragrant steam. Botanical matter floated atop water as tallow candles burned about its base in this most sacred space.

It lay there, draped across a stool at the tub's end—the white cotton sheath.

The ritual waited, ready. *Welcome to the waters.*

It was a voice like Knowing's, like NuNu's, multi-layered with legacy. Accepting the invitation, Taffy relished the undressing.

Naked as birth, she entered the tub, surrendering to the waiting well both musky and sweet. Steamy water licked the nape of her neck as Taffy leaned into a lovingly prepared, and desperately needed, luxury. She was tired of holding fast to the self others tried to drown. Grandmother Lacy. Alfredo. Rachel to unconscionable degrees…

Rest.

Obediently, Taffy yielded, allowing weariness to lift as water washed and purified. Old poison was thick, as were her wounds. But so, too, was this healing, the uncoiling of anger, hurt, even hate. Here in the sanctuary of a crude cabin, she made a lavish choice long overdue. Relinquishing retribution and reaching for perfect peace, Taffy chose to live free.

She was awakened by a warm waterfall—an aromatic libation poured atop her head.

Disoriented, Taffy tried rising from the tub but was stilled by hands made strong by decades and situation. "Rest yourself, Little One."

Taffy whirled, coming face-to-face with timeless eyes and smoky skin. "*NuNu!*" Shamelessly naked, Taffy fell onto her grandmother's chest fragrant with earth, work, a hint of ginger and much living.

"Welcome home, Little One," NuNu hoarsely whispered, clutching her namesake and jewel. Massaging the sleekness of young skin, NuNu's gnarled hands explored Taffy's face. High forehead. Sleek slant of cat-gray eyes. Jutting cheekbones and proud nose. Full, rich mouth and defiant chin. NuNu beamed. Her precious one was here.

Taffy did her own searching, assuring herself NuNu was well despite infinitesimal changes.

NuNu's skin was still smooth, bittersweet chocolate, but her short-cropped hair had finally surrendered to silver. Shoulders retained erectness, making her appear taller than her six-feet. There was softness in NuNu's movements, and sharp eyes had absorbed a milky ring. Still, Taffy wasn't fooled. Her daddy's mother saw more than her share.

"I can't ever sneak up on you," Taffy laughed, indicating the tub and candles NuNu had prepared.

"These old eyes still see their share," NuNu chuckled deep and earthy. Kissing Taffy's forehead, NuNu pushed her back into the tub, Taffy's temple a semblance of her own before gravity and time. "Sit your nakedness down and finish this cleansing."

"I need it more than you know."

"Then you need it bad."

Removing hairpins, NuNu lathered Taffy's thick mane with homemade ginger and citrus soap. Taffy felt pure, skin caressed by the breeze flowing through an open window. The breeze set candlelight to dancing across the walls, the ceiling, and out the back door. Taffy's breathing deepened. Cares receded. And NuNu launched into legacy without preamble.

"Where you come from, Little One?"

Glancing at the simple garment draped across a stool, gleaming in candlelight like the bride's garment it was meant to be, Taffy's answer was simple. "From the keeper of the sheath."

"Tell her tale," NuNu commanded, lathering Taffy's back—smooth and unbroken by slavery, unlike NuNu's.

Gaze fixed on that aged, white garment, Taffy dutifully spoke of an African girl snatched by opportunistic slavecatchers long after slave trading was done. Arriving in a strange land with a renegade sailor's baby forced in her belly, she was purchased by a Tennessee banker. Branded "Octavia," she hid her African name beneath her tongue, lest it slip across the waters leaving her lonely.

NuNu nodded, gratified her granddaughter recalled. "Folks said she was too evil to claim 'Octavia'." Heat sprang from NuNu's eyes. "My MaMa was just proud African, new, not seasoned…tryna keep a taste of home."

"You were her treasure, the forcefully conceived," Taffy intoned, touching her grandmother's sable-rich skin looking like Africa spit out that white sailor's blood and swallowed NuNu entirely.

NuNu grunted. "MaMa gave me her new name, but she taught me old, African ways. My girl child would've known 'em too, but she took her first and last breath in one day." NuNu's smile was soft, yet proud. "My Octavia walked across the waters in MaMa's arms after leaving her portion of The Gift for you, so never forget who you are or what you have."

"Octavia: four-deep," Taffy uttered.

"We share The Gift and the name. MaMa, me, my child, now you, Little One. You'll tie up loose ends."

Taffy frowned. "Meaning?"

"Your way's hard 'cause you're double-portioned, but that double-dip's gonna help you settle some things," NuNu soothed, feeling Taffy's spirit flinch. NuNu draped the wet rag across Taffy's chest, covering nakedness as well as wounds. A rustling chuckle sprinkled like dry leaves from NuNu's lips. "Didn't have to teach you much. You came here knowing. Wasn't born with a veil on your face like us other Octavias. You come out your mama's belly eyes wide…and white. Nearly scared Lacy to death."

"Wish I had," Taffy mumbled.

NuNu stilled. Her voice was hard and insistent—a walking stick pounding dry ground. "Don't eat poison someone else serves. What's done is done." NuNu's voice melted slightly. "Let it go for your good not hers."

Taffy returned her grandmother's stare. Had NuNu glimpsed truth regarding Taffy's Up North exile or had God blocked her view?

"'Sides," NuNu continued, "It's coming out in the wash real soon."

☙

They sat in harmonious silence—Taffy's skin oiled smooth, hair still damp and hanging heavily—a large hurricane lamp illuminating the space between. "You ready?"

Offering her right hand, Taffy nodded, seated at her grand-mother's feet. Biting her lip against the pin prick, Taffy watched a red pearl sprout from her fingertip.

"The life of all flesh is in the blood," NuNu quoted, pricking her own finger before pressing hers against Taffy's. "Take all my good and none of my bad, and weave yourself a world right for you."

Sacred moment passed, they wiped hands on an old towel before spreading the sheath. It was little more than a castoff undergarment embellished by the first Octavia. Transformed into bridal attire fit for her child, it became Octavia's shroud. Now her offspring beautified the sheath with intent and painstaking embroidery. NuNu insist-ed Taffy take the sheath when she left Bledsoe this time. Wrapped in muslin and tied with hope, the simple cotton heirloom offered a promise more poignant than satin or silk when worn to a mar-riage bed of real love. NuNu bristled knowing a union with Alfredo couldn't grant Taffy a worthwhile thing. Her granddaughter needed a different bed and a different love…

"NuNu, Alfredo's connected to Greenville," Taffy disclosed, halting NuNu's musing. Greenville: the word she'd whispered, causing Alfredo's face to concave in fear.

"That mess-of-a-man you married got something to do with your Daddy's being jailed?" NuNu sharply demanded.

"I don't know," Taffy admitted, "but Greenville's heavy on him."

NuNu snorted. "Bet Imogene knows but she ain't told the truth since conception." Silence swelled until NuNu decided, "Lord knows. He'll show," before lapsing into rhythmic humming meant to soothe the soul.

Hearing a second voice—higher, clearer than NuNu's—Taffy's

head snapped up. Looking towards the washing room, Taffy recognized the hazy outline of The Gift reaching into the tub to extract an ugly, odious thing. Smiling her approval, Knowing walked out the backdoor triumphantly.

NuNu's voice was filled with wonder. "You see her?"

Taffy answered reverently. "Yes…but never her face…at least not clearly."

"Don't matter. God's gifts are in His image. So are you. When you know yourself, you've already glimpsed His gifting." Still, NuNu looked about hoping to see what Taffy saw. "The Gift ain't wasting daylight, Little One. She means for you to hear, see, and obey."

In NuNu's eighty-plus years The Gift never manifested herself like this. But if the Holy Spirit could transfigure into a dove certainly God's Knowing could inhabit feminine form. The transfiguration left NuNu worried that there were turbulent times ahead. How to mitigate the pitfalls in Taffy's path? Humbly, NuNu bowed her head. The matter wasn't in her hands. This was but a beginning. And pain was part of Taffy's process.

CHAPTER NINE

Girls were a "colossal waste" of God's time better spent making frogs, lizards, snakes…anything *but*. Peanut butter toast was a treat for kings. Willie Ray Williams III was still his best friend. And school was a chore even if he did get mostly A's.

"Better not let M'Dear catch you bad-mouthing school," Taffy teased, Angel skipping alongside the next morning to meet the school bus, having updated her on his current worldview.

"It's icky having a schoolteacher at home," Angel confided.

"*Former* schoolteacher," Taffy modified.

"She still won't let me have bad grammar or nothing."

"Or anything."

"See! Just like that."

Taffy laughed.

"Thanks again for the model plane, Taf. It's same as the one I saw!"

"Sears and Roebuck catalog?"

"No," Angel tapped his forehead. "I saw it before I got it. Usually do."

Taffy's steps slowed and she watched Angel closely. He couldn't have The Gift…

Taffy juggled curiosity and hesitancy. The former won. She pushed away from herself and towards Angel, spirit glimpsing inner realms. But she couldn't stay. Something was in his blood. Shocked, Taffy withdrew.

The Gift came only to the females in Octavia's line, hadn't chosen since Taffy, and Knowing *couldn't* come to Angel unless…

See what you know and know what you see.

"Lord, no," Taffy barely breathed. Facing a mountain too high to manage, she let truth leave. Reeling, Taffy took Angel's hand, intent on stabilizing herself with his sweetness. A jolt shot through their connected palms, signaling deep legacy. Taffy opened her mouth in question but Angel released her hand and bolted toward the hilltop.

"The new bus is coming!"

Taffy heard it before she saw it. Like the text books courtesy of Richland Elementary, it was white folks' cast-offs. "Lord, Miss Delphie can hear that thing."

Angel giggled. "Miss Delphie's deaf and over a hundred."

"Precisely! And who's driving?" Taffy asked, as the bus wobbled their way.

"Deacon Williams. Stand back if you want your feet."

"Deacon Williams as in Willie Ray's grandfather?" Taffy trilled.

Angel grinned. "Lord-a-mercy! Deacon Williams used to cart us on a mule-drawn wagon, and he was hazardous then."

"Hey, Angel boy, welcome aboard!" William Ray Williams Sr. boomed as the bus rocked to a perilous halt. "Sister Rachel! How you?"

"'Morning, Deacon Williams. It's me, Taffy."

Deacon Williams lifted thick spectacles from the bridge of his nose. "Whoa and behold! Thought you was looking a little tall and dark to be your mama. Sho' miss her at the schoolhouse. Miss Rachel was one of the best teachers Bledsoe Normal ever had. Gal, when you get back? Ain't nobody said nothing 'bout you being here."

"You must still be holding out against a telephone."

"Ain't no need for gadgets like tellyphones and toilets. They spoil folks, make 'em lazy. Can't walk to neighbors to say 'how do?,' and won't go to no outhouse to handle business. Me? I'mma talk to friends face-to-face, and leave my stinky outside."

Taffy had to laugh.

"Well, how you doing, Taffy-gal? How long you here for? Heard your daddy's out hunting. Tell 'im I'mma join him when my new spectacles come in. Cain't be aiming at deer and shooting folks dead. Gotta go. Tell your people I said howdy. "

"Yes, sir," Taffy replied, head rocking with Deacon's rambling word storm. She hugged Angel, releasing him to board the bus but Angel held fast. "What's wrong?"

"I don't feel good."

"Scolioitis acting up?"

Angel giggled. Taffy bent so they were eye-to-eye. "I'll be here when you get home, baby. I promise."

"On a penny?"

"Take a kiss instead?"

Angel didn't mind the series of 'ewwws' and 'yucks' erupting aboard the bus as schoolmates pressed against windows. Content, he let Taffy urge him forward. "Wait! Can we play ball when I get home?"

"Yes, Angel."

"And bake something? Apple cake, three layers, chocolate frosting and peanut butter with strawberry jam in between?"

"Cookies are easier," Taffy suggested.

"Cake is bigger."

"Get on the bus, Angel."

"Okay, cookies. Can we go night fishing, too? Papa should be back from hunting by then, and you know he likes his night fishing."

"Deacon, you can shut the door," Taffy stated, stepping away from the bus and waving as Angel's peers laughed. Unfazed, Angel moved up the aisle, calling out suggestions for his pleasure until plopping onto the empty seat Willie Ray had saved.

Deacon Williams opened the door again. "They're a notion ain't they?"

"And then some," Taffy agreed, waving until the rickety rectangle-on-wheels disappeared from view. Smiling, Taffy turned and headed towards family land. "Time to see the rest of my crazy Bledsoes. Lord, give me strength."

❦

It was high noon and hot by the time Drew Bledsoe made it in from the fields for his midday meal. Animated voices bouncing across his yard escorted him through the gate. His wife's bell-like voice was elevated in pitch and pleasure. Instantly, Drew knew: his cousin was home.

Stomping up the porch, he yanked open the screen door. "There best be some cooking amongst all this cackling!"

"Chloe, your caveman done come," Taffy slowly drawled.

Chloe Bledsoe snickered. "Lord, here they go."

Eyeing NuNu's loose-fitting housedress sagging on Taffy's tall form, Drew smirked. "Your wardrobe didn't get the news slavery ended?"

Chloe howled. Taffy pounced.

"Quit baying at the moon and gimme love," Drew ordered, catching Taffy in a bear hug. Holding her at arms' length, Drew decided, "Cousin, you looking alright minus this follow-the-Drinking Gourd-get-up and them Mammy-made braids 'bout your head."

"And your wife's looking less virginal than before." The women's hysterical laughter thrilled the air.

"Yeah...well." Drew rubbed his wife's distended belly. "I do good work."

"Andrew Bledsoe!" Chloe shrilled, wide-eyed. "Lord Jesus, did this man say what he said?"

"He did," Taffy instigated.

"Baby, go wash up so you can eat."

"Ain't enough soap in the world," Taffy teased.

Wagging a fist Taffy's way, Drew hugged what used to be his wife's waist before leaving to do her bidding.

"Y'all look good together, Chloe," Taffy acknowledged once Drew was out of earshot. Drew—ranch-hard and ebony—complimented Chloe's soft, golden glow. Despite her own losses in love, Taffy admired the man-woman passion always evident between the two. "Still in love?"

"Amen and always," Chloe affirmed, unconsciously rubbing her protruding belly.

Taffy smiled, noting the gentle, pink haze about Chloe's head. "You tell him I'll deny it, but Drew's a good man, so I'm glad."

"Speaking of, Taffy, when—"

"Chloe," Taffy interrupted, tone warning, "don't start."

"You don't even know what I was gonna say," Chloe protested, pulling Taffy down onto a kitchen chair.

"Something meddlesome as usual."

"No, I was 'bout to ask when you gonna locate some loving of your own."

Taffy snorted. "That's not meddling?"

Chloe's bell-like voice launched into a familiar lament. "I'm interested in your best and what you have isn't it."

"Nothing subtle 'bout you, girl. You plunge head-first."

Chloe covered Taffy's hand with her own. "I worry about you, Taf."

Taffy looked out the kitchen window away from the flashflood of light rushing from Chloe's soul into her own. Though irritating at times, Taffy knew Chloe's meddlesome tendencies were rooted in affection tried and true.

Born weeks apart, the two shared a bassinet when their mothers' came calling, which was often—Corrine Randolph and Rachel Bledsoe being bosom friends since picking-berries-by-the-lake-days. Chloe and Taffy grew up heart-to-heart, their joke being: "we're bound from cradle to crypt."

Their kinship conquered the imposition of Up North distance. Chloe was friend, sister, and confidante helping Taffy keep her mind through trying times. When Taffy's insides went weak with absence, Angel's photographs and Chloe's rambling letters softened sharp reality. Now, photos, letters, and Octavia's sheath lay cushioned in the mahogany box in Taffy's suitcase—treasures side-by-side.

"I'm fine," Taffy insisted, cupping Chloe's belly. Strong, staccato bursts vibrated beneath Taffy's palms. Beaming, Taffy offered, "She's gorgeous."

Chloe sharply inhaled. "We're having a girl?!"

"A *gorgeous* girl, and she's not long in coming."

Chloe squealed. "He swears we're having a boy so don't tell Drew—"

"Don't tell me what?"

The women looked up to find Drew entering the kitchen, slinging soapy water from his hands.

"Lord, you can't teach a donkey nothing," Taffy mourned, shaking her head. "Dry those hooves on a hand towel."

Drew smiled. "Yessuh, bearded wonder."

"Best sleep with your good eye open."

Pushing away from the table to fix Drew's midday meal, Chloe tittered, "One day y'all gonna pretend you got good sense."

"Today's not that day," Taffy promised, nudging Chloe back onto her chair. "I'll fix the plates, Chloe. Sit and rest with your jackass."

CHAPTER TEN

Meal finished, dishes cleaned and Drew back on the ranch where he belonged, Taffy and Chloe sat on the porch swing, gently swaying, arms linked.

Sunlight kissed day with sweet affection. A flock of birds burst upward, frightened by a bounding jackrabbit zigging and zagging until swallowed by growth bordering the fenceless backyard. The foliage surrounding the tiny, two-story frame house was well-manicured, but ten yards out, Drew let nature have her way. Blackberry bushes formed a natural demarcation, separating tame from free. Taffy inhaled their sweet perfume.

"Berries smell wonderful, huh?" Chloe offered. "We should pick some for a cobbler tonight. Nothing like warm cobbler with fresh cream."

"Mmm-hmm," Taffy murmured, enjoying this camaraderie so like a blanket on a clothesline warmed by the sun. "Everything's okay down here, downhome?"

Chloe brought Taffy up to speed since their last conversation on who'd been married, buried, moved away or come to stay.

New families had flocked to Bledsoe, fleeing a Depression denting preexisting deficits. Like some old prophetess, NuNu warned, "Famine's 'round the bend." Told folks to snatch their money out "buckra banks" long before Black Tuesday wrecked the white man's world and he threw himself off high-rise buildings like God gave him wings.

Those who valued NuNu's sight saved their cents and armed themselves against turbulent times. Mutual Aid accelerated. A community pantry was formed, stockpiling sundry essentials. And when the bull market burned, Bledsoe had enough to share. Share it did with nearby sister towns, Drexel and Winter Cove—their Colored residents finding assistance in Bledsoe and fair credit at Tinsley's General Store. Through collaborative efforts, Bledsoe survived. A refuge to

Colored folks in need, the town had doubled in size.

"But we're still Bledsoe and still Black. Like Poppy preaches 'ain't nothing white here 'cept milk and teeth.' So thank God for good things. And I'm still worried 'bout you, Taf," her heart-sister lamented.

"Like a dog with a bone," Taffy mused at Chloe's picking up the untied string.

Chloe sat forward, talking fast. "I don't understand why you stay, Taf. Al Freeman ain't no good to nobody save himself and the dead folks in your downstairs deep freeze."

"You're preaching to the choir, Chloe."

"Honey, you know I don't advocate breaking up marriages. What God joins man shouldn't undo—"

"Don't blame this on God," Taffy interjected. "It wasn't His idea."

"Amen to that! So…when you gonna handle it and how?" Chloe persisted.

"It's already handled. I'm not going back. Angel and I are leaving—"

"*You and Angel*? Leaving?!" Chloe stopped the swaying swing. "For…?"

Taffy inhaled cautiously. "I can't say just now."

"Why not? You don't know?"

Taffy nodded, feeling a soft blooming inside at the thought of escaping her marriage's coffin-like confines. "Of course, I do. But you don't need to. Not yet."

"Why not?" Chloe asked, clearly vexed.

"Once Alfredo knows I'm gone, who you think he's gonna interrogate?"

"He can bug and bother all he wants! I wouldn't tell that man a thing and you know that, Taffy!"

"I don't want you lying for me, Chloe."

"Wouldn't be the first time, won't be the last." Chloe overrode Taffy's laughter with, "Well, if you won't tell me where, at least tell me when."

"Tomorrow—"

"*Tomorrow*?!" Chloe shrieked. "Unh-uh, no ma'am, you can't just come home one day and disappear the next. That don't make no sense!"

Taffy pushed the swing back into motion, certain of God's direction. "Actually, it does. Alfredo thinks I'm here for Founders' Festival. That's not until next week. By the time it's over and he realizes I'm long gone, I'll have a week on my side."

"Taf, you deserve more than what you have, but this don't sound right. You can't just take Angel and disappear heaven knows where."

"Watch me."

"Lord… Okay, at least tell me if it's Harlem? I know them riots tore you up inside, but they've passed, and you always said Harlem *if* and when you ever left. You said that—what's it called?—August Savon Studio for Colored Crafts…"

"Augusta Savage Studio of Arts and Crafts," Taffy provided.

"Right! That! You been drawing and painting since we were kids. You seamstress so good on account you make art with your seamstressing! Is that where you're headed? That Harlem studio?"

"Chloe, quit fishing."

"Detroit? Philadelphia? You going north, south, east or west?"

Taffy took to humming, ignoring Chloe's dogged questioning.

"*Ooo*! You so willful! This has been building a while, but it feels sudden."

Taffy quieted. Yes, Chloe understood how Harlem's riots tore her up inside. But would Chloe understand recurring, disturbing dreams? Since Grandmother Lacy's death, nightmares walked at will. Most were mind-numbing and thankfully forgotten upon waking, leaving vague imprints of an empty, open casket or grave. But yesterday morning Up North, dreams twisted, placing Taffy dead center, running for a train and her life, blood flowing from her back fountain-like.

Only in part, Taffy disclosed the dream. Chloe gripped the swaying swing.

"Ask your gift to find you another something to think on. I'm not liking this."

Taffy snickered. "I learned long ago my gift can't be manipulated."

"Why board a train going wherever you going, just to be snarled at by some twisted up, ugly thing?"

"I'd rather leave bleeding then stay put and die."

"Hmph!" Chloe nodded her agreement and understanding. "Lord knows you been tied up too long." Rubbing her belly, Chloe sighed. "Maybe this is best."

Taffy laid a hand atop Chloe's. Together, they rubbed her baby belly, drawing peace.

"Call me when you get where you're going so my mind can rest."

"I will," Taffy vowed. "And, I'll tell you everything soon enough, Chloe. Just let me get settled."

"Don't get where you going and get all swallowed up. We got any kin where you headed?" Chloe interrupted Taffy's comeback. "I'm just making sure you and Angel got a soft place to land. I don't want y'all poor on some big city street."

Taffy patted the bills folded against her breast. "I got something saved, and you know good and well I don't play with Angel's well-being. We'll manage."

"Taf, I don't wanna see you go, but I can't stand you being with Alfredo either. Leaving'll be the lesser of two evils. Right?"

Eyes fixed on the beauty of day, Taffy told Chloe about the ugliness of yesterday morning and finding Jonnie Mae. Chloe covered her mouth in disbelief. "Chloe, every day I stay, it's harder to breathe."

They sat in silence as Chloe held Taffy's hand. "Aunt Rachel and Uncle T. made peace with Angel's going?" Chloe asked softly.

"They don't know yet."

Chloe leaned away for a better look at her dearest friend. "You gonna tell 'em before or *after* leaving? Angel's been here since he was three. Bledsoe is all he knows."

"Time he knew something different," Taffy replied, jaw set, eyes smoky.

"You still look like a cat, like you can see in the dark."

"Used to think I could, but look where that got me." Her gift of prescience hadn't prevented damnable things. Yawning, Taffy stood, stretching, tired of bending a mind-numbing matter. "I'm taking a bath and scratching up a nap. NuNu had me up all night talking and stitching. Walked Angel to the bus then stopped all along Bledsoe Boulevard this morning," Taffy relayed, playfully referring to that long stretch of road inhabited by family.

"Gon' up. Your room's ready. I'll wake you in time to meet Angel." Troubled by all she'd heard, Chloe sat pensive, completely forgetting and failing to mention what Taffy need know about Bledsoe's most recent arrival. "Taf, what'll you do if Alfredo finds you?"

Taffy's answer was a mysterious, rather dangerous smile.

CHAPTER ELEVEN

Bledsoe was more beautiful than memory allowed. Emerald grass. Sloping hills. Untamed acreage cohabited with wild weeds. Creeping vines and fruit-burdened trees showed evidence of good spring rains. Deep green grass cushioned Taffy's naked feet that still refused shoes. A crystal stream cut through earth like a ribbon, courtesy of Lake Florence. Poplars, crepe myrtles, camellia, and myriad fruit trees bloomed as neat rows of crops spread like puzzle pieces lovingly placed. Azaleas, sweet peas, and gladiolas with a curious spattering of out-of-place blood red hibiscus—that NuNu claimed came from Poppy's veins—created an earthbound rainbow.

Solomon's glory couldn't compare.

God had kissed Bledsoe, transforming it from disregarded wasteland to prime, precious terrain. Even so, she couldn't receive the rest found in this sanctuary. Thoughts stretched her mind. Seeing Angel home to his chores, Taffy went in search of solace. Lake Florence rippled, waiting.

She sat, dipping toes in welcoming waters before wading in. Sprinkling cool drops onto her face, Taffy prayed her actions were right with God's want and will.

"Lord, you know I *can't* stay with Alfredo and survive."

He wasn't altogether worthless always; might've been appealing beneath a different sky. Wasn't charming, but in the beginning Al was somewhat kind. But Alfredo proved loathsome, yard-dog mean, over time. With his indecent magazines, habitual adultery, Al openly flaunted his foolishness while daring Taffy to seek outside intimacy.

Step out on me and I'll write you up so wrong that boy'll be lost to you forever!

And Al's kindness dried up faster than a low creek in July, all because his wife simply didn't want him *that* way.

Lord knew his consorts were welcome to him. But now, unfortunately, Taffy knew faces and names: Truly Earl, her oldest, and Jonnie Mae.

"*Whew!*" Taffy was sick of stupidity. She felt stretched. Pulled. Wanted to return to NuNu's bed, burrowing against her grandmother's scarred back, cradled in safety.

She'd been careful not to awaken NuNu this morning, climbing from bed and dressing quickly—eyes locked on the muslin-wrapped sheath over which they'd labored lovingly. Its miniscule pattern of flowers the first Octavia began might've been completed decades ago had NuNu's infant Octavia lived. But she hadn't, and time passed until Taffy arrived, ready for a rightful role. Now the cotton sheath, softened with years, was complete despite there being no one to wear it as the wedding garb it was meant to be.

Taffy hadn't been allowed. Married in a rush-and-a-hush, there was no family tossing flowers at her feet, bestowing blessings. Just Lacy paying some apathetic justice of the peace as Rachel stood witness, shedding alligator tears.

I don't and won't were the vows Taffy should've screamed. But Grandmother Lacy—spearheading the abominable—held infant Angel, steely eyes daring Taffy to do one contrary thing. For Angel, Taffy acquiesced, reciting vows like prefabricated lies.

Now you're a real woman, honest and reputable again, Lacy had declared, returning Angel to the safety of Taffy's arms, marriage certificate complete. *Don't sully your married name. Cook, clean, and keep the man content.* Protests were silenced, by backhand if necessary. *That marriage bed is your burden. Pleasure is a myth. Endure!*

Taffy snickered. "Not as long as I'm breathing and a Bledsoe." She'd sacrificed too much to choke on bitter things that should be sweet. But what sweetness existed after being a bartered and bewildered bride, married off to some ancient, little known tyrant at the age of sixteen? There'd been no courtship, just backwards transactions void of affection before being unceremoniously shuttled Up North where Taffy struggled to make a home not built on hate and rage.

"Forget those things that are behind," she commanded herself. "Press on."

Needing full relief, only the thought of someone venturing to the lake and catching an eyeful kept Taffy from disrobing. Instead, completely clothed, Taffy waded deeper in Lake Florence's liquid embrace to wash stained memories away.

⸎

She hadn't meant to nod off. But a cool breeze and the lake's tranquility combined with limited sleep left Taffy dozing beneath a shade tree. Waking, she knew by the lazy slant of the sun that day was near done. Hopping up, she stretched, sundress now dry by day's warm touch.

Heading towards Drew and Chloe's, Taffy's thoughts were like pulpy lemonade, bitter but sweet.

Tonight was her last in Bledsoe for God knew how long. Long enough for Alfredo to exhaust his search? He wouldn't easily quit. He held on for money.

Taffy had watched Alfredo's rise, the acquiring of the funeral home he so wanted, his staying afloat while The Depression slammed better men to the ground. Because he had backing. Lacy.

Lacy paid blood money, buying Alfredo, trying to own Taffy. Love of Lacy's filthy lucre had Alfredo holding onto a marriage wrapped in icy sheets and not worth spit.

"I already washed myself of bitterness," Taffy reminded herself, entering Drew and Chloe's backyard. Choosing joy, Taffy headed for the berry bushes. Ripe, succulent, they begged her picking for a cobbler that would scream good and sweet. Grabbing the basket Chloe kept on the back porch, strong voices grabbed Taffy. Jovial. Lively. Deep, resonate, and perplexing, one voice meandered out from the others.

Breath snatched, heart hammering, Taffy stood frozen by time. Only her mind moved, begging retreat. But a contrary heart had its own thoughts. A strong baritone erupted with laughter that exploded in the pit of her belly as Taffy slowly mounted the steps, opened the backdoor. She approached the kitchen, trembling. Swinging the door open, Taffy stood immobilized as her world wobbled and fractured beneath a haunting potpourri of red warmth, peppermint, and long, lost love.

CHAPTER TWELVE

Running was futile. Still, she tried.

Heart pounding, pace furious, Taffy put as much distance between herself and Chloe's kitchen as possible, trying to outrun the man she'd left behind.

She had to get Angel! Grab their things. Be on that train a day early. Richland's one and only Chicago-bound had already departed this morning. Didn't matter. They'd hightail it to the station in Trenton, all forty miles on foot if need be. Anything to escape Roam Ellis, the man Taffy meant to marry.

Confusion had Taffy spinning. Taffy headed one direction, then turned and went the other. She stopped abruptly, yelling her agony at the sky. *"Lord, why?!"*

Roam Ellis had violated the silent rules of their separation! They were partners in a well-synchronized dance of avoidance, elaborately ensuring their paths never crossed. And they hadn't. Not since he'd given Taffy his heart and she'd produced another man's child.

Now, Roam was home. Where'd he come from, and for how long?

"Dear, Jesus," Taffy moaned. Seven years after the fact, memory of the pain that ravaged Roam when seeing her with newborn Angel in arms the first time ripped a fresh hole in Taffy's heart. She'd shattered the man. His love. And the future they'd dared to dream. Subsequently, Roam boarded the rails leaving Taffy to Alfredo and their newly created family. Now Roam was here. Unannounced. Without warning.

Taffy never believed in coincidences. Just divine timing...

What had Knowing said? *God controlled the reckoning.*

Weighted truth had Taffy bent at the waist, trying to breathe. She struggled to quiet a raging heartbeat as a mountain of loss straddled her back. Gripping her sides, Taffy's hands slowly slid to her knees. Old tears sprang fresh and fierce in her eyes, taking their sweet time to run new rivers.

Slow minutes passed before raw shock lost its edge and Taffy could right her posture. "Pull yourself together," she grit, wiping wetness from her face. Taffy set her mind right and her feet in motion. Still. "Meddling heffa could've said *something*." Taffy kicked rocks from her path, seething at Chloe's scheming and Drew's sitting smug as an ass-up donkey.

Seven years ago Taffy would have rejoiced at an audience and opportunity with Roam. Now, it was too much, too late. Roam Ellis had to go!

"We can't both be in Bledsoe," Taffy decided, thoughts flying fast, furious, and plain... "Foolish!" Roam had every right to be home. "And I have every right to leave!"

Like she'd left Chloe's? Overly affected, shamefaced with evident longing?

"Lord, I hope those fools didn't see all up in my feelings," Taffy fussed, walking nowhere fast. She was embarrassed by her crazed reaction, but *Lord, Jesus*...Roam Ellis had become some kind of something! Nothing like the boy she'd thought beautiful since the night he stole her heart when Taffy was fourteen.

Back when he was little more than a musty-butt boy running rag-tag with Drew, Taffy ignored Roam and his constant "threats" to marry her soon as she finished school. But she turned fourteen, Roam seventeen, and Taffy's interest bubbled to bursting.

Suddenly, he smelled good. His deepening voice and broadening form were far better. But the night Roam pulled Taffy from the church basement, confronting her for choosing Elton Young as her date to the Sadie Hawkins dance, kissing her with a tender anger that left her weak, Taffy fell in love neck-deep.

Two years they courted, daydreaming life and love until...Taffy went away, returning with a baby, body changed. But truth was? Love remained?

"That's a lie from the pit!" Taffy protested, staggering at an altar of complicated affection. Taffy did her best to negate this ungodly encounter, heaven's stopping and the earth stilling as shockwaves roared between. Tried not to be a cauldron of emotions liable to spill all contents at Roam Ellis' feet—every truth, secret, and lie contrived. Did her best to be unaffected by the lopsided grin of the boy she once loved, fought to ignore an unwanted thirst for the man he'd become who looked dangerously delicious.

"Don't let your thoughts send you to hell in a handbasket," Taffy warned herself, trying to holster errant thinking. Still, her traitorous mind took its time remembering entering Chloe's kitchen like a sleep-walker and finding an incarnation of forgotten dreams, a man worth the sinning.

What had he grown to? Six-four, five? Two-hundred-fifty-plus pounds of hard-bodied muscle and shoulders wide? That anemic cat-erpillar that once populated his upper lip had gone and found friends, blooming into a moustache that would tickle, thick against her skin. With copper-penny complexion and familiar red waves like low-burn-ing coals atop his head, this Roam was tantalizing, frightening. Remarkable face, clef chin, sculpted lips, grin mischievous, and teeth too-pretty-for-a-man. Beneath this polished façade Taffy glimpsed Roam's force and power within. Raw strength met fresh rhythm and flow. Roam Ellis had gone off and grown into himself. And Taffy's re-sponse to his newness had been nearly as bad as the slow, unrighteous scrutiny Roam had raked over her body and being.

Leaned up against a counter, a spoon in his mouth, a bowl of something savory in hand, Roam's posture had changed from loose and easy to ramrod straight. Roam's visage had been a nickelodeon at fast pace. Hot fury and dense pain flashed before fading. Then soft as cotton, indifference masked Roam's face.

Resuming his lounging posture, Roam had eased back against Chloe's counter, his indifference replaced by something warm. Dan-gerous. Taffy felt pure heat as Roam eyed her in an excruciating trek, head-to-toe and back again—all the while slowly wrapping his tongue about that spoon, licking it clean, gently as if her body…

Stunned by her wanton turn of thought, Taffy angrily fanned herself beneath the evening sun. "He had no business looking at me like that!" With an intense heat like hot fingers on Taffy's flesh setting something unexpected ablaze. His stare was boldly intimate when meeting Taffy's paralyzed gaze. A lazy, lopsided grin lifted Roam's lips as—bareheaded—he'd tipped an imaginary hat and offered a greeting.

"Miz Freeman." His baritone rumbled a simple salutation that was water on fire.

Freed from whatever the spell weaving its wonder, Taffy had shot Chloe a searing look before pivoting. With loud indignity, the screen door slammed behind her in farewell.

Now, here beneath nature's glory, Taffy picked up a rock, hurled it at a tree. "I'm done with stupidity!" Done with sweet thoughts of lost dreams. She'd long abandoned thoughts of confrontation, *never* fathomed reconciliation. And Taffy didn't have time for fantasy. Or lustful longings, and a momentary envy that Roam had prospered without her. She'd been left behind as if they'd never exchanged promises to build a house and make a home grounded in love, faithfulness, and fidelity.

Taffy snorted. "Honey, you're the one went off and married another somebody." And being in Bledsoe with Roam could only precipitate a catastrophe, Taffy concluded, spotting in the distance the pumps she'd flung aside yesterday to give Angel a run for his money. Angel still won.

"And you still walking 'round looking country," Taffy scolded, examining her bare feet. "Shameful!" The scarlet toenail polish, the fact that she was content being shoeless, or that she was troubled by a man beyond her reach?

Eyes narrowing, Taffy harnessed her thoughts, tight like the sundress she hiked between her legs to mount the fence boarding Bledsoe land. Once upon a when, she could easily shimmy her girl-narrow self between the slats. Too much extra to try now, Taffy pitched herself over the top rail, hopped down the other side.

Walking the short distance to where her shoes and stockings lay, Taffy picked them up but refused putting them on. Like she refused trouble's call.

"Can't waste daylight agonizing over what coulda been." Still, Taffy couldn't shake heavy sorrow. She headed for the back road deciding prolonged grief didn't do anyone any good. This time tomorrow she'd be in Illinois, and desolate thoughts of Roam Ellis would dim and fade. Eventually.

CHAPTER THIRTEEN

He wasn't spying, simply driving. Excessively slow. *Sight-seeing*, he called it, privately savoring a scandalous meta-morphosis.

Good damn *gal…you got grown!*

As a Pullman porter, his routes on the rails had taken him coast-to-coast. He'd enjoyed many pretty Colored women, layover lovers who shared his downtime. But this right here, sashaying up the ways, was altogether outrageous.

Roam Ellis whistled low. "That there's more than a 'pretty brown-skin with a shape hittin' ninety-nine'," he muttered, using porters' speak meant to describe a Colored woman's glory. This here was dark velvet on a coke bottle streaking past two-hundred-and-two. "Oughta be a law."

Where was the fresh-mouthed know-it-all with the eerie ability to tell folks their business before they knew it—whose pigtails he pulled just to set feline eyes aglow? Long gone, the young lady who'd prom-ised her heart while holding his was mere shadow moving under-neath. This here was a *real* woman, grown decadently.

"*Damn!*" What was previously a hint was now a holler. Healthy-bosomed. Body tucked narrow in the middle. Limitless legs. Homegrown hips and heaven-built backside, flowing full, high, round and wide, all about the outside. An hourglass-on-overtime, she was sensuality personified. At Drew's, she'd kept her distance, still he'd caught her honeysuckle-and-ginger scent. Despite thick backwa-ter braids, she was silk and sunshine, her obscene bounty enough to make a dead man rise.

His whole being responded honestly; body thickening, anger sparking. Roam squashed the absurd rush above and below the belt-line. Wasn't interested in tangling with Taffy Bledsoe. Did it once and had the bruises to prove it. Took forever to fix what she'd wounded, but he was a better man for it. Her deception afforded Roam *carte blanche* to travel faster, farther and wider. And he thanked her for it. Still, displeasure rioted at Taffy reentering his world without warning.

So, this was Drew's "surprise".

"Dumb nut!" Roam could do without his closest friend's twisted humor. Granted, Roam had barely hugged Chloe before making a beeline to her percolating pots. But by the time Taffy walked in, he'd downed plenty red beans and rice, time enough for Drew to tell what needed to be told. "Fool, why didn't you tell me Taffy was here!" Roam shouted after Taffy exited, leaving thick tension behind.

Drew had merely laughed. "Man, don't play stupid as you look. You know good and well Taffy comes home every Juneteenth, which is precisely why *you don't*!"

"Plus it's Founders' Festival next week, so where else would Taffy be?" Chloe had added, looking innocent when, knowing Chloe, she'd had a hand in this.

Now, driving along, Roam stopped drumming the steering wheel long enough to extract customary peppermints from his pants pocket. Unwrapping two, he popped them in his mouth—sucking, tussling.

Might as well concede the inevitability of Taffy. *That's why you're here a week early*, Roam admitted. Planned to visit long enough to satisfy his parents. Hop back on the rails and be long gone before Founders' Festival began. And if chance should cause an encounter, it would be minimized, padded with apathy. He'd be ready *if*. Roam was wrong. Wasn't sure what he'd expected, but good God in Zion, *that woman* wasn't it!

Roam fiddled with an ever-present cigar tucked behind one ear. A college professor-turned rail chef due to circumstance, "Doc" gave Roam his first stoagie, declaring, "it'll let that fine mind unwind." Sitting there, Roam's mind was wound up tight. Advance warning might've bought him some time, but it wouldn't have been enough. Seeing Taffy snatched him back seven years. Something raw rumbled within. Roam slapped constraints on it. What was, was. "What is, 'sho 'nuff is," Roam allowed, enjoying the pleasure of watching Taffy unawares.

The longer Roam watched, the more he wound up liking the wave of her walk. The more he wanted to lick and lap her most sensuous secrets, despite the past.

Regrettably, matters hadn't turned out on last night's pit stop in the nearby town of Trenton, before winding up downhome in Bled-soe. East of Bledsoe, Trenton was the closest thing to a big city in Progress County. And in that town sort-of-like-a-city was a woman worth seeing. Clean-suited, he'd called on a layover lover, intent on enjoying sweet brown honey before heading home. Wasn't much company, but she warmed a bed. More than once he knocked. Time lapsed. She'd opened the door a mere crack. From her meager at-tire, tousled hair, and the male voice demanding fulfillment, Roam deduced she was already occupied. Tipping his hat, Roam left her and her greedy, unapologetic eyes. They had no exclusivity. He left unfazed, yet unsatisfied. Watching all this homegrown heaven here, Roam experienced an intensely heavy, low-lying ache.

Slowly accelerating, Roam reminded himself, "That's a married woman, Ellis. Look all you want, but you'd better not taste."

CHAPTER FOURTEEN

Equilibrium mildly restored, Taffy walked the road, headed home. At the sound of an approaching vehicle, she moved over ready to wave at whoever passed. Instead, the car inched up beside her, driver in full-view.

Lord, I thought you loved me! Taffy redirected her attention to the road ahead. Taffy recalled the train ride home and holding her breath as Pullman porters came and went, fearing *he'd* somehow appear. When he didn't, Taffy relaxed, focused on getting Angel and heading to Cousin Gracie's. Now, miraculously, here he was harassing her tranquility. Taffy prayed Roam would drive on. But ever the tormentor, Roam couldn't leave her to struggle unseen.

"Doing alright, Miz Freeman?"

"Yes, thank you."

"Need a ride?"

"My feet'll find their way."

"Carrying your shoes so your feet can see?"

Taffy shot Roam a sideways glance. He sat behind the wheel cool-as-casual, that signature lopsided grin that used to make her belly flip-flop decorating his too-fine face. Resistance wobbled, but her voice was sure. "You need something?"

"Once upon a when I did but she got away."

Taffy stopped suddenly, forcing Roam to hit the brakes. Arms crossed, shoes dangling in hand, Taffy stared him down, talking tightly. "I'm in no mood for your foolishness, Roam Ellis. You need to say something? Say it. Otherwise leave."

"You're losing a leg."

Following his gaze, Taffy noted the stocking escaping the pocket of her sundress. Taffy left it like it was. "Anything else?"

"Yeah." Reaching over, Roam pushed open the passenger door. "Get in."

"I wish I would!"

"I wish you would, too, so do it."

Command ignored, Taffy resumed walking. She heard the door close and the crunch of road beneath wheels.

"Still calling the shots, huh? Fine. It's your game, Taffy Lou. Let's play your way. Get in and let's go sip sassafras and discuss the weather and whatever asinine drivel women like you prefer."

"Women like me?"

"Weak. Scary-assed. Two-faced, deceiving kinda women sidestepping issues 'cause you're too pathetic to handle them head-on."

Without thought Taffy marched into the road and across the car's path. It jerked to a halt. Stopping abreast the driver's door, Taffy leaned into Roam's space. "Listen closely, *Mr.* Ellis! This 'weak' woman's faced and fought more devils than you know, and lived to tell the tale. If I'd rather not deal with you right here and now, Demon-of-the-Day, that's choice not fear. Now, sidestep that, little knuckleheaded Negro."

Taffy had to jump back to avoid the opening door. On his feet and in Taffy's face in a heartbeat, Roam's baritone was gritty. "Ever know me to mince words?"

"You're straight no chaser," Taffy slung, using Roam's oft-spoken motto.

"And I ain't changing. So deal with this, Taffy Bledsoe—"

"Freeman," she inserted with twisted glee.

"You were damn wrong! Leaving us like you left. Mine one day. Gone the next. No warning. *Nothing*!"

Taffy's voice rose in exasperation. "It didn't happen how you think—"

"How the hell would you know what I thought?! You didn't care enough to ask *or* tell a thing. I found out like the rest of Bledsoe. *After the damn fact*!"

"Roam, every time I reached you refused, and you know it!"

"*Damn right*! Had nothing to say to you then, crazy for fooling with you now."

"Roam, how—"

"What did you wanna hear, Taffy? *Huh?!* 'Congratulations' for going off and having another man's child after promising me certain things?"

Hands on hips, Taffy needlessly demanded, "What things?"

"*Every*thing," Roam growled.

Taffy studied Roam long and hard, sensing something fragile beneath Roam's fury. That fragile thing plucking her conscience, Taffy's ire slowly deflated. She was left consumed by an overwhelming need for touch and forgiveness. Swallowing pride, Taffy looked up into the dark storm brewing in Roam's eyes. "It *can't* suffice...but I'm sorry."

Roam snorted away the soft-spoken apology.

"If I could wish away my wrongs, Lord *knows* I would but I can't," Taffy offered quietly, humbly. "Sorry is too, too simple, but I need your forgiveness. Please."

"You need?" Roam scoffed.

"I do."

"Simple as that?"

"That simple. I can't grovel, Roam. I've been stepped on enough."

"By whom?"

Taffy ignored the inquiry. "And, no, I didn't show you the respect you deserved, but more was at stake than I can say. I was sixteen doing what I could with what I had. Can you accept that?"

Roam's brooding, long-held silence was its own reply.

Taffy sadly exhaled a heartbroken sigh. "Good night, Roam."

"You're walking away *again*?!" Roam hurled as Taffy did precisely that. "So, it's 'hello and goodbye' huh, Taffy? *Taffy*!"

She didn't dare look back. There was much there she wanted to fix, might've fixed...but for Angel.

Moments later Taffy felt the friction of crumbled connections as Roam's vehicle barreled past. Her heart constricted. "Jesus, Lord..." There was little she could do to fix herself or him. So she let Roam go. "Like a fool, again."

It was best, despite wretchedness. No good could come of loving the right man at the wrong time. This here hurt something fierce, but she'd go on living. Better. Without self-sacrifice. She'd take delight when and where she could. Soon as her feet touched Chicagoland.

Stubbornly set on possibilities, Taffy approached a tree-lined bend where the road narrowed drastically. Rounding the curve, she froze.

Car perpendicular across the narrow outlet, Roam stood propped against automobile, muscled arms folded across a wide chest, Taffy's path unquestionably obstructed.

Taffy made ready to fuss him out only to reconsider. *That steel-headed man won't move.* She would. Taffy eyed the fence, knowing she'd earlier hopped it with ease. But she couldn't hike her dress up before present company.

"Go ahead," Roam goaded, popping peppermints in his mouth, ready to enjoy the spectacle. "I'd like to see you try."

Options were few with the opposite side of the road lined by a ditch and a frighteningly out-of-control briar patch. Taffy could reverse her path. *I'm not!* Taffy had long ago learned how to do what she had to.

"You 'bout to break something," Roam warned, shaking his head as Taffy prepared to climb. "Gal, quit acting up and walk this way."

Ignoring Roam, Taffy hoisted herself onto the bottom rail. Fumbling, she tried climbing with shoes in hand, finally dropping them over the fence, onto the other side.

Roam moved quickly before Taffy, too, was beyond reach.

Taffy felt an arm snake about her waist, effortlessly hauling her backward as if it didn't cost Roam a thing. *"What're you doing?!"*

"Whatever I want," Roam responded, setting Taffy on her feet, anchoring an arm about her waist when Taffy spun, spitting heat.

"Move, Roam." Taffy strained against Roam's iron hold. "Get off me before I hurt you!"

"Already did."

Her fire fizzled. Voice softened, tongue tasted regret. "Roam, what do you want?"

"You." Taffy stilled. Roam reinforced his hold. "Two things I won't do with you: mince words or waste time." Lifting her chin, claiming her mouth, Roam proved his point.

His lips were hot, soft, sweet. Taffy got lost savoring them and him, and the bombarding emotions of mere moments before became nonexistent. *Oh my blessedness,* Taffy inwardly purred, feeling a slow, unsanctioned melting. They'd shared quick, quaint kisses in adolescent sweetheart days. *Never* this. Never with man-to-woman *savoir faire.* Resuscitated passions exploded and multiplied. Taffy could barely breathe let alone think, so she followed love's lead and held on for the ride.

The ride was provocative, evocative, and disconcerting with Taffy melting and meshing against Roam like where she was was where she wanted to be...

Roam broke his hold, easing Taffy back a bit. He was too willing, she too ready, flowing into him without vacillation, with a whole lot simmering underneath. Roam passed a hand over moustache and mouth, not wiping, but sealing. "Woman, what're you doing to me?" She was silk and sugar slamming him against a brick wall head-on.

Lord, what are *we doing?*

Taffy struggled to get her bearings, Roam's unique taste branded on her lips. Too easily, they'd stepped into a sweet spot as if time hadn't passed when truly it had. The solid strength of Roam's body was proof enough. *Amen!* "I apologize for acting a sin and a shame," Taffy offered.

"Tell that to a blind man."

"Fine, I'm not sorry, but I need to be."

Roam chuckled unexpectedly. "That makes two of us." Sobering, Roam released Taffy completely. "Didn't mean to disrespect you or your marriage."

"I married you first," Taffy quietly reminded, remembering that Tom Thumb wedding her bossy-busy oldest cousin, Dena, strong-armed Roam into. Taffy was a bored bride of nine and Roam a grumbling groom of twelve when Dena officiated their nuptials. No kiss, just a clean handshake. No vows, just a promise not to feed each other frogs. Honeymoon was misinterpreted honeyed coon. Both declined. Taffy received a ruby ring, courtesy of Cracker Jack, making them boy and bride.

Roam stood silent, considering. "Yeah, well, that's neither here nor there."

"I still have that ring," Taffy confessed. "It's a reminder of who was once my sweetest thing."

Without comment, Roam reached for her hand. "Let's get you home."

Taffy slid away. "I'll walk."

"Still stubborn."

"Just needing the night air," Taffy amended, noting evening's final descent. *So I can clear you out my mind.*

"I'd rather cart you home."

"This isn't the big city, Roam. I'm fine."

"That you are," Roam stated, his eyes doing a slow dance down her physique.

Taffy ignored sudden heat. "Turn around."

"Why?"

"Just do it."

Dubious, Roam complied.

"And why're you here anyhow?" Taffy demanded. "From what I know, you haven't been home in a minute, and you *never* come home during Juneteenth."

"Founder's Day happens once every ten years," Roam replied. "Not here for anyone or anything more."

Roam was still honest to a fault, not sugar-coating the fact that he'd meticulously, painstakingly avoided her for years. They both had. Still, truth hurt. While Taffy evaded Roam out of shame, she couldn't fault Roam's preserving his well-being by avoiding her: *his* painful past.

Climbing the fence and hopping down the other side, Taffy righted her clothing. "Finished."

Turning, Roam shook his head, semi-grinning. "You're a predicament, Taffy Bledsoe."

Smiling ruefully she added, "Freeman." *But not for long.* "I'd better go."

"We're not finished." Roam's tone hardened. "You're holding a story untold."

Startled, Taffy merely nodded, afraid to open her mouth for fear of unearthing truths long buried. Softly, Taffy spoke after a long silence. "If and when talking time comes, you'll understand more craziness than you care to. 'Night, Roam."

Taffy was a distant, indefinite figure in the distance when Roam's pulse normalized enough for him to emit a low, deep, "Sweet dreams, Dollbaby."

CHAPTER FIFTEEN

Traveling doggone dusty roads of her downhome, he'd been anxious to be wife-free. Now, back North, Alfredo meant that. Literally.

"Sassing in my face talking 'bout I can sleep in her bed 'cause she ain't in it! Correcting me in front that old, tired-out Tinsley!" He ranted, raved, hiding fear beneath insult and indignity. He forgave himself for ever wanting to ride her unfettered hips that moved like a wave of some great sea. Forgave his britches for growing snug just looking. Marriage to a young, lush girl should've been divine, but she defied his pleasure repeatedly.

Now, two years shy of twenty-five, Taffy was age-advanced for Alfredo's taste, yet young enough to manipulate. Or should've been. Rock-solid and willful, his wife knew what she wanted, and it wasn't him. *She* made him favor tender females, sliding past puberty, sauntering along the fringes of womanhood, pliant and pliable—molded at will. Alfredo's bent desire was his wife's doing.

The longer he drove, the more blame Alfredo piled on Taffy's head. Her fault he'd resorted to multiple means of relief because she wouldn't surrender, legs spread. Brothels. Strange bedrooms. Outhouses and backseats. And his clammy, undertaker's hands that kept the car from veering.

"Shoulda took it," Alfredo spat, apparently forgetting he'd tried. He'd stumbled from Taffy's bedroom four years ago, sewing scissors sprouting out his spine.

Alfredo rubbed his back against the seat, unconsciously scar-scratching. Took Mr. Johnson next door to extricate scissors that ended futile attempts to copulate. Left Alfredo bumbling a cockamamie tale of accidental self-infliction. But neighbors knew Freeman was too weak to tame a wild wife, that his marriage was far from good.

Alfredo pounded the dashboard. "What they know?!" he shouted.

Not one was married to a hoodoo woman. He could only push so far. And push he constantly did. But yesterday she'd fought dirty, forcing his littered past down his ear.

Greenville.

Avoiding southern soil housing his skeletons, Alfredo Freeman rarely accompanied his wife on her jaunts downhome. He'd done so yesterday to throw her off, to remind Taffy who held power. Now she knew about Greenville? How? And how much?

Angrily, Alfredo swerved off the highway searching for a telephone booth. He had an inkling.

Ten minutes later, back on the road, Imogene's mocking laughter still rattled Alfredo's skull. She hadn't told Taffy a thing. What Taffy knew wasn't her concern. Alfredo doing what he was paid to was.

That's going up fifty! Alfredo threatened, demanding increase for his suffering. Seven years married! For what? So that gal could have his name, giving nothing in exchange except a business and an empty bed?

Had to admit, Lacy set him up nicely, even hung the door shingle over *Freeman's Funeral Home*. He had plenty when others ate poverty. He was a Colored man without cares…save one frigid, abnormal-un-natural wife too many.

You talking sorry, like a man who can't get in his woman's pants! Snatch is snatch. Get it elsewhere, Imogene had taunted over the telephone.

Imogene: evil. Lacy: lying, claiming Taffy would come around. Female parts needed repairing after birthing a baby. Give her time.

He'd given plenty—months melding into countless many until his loins were leaden. He'd demoralized and demanded, finally storming her bed. Evicted with scissors decorating his back, that ended that. Others alleviated his needs, assuming his wife's responsibility—making Alfredo a sinner seeking outside relief. Lacy and Imogene had asked too much of a man.

"Shoulda never mixed up with them in the first place!" Lacy. Frilly-fancy on the outside, but Hades-and-a-half within. Imogene? Playing store owner when he'd paid to lay with her kind. He despised them both. Twisting, corrupting his existence with dirty, blood money. Were his hands filthy, too? "Lord, now, you know I only did what Miss Lacy asked," Alfredo rationalized. *Lacy* plotted and planned that gal's life away, had her hemmed up and hapless. "Wasn't my doing."

Still his deal with Lacy was one with the devil for which Alfredo might eventually pay…because Imogene, too, knew what he'd left in Greenville.

"How, dammit?!" Alfredo couldn't say, other than Imogene was nosey and dog-low. He was convinced she'd told Taffy, spilling Greenville and the names it contained.

Creola. Nedradine. Rosalee. Underage pursuits, each. He was still outrunning the fourth one, whom he refused to name. Told her he didn't want offspring! Gave her money to visit the root woman before too late. But she'd waited, got taken by the grave. Her narrow hips and unwomanly womb weren't wide enough to birth the unborn. What, pray tell, had that to do with him?

He'd paid his debt, did three months in Greenville over that thirteen-year-old; more accurately, for the boss' car she'd bled out in, trying to birth his seed. He'd wrapped her body in old rags and, weighted by bricks, fed her to the river before cleaning the car best he could. Blood didn't go easy. Charges racked up. *Temporary theft. Neglect. Unlawful use of property.* Nothing was known of his secretly trying to cart that Colored girl to a midwife while on duty. After all, his job was chauffeuring, not using the boss' car for personal needs. Imprisoned for crimes against a car, Alfredo swore he'd never work for white folks again.

He served time for crimes against a white man's car. Courts need not know, and wouldn't care, about a missing Colored girl's hemorrhaging.

"She shoulda seen the root woman like I said," Alfredo mumbled, feeling exonerated having paid society's debt in Greenville. *I don't owe nobody nothing!* "They owe me," he ranted, rubber eating asphalt at increased speed. But Imogene was stingy.

"Sorry 'bout your troubles, honey, but that agreement's fixed. We bought you and your name. You staying married and keeping Taffy Up North where she ain't a nuisance, and you gonna do it without one more dime than you been getting." Imogene's voice had been hollow across the phone, but her menace was concrete. She'd continue Lacy's posthumous payments. "However, I *ain't* Lacy. My cousin was sweet. Me? My past is mean as yours. I can pull it up if need be. So don't try me. Your money's coming…as is."

"As is," Alfredo repeated vilely, clutching the steering wheel.

He needed the extra. Truly Earl and them brats wanting to eat.

Hughes Street Brothel increasing their fees. Was this God testing? Proving?

"Won't fail you Lord," Alfredo promised, slowing the car enough to pick his way through the unfamiliar neighborhood, thinking women a worthless drain, his wife primarily. Wasted enough dollars on harlots waiting for Taffy's nonexistent womanhood to rise. *Lacy's fault that gal has no pleasuring parts.* Still, Alfredo provided shade and shelter, didn't beat her like a lesser man would. But Alfredo was through with that foulness. He would help God by helping himself.

He parked the car, patted his suit jacket, making sure the envelope was pocketed. He'd have to grease this man's filthy palms. Hated dealing with riffraff and miscreants. They brought the race down. Still, riffraff let the God-fearing keep clean hands.

Alfredo worried his ready cash wouldn't meet the mercenary's fee. Could he buy a crime on time? Make a down payment and pay the balance when the insurance money arrived?

Alfredo knew the insurance man personally, had taken extra care laying out his vinegar-smelling mother so that she looked to be truly sleeping. Surely the man would expedite the policy's payout in light of Alfredo's grief.

He smiled, already relieved. Imogene could keep her money. The policy was plenty. And Taffy could stay right down there in crap-bowl Bledsoe, crying behind that Ellis boy before her living days were done.

"She think I didn't see her go all quiet when Tinsley mentioned them Ellises?"

Her former betrothed had never surfaced between them. Taffy always refused to resurrect him. Knowing Taffy couldn't offer nothing but ice-cold loving, Alfredo never cared. Tinsley said that Ellis boy rarely came home. But what if some stupid fluke matched them up this time?

Alfredo soured at the thought of Taffy trying on adultery, betraying him after all he'd done for her. Could be, she was already guilty. His pa always said, '*what a woman ain't giving somebody else is getting*'.

"Don't matter now," Alfredo decided, knocking. "That cat-eyed bitch is 'bout to lose all nine lives." With God's blessing—and a reliable reference from a Greenville cellmate—he'd soon be a widower, courtesy of one Dempsey Dupre.

CHAPTER SIXTEEN

Thaddeus Bledsoe wasn't well. His fifty-three-year-old body fit from a life of manual labor was, according to Dr. Blue, exceptionally healthy. But his hearing was sick, perceiving the senseless. God had left his ears.

Taffy's Daddy and NuNu's last born didn't have special sight. The Gift kept herself sacred for the females in Octavia's line. Nevertheless, as NuNu proudly proclaimed, angels kissed her baby boy's ears. And when they did, Thaddeus intuited things from other realms.

He remembered when the phenomenon first occurred, the day he heard Rachel peeking through bushes as he swam nude. He heard a rioting heartbeat, blood flooding virgin veins as Rachel ran from the lake, confused.

That special, acute hearing happened each time his seed created life in his wife's womb. Even heard the first three leave her body and go home to God. Angels kissed his ears at will. And right then angels were working overtime. Yet, all Thaddeus deciphered was a high-pitched buzzing that made his skin crawl.

"Papa, Mr. Haynes says they're just about through with the back acres."

Thaddeus smiled at his grandson bounding his way. "Do you ever walk, son?"

"Sometimes," Angel answered, "but I'm practicing."

"For?"

"The Olympics."

"You and Jesse Owens, both," Thaddeus commented, pushing pitchfork prong-first into the ground.

"Yep, and Taffy said she'd give me a ten."

"She's partial to you."

"I thought so, too, but Taf said she didn't like me that much."

Thaddeus chuckled soundly. "We both know that's a bald-faced one," Thaddeus offered. Without question, his girl loved this boy.

Thought Taffy might lose her mind when Freeman sent the boy home for him and Rachel to raise. Freeman's accusations didn't sound like right, thought the man was padding his tale. Didn't think Taffy capable of wild living, as Freeman claimed. But then again, Thaddeus never thought she'd be unwed in a family way, either. Something odd jumped in his chest, thinking back on his daughter's being with a child no man would claim.

He hadn't condoned the situation, yet Angel wasn't the first to get here as he had. Mankind was prone to mishaps. Look at Deacon and Sister Williams' middle girl, Jean Etta. Had a shotgun wedding in March, said hello to a fat, healthy baby come May. Wasn't the first and as long as flesh felt good, wouldn't be the last. But at least Frank Howard owned up and did right by Jean Etta. Taffy's situation differed back when.

Folks whispered and wondered and treated his child like a disease because Taffy wouldn't name the responsible party. Angel was a month living before Freeman showed up, hat in hand, looking like last year's crop left in the rain.

Perceiving the unhappiness his daughter now masked, Thaddeus blamed himself, wondering if any of this would've happened had he been home where he belonged. But the Great Mississippi Flood of '27 found Thaddeus chained to a gang.

He'd gone next door to Mississippi, intent on the business of Colored men. Farmers and ranchers banded together in solidarity, praying power in numbers, daring to stand and fight, hoping for equity. Supplying white grocers, many received bottom dollar on their crops. Some were promised pay *if* their "inferior" harvests sold, even though those products often made it on front display. Others who'd miraculously managed to get and keep Reconstruction's forty-acres-and-a-mule saw the federal government eyeing their land, dividing it for itself, and other whites demanding their 'rightful' piece of American pie.

Armed with an agriculture degree, Thaddeus went despite his wife's pleading. It was dangerous. Black men had been strung up for less. The clandestine meeting a success, Thaddeus headed home heart light. But torrential rains suddenly plummeted, drowning earth many months like God had tired of man again.

There was no ark this time. Homes were swept away. Levees

broke. Lives were lost. There was no way in or out. Mankind was trapped, corralled by rivers of rain, seeking refuge in segregated Red Cross camps where rations were doled as Jim Crow dictated.

When the heavens tired of her onslaught, over two thousand Colored men were assembled into work crews, salvaging the mess nature made. Like slaves, they were forced into chain gangs at gunpoint. Convicts *and* free men labored day into night.

I remember. Thaddeus recalled every grueling, back-breaking day, and being stopped on a rainy road, trying against all odds to reach home. *Papers?!* Slavery was over; he was his own master. Guardsmen with guns decided otherwise.

Thaddeus was shackle-bound like the rest, working nonstop, repairing levees. Wasn't allowed to write home. Tried notifying family as best he could. Word-of-mouth was the only means. Released men served as couriers for the retained. Weeks became months, and seasons changed. Still Thaddeus was a barely-paid slave, and he had the gall to question too-short earnings one day.

College educated, he could count, and two-plus-two wasn't adding up to four. Dubbed 'uppity trouble-maker', Thaddeus caught the butt end of a rifle. Regaining consciousness, he found himself property of the state pen for damn near two years...

"Angel, you baling hay or climbing mountains?" Thaddeus asked, yanking self from the past to enjoy his grandson's antics.

"I'mma help, Papa. I just wanna see how high this hay is."

"Well, hurry now, before supper break ends and you gotta get back to school."

"Yes, sir. Okay, Papa, you watching?"

"Don't have a choice but to," Thaddeus replied good-naturedly.

"I'mma fly like Bessie Coleman."

"Lord, forbid you crash like her, too."

"Was she really a Colored woman, Papa?"

"Colored as us," Thaddeus assured.

"And she really was the first Colored to have an international pilot's license?"

"Yep."

"Okay, this one's for Captain Bessie!" Angel yelled, jumping from a six-foot high stack of hay. "How was that, Papa?"

"Right fine for a boy with no wings. Now get that pitchfork over yonder and work like John Henry."

⌘

Matthias "Poppy" Bledsoe had nothing to prove. Having tilled, planted enough in his near ninety years, he could lounge on a chair in the shade and watch his boy work.

Thaddeus was a powerful laborer, Poppy and NuNu's one son attached to the soil. Their other four followed different dreams, pursued lofty degrees, but Thaddeus—having ground roots—majored in agriculture and husbandry. Poppy cherished his children, would die for each, but his connection to Thaddeus was deep. This one knew what it was to sow himself into the soil and reap life in exchange.

Listening to his son talk, Poppy's gaze wandered to the young men working his fields as he once did. Sweat poured off their bare backs like rain. Poppy grunted. God had been gracious and good to this land, bought with his blood and tears. The land was all, still he thanked God his oldest, Augustine, chose law.

Auggie's legal expertise got T.'s sentence reduced. Poppy grunted again, thinking on his boy being chained to Mississippi like a common criminal, charges mounting to nothing more than being bold and Black in a white man's world. Grinding toothless gums, Poppy remembered experiencing that kind of injustice firsthand...

Poppy fingered his left temple, boasting his battle scar. He'd fought hard. Even winked at death. But when he rose from his convalescing, he fixated on a white-free life. Living with might mean *their* bloodshed.

A dog barked. Poppy and Thaddeus looked past the fields.

"That dog'll follow her 'til he dies," Thaddeus mused, watching his father's hound loping arthritically at his daughter's side.

"Old Boss is a fierce protector," Poppy bragged. "Augustine did good in gifting him to me."

Thaddeus grew quiet. His eldest brother had been gone a year now, suddenly dead of a heart attack, presumably. Never knew for sure since Vesta, Augustine's widow, decided no one was cutting her man, even in autopsy. Now, Auggie was ground-deep out back, beside their newborn sister whose birth and death occurred in one day.

"What's all this pretty doing out here?" Poppy called.

"Came to see all this handsome," Taffy replied, kissing her grandfather's near-baldness and wrapping her arms about his neck from behind.

"Don't blink 'cause I ain't got much left."

Thaddeus joined their laughter, but inside he was frowning. It was around Auggie's death that his ears took to buzzing out-of-sync. Certainly was about that time that he found himself unable to please his wife.

Honey-Love, what is it? Rachel repeatedly asked, but Thaddeus couldn't rightly tell. Just knew he couldn't touch his wife with real power or purpose. Couldn't sustain or maintain relations. And the seeking-to-satisfy-her motions of his hands wasn't enough for Thaddeus. His hands were a secondary source for Rachel's pleasure—like gravy on meat, never primary like the meat itself. Experiencing uselessness, Thaddeus threw himself into his work and gleaned the fruit of his labor while a wall planted itself down the middle of his marriage bed.

Could've asked his mother for a healing, but was too proud. Couldn't do a thing but take it to Jesus in prayer. So far, the Savior hadn't resurrected the limp and the dead.

"Hi, Daddy." Taffy abandoned Poppy long enough to peck her father's cheek.

"Heya, Taffy Sweet. Whatchu and Boss up to?"

"Walking off Mama's persimmon bread. And no, Poppy, Boss didn't have any."

"Better not! I'm tryna keep this dog long. Can't trek like he used to, but he's still good company," Poppy declared, scratching Boss behind floppy ears.

Having his fill, the old canine plopped down on the grass where Taffy now sat. Glancing back and forth between the dog and his daughter, Thaddeus' ears took to humming outrageously. Something about Augustine...

Augustine... Taffy... his brother... his baby girl... Angel having extra good Bledsoe genes... His head whirled with senselessness, leaving Thaddeus weak.

"Daddy, you okay?"

"Old man's just hot and tired in this June heat," Thaddeus downplayed, collecting breath and patting Boss' rump.

"Glad I brought this." Taffy offered the thermos she'd placed at Poppy's feet.

Thaddeus took a satisfying swig. "Wooweee! Your Mama's peach and mint iced tea!" He offered the thermos to Poppy. "How're you and your mama doing?"

"We're alright, Daddy." Taffy patted the ground. "Sit and rest yourself."

"Don't turn my boy lazy," Poppy warned. "His job don't include loafing with pretty women."

"Daddy needs a new job."

Thaddeus laughed. "If I get down on that ground, you gonna help me back up?"

"Daddy, stop playing old," Taffy chided as her father sat, looking years younger than fifty-three. "You work this ranch better than Drew and the rest of 'em combined."

"You're stretching truth, babygirl."

"Barely. But I bet you can still outrun me."

"Don't know about running but I can out-swim you, hands down."

"Ha!"

"Babygirl, I'm the one taught you! Meet me at the lake. Loser buys winner a new plow."

"I don't need a plow," Taffy protested.

"You being presumptuous, but okay." Thaddeus winked at his father enjoying the banter. Poppy missed his granddaughter. Didn't know why she was Up North with that no-good no how. "Winner buys loser a new combine," Thaddeus altered. The breeze brushed their shared laughter across the field. "So...speak truth and shame the devil, how're you and your Mama?" Thaddeus still struggled to comprehend the wedge between the two.

He'd come home after being incarcerated to find his daughter with a baby and at odds with his wife when they'd been heart-tight before. Folks, mainly Mother Lacy, said Rachel and Taffy were too close, that they doted on Taffy inordinately. But after three miscarriages Thaddeus and Rachel held their breath until Taffy was born. And when she was, she changed their world.

All that power and presence in a tiny squalling ball crying lustily until bundled at her mother's breast. She latched on greedily, exerting rights and pulling down mother's first milk until satisfied. Before drifting off to her first sleep this side of life, she opened changed eyes.

White eyes! Gifted eyes, his mother said, like the first Octavia claimed chosen ones were born back across the ocean. He was accustomed to his mother's African myths and strange phenomenon. Still, the sight of his infant's colorless gaze was disconcerting. "*This one is special. The color will come,*" NuNu promised. And it did. Gray like her mama's.

Rachel left teaching to give Taffy her undivided attention. They spoiled her rotten, doted on her maybe more than due. But she was their first and only, a consolation and crown. Now there was enmity between the two. Mother and daughter fixed polite faces, spoke in tones suitable for well-bred women. Still, Thaddeus detected vicious rumbling and a broken union.

Pulling blades of grass and sacrificing them to a warm breeze, Taffy let a long silence unravel before answering. "We're good...considering."

"Considering what?" Thaddeus demanded.

"The child's grown, T. Don't pry."

"It's okay, Poppy," Taffy assured, sitting cross-legged like a girl playing dolls. "Nothing new, Daddy, just old things."

Like...Rachel siding with Lacy and saddling Taffy with a marriage not heaven-made. It was only right when Freeman finally showed up ready to act like a man and take on responsibility. Then, Taffy faulted Rachel for standing idle when Alfredo shipped Angel downhome knowing Taffy was capable, had in fact taught Taffy what she knew about domesticity and motherhood. As if Taffy's loss was Rachel's doing...

"Be careful carting old things, Taffy Sweet. They start looking and feeling familiar even when they're no good and need releasing."

Poppy grunted.

Taffy exhaled through pursed lips. "Daddy, sometimes forgiving's easier said than done."

"What is it you have to forgive?"

Taffy sat plucking grass, chewing her bottom lip, fighting the urge to speak the unspoken. "I'm sorry for acting ungrateful. I appreciate you and Mama for doing for Angel."

"I love that little knotheaded boy as much as you, so he's welcome here." Thaddeus paused, chugging tea. "But this was supposed to be temporary so answer me this. Why's Freeman still so set against his own child?"

"It's more complicated than I can tell," Taffy confessed, stroking Boss' head resting on her lap. "Things weren't right between us and Al decided Angel ought to be here."

"Without your consent. And those things still aren't right after four years?"

Taffy shook her head. "Never will be."

"So Angel's your Mama's and mine to finish raising? You send money for him every month and keep that boy opening gifts, but that's beside the point. He's yours, Taffy. He oughta be with you."

Taffy touched her father's hand. "When I leave this time, Daddy, he will be."

"Leaving...? When? Whatchu talking?"

Taffy exhaled long and hard. "Angel and I were leaving today—"

"Where you headed?" Poppy inquired, ignoring his own advice to stay out of his granddaughter's affairs. "And why?"

Before Taffy could answer her grandfather, Thaddeus was nearly shouting. "You just gonna come home, snatch that boy up, and leave without telling your mama or me?"

"Daddy, wait, I *was* leaving...I mean, I *am*...but not today, or right now."

"Well, where you headed, and why you still here?"

"Need time to think," Taffy admitted. To unfurl conflictual, confusing thoughts cramping the corners of her mind. Things were happening that Taffy didn't appreciate, anticipate, or understand. *Good sense would've got you on a train last night! Right after you saw* Him! But, here she was, still here—married and looking over the fence at what she wanted but couldn't have.

Taffy wanted to laugh. She was running to the Windy City away from matrimony. Yet, here she was using marriage as avoidance so she wouldn't love *that* man. Sober moments passed and Taffy did laugh. "It's part of the reckoning."

"What is?"

Taffy looked at her father. "Getting unmarried."

"What in the..."

"Ooo, Jesus," Poppy prayed.

"Listen here, Taffy Sweet, that thing you have with Freeman isn't good, but I can't have that boy pulled between you two in some crazy war behind you tryna get yourself 'unmarried'!"

"He won't be. I promise," Taffy added at her father's dubious look.

Thaddeus studied his child. She'd been a good girl. Wanted to be a nurse back when. Told her she could be a doctor if she wanted, even put money away for her schooling. But she got sidetracked. Still, she was a fine young woman making her way Up North. He'd taught her how to handle money, and she had a sound head on her shoulders. Wasn't sure he'd favor them all, but whatever Taffy's plans, she'd do right by Angel. Still…

"Where *were* you headed, Taffy?"

Knowing she needed to be forthcoming to secure her father's cooperation, Taffy conveyed her plans.

Thaddeus shook his head in reply. "Oh, no, indeed! You're not taking that boy up to Gracie's. She's got enough on her hands."

"Her husband break his back last year, no?" Poppy asked.

"My back would be broke too, with seventeen younguns!" Thaddeus replied.

Taffy smiled at Poppy's raucous laugh. "Daddy, it's only temporary." The majority of Cousin Gracie's large brood were grown and gone. With working as a domestic and her husband being disabled, living was lean. Still, Cousin Gracie offered a safe place for Taffy and Angel to lay their heads. "I pray we're not there but a minute. Just long enough for me to find a job and get a place. Two of Gracie's daughters sew in one of the factories. They'll put in a good word and help me get on."

"Your marriage that bad you willing to take wild risks?"

"Daddy, you know it is."

Exasperated, Thaddeus scratched his head. "Babygirl, if you gonna do it, do it right. Gon' up to Chicago if that's where you feel you need to be. But go by yourself. Set things up like you said. *Then* come get Angel. No need exposing him to instability."

"Daddy, you just said Angel ought to be with me. So, when I go, Angel goes. We'll be fine."

Thaddeus opened his mouth, hot with objections. Only the cautionary look on his father's face stopped the flow. "Granddaughter, sometimes you gotta do what don't make sense to nobody but yo'self." Poppy locked eyes with Taffy, spoke from experience. "Might catch some laughter, or a 'lil scorn. But if you big enough do it, then do."

Seeing Taffy's smile, Thaddeus sighed, relenting. "I'm not agreeing with your old granddaddy, so we gonna let this hold 'til later…" Thaddeus' words trailed off as revelation hit him like a shoe upside the head. "You getting 'unmarried' got anything to do with that youngster out there working the fields?"

"You talking Roam Ellis?" Poppy interjected.

"Yes, sir, indeed!" Thaddeus exclaimed.

"Savior," Poppy droned. "Not my granddaughter. This child here got better sense than to play like she don't."

"Good sense gets slippery with the young and silly."

"Yeah, but that Ellis boy just pulled in here last night."

"One night's enough," Thaddeus supplied.

Taffy hopped up, laughing. "I'm finished with you two sitting up discussing me like I'm not here. Roam Ellis has nothing to do with nothing. My personal decisions are just that. Mine."

Thaddeus studied Taffy a while. "I'mma take your word on it for now. Here, help your daddy up off this ground. My work's waiting."

Boss by her side, Taffy offered Thaddeus a hand. He played dead weight. "Daddy, you gonna make me lose my footing. Get up."

Thaddeus did, chuckling. "You getting weak, little girl."

"That or you had three too many helpings last night." Taffy patted her father's still-firm midsection.

Gazing at his daughter, Thaddeus cautioned, "Do right, Taffy. On all accounts."

She nodded. "Yes, sir. Love you."

Echoing the sentiment, Thaddeus kissed her forehead, watched her hug his father before leaving, dog at her side, a field holler floating like a halo about her head.

"That's some stubborn right there."

Poppy grunted. "That's the apple. You the tree."

Thaddeus chuckled but briefly. Troubled, he redirected his attention to the men in the crops, singing field songs passed down from slavery. They toiled three-, four-deep to a row, mirroring his time on the work gang. He surveyed them with appreciation knowing they were compensated for keeping his family's land plentiful. Watching the men, Thaddeus' gaze landed on one, and memory flashed back to the day he asked for Taffy's hand.

"Excuse me, Mr. Thaddeus, may I speak to you a moment?"

He'd been with his brothers at the time, sitting, talking, doing what brothers do.

"Best go see what Little Mr. Ellis has to say, T.," Augustine had teased. "Looks like something serious is on that youngster's mind."

Thaddeus had followed Roam out the yard and earshot of others.

"What can I do for you?" he'd inquired of the fourteen-year-old.

"Sir, I intend to marry your daughter if that's alright by you."

"I see. Why?"

"I think I love her."

"Because..."

"Because she's smart and pretty and feisty and tall and she wants more from life, like me. And I guess she'd make a good, honest wife and mother."

"You can tell all of that looking at my eleven-year old child?" Roam nodded at Thaddeus' query. "You can't find a young lady closer your own age?"

"Yes, sir. I can, and I have...before...but I prefer Taffy."

"So Taffy's not your first love?"

"I've had other affections."

Amused, Thaddeus asked, "For how long?"

"A week or two, but I was immature then."

"I see. You like her?"

"Sir?"

"Do you like my daughter?"

"Mr. Thaddeus, I just said I love her I think."

"Young man, I heard what you said, but love's funny, showing up strong one day and low the next. Like the ocean, it ebbs and flows. Hot to cold. But like'll help you tolerate things you thought you loved about a woman when she gets to doing something other than what you want. You like Taffy enough to keep her when dinner's burnt, babies are crying, your best shirt changed colors in the wash, and you can't find a clean place for hat or head?"

Roam couldn't answer.

"Just a little something to think on. Come back and talk to me once you do," Thaddeus said, returning to where his brothers waited, keeping his chuckle low. Just then Taffy, Chloe, and an ever-present gaggle of girlfriends came bounding out the house. Taffy took one look at Roam and stormed down the walkway.

"Roam Ellis, what're you doing in my yard?" the eleven-year-old demanded.

"Talking to your daddy."

"About what?" she'd shot, hands planted on her imagination.

"Men's business."

"Must've been a short, one-sided conversation since you ain't a man."

"Man enough to ask for your ashy hand in marriage," Roam retorted.
"Marriage?!" Chloe erupted. "Taffy doesn't love you."
"Sure don't," Taffy sassed.
"You like me?"
"I guess, 'bout as much as I like school, but—"
"That'll do," Roam decided walking away.

Clear memory got Thaddeus to thinking. He'd known Roam since the Ellises moved to Bledsoe decades before. Thaddeus worked Roam hard alongside Drew and other nephews come weekends and summers since Roam was old enough to earn his keep. But standing there watching Roam Ellis watching his daughter, Thaddeus didn't recognize him. Roam had the starved, focused look of a hunter deprived. He was wounded and resolute, a hunter determined to possess his prize come hell or high water, consequences be damned.

Thaddeus had known that hunger for a woman, and he'd married her despite her mother's dislike and protestations. So he understood Roam's determination. But it was desperate, dangerous. Surely, Roam knew better than to pursue what wasn't his? Or at least hold himself together until Taffy was 'unmarried?' *If* Taffy even thought about Roam that way. Which wasn't likely seeing as how bruised blood flowed between them.

A workman said something Thaddeus couldn't hear. A round of laughter went up. Roam shot one last longing look in Taffy's direction before slinging that hoe like an ax chopping something in two. Thaddeus decided it was praying time. "Sir…?"

Staring at nothing in particular, Poppy repeated what Thaddeus hadn't heard. "Our girl's carrying memories don't belong to her."

Thaddeus frowned. Did unjust memories factor into Taffy's predicament with Alfredo, Roam…and, *God forbid*, Augustine?

CHAPTER SEVENTEEN

Seven years of six-week stints necessitated downtime, reclaiming rest from the rails. Layover pattern well-established, he came up for air only after hibernating. Hibernation over, he groomed up, splashed on smell-good, and made his way to a Porters' Club for cards, sweet music and, if the stars aligned, layover love. Not this time.

He'd worked the fields that day—early, long and hard—because sleep wasn't working for him. Inordinate energy had Roam Ellis wound up and restless. Better to burn it honest than do what he ought not. Like kissing, caressing, and blessing that woman until barefaced hunger was fulfilled.

Of their own volition, Roam's feet tapped an aggravated cadence on the bottom of Drew's boat. All because she had him. Still. Could twist Roam and tie him with a look. But this blazing, newborn, pure-D...*lust?!*...was something-altogether-else. Had him acting unconscionably, wanting forbidden sweets when he'd prepared for war.

Old wounds trotted themselves across the battlefield the moment she'd entered Chloe's kitchen yesterday, but Taffy's simple, honeyed repentance left Roam staggering. Dropping weapons, he reached for Taffy. One touch sabotaged resistance and killed Roam's resolve.

Better buck up, Roam had warned himself. And he thought he had. Until she sashayed heaven-sent hips across her family's fields today. Sun high, she'd moved like cool waters, thirst-quenching. Satisfying. And she'd avoided him, intentionally navigating a wide arc far from the rows he hoed. Didn't matter. Overly conscience of her lounging with her father and Mr. Matthias, Roam's interest burned enough for them both. Too grown to act like some under-aged, pimple-faced fool, Roam had resumed his task with a vengeance until, unable not to, he'd paused to watch Taffy saunter away. Staring-like-stupid had earned him some ribbing from his work companions.

"Ellis, you'd best blink 'fore your eyes pop out your head."

"Better do more than blink before that other thing breaks his britches!"

Roam had laughed along, thoughts uneasy. His first love had become a conundrum. But, forever fascinating, *this* Taffy Marie Bledsoe harbored a mysterious, undecipherable thing. The unknown didn't sit well, left Roam cagey yet intrigued.

Intrigued, hell! Man, you're spellbound.

"Whatcha mumbling about?"

Unaware he'd voiced his plight aloud, Drew's question caught Roam by surprise. "Not much," Roam downplayed, too stubborn to admit he was absorbed by a feminine enigma he couldn't have or comprehend. Innocence. Intoxication. Hers was a dance and a duel wrapped in ribbons of effortless sensuality that left Roam wanting to access the altar of Taffy's mind and body, palm the curve of her trim waist only to venture high or low, knowing either direction held treasures he'd worship one voluptuous inch at a time.

Yeah, Lord. Roam grinned unconsciously, imagining some sweet sinning. Backwards men didn't sanction a woman's pleasure. For them, intimacy meant coupling and coupling was a man's cream to swallow whole. Forget a woman licking her lips as well.

That woman's got lips worth licking, Roam mused, recalling wisdom gained. If ever inclined to forget his father's tutelage he'd remember two things. *Son, treat women like you want your mother treated.* And, *give pleasure before you get it.*

Lulled by the moon's play across the lake's face, Roam decided Taffy was pleasure-less, like Freeman had yet to touch her the right way. She'd meant the world to him once. Secrets were shared, a future plotted and planned. He'd invested himself in her, and would've moved hell and high water to give her what she wanted let alone needed. Seven years and a marriage later, there was hell and high water between them. Yet, divine connections prevailed. Connection enabled insight, exposing discontent; and discontent, vulnerability, as if what Taffy lived wasn't love.

That's not my concern, Roam insisted, leaning back on a yawn. Caring for Taffy came with consequences and he knew better than to walk that route again. Roam would never grant that woman access to his insides. Didn't matter that he was starved and craving Taffy with an infinite lust he couldn't explain…

"What?!" Roam demanded when Drew rapped his fishing pole against Roam's rapidly bobbing leg.

"Man, you can't be still for nothing!" Drew complained. "You gonna chase off the fish. Bouncing those big feet in my boat!"

Laughing, Roam relaxed in what felt like the first time in forever. His motion slowed, but didn't still. Shoes drumming a soft cadence on the boat's bottom, Roam expended restless energy, not caring if fish bit or stayed away. "Been moving too much since birth. Can't quit now."

Drew snorted. "That's what happens when you're high-faultin' and get born at a hospital instead of home."

Roam's chuckle drifted across the lake's moonlit face. Story was, nurse at the Colored hospital misspelled his name at birth. Should've been that ancient, cultured city of mythic proportions. Came out, instead, like something without restraint. His mother requested a correction. His father, the right Reverend, said it was the Lord's want and will. Now, he was a man of restless soles.

"What kinda country contraption you got going on here?" Roam rocked back, testing Drew's rigged-up seating. Legs removed, two lawn chairs had been propped and affixed to the rowboat's bottom slats, providing questionable, yet comfortable seating.

"Don't worry. It'll hold your big ass."

"It better," Roam rumbled, double-checking the live bait on his line. Drew stuck to worms. Roam preferred minnows for night fishing, claiming the iridescent sheen of their scales proved more visible in dark waters. With an easy motion, Roam cast his line.

"So, tell me something good."

Roam snorted. "Man, quit riding in my pocket and buy your own ticket to somewhere."

Drew's easy smile flashed bright against night's tableau. "Why should I when you're my pipeline? So…how's that iron horse kicking?"

"Hard! This last route had me eating cabbage and crow." Minding his line, Roam filled Drew in on his pay coming up short, thanks to a passenger's inebriation. After excessive indulgence, said passenger stumbled into Roam's car, and upchucked on a female guest before passing out in the aisle. The desecrated woman rider was inconsolable, and wouldn't rest until compensated for her suffering. "Who you think had to compensate for that mess of a dress?"

Even in the dark, Roam saw Drew's eyes grow wide. "Stop lying! Why?"

Roam shrugged. "It happened in my car, on my watch. White man craps. It's ours to clean." Days removed from the incident, anger spent, Roam could be mellow-headed about it. "Drunk skunk comes to, cussing up a storm. Naming me all kinda 'niggers' I ain't never been or ever will be. He's tipsy as hell, blaming me for his gut-spewing, like I got something to do with his inability to hold his drink. So the fool rags to the conductor, demanding *I* atone for that white lady's junked-up dress."

"Man, what'd you do?" Drew questioned, curious and amused.

Roam stretched long, well-muscled legs, a smug grin on his face. "We pull into Boston 'round midnight. The conductor wires the office man to dock my pay five dollars for that raggedy-ass dress not worth fifty cents." Roam held up a wide palm, stifling Drew's response. "So, good Pullman porter that I am, I help the drunkster and his bags aboard his sleeper connector to Washington."

"Yeah…" Drew waited.

Roam pantomimed a subservient tone. "Sorry for his trouble, but you know us culluds ain't got much schooling. Gotta Washington state…*and* a D.C.?" Snickering, Roam ended his pantomime. "He wanted the capital not the coast."

"Naw, you didn't! You sent 'im out west?"

"Happy trails, muthasucka."

Drew laughed 'til he cried. "If he raises sand, you gonna be unemployed in the soup line."

Roam sucked his teeth. "Nut was so toasted, he wouldn't know me from the next Negro. Besides, the Brotherhood handled it," Roam confidently stated. Theirs was a fraternal order, A. Philip Randolph's Brotherhood of the Sleeping Car Porters. The first Colored labor organizations of its kind, the Brotherhood fought to secure fair practices aboard the railroads, particularly George Pullman's luxury sleepers. The labor-focused organization swiftly became a tight-knit network, an extended family of Colored men who looked out for each other's interests, on and off the rails. Their Grapevine proved an interconnected system allowing porters to move information faster than the trains they traveled. So when Roam deposited his offensive drunk on that westbound bullet with a quick, quiet summation of the situation, he received a promise.

We'll keep the liquor loose.

"So what happened?"

Feeling a tug, Roam reeled in his line. "Last I heard, he woke up piss drunk in a Washington *state* train station."

"Y'all some cold Negroes," Drew chuckled, admiration in his tone.

"Comeuppance tastes best that way. And I ain't worried about my job seeing as how Drunk Mister needs to keep his wife ignorant of the companion he boarded and bedded with."

"Another woman?" Drew ventured.

"Try another man," Roam supplied, lifting his pole and whistling at a large catfish flapping wildly on his line. "Looka here, looka here! Catfish don't usually join the night feeders." Roam carefully deposited his catch in the large bucket at the boat's prow.

"What's that? Four to my ten?" Drew goaded.

Better-than-blood brothers since the Ellis family moved to Bledsoe some twenty years back, the two still tended to be competitive in some things. Particularly fishing. "Whatchu got?" Roam challenged. Aided by the light of the lantern lifted on a raised hook attached to the prow, Roam inspected Drew's haul. "Some crippled-ass bass, five lost-looking perch, and half a snapper? Who's eating that?"

"You!"

"Damn straight," Roam chuckled. Attaching new bait and readjusting his lure, Roam sat and recast his line. Within moments, he was yawning, wide-mouthed.

"We ain't been out here but a minute. You ready to call it quits?"

"Naw…this is good," Roam responded, the tranquil essence of home seeping into his soul. A big man well-suited to his position, he gladly rode the rails state-to-state, coast-to-coast. Hoisting luggage, serving passengers, Roam worked six-, seven-week stints surviving on catnaps and stolen sleep, until a layover allowed real rest. All because a Pullman porter's nomadic existence met his needs. Taxing as it was, a wanderer's life on the rails rendered Roam carefree. Yet. "I need and miss this."

"You growing tired of rail-riding?"

Roam's thoughts cycled back to childhood and his inordinate interest in trains. Racing along tracks at the backside of town, or lingering about the depot in nearby white Richland, Roam could be transfixed for hours—watching passengers come and go. Tired of watching, he'd assault ticket master Mr. Gorman with a barrage of questions—his analytical mind needing to understand the engine and its intricacies. Vexed and red-faced, Mr. Gorman would shoo Roam away, having had enough of "that Colored child's curiosity". But the ticket master's impatience did little to reduce Roam's interest. He'd determined at a young age that God made the rails for his riding.

Watching the gentle motion of the bobber atop the water, Roam exhaled a loaded sigh. "I can't complain. The good Lord's blessed me to travel this country and see more in these past seven years than most Colored men can. Pockets are lined with a steady wage. And I appreciate it. But Drew…man…sometimes I feel like sitting down, doing what you and Chloe did."

Drew took his time pouring from the coffee thermos his wife had prepared, before passing it to Roam. "First Lady been in your ear?"

Roam's sculpted mouth lifted in a grin. "Yeah, Mama's canvassing. Pops, too. Pops still calls me a wanderer, and thinks I oughta give up—and I do quote—'traipsing about God's countryside unattached, like a vagabond in a monkey suit, kowtowing to white folks' whims, and latch onto legacy'."

"They still talking seminary, like the pulpit's your place?"

"Do I look like somebody's preacher?!"

"Hell naw! But man, y'all Ellises been preaching more than a century," Drew needlessly reminded, leaning over and using a net to secure a fish shimmering on his line.

"Since 1829." Roam couldn't forget a lengthy legacy, would proudly cite family history in a heartbeat. Freemen of Color since 1829, Ellis men were literate preachers and abolitionists advocating emancipation while undermining slavery as operatives of a Railroad underground.

Roam witnessed that communal pride and obligation in his father's acts as the right Reverend, his mother's charitable giving. He was taught to be selfless to a degree. Still…Roam drew the line. Despite his parents' insistence, preaching was neither passion nor purpose. Rail-riding was. Moving far and wide was in his veins and his name. Besides, Roam knew he was nobody's preacher capable of saving souls, especially his own. "But we both know it ain't my not preaching that got them campaigning. And I'm faulting you for it."

"What'd I do?"

"Put your wife in a family way," Roam jokingly accused. "You know what the Rev's all about." Roam mimicked his father to a "T." *Honor. Dignity. God. And Family!* "Pops takes a breath, and Mama comes in swinging. I barely get in yesterday, and here's Mama. 'Roam, honey, you're four-years-short-of-thirty and no marriage, mortgage, or baby in a wife's belly. You keep riding that railway without a woman, you'll wind up old, dusty *and* musty'."

"First Lady's got a point," Drew agreed. "It takes a good woman to give you shine. So, how long you think you gonna lick up all that luxury?"

Roam snorted. George Pullman's Luxury Sleepers, with their posh accommodations and pull-down beds, were idyllic. For *them*. White riders. But for Roam and fellow porters, those sleepers could feel like quasi-plantations on wheels. Long, hard hours and sleep-deprived nights answering passengers' querulous calls. Being financially penalized for items missing at the end of a porter's shift. The innate demeaning of Black men—attending unattended children, declining intimate propositions, dealing with tipsy white men and their ways. No route ended without his confronting bodily wastes, expelled from one orifice or the other, triggered by intemperance. Excess liquor, smoke, or food. Secretions of a private nature equally foul from folks cramming bodies in miniscule berths to satisfy the flesh—leaving prophylactics and private markings behind.

Few stopovers, too often brief or full of cat naps. Only long layovers provided leisurely opportunities. Still, negatives paled beneath benefits. Steady wages, respect within Colored communities, and entrance to Pullman clubs eased the weight. No, luxury wasn't his. Indeed, Roam learned long ago how treacherous the rails could be, and rode them strapped about the ankle, pearl-handled loaded at the ready.

He'd seen and heard too much not to.

Black men pulled from Colored cars in the middle of the night for infractions, real or imagined, never to surface again. Negro women snatched into white cars against their will. Let it happen on his route. He and his pearl-handled would have to disappear. Protecting a Colored woman's honor was something ingrained, especially if she was his.

"Not sure how long before I quit the rails, or the rails quit me. That smokestack-of-an-iron siren ain't lost her lure, yet. We'll see.

'Ey…congrats, again, to you and Chloe." Roam heard pride and humility in Drew's 'thanks!' After seven years of marriage, Chloe and Drew were expecting their first child. Thinking back on it, Roam realized Drew and Chloe's wedding marked the last time he'd laid eyes on Taffy. Until yesterday. Standing as best man, Roam didn't bother changing his suit after the "I Do's". Rather, Roam left the sanctuary, bags packed, heading straight for Richland's train station. The ink on his high school diploma barely dry, Roam signed on George Pullman's dotted line, leaving heart-wreck and Taffy Bledsoe behind…

Roam snatched a sandwich from the basket near his feet. Unwrapping it, he tore into it, biting off a sizeable hunk.

"I know First Lady fixed enough for me," Drew prompted, watching Roam chew stiff-jawed, like something distasteful seasoned his mind. Roam handed over a sandwich, absentmindedly. "So…since preaching's out, what about that other thing?"

Roam talked around chewing. "I'm squirreling it away. Half of my pay, *every* payday."

"Gonna be able to study *and* rail-ride simultaneously?"

"Usually sitting up with a book in my hand in between duties as it is. It could work." Roam scratched his brow. "We'll see. In the meantime, gonna keep doing what I do."

"Riding that iron horse and enjoying the cities. How's Harlem?"

"Not bright as she used to be, but she's still sweet like honey."

He'd seen many cities. Houston. Detroit. Chicago. Kansas. Dallas. Memphis. Los Angeles. Santa Fe. Philadelphia. Many more. With its mad jazz, rich and cultural arts, and Savoy stomping, hands down Harlem topped Roam's favorites. As a Colored man, Roam was proud of and impressed by what was accomplished there. Ragtime. Swing. Hot, "hell-sent" Jazz. Books born in Negro minds. Art gloriously divine. New and dizzying politics preaching pan-African unity. He'd witnessed it all up close. Waning or not, Harlem and her renaissance still had shine.

Roam extracted a magazine from the sandwich basket. "Here. Forgot to put this in with Philly's *Courier* and those other newspapers you like so much."

Drew leaned towards the lantern. Of all the Colored newspapers and periodicals Roam sent home for consumption, *The Crisis* was Drew's favorite. An Aaron Douglas print consumed the cover, beautiful in all its Blackness. Drew smiled big. "Well, I'll say." Quietly,

Drew skimmed the content. "I sure like this *Crisis*, but sometimes I think Dr. Du Bois ain't seeing clearly."

"Why? 'Cause he's more radical than Booker T.?"

"Yeah…maybe… I mean, I respect Dr. Du Bois for being the first Colored to graduate Harvard with a Ph.D. in sociology. The man's brilliant, but he's—"

"Self-indulgent? A color-struck, narcissistic elitist with his Talented Tenth?" Roam posited.

Somewhere an owl hooted, nearly in sync with Drew's laughter. "Yeah, that. But I guess that's better than 'lowering my buckets' back into slavery with ol' Booker."

"Naw, I don't think that's what Washington really wants. He's using subtle tactics to hack at this inequality thing." Roam thought on the conditions in Colored cars. Wasn't much better now than when Plessy challenged Ferguson. Still hot, still cramped. Still separate and bearing no semblance of equal. Wasn't right on land, felt more oppressive on wheels. "I prefer thinking ole Booker's tryna get what Colored folks need without alerting the white artillery. His theories don't always sit right with me, but I understand his methods." Even so, Roam didn't subscribe to assimilation and accommodation as a means of improving race relations.

"So, if assimilating and accommodating could kill Jim Crow's crazy ways, is it worthwhile?" Drew challenged.

"Man, we been accommodating since being dragged onto U.S. soil! Can't bend much more," Roam stated, thinking on the hot, cramped Colored cars hooked behind the engine—flipping "white folks first" so that Colored riders swallowed engine noise, flying cinders, and fumes. Used as storage facilities for white folks' luggage, there was no onboard luxury. "And assimilating?" Roam made a derisive sound. "I'm not interested in integrating, giving up aspects of myself, and taking on white ways. Still, Colored folks oughta have the right to live and educate and shop where we want. Our green money spends same as theirs. I don't want what they have. I want mine. We keep accommodating? Shoot! They'll keep feeling exonerated from social responsibility, and stay blind to the need to affect *their own* moral changes—"

"You talking status quo?" Drew interrupted.

"Nail on head," Roam affirmed, tossing his balled up sandwich paper back into the basket. "Nothing changes when you live that way, and white folks won't ever tire of giving us less."

"Don't get all ornery and tip this boat over, but I'mma ask you something. Ain't part of being a porter, assimilating and accommodating?"

Roam considered the starry sky. A study in fortitude and self-control, Roam daily insulated his psyche. Though courteous, he refused to be obsequious. Carriage remained upright. Spirit wouldn't bend. Despite being hailed as "*boy!*" or "George" as if he too—like the luxury cars—was Mr. Pullman's *thing*. "Being a porter's not the sum total of my being, Drew. It's a payday, not my person. And I do what I do without skinning and grinning."

"Amen! But being a porter, *do you* affect improvement for our people?"

Roam did what he could to make travel tolerable for Colored passengers. Secreting pillows to expectant mothers and the elderly, blankets to small children, and a little something to those who couldn't afford to board with grease-stained bags didn't social change make. Circulations discarded by white passengers, Negro newspapers collected in big cities—Roam dropped some in the Colored cars, shipped most downhome to keep people in the know. Along with those newspapers, he often included cash in an envelope with instructions to his mother: "help whoever needs helping." Small acts of kindness alleviated immediate needs, but their scope and impact, Roam admitted, were limited.

"Might be small to you," Drew reasoned, "but it's something to somebody."

"Yeah…but we gotta do more to lift ourselves."

Drew nodded. "Think that's what Harlem's renaissance was all about?"

"Maybe. Maybe not. Coulda been just the phenomenon of an enclave of Colored artists exhibiting their gifts, not even thinking about racial uplift individually or initially. But let's be real: race will always be attached to whatever Colored folks produce," Roam stated, inherently pragmatic. "That's the cost of living in America."

Securing his fishing rod between his legs, Drew leaned back, arms folded behind his head. "Well, I oughta take Chloe on up to Harlem after the baby comes, so she can see all those big buildings. It's nothing but Colored folks there?"

"Mostly," Roam answered, absentmindedly tweaking the red-gold hairs of an immaculate moustache. "In that aspect, Harlem's kinda like Bledose. But then there're times when you walk into a Harlem club or a Colored restaurant and find nothing but white folks. Mixing in, wanting what we have." Roam sucked meat from his teeth. "Ain't doing much more than indulging "dark desires" by walking on the wild side. They visit our establishments, buy a little Negrobilia, and go home to lily white land, thinking by hearing our music and buying a piece of Negro art they've overturned social ills."

"Sounds like patronizing," Drew decided. "Infiltration of the enemy."

"Exactly! Patronizing's not the solution. Policy change is. I mean, that dollar they spend on a plate of chicken and blackeyed peas helps keep that Colored cook fed. But it's time to change policy and practice, not just preference or privileged participation. After all, policy dictates. Policy-*makers* dominate."

"True. Now shut up so the fish can think."

Both chuckling, the two settled back in comfortable silence. There was a calm, out here at night, with no other fisherman. Bullfrogs bellowing, cicadas singing, it was a serene atmosphere Roam relished, even craved.

Thank God for home, he thought, a plentiful place founded by freed slaves. Home was decent, occupied by folks caring for their own. If someone was hungry they got fed. If clothes were needed they got shoes to boot. Wasn't nothing like the hobovilles and shantytowns swelling along the rails. Or cities of homelessness, increased vagrancy, desperate gambling, and soup kitchens feeding the empty-mouthed-and-belly-lean. No overcrowding and living atop each other in tight shoeboxes stacked stories high. Home was peace and plenty. Bledsoe had her share of ills but they got handled best they could and the town survived.

He had more than enough time on the books. Still, Roam didn't plan to linger, maybe long enough for the Founders' festivities opening ceremonies. Seven years he'd been riding the rails, padding his small-town origins with the fat of the world. Evolving. Becoming. He'd been wide-eyed and slack-jawed in the beginning, overwhelmed and impressed by new sights and sounds. Now, after years of six-weeks-on-one-week-off cross-country trips Roam was nearing saturation. He needed this downtime to recollect himself...and rest from the something, unfurling like smoke, itching and clouding his mind.

Without a woman, you'll wind up old, dusty and musty.

Roam shifted. Home had a way of calling into question his nomadic state of being. Made Roam sit a while, soul naked without the psychic costume behind which the world required a Colored man hide.

Suddenly pensive, Roam watched the lake's mirror-like face. Some insect or other, skimmed across the water, interrupting its placid surface. Ripples danced with moonlight. Roam closed his eyes.

He wouldn't ride the rails forever, was working on a plan for when his Pullman days were done. Might make his mother happy and include a wife. For now, Roam enjoyed layover love.

The rails afforded access to many a fine Colored woman across the continental U.S. Some polite and reserved. Others putting it out there for the tasting. Some holy, some hellish; others occupied a sweet, even place in between. Was up to him to know the difference—which fruit was best, which forbidden.

Admittedly, he'd been wild in the beginning, like a greedy child loosed in a candy store. Overindulging here. Nibbling there. Without thought, or consequence until Doc, prized chef and seasoned vet of the rails who'd watched those rails turn family men into philanderers, pulled Roam under his wings. *"Youngster, you'd best temper yourself 'fore you leave a messed up trail you can't clean."* Roam learned to minimize.

Inhaling clean, country night air, Roam decided he wasn't a womanizer, yet he never lacked options. Had a familiar female at any given layover, should a craving call. He tried treating layover lovers like more than mere stops along the way. But truthfully, women and cities had started blurring together until consorts became synonymous with geographical terrain.

St. Louis was caramel-skinned with a high laugh and low moan. Detroit slept all day and played hard at night. Memphis was smooth juice until departure time; then she became a scene from hell Roam refused to revisit.

They were among a line of women treating Roam like cane syrup on griddle cakes, something to sop up and savor. Exuding southern charm, he was generous, a luxuriant lover, like smooth river water beneath a bridge. Controlled motion in his movements, Roam was steady, unhurried as if molasses thickened his southern blood. Quick when quickness was needed. Well-versed in the wonders of female

flesh, he knew how to give and receive sensual satisfaction while basking at its shrine. If the many intimations bore proof, Roam Ellis was
well-equipped with the goods settling-down women wanted. But was
he ready to settle?

Easing deeper in his seat, Roam's foot tapped a rhythm. His
thoughts kept their own cadence, forcing Roam to confront that itch
that was twitching long before coming home. It had been with him
a while now, subtle yet present, like muscle and membrane beneath
skin…

"So, you thinking on something that'll keep you past a Saturday
night?" Drew's question cut through the calm, paralleling Roam's
drowsy thinking.

"You sounding like my mama," Roam answered, stretching.

"I'm not my wife, so I don't meddle, but you said you thinking
along the lines of what Chloe and I did—settling down somewhere
with something other than a Saturday night fire? Hot stuff might
taste good for the minute, but man, loving the same woman every
day is something sweet."

There it is, Roam thought. *That's* what he craved. *Consistency*! Not
just an ever-ready supply of open thighs. Something more than copu-
lating for convenience and mere carnal contentment. Twenty-six *was*
well-past prime settling-down time. He was a good man deserving a
good woman, not just tawdry hellos and indifferent goodbyes.

Stroking the underside of his jaw, Roam sat with truth a minute.
He *was* tired of changing beds and bodies. Time to stop bed-hopping
and build a home. Time to quit all this coast-to-coast running, sit
himself down somewhere, and cease trying to find *her* in every woman he finessed.

Roam sprang forward, jolted by naked truth and a violent tug on
his line. Refuting asinine correlations between endless journeys and
broken-heartedness, Roam focused on capturing his catch.

He wasn't running! Even as a youngster, he'd planned to journey
beyond Bledsoe and the South. But back when there was love between them, Roam never imagined going alone. Always pictured *her*
as bride-at-his-side. But Taffy split his heart in two, choosing another.
Roam chose to keep his mind. Betrayal burned like hell still he took
rejection like a man: he moved on. Hadn't stopped since.

"There're a couple of nice, unattached sisters here in town who'd
be more than happy to have your company." Drew's words bounced

off Roam's broad back.

"I'm not interested in none of your knock-kneed, snaggle-mouthed kin."

"Watch out, talking 'bout my family! Snaggle-mouthed maybe, but ain't none of 'em knock-kneed."

Using hands to sculpt air in visual demonstration, Roam escalated their laughter with, "Keep all that and put me first in line for a big-legged woman with some grits-eating hips and a sweet...round...*high and mighty* homegrown behind! I need a woman I can't snap in half. Speaking of..." He sobered quickly. "You shoulda told me Taffy was here! Your jokes are janky, man."

"Did I get you?" Drew gloated.

"You 'bout to get got."

"Yeah, well, I thought she was coming next week. And whatchu doing looking at my cousin's backside?!"

"Focus on the point at hand."

Drew cut Roam a look before offering, "Y'all been dodging each other long enough. Can't do it all your lives."

Roam's jaw tightened before relaxing. Taffy was his past. And the past was just that. Gone. Still...she'd been running loose in his mind, since tasting those lips. Feeling that real woman body up against his. *Better* than he liked. Soft but firm. Juicy. Thick.

"How long you staying?"

Reclaiming his seat, Roam patted his hard belly. "Long enough to get fat off Mama's homecooking." Laying fishing rod aside, Roam toyed with the ever-present cigar tucked behind one ear. "That's all I plan on doing. If I'm not eating, I'm sleeping. In fact, wrap up this sorry fish trip. My bed's calling." Roam was ready for that feather mattress in that tiny house on the edge of town.

While his parents inhabited the parsonage behind First Zion, Roam preferred that small, uninhabited house his parents built when first coming to Bledsoe. Flooded with sentiment, the house was too precious to sell. Sometimes rented to migrant workers or families fallen on hard times, the house most often sat empty until Roam's return.

"Begging pardon, but only sorry thing out here is the fisherman holding your line," Drew taunted, getting up and reaching overboard for the anchor.

Unable to bypass an opportunity, Roam took aim. His foot landed firmly on Drew's derriere, knocking him overboard. Roam's laugh cracked the night. Spluttering and spitting, Drew resurfaced, cussing and fussing. *"Fool, what's wrong with you?!"*

"Nothing wrong with a little surprise. Right?" Roam's grin was satisfied. "Next time, tell me your cousin's home *before* I see her."

Sopping wet, Drew pulled himself aboard, dripping up a storm. "I oughta knock you into next week."

"Gonna need an army."

Grumbling, Drew began removing sodden clothing. When he reached his underwear, Roam hollered. "Naw, sir, this ain't that kinda boat ride!" Pivoting, Drew lowered his underwear, flashing Roam his behind. "Aw hell…" Roam plunked down on a chair and covered his face.

Shivering in soaked skivvies, Drew grabbed an oar and took a seat as well. "Get to rowing, man, so I get home and get dry. You alright?" Drew asked a shuddering Roam.

Roam groaned. "I wanna pluck out my eyes."

CHAPTER EIGHTEEN

A ngel Baby, sixteen plus seventy-three isn't ninety-eight."
"What is it?"
"That's for you to figure."
"You can't tell me?"
"I could but that wouldn't make you wiser, would it?"
"No, but I'd be happy."
"Angel, rework the problem."
"Yes, ma'am."

They sat at the dining table, Angel's schoolwork spread before them. He'd brought home a less than acceptable mark on his math exercises. Usually happened whenever Taffy arrived. Unfocused and excited, it took a minute for Angel to settle himself. Understanding the distracting thrill of resurfaced love, Taffy patiently helped Angel correct his mistakes.

She felt bound to make a mistake, being here distracted, instead of Chicago-bound. Should've boarded that train first thing this morning, yet Spirit repeatedly cautioned, "*Stay.*" Stay for the upcoming opening ceremonies of the Founders' Festival and Angel's poem recitation. Stay for the pending Bledsoe family photograph beneath a one-hundred-year-old oak tree. Stay for the opportunity to confide in a man whose heart she'd broken beyond belief? What sense did that make? Taffy reasoned with God, wrestling like Jacob with his angel, until exhausted. Now she was anxious and confused, heart pumping, body rebelling.

Should've stayed indoors.

Could've done without seeing that shirtless man sweating beneath the sun this afternoon, built like God liked him. She'd ignored him best she could, out there working the fields. But love, and maybe lust, was intent on having her way. Taffy swore she'd keep her distance. No need stirring memory of his kiss, warm lips, the rebirth of dead senses. She could do without fleshly insurrections.

Hadn't her mother relentlessly drilled 'monogamy'? But what was Taffy faithful to? A philandering spouse consumed with carnality?

The ringing telephone suspended Taffy's musings. Her parents were in the front parlor. Her mother would most likely answer. Sure enough, Rachel's clear voice offered a greeting that made Taffy's blood still.

"Big Baby! Oh, my, it's been a while. Family's fine, and yours? No need to apologize. You would've been there if possible. Yes, the service was lovely. Did you receive the copy of Mother's obituary?"

Taffy anchored her mind on Angel. Still, her hands trembled as she struggled to pull her attention from her mother's conversation, knowing the evil on the other side.

"Taffy... *Taffy!*" Angel had to shake her for her to hear. "Is this right?"

"Yes, sixteen plus seventy-three is eighty-nine. Good job."

"Oh-h-h! I had the right numbers but I twisted them."

"Mmm-hmm." *Twisted.*

"Taffy, you okay?"

She sat staring at yesterday. "I'm fine." She found a smile. "Bath time, Mr. Man."

"Bath's are for girls," Angel protested.

"And little boys who don't wanna smell like fried polecat."

Taffy lay atop the bed humming for Angel's benefit as well as her own.

She'd like to see the baby.

Just a day trip, nothing strenuous. Al would cart them. A visiting Grandmother Lacy knew the way—after all Big Baby was her kin. Taffy hadn't encountered Big Baby since her own infancy, but she was welcome to stop by. Grandmother Lacy said Big Baby didn't get around much, gout or rheumatoid arthritis or some other illness contrived. Alfredo chauffeured the thirty-minute ride.

Dressed in white, house smoky with the scent of acrid leaves, Big Baby got around just fine—playing hospitable, offering viscous, odd-tasting tea. Hated declining hospitality, but Taffy couldn't manage more than a few mouthfuls. Such was enough. Taffy grit her teeth, anger sparking when remembering fighting for consciousness. Casting off hands pinning her naked, legs parted, on a cot in a room floating with women in white, the scent of burning lye, and an intrusively inserted thing. Called it purification. Blood-letting. Eradicating the sin blocking her from her husband's intimacy.

Spotting, cramping, she managed only to care for infant Angel the next few days. Tried escaping back to Bledsoe, but Grandmother Lacy blocked the path with poisonous threats. Never hated like she did Lacy and Alfredo then. Kept her promise never to look on Lacy—dead or alive—again; vowed Alfredo would never touch her unless *she'd* ceased to live. Moved with baby Angel to the spare room at the end of the hall, where the locksmith fixed the door and presented Taffy the key. Reliving the extremes to which Lacy would go to keep secrets concealed, Taffy eased onto her side, wiping a solitary tear.

According to the chime of the grandfather clock, midnight came and went, finding Taffy sleepless. She'd counted stars, the chirp of cicadas. Nothing soothed. Irritable, Taffy climbed from bed, tucked the cool cotton sheet about Angel and tipped from the room. Quietly, she descended the stairs, heading for the kitchen and milk to warm. High-beams flashing across the wall sent her to the backdoor instead.

Cautiously she peered out, instantly recognizing the pick-up entering the gravel drive. "Drew?" Alarmed, Taffy prayed nothing was amiss with Chloe. Grabbing her mother's sweater from the coat rack, Taffy tossed it over her shoulders, reaching the back porch just as Drew's passenger pulled something from the truck bed.

"Hey, Taf, I promised Uncle T. we'd bring him a line," Drew called from the driver's seat, passenger already approaching the house with a string of fresh-caught fish.

"Where would you like these?" Roam asked, mounting the porch.

Tightening her mother's sweater over her nightclothes, Taffy refused answers involving the man's anatomy. "The kitchen sink's fine." Holding open the screen door, Taffy let Roam pass while glaring at Drew, wishing she had a brick for his head.

"You still know how to clean and gut fish, Miss Cosmopolitan?" Submerging the catch in a sink full of water, Roam looked over his shoulder at Taffy, hovering at the kitchen entrance, silent and not amused.

"I'm sure my father thanks you, but those fish could've held 'til morning." Nervously, Taffy fumbled with her sweater as if needing a shield.

Roam snickered, having already envisioned her in nothing but skin. "You okay?"

"Are you?" Taffy snapped, wishing up an extra brick.

They stood eyes locked, heat flowing between them. Roam approached. Taffy moved from the doorway, granting Roam room to leave. Instead, Roam leaned down, whispering, "I'll be real good once we get some loving."

"Satan is a lie, and Hell has room! I'm not interested in playing games in the backseat of some car with you."

Roam laughed, low and deep. "Dollbaby, trust me, we won't be playing."

Ignoring the thrill shooting up her spine at the old endearment, Taffy held the door open. "Go home, Beelzebub. You're wasting my life."

Staying put, Roam chuckled before advising, "Lemme tell you like the Apostle Paul. 'When I was a child I spoke like a child. Now that I'm grown I've put away childish things'." Roam moved closer. "Backseat business is for hormonal kids. I'm all man. Our love-making won't be kiddie-quick in the confines of a car." Roam's baritone dipped deeper. "Gonna use whatever room we need and take our time spreading all this heaven," Roam slowly caressed Taffy's hip, "real nice...and wide." Grinning, Roam walked out, leaving Taffy utterly tongue-tied.

Drew's truck was down the road before Taffy thawed enough to holler, "Red-headed crazy!" She doused the kitchen lights, fish forgotten, and mounted the stairs. Midway, Taffy plopped onto a step, leaning against the stairwell, head in hand. Roam Ellis was out of his unnatural mind and in need of an exorcism, if not an enema. Just the same...Taffy was stuck on Roam's arrogant assertion.

"...once we get some loving."

Roam's sensual prediction incessantly circling her skull, Taffy uncomfortably squirmed atop the steps, something warm like bathwater seeping between her legs.

CHAPTER NINETEEN

Perverting scripture and blaming his filth on Apostle Paul," Taffy fumed. "I'm not here for this."

What 'this'? questioned The Gift. *Flesh? On Fire?*

"No…maybe…nearly," Taffy wrestled, tugging a dress over her head.

It either is or it ain't. Make up your mind.

"That's what I need you to do."

Me settle your thinking? The Gift smiled. *You know that's not my purpose.*

"Well, I'm sick of Roam Ellis, and I'm not dealing with any of this," Taffy stubbornly stated, pinning braids atop her head.

Yes, you will, 'cause a heap see but few know. Or like the Good Book says, many are called but few are chosen. You're both, so you can't choose willful ignorance.

"Knowing, *please*! Give him a disease or strike him ugly or something."

Knowing laughed until even Taffy felt good. *God doesn't use the devil's devices.*

Taffy shrugged. "Fine. I'm grabbing Angel and getting."

Coward's blood ain't in you, Knowing chastised. *Run now. Run the rest of your life.* Knowing made a silencing gesture at Taffy's intended interjection. *Taffy Marie, I've had the pleasure and pain of watching you become who you are, but all things aren't ours to dictate. God has the final say. Still, you have choice, which is part of growth. So choose wisely 'cause love ought to be lived right.*

Afraid sound judgment would be swayed by sensual craving, Taffy smoldered, wondering what good was second sight if she couldn't see?

I own you or you own me?

Instantly, Taffy stilled. "You don't possess the gift," NuNu always instructed, "and she don't own you. You both belong to God."

Knowing nodded, satisfied Taffy recalled. Certainly, she did. Remembered growing up different, often teased, other times treasured for her ability to see. Never understood the commotion Knowing created. Glimpsing hearts and minds and colors that exposed the spirit was natural, Taffy's normal. But some treated Taffy differently, offering pennies or sweets to foretell a future and harvest a hope, or locate lost love.

NuNu positioned herself like a barricade between Taffy and ignorance. "You ain't no circus sideshow, Little One. You see what you see for the good! Not for filthy gain or trifling folks too lazy to view their own selves. If you let 'em, folks'll suck you dry," NuNu warned, preserving sanctity while helping Taffy navigate a supernatural path.

"We both belong to God," Taffy answered humbly.

"Taf, who you talking to?" Chloe asked, scoping the empty room when entering. "Never mind," Chloe amended, noting the oddity of Taffy's eyes. "And why're you dolled up? We're just going to town."

Taffy downplayed her finery. "It's a piece-of-dress, Chloe."

"*This* is a dress." Chloe plucked the fabric of her own garb. "That there's something altogether else," Chloe concluded, admiring Taffy's ivory and periwinkle silk. "Lord, I used to have a figure," Chloe reminisced, rubbing her baby belly. "Aunt Vesta called. Drew can't leave the stables. A mare's foaling. Can Uncle T. drive us to town?"

"Daddy's over in Drexel until tonight," Taffy provided, perching on the bed's edge, massaging scented oil over her legs.

"Guess we better wait 'til Drew's free or go tomorrow."

"You need things for tonight's fish fry and I'm not going to Miss Marva's on a Saturday. Every woman and her mama'll be there getting cute for 'Come Sunday'."

Chloe rifled through her pocketbook, smiling when producing keys. "We could drive."

Eyeing each other, they snickered.

"Between the two of us, I'm the better driver and that's not saying much," Taffy admitted, easing stockings up legs. "I gotta wear shoes?"

"I'm not going to town with a barefoot cave creature, so put something other than downhome dust on those feet."

Easing into leather pumps, Taffy tottered about the room. After much freedom, her feet resisted stylish confines. "Remember how we took down Deacon Anderson's mailbox and his blue ribbon goat?"

"*We*? You were driving. Poor goat had a three-legged limp thanks to you."

"I was twelve."

"You were silly, driving your Daddy's truck on a dare. Who was it dared you?"

"Guess," Taffy sneered, grabbing her pocketbook and heading out the room.

"Oh, yeah, that big penny-red. That man's been crazy since the crib."

"You don't know the half," Taffy agreed, reliving last night's exchange, and Roam's presumptuous, sensual prediction that awakened something needing relief.

"That man showed up here come dinnertime yesterday acting like he'd come for my food and some fishing." Chloe's voice turned sly as they descended the stairs. "What he really wanted wasn't on his plate. How you plan on handling that, Miss Taffy?"

"Roam Ellis ain't nothing but breath and britches," Taffy breezily replied, sending Chloe into a peal of laughter as they headed out the door.

"Oh, wait! Aunt Vesta wants us to pick up a few items. You wanna call your mama and see if she needs anything?"

"No."

"You ain't right, Taffy. You know we check with each other to see who needs what from town."

"Fine, Chloe Jean, go call Mama and stop meddling."

"I'm not meddling!"

"You're tryna fix something that's not yours to mend, so either get in this old rusty Ford or I'm gone."

Drew's counsel was similar. *"Babe, grown folks'll fix themselves. Let it be."*

"I'm *not* meddling, Taf! I just want you and Aunt Rachel to be right again, to get your closeness back. Okay? Taffy...?"

Taffy started the car.

"Fine! I'm coming," Chloe huffed. "You bullheaded Bledsoes are enough to make me pee."

"Taffy, you 'bout to hit the curb!" And she did, like Satchel Paige out the park. When the Ford stopped rocking, the two fell into a hysterical fit, relieved they'd made the journey to town with only one near-casualty. "Never thought I'd see Olivette Williams run for something other than a rib," Chloe choked, laughing.

"I didn't see her," Taffy insisted.

"You can't *not* see Miss Olivette! She's five-feet tall and six-feet wide! She ain't hard to miss, but thank God you did, or the front of Drew's Ford might be missing," Chloe remarked, sending them into a fresh, irreverent fit.

"Find a dollar and buy yourself some sense," Taffy managed to breathe.

"I know. Lord, forgive us," Chloe repented. "See what happens when I'm with you, just get all uncouth."

"You were a spectacle before I got here. Get out the car and let's go."

Exiting the haphazardly parked vehicle, they made their way onto the wooden, raised platform accommodating downtown foot traffic. Having only witnessed this new Bledsoe in the waning light of day, Taffy was better able to appreciate how its hub had changed. New businesses sat beside old, both spruced with coats of fresh paint. Still, nothing outshone that paved road. No more muddy rivers in winter or droppings from horse-drawn wagons. Passage had been improved.

"Wanna stop by Tinsley's first?" Chloe questioned as they leisurely strolled.

"I'd rather dodge Cousin Imogene's venom, but I promised Angel some sour balls," Taffy conveyed. "Plus, I told R.J. I'd stop and see him again."

"Well, let's get in and get out."

Heading that way, Taffy matched Chloe's wobbling pace. "What's this?" Taffy paused outside Tinsley's before a notice announcing a meeting for a proposed library.

"Gon' and read up on it," Chloe suggested. "I'll start shopping."

Taffy nodded, already engrossed. The closest Bledsoe came to a library was Matlock's Barber Shop. Like her grandparents, Old Man Matlock couldn't read, but he loved books—their smell, the pictures that allowed him to concoct his own fanciful tales. He coveted them, only offering picture books to a fretting and wiggling child to keep him still. When The Depression hit and folks couldn't rightly afford to pay, Old Man Matlock asked for unwanted books instead. Now he had stacks of them. Reading the library proposal, Taffy wondered if he'd donate any.

"Taffy?"

Taffy looked up to find a well-dressed woman coming her way. "First Lady!"

"My dear, how are you?"

"Well." Taffy returned an affectionate embrace. "How're you? Reverend Ellis?"

"We're both living off God's good grace," replied the First Lady of First Zion African Methodist Episcopal.

"Well, grace is surely good," Taffy complimented. A slender woman a few inches shy of Taffy's height, First Lady Ellis' Seminole heritage was evident in her sharp nose and jet black hair, and the skin coloring bequeathed to her only child.

"Flatter an old woman and she'll want you to do it again." Shared laughter was sweet. "You do look wonderful, Octavia," First Lady remarked. Taffy hadn't been home but two days and already the gossip mill was overflowing. Folks said big city living finally caught up with Taffy and she was inches from leprosy and lesions. First Lady smiled, seeing truth wasn't in lies. "Just as lovely as always."

First Lady's voice rang sincere despite failed love. Holding a torch for this girl, her son's intentions were once clear. Taffy would've been daughter-in-law but matters hadn't worked Roam's way. First Lady had shared her son's ache, even his anger. And while Roam long possessed an affinity for the rails First Lady knew his fierce attachment was partly an escape from brokenness. First Lady struggled mightily to do the Christian thing and not hold animosity. Years and distance helped. She conceded all were prone to mistakes, especially the young. Besides, First Lady knew enough to know she wasn't privy to all things. There were three sides to this story: Roam's, Taffy's, and God's. And only the latter's told all. "How's Mr. Angel Sir?"

Taffy's answer was interrupted. Red warmth crept up her spine before he appeared, and when he did she willed herself to calm. Taffy preferred being anywhere but here with him. She was still outdone over his indecency and the unrighteous impact of his carnal threat and prophecy. But truth be told Roam Ellis—suited like Sunday— looked good enough to forgive.

Following Taffy's intense gaze, First Lady found it locked on her child and her child's on Taffy. "Son, look who I found standing here sweet as springtime."

He came up the walkway loaded with packages. Shifting his burden, Roam freed a hand and tipped a real hat this time. "Miss Taffy."

"Mr. Ellis. How're you?"

"Could use a few winks after night fishing…and *whatnot*…but I'm otherwise good," Roam answered, grinning devilishly.

"All my child does on layovers is sleep."

"And eat," Chloe added, coming their way. "Still parking those big feet under my table tonight, Little Mister Ellis?" Chloe asked, kissing First Lady's cheek. "We gonna need to repopulate the Gulf once your greedy gets done?"

First Lady couldn't help laughing. "You know him well."

"Ooo, First Lady, come see this new fabric that just came in," Chloe suddenly invited, linking arms with her pastor's wife and steering her towards Tinsley's. "Take your time, Taf. I'll get Angel's sour balls."

Taffy shot Chloe a hot look, knowing she was up to no good.

"See you Sunday?" First Lady called over her shoulder.

"Yes, ma'am. Please give the Reverend my regards." Taffy turned away, only to be halted by a firm touch on her arm.

"Mind waiting while I put my mother's packages in the car?" Roam requested.

"Can't. I'm in route to Miss Marva's."

"I was wondering when you'd stop looking country 'bout the crown and handle those picky plaits atop your skull."

"Roam, the more I see you the less I like you."

His booming laughter was a peppermint-scented wave against Taffy's face. "Always loved teasing you. Still do. Still love you, too. Wait, now, don't stomp off." Roam held her arm as Taffy attempted to do just that. "Let's walk and talk."

Ignoring the jolt caused by Roam's touch, Taffy snorted. "Not with all these nosey folks 'round here."

"Just look straight ahead and pretend you're not enjoying my company."

"That won't require acting."

CHAPTER TWENTY

I was out of line last night. I apologize," Roam quietly offered, casually strolling.

Looking in shop windows, Taffy exhaled, relieved. "You're forgiven for talking out the side of your nasty neck—"

"'Ey, I don't apologize for stating what I want. I'm sorry it was crassly done."

Taffy stopped and stared. "I thought you'd have better sense in sunlight, but you're still showing your backside."

"I prefer honesty to your playing like you don't want us, when truth is—"

"Truth has nothing to do with this, Roam Ellis. Neither does love," Taffy insisted. "This is you pissing on turf like some animal warding off a rival."

"Don't use unladylike language. Urine's preferable to piss."

Taffy had to laugh. "Ooo, I wanna hit you!"

Roam extended an arm. "Go ahead, its deserved." Pushing his arm away, Taffy moved on. "You get points on the rivalry theory," Roam conceded, matching Taffy's slow stride. "You said it best: you were mine first."

"I never said that, Roam."

"Thom Thumb wedding," Roam reminded, voice haunted by want. "You married me first. I have a right to mark territory when deprived of what's rightly mine."

"That was kids' play. *And* I'm not a possession."

"Not implying you are. But, Dollbaby, you—"

"Don't call me that."

"Fine, Taffy Mae."

"You know my middle name as well as your own, and Mae isn't it."

"*As I was saying*, Taffy Jane!" She sighed. Roam briefly grinned, offering Taffy a peppermint before popping two in his mouth, thoughtfully sucking, swirling before continuing. "Listen, I've always been forthright to a fault. Especially in important things. Not aiming to shock or offend, but we've lost enough time, and don't have any for game-playing."

Exasperation coated Taffy's tone. "That's precisely what this is, Roam, a game. We're face-to-face for the first time in eternity and you wanna talk troubling things?"

Roam held Taffy's elbow with a courtly, tender touch as they descended the end of the walk. Crossing the street, they greeted familiar persons, ignored curious stares.

Roam was first to speak. "What's troubling? That I love you or that I want you?"

"Roam, *stop*."

"You think I *want to* want you?" Roam chortled. "Nothing doing! But if I'm feeling this, so are you. Deny loving me," Roam challenged at Taffy's scoffing laugh. Her sudden silence was conceding. "Mmm-hmm," Roam gloated. "It's like this. Putting a pot on low heat, leaving and walking off, doesn't mean food's not cooking. Come back and crank up that heat and see if that pot don't boil quick-like…'cause it's been simmering all along."

"You haven't been 'simmering' for me! You've gone on with life."

"Did you expect me not to?"

"No, a man like you doesn't sit around pining."

"A man like me?"

"Shoe hurts on the other foot, huh? A man of the world, too handsome for his own good, who's intelligent and well-traveled isn't lacking options. I bet green money there's a lady friend at every layover. Can *you* deny that?"

"Dollbaby, that's physical release, not heartstrings."

"I wonder if your lovers agree."

Roam paused, cornered and confronted. "Listen, Taffy Lee, I'm not callous. I simply don't delude myself fabricating what doesn't exist. This here does. Obviously, it's been on the backburner."

Taffy focused on their pathway as if helping her thoughts to move. "Backburner or not, Sweetness, I'm someone else's wife."

"And that's working for you?" Taffy stumbled. Roam steadied her. "You okay? That's what I thought," Roam decided in Taffy's silence. "Life's not right in paradise."

"Doesn't matter. I took vows."

"Til death do you part? Got news for you, Baby, and I truly pray you realize this. You're already dying."

Taffy shivered. Her tone turned sharp. "Roam, I'd rather not do this!"

"I'd rather it not be done. Rather you not be married, but you are so I'll say this and I'm finished. I thought I was through with you. Told myself you were bitter water under my bridge. Did my damnedest to stay far away from you. Still, here I am."

Taffy waited expectantly, but Roam left it like it was. "Here *we* are," Taffy quietly acknowledged, deciding denial was synonymous with a lie. "Pot on the stovetop," Taffy mused, wishing she'd kept to her plan. Being in Chicago, she could've avoided ripping scars off old wounds. "I'd better not keep Ms. Marva waiting."

Roam glanced up noting their arrival at Taffy's destination. "So conversation's ended?"

"For now. Tip your hat real formal-like in case anyone's looking."

"Dollbaby, this here's front page news," Roam jested, touching her hand. "Two things. One: you realize you called me 'Sweetness'? Haven't heard that in a heap. And two: am I too handsome for *your* good?"

Glancing across the road and finding Cousin Imogene watching from the window of Tinsley's, Taffy merely smiled before leaving Roam where he stood.

"You gonna fess up real soon, Taffy Faye," Roam taunted. Amused, he moved on.

Neither noticed the man at the end of the road. He'd stood under the cover of a partially completed building trekking the pair the entire time. Now he dropped his smoked-to-the-stub cigarette, crushing it underfoot, extinguishing a burning thing. If looks could be believed, something was burning between those two. *Coon courting's going on.* Wasn't right, and he had no qualms about blotting the woman out. Not now. God wasn't pleased with her wicked ways. Neither was he.

CHAPTER TWENTY-ONE

T he bell above the door of *Miss Marva's House of Style* chimed a new arrival.

Lowering a dryer atop a client's head, Marva Morrison looked up and nearly lost what wits she had left. "Hey, now, gal! Get your long self over here!" the proprietor commanded, giving Taffy a sound embrace. "Grapevine said you were back. I figured your mess-of-a-head would find its way here eventually."

Laughing, Taffy squeezed the contradiction-of-a-woman with her Hollywood hairdo and denim dungarees. "Have space for a walk-in?" Only Miss Marva could truly subdue Taffy's indecisive mane. Curly, kinky, straight: Taffy's hair wouldn't choose. Miss Marva brought her hair under subjection and made it behave.

"Child, I don't do walk-ins no more. Better be on my books two weeks in advance or you leaving here nappy and unhappy. But lemme check... Dottie, who I got next?"

On the far side of the salon, a woman in a pink smock with *House of Style* embroidered on the breast pocket consulted an appointment book. "Miss Olivette."

Miss Marva sighed. "Tired of Olivette rumbling her moon ass in here late. If she's more than five minutes behind you got her spot... and she will be, so come on back."

Taffy quickly looked about, admiring a table bearing a vase of wildflowers. Fluffy pink draperies bordered windows boasting a gold-scripted list of services in lieu of the old, beat-up cardboard sign. "Nice changes, Miss Marva."

"Ain't much but it makes folks feel nice in a world tryna pull us down."

"Business must be good if you no longer take walk-ins," Taffy observed, following Miss Marva to her private station atop a small platform in the back.

Miss Marva chortled. "*That* has definitely changed. You wasn't but a little thing back then, so you may not remember how these doors were open and my chairs empty when I first came to Bledsoe after slaving in that meat factory back east."

"All I remember, Miss Marva, is you scandalizing Bledsoe's prim-and-proper with your steel-toed boots and chewing snuff."

Miss Marva bent sideways with laughter. "Girl, you a hoot and a holler! But you're right. These skirt-wearing women 'round here think I don't know they used to call me 'Mister Marvin'. Just 'cause I could out-cuss and out-drink bigger men. These women thought I'd contaminate their precious hair 'til Corrine Randolph came crawling in here, tail 'tween her legs."

Taffy smiled, clearly recalling Miss Marva's shop being open and absent of customers nearly two months. Then Aunt Corrine, Chloe's mother and Rachel's dearest friend, mixed some lye to "loosen" her curls. Brains nearly burnt out, she hopped around Rachel's kitchen, half her head afire. Rachel couldn't fix Corrine's mess. No one could. Except 'Mister Marvin'. Desperate, Aunt Corrine slid on over, humble as pie, begging aid. A graduate of Madame C.J. Walker's Lelia College for Walker Hair Culturists, Miss Marva resuscitated Aunt Corrine's hair until it flowed like a living thing. And so *Miss* Marva was allowed to stay despite her peculiar ways.

"I'm on my feet so long I can sleep standing. I go home smelling like hair lye and hickory from Moody barbequing next door, but I'm grateful. How you and Angel fairing?"

Taffy's face lit up as she launched into a seamless stream of Angel's doings. They'd resumed an easy rhythm that defied lost time. Taffy never forced her affections. Didn't bother assuming a role or object to his calling her by name. She let Angel set the pace. Their moments were treasured—gathering tadpoles in the back pond, climbing trees and other pastimes that heightened his pleasure. Truth be told, Taffy gleaned satisfaction as well. Forced to grow up faster than her years, Angel afforded Taffy a second pass at childhood.

"Hold up! I don't want no dissertation on ashy-kneed Angel Freeman. That boy runs 'round here enough for me to know what he poops and pees," Miss Marva complained as Taffy laughed. "Just wanted to know how y'all fitting in with each other?"

"We're fitting fine, Miss Marva."

"Good." Miss Marva reached up and tugged a braid coiled atop

Taffy's head. "What the Hades you doing to your hair?"

"Nothing—"

"That's obvious!" Snatching a fresh cape from a shelf, Miss Marva snapped it open, secured it about Taffy's neck. "Sit down and let's work some magic on this mess. Oh, Lord, I hope this cow ain't coming in here," she muttered, looking out the window.

"New to town?" Taffy asked, watching the woman—thirtyish, petite, and attractive in a deceptive, decorative way—saunter through Miss Marva's front door.

Miss Marva snorted, eyeing the woman headed for the one called Dottie. "Nothing new about that heffa. Those cookies been 'round the block and back. Bledsoe's prim-and-proper been tryna get rid of her since she came."

Curious about an array of off-colored lights sparking wildly about the woman, Taffy refrained from commenting. Even Miss Marva hushed and observed the two women huddled up whispering until Dottie realized she was under scrutiny. Hurriedly, she returned to business as the visitor took her time sashaying out the salon.

Sucking teeth, Miss Marva left that alone. "Finish your schooling?"

Forced to leave school when Angel was born, Taffy had recently reenrolled and finally completed her graduation requirements earlier in the year.

"Good for you, baby! Now you can make your way a little better, do all that drawing dresses you like so much." Miss Marva pulled a chair lever, elevating Taffy's feet. "Colored women don't get the chance to reconstruct ourselves. Most of us doing what we have to, not what we want. So you and I are blessed in having a chance at what we love."

Taffy agreed she was blessed and beyond grateful for God's goodness. But did she have what she loved, let alone love what she had? "Miss Marva, can I ask you something?" Though distanced from others in the salon, Taffy lowered her voice. "What would you do about inappropriate affection?"

Miss Marva turned off the water she'd been running to warm. "Is it affection you have, or somebody having it towards you?"

"Both."

Miss Marva hesitated before securing the pink privacy curtain about her station.

"Baby, I might not be the best kind of person to answer that."
Miss Marva scratched her chin. "Then again maybe I am." Turning the water back on, she undid Taffy's braids. "Gal, you still have
enough hair on your head for two. Lay back," she instructed, waiting
as Taffy obeyed. "I'mma tell what I usually don't, 'cause it might help.

"My folks put me out when I was fifteen after my mama came
home from work ailing one day and found me and my best friend,
Francesca, touching each other. We were on my bed, *inappropriately
exposed*." Miss Marva breathed slowly before continuing. "My parents said I was dead to them, so I packed my bags, headed who knew
where. I asked Francesca to come with me, but she was scared to try
life our way." Miss Marva gazed into space. "When Franny's pa found
out about our goings-on, he beat her so bad she lost her right eye."
Miss Marva shuddered with memory. "So, yes, I know about inappropriate fondness. Experienced it before," glancing up as if seeing
through the curtain and across the salon, Miss Marva added, "still
do."

"No easy way around it?" Taffy questioned, soothed by the water's
warm cascade, tempted to unburden seven-years of falsity. Miss Marva wouldn't condemn.

Miss Marva frowned. "Baby, no, you gonna struggle with that
kind of love."

"I'd rather not."

"You will if you want it. This business you fretting over got anything to do with that seven-foot Seminole walking 'round here with
his mama earlier today?"

"Six-four or -five," Taffy corrected.

"Mmm-hmm. Y'all found your way back to each other, but you
got Al Freeman 'round your neck." Truth left a bad aftertaste in Miss
Marva's mouth. She was silently thoughtful a while. "Sorry, I don't
have a magic fix. This here's your row to hoe. But I'll tell you this:
you gotta decide if you want it...or if it's best like it is." Miss Marva
quieted before laughing. "I hear it's cold Up North where you live."
Miss Marva nudged Taffy with her hip. "If I were you, I'd cozy up
with that Roam Ellis and have that big ol' boy bake my cookies with
that hot southern comfort packed in his pants."

"Miss Marva, I'm not fixin'-ta-bout-to!" Taffy squealed. "Do my
hair, please."

The hair culturist chortled wildly. "What we doing to this stuff anyhow?"

"Whatever you want," Taffy moaned.

"One masterpiece coming up." Miss Marva paused when hearing the bell chime above the front door—listened to make out the voice. "Come on back, Chloe Jean!" Pink curtain opening, Chloe appeared. "Hey there, big belly, when you spitting out that thing?"

"Nice seeing you, too, Miss Marva," Chloe replied, easing onto the dryer seat.

"How's Drew? And when you gonna let me get 'hold of that head?" Miss Marva shrieked, frowning at the demure bun at the nape of Chloe's neck.

"Drew's good. And what I need to be all spruced up for, with my expectant self?"

"Being spruced up got you *knocked* up."

"Lord, Miss Marva…"

"Don't 'Miss Marva' me! That hair*don't* is 'bout as appetizing as piss-and-grits."

"Not funny," Chloe droned above Taffy's ringing laughter.

"Sure ain't! It's sad," advised Miss Marva. "*You* might be with child, but Drew ain't. Spruce yourself up if you wanna keep some pleasure on his pipe."

Chloe looked at her curiously. "Ma'am?"

"In-a-family-way or not, I know that farm-fed man's still tryna crawl in your cookies. But the way that hair's looking your cookies is crumbling."

"Miss Marva, if I was Catholic I'd 'Hail Mary' myself to death over you," Chloe stated with an exasperated shake of her head. "Taffy, hush! It ain't *that* funny."

"And *you* lay back so I can soften this bush," Miss Marva ordered, smoothing a homemade treatment over Taffy's hair. Valuing her "backwater ways", Miss Marva solicited NuNu's counsel in concocting a proprietary blend of honey, olive oil, coconut milk, licorice root and other herbs and extracts she refused to name. "I ain't offering no more man-related advice today. Y'all gonna figure the rest for yourselves. And… Oh, hell-no-no, she ain't coming in here thirty-five minutes late!" Miss Marva took off marching towards the front door, pink smock slapping about her dungarees. Turning the lock with satisfaction, she retraced her steps.

"What's wrong?" Taffy inquired.

"That," Miss Marva replied, nodding toward the door where Olivette Williams stood unsuccessfully trying to enter. "That'll learn her. Fat meat's greasy and my time ain't for play. And, you, Sweet Water Taffy—get up from this washbowl so I can whip some order back into this nest you passing off as hair."

CHAPTER TWENTY-TWO

Somebody sure is driving slowly," Chloe observed. "Don't want the wind blowing your precious curls?"

Taffy admired the sophisticated upsweep in the rearview mirror. Miss Marva knew her stuff. A client could enter her shop with a magazine picture asking 'can you do this?' and Miss Marva would do one better. "That woman's a wonder," Taffy praised.

"That woman needs dipping in holy water."

"Miss Marva just speaks her mind and her truth as she sees it. And the day she changes is the day she's dead. She means well."

"She does," Chloe agreed, "but that don't mean she ain't a mess."

"And more," Taffy concurred with a laugh.

"Folks say that shampoo girl, Miss Dottie, and Miss Marva are… *special* friends."

Taffy didn't feign ignorance, not after the confidences Miss Marva shared. Not to mention grown folks whispering too loudly when Miss Marva came to town about her manner of dressing and drinking and *unholy bedroom tendencies.* "Hmmm," was all Taffy allowed.

They fell silent until Chloe suddenly blurted, "I'm missing my Mama. Mind if we stop by?"

Taffy glanced at Chloe's profile. Her eyes were wet, soft. Taffy reached for Chloe's hand. "Of course not."

Chloe exhaled. "Been gone two years and I'm still not used to it. Sometimes I pick up the phone or head out the door, intent on talking to Mama, only to remember Jesus has her." Chloe gave Taffy a wan smile. "Promise I won't stay long."

Taffy patted Chloe's hand. "Sweetie, take your time."

They made their way across well-kept grounds to the tombstone marked with the details of Corrine Randolph's life, her rising, her setting, and the epitaph, *"Her virtue excels them all."* Placing gathered sunflowers in a brass urn, Chloe kissed the stone.

"Hi, Mama, I brought someone to see you."

Taffy caressed cool marble. "Aunt Corrine, Drew's doing good by your daughter and this beautiful baby she's baking. Chloe's just fine."

Smiling, Chloe dabbed her eyes.

"I'mma let you two have your time, but I sure miss and love you, Aunt Corrine, *and* your pecan pies," Taffy said, squeezing Chloe's hand.

Watching Taffy move on, Chloe could've sworn Taffy's fingers felt like her mother's own.

She strolled the graveyard, reading markers; most familiar, some unknown. *Amazing,* Taffy thought, how life could be narrowed to a matter of dates and inscriptions, incapable of conveying the breadth and depth of one's being. She wondered what her own tombstone would read…

You're already dying. Roam's pronouncement reverberated painfully.

She was the one gifted with sight, yet Roam had always seen her clearly. Taffy resisted notions of dying. She'd learned how not to drown. But was that the same as living? She'd fought too hard to maintain life, and if the fight wasn't finished neither was Taffy.

A rustling sound interrupted Taffy's train of thought. Turning, Taffy saw an old woman in the distance, a wicker basket filled with orange daffodils slung over a pale arm.

What was a white woman doing in the Colored cemetery?

Head cocked, Taffy remembered: Goldie Hale Thornton, wife of Richland's "The Judge".

Goldie Hale Thornton was Bledsoe's boogey phantom with which children terrorized each other by night. Here she was in broad daylight, tending the graves of five Black babies.

Folks said she was crazy and that The Judge feared Bledsoe because of those Black babies birthed by her white body. NuNu never confirmed or denied, just said 'let it be' whenever Taffy questioned legend's veracity. Were Miss Goldie's babies Colored because of NuNu conjuring?

Legend was near slavery's end Goldie's pa, Preacherman Hale, took a second wife upon the demise of his first. That marriage led to property: NuNu and her baby brother, Elias, acquired like wedding china. Orphans. Mother dead over master's greed...

Mending and embellishing the sheath rescued from the rubble heap, Octavia and child were terrified by Master's storming their candlelit cabin, looking on Octavia's twelve-year-old treasure, something tight in his loins and eyes.

Octavia offered herself. She was shoved aside. Tender meat was Master's.

Africa still thick on her tongue, Octavia heaped curses on Master snatching at his property, but her Treasure. Reliving the raping aboard an enslaving vessel, Octavia bit Master's ear off. The overseer strung Octavia up, beating until blood ran a river.

Master defecated on her wounds. Slow death set in. Days later, Octavia walked home across the waters, leaving orphaned children on northern shores.

But morning after, Master's body erupted blood and ooze, smelling of defecation, death, and delirium. Withered by her father's demise, Master's youngest accepted old Preacherman Hale's marriage proposal, agreed to finish raising his motherless child.

Heading further south, Octavia's orphans in tow, the newlyweds' forged an existence beyond Master's misery and Octavia's mutiny. Only the white cotton sheath hid beneath NuNu's clothing survived when Octavia's everything was spat on and burned.

NuNu cherished her mother's African ways, and Preacherman favored NuNu's baby brother, Elias. He was quick of wit and intelligent. Allowing the boy to eat and sleep in the family's abode, albeit the cellar, an indulgent Preacherman watched Elias become a fine buck, but failed to watch his daughter, Goldie, watching Elias as well.

Eyes filled with the charms of a slave girl on a neighboring estate, Elias was blind to Goldie's abnormal interest. NuNu—newly wed and expecting—warned her brother, beware. Elias laughed at the lunacy of a white female's infatuation until accosted by Goldie's petulant whims. She demanded the same affection he gave his slave gal. Elias refused, preferring life.

Jealous, she lit into him, scratching, biting. Deflecting Goldie's blows, Elias unintentionally struck her in defense. Nose bleeding, Goldie cried the highest foul. The nail tracks on his face, her weeping and wailing were proof: Elias had niggardly intent.

Turning his back on the Black defiler he'd help raise, Preacherman

Hale watched the mob descend. They were judge and jury, executing southern justice with a noose and the sturdy limbs of a century-old tree.

First mother, now brother. If not for her man, Matthias, NuNu might've gone mad. Momentarily, perhaps she had, stalking Goldie Hale, leaving earth-filled sachets about her door. But it came to a head the day NuNu prophesied.

White veil claiming her eyes, NuNu walked a figure-eight around Goldie, growling, "My brother be with you always!" Jabbing fingers against her enemy's white belly, NuNu left Goldie to her laughter that dried up three years later when Goldie birthed her firstborn.

Married to the man destined to be The Judge, attended by a Colored midwife, Goldie gave birth to her first mulatto child.

Sending the Colored midwife back east where she couldn't tell a soul who cared, The Judge confronted the tar-touched baby in the birthing bed. Orchestrating that hanging in her honor, he knew Goldie abhorred a Colored man's touch. Yet, he made her swear atop Bibles that she hadn't sullied their marriage or been defiled.

It was that 'black beast, Octavia!' She'd put roots on Goldie's womb.

Wrapping living baby and lifeless afterbirth in an old knapsack, Judge went hunting for a witch. Would've killed NuNu with his bare hands, but he fell near dead at her feet. Only Matthias could make NuNu take death off The Judge, convincing her they'd be, like Elias, swinging from a tree. Who, then, would care for their newborn, Augustine? NuNu withdrew death, but left a raised marker and reminder on Judge's neck.

"Come near me or mine and that welt will bore into your body and eat you from the inside out 'til ain't enough of you for a maggot's meal," *NuNu vowed.*

Goldie and The Judge might have convinced themselves the ordeal was little more than a vain imagination, except four more pregnancies produced beige babies. More Colored midwives disappeared, and little mounds of dirt multiplied in Bledsoe's cemetery.

Taffy watched Goldie Hale Thornton place orange daffodils atop tiny, cross-guarded mounds. Miss Goldie prayerfully knelt at each before toddling several rows to a newly erected, ornate headstone Taffy didn't recognize.

Sitting delicately, Miss Goldie pulled a wrapped sandwich from her basket and proceeded to break bread. Tiny bits she gave to herself, then the ground, fingers digging holes in the soil into which morsels were fed.

"Twin, mama says you gotta finish dinner, else we can't have dessert, so eat up."

Taffy didn't fear the dead; had found her best Hide-n-Seek spots here in the graveyard where bones rested after the soul separated. Death was as natural as life. It was the manner in which death claimed a body that could prove the problem. So, Taffy was without dread. Still, the sight of Miss Goldie feeding herself and the ground was nearly as startling as the sudden appearance of an ageless being standing beside the grave.

Knowing? Taffy marveled, viewing more of The Gift than ever manifested. The Gift waved Taffy forward, inviting her to see who it was Miss Goldie fed. Taffy turned tail and went the other way.

CHAPTER TWENTY-THREE

Chloe's kitchen bumped and bustled, every conceivable space consumed by colorful spirits and liberated souls, effortless laughter and Friday night freedom.

The work week with its cares was over. Masks worn in the white world were stored. Women were home where they mattered, with names other than 'gal' and faces refusing to meld into a monolithic nonentity. Having no one to satisfy save themselves, they threw pleasure in pots and seasoned food as if fixing life up right.

Downhome smells of snapper, butter fish, gulf-fresh shrimp and oysters tempted Taffy's hungry stomach. She inhaled bright frivolity while whisking a wooden spoon about the large bowl cradled in the crook of her arm. She was engulfed by a cacophony of effervescent energy, vivacious spirits like the vibrant plumes of some exotic bird. True to form, these women laid love at her feet when welcoming her back into the fold.

"Taffygirl, those pretty city fingers remember how to make batter?" boomed Vesta Jo Bledsoe, her voice a flying crescendo above the din. Aunt Vesta was loud like that; never learned to whisper, never thought she should.

Widow of Poppy and NuNu's eldest, Augustine, Vesta Jo Bledsoe darted about the kitchen in her regular role as commander of the Friday Night Fish Fry, holding a place of honor and freely flowing where others didn't dare.

Friday nights at Chloe and Drew's were reserved for the "third-line younguns," Poppy and NuNu's descendants two generations removed. While the second-line—the sons of the founding family and their wives and comrades—gathered on somebody's porch or parlor it was, in Vesta's opinion, sedate compared to what jumped off down here. So Augustine's childless widow claimed her weekly spot in Chloe's kitchen, come rain or shine, long enough to get her fill of young energy before moving down the road.

"I have enough country left in me to bake a proper pan of corn-bread, Aunt Vesta," Taffy assured, loving her aunt's robust energy and refusal to go silent and unseen.

"This child's still country *and* corn-fed," remarked Dena Bledsoe Hampton, patting Taffy's backside. The firstborn grandchild ten years Taffy's senior—officiator of Tom Thumb weddings and backyard revivals, where "parishioners" beat pie tins like tambourines and caught the Holy Ghost on cue—Dena was of that new, unconventional generation of Bledsoe women keeping their daddy's name while gluing their husbands' behind.

"Like your stuff ain't bubbling over," Taffy sallied, bumping her cousin's prosperous posterior.

"Bounty's in the Bledsoe blood, Miss Pretty City," Dena retorted. "Just make sure you make corn*bread* not bricks."

"Stop all the Who Shot John 'fore y'all sour something," Aunt Vesta hollered above the laughter-splashed room. "And Dena darling, ain't *nobody* wanting no fancy flavorings in that pound cake. Vanilla, almond, or lemon. Understand? Not that cayenne and clove mess you made last week."

"Funny how it disappeared," Dena mumbled, mentally concocting a blend of cardamom, nutmeg, and sage while whipping sugar and butter into a smooth paste.

"And Boss thanks you!" Aunt Vesta chortled, peeking over Chloe's shoulder. "That potato salad needs more onion powder, Chloe dear. And a dash of dill." And on Aunt Vesta went, editing and tasting until the spread bore her approval. Removing apron from her thick middle, she hung it on a hook. "I'mma gon' up the road and sit with the oldsters."

Like clockwork protests sailed about the room urging Aunt Vesta to stay. As always, Vesta declined, claiming she was too seasoned for young fun.

"But if one of them youngbloods liking aged meat strolls through here, looking fine in his Friday night feel-goods, send 'im my way. Your auntie's got something he can gnaw on other than a bone," Vesta advised with a saucy swirl of hearty hips.

The room erupted. "Oh, Lord, Aunt Vesta, you nasty!" Chloe shrilled.

"That big belly says so are you," Aunt Vesta teased. "Lemme make my plate and I'm gone."

"Taf, think Aunt Vesta'll marry again?" Chloe questioned as they donned their own Friday Night feel-goods.

"I've no idea," Taffy murmured, dabbing her lips with a hint of color.

Chloe ran a brush over the downy soft hair released from the bun at her neck. "Thought you had insight."

"Hmph!" Noting the soft-as-a-kiss cosmetic color highlighting Chloe's face, Taffy teased, "See you took Miss Marva's advice to spice up your life."

Chloe rolled her eyes dismissively. "Seriously, Taf, Aunt Vesta's too vibrant to be fading away man-less—"

"That's not for you to decide, Chloe," Taffy interrupted, gently patting Miss Marva's upswept masterpiece.

"She says Uncle Auggie was all the man she needed." Chloe was too caught in her meddling to notice Taffy's sudden stillness. "But Uncle Auggie's gone and Aunt Vesta's here, and a woman should live *and* love."

Taffy shook off the eerie distress that always accompanied her uncle's mention. "If a mule kicks Drew in his melon head and he goes to glory, you'd jump the broom again?"

"Don't be morbid; and no, Drew's my one and only."

"Then you understand Aunt Vesta's point of view. She's satisfied."

"Are you?" Chloe challenged. God had a way of working wonders. Didn't mean God didn't want a little earthly help sometimes. "If not, I know a big redbone who'd be more than happy to sweeten your tea."

"I'm not fooling with all that, Chloe Jean," Taffy warned, backing away from the looking glass. "You 'bout ready?"

"Yeah," Chloe sighed before brightening. "Let's get you downstairs, 'cause the way that dress is fitting, I'm putting a curfew on it and you."

By nine that night, Drew and Chloe's pulsed and throbbed with living from the center of the satisfied. Clusters, pockets, and paired-off people decorated the tiny space like living, breathing fixtures. Human revelry mixed with the phonograph's sounds, tumbling out windows into the warm arms of a night soaked with pleasure and promise.

A near-empty plate in hand, Taffy made her way through a liquid rainbow, its multihued rush dripping nectar sweet. Every conceivable seating surface was covered. A boisterous mix of deep, masculine instruments blended with female sweeps and trills creating a human symphony. Conversations were as vast as the gathering—fast and furious or smooth and free.

There was much pontificating and gesticulating over the vices and virtues of Negro America. Names floated like clouds. Marcus Garvey. Mary McLeod Bethune. "The Brown Bomber." Golden horned "Satchmo." Ethel and Billie, who sang with souls in their throats. Mr. Paul "Renaissance Man" Robeson. Current affairs, problems of securing the vote, and electing officials representing Colored interests. The world at large blended with local places and celebrated faces; the newest hairdo, fashion, and the goings-on in towns next door. All were served on platters for the picking, seemingly endless in possibility. Still, Taffy was caught off-guard when walking into an incredulous hiss gushing from Cousin Dena's lips.

"Who invited that unholy heffa?" Pausing, in her journey to the diningroom sideboard, Taffy turned a questioning look on her cousin seated in female company. Following the direction of Dena's frown, Taffy saw the subject in question. "Look at that mess! This is not the Lord's house. All *ain't* welcome here," Dena uttered, eliciting laughter from the flanking, feminine circle.

"Dena, stop," Chloe managed around a giggle, "she's not doing any harm—"

"*Yet!* Y'all best count your men, make sure ain't none missing."

Taffy eyed the woman chatting up Dena's husband, Bufford Hampton, best known as Hamp. The same whirlwind who'd breezed in and out of Miss Marva's salon. Her tangerine and lime pant ensemble and sunset orange fingernails matching the four-inch stilettos encasing dainty feet was decidedly festive. Yet, Taffy noted, the woman lacked light. Taffy questioned her identity.

"That's Paris Brown, but Dena calls her The Paris Hotel," Chloe supplied.

Dena answered Taffy's questioning stare. "The *ho's tail* is always open for business." Taffy couldn't help laughing with the rest. "Busier than a two-legged mule at an ass-kicking contest."

"Lord, y'all ain't right," Taffy sputtered. "If she's that terrible, why're you sitting here while she's over there chatting up your mister?"

"Hamp's no brain doctor, but he knows I'll cut it off and serve it fried."

Perhaps sensing the heat of female stares, Dena's mate looked their way. The center of unwanted attention, Hamp quickly excused himself to join a domino game.

Paris acknowledged Dena with a coy, cool smile before thrusting out her small chest and smoothing a hand over tight pants strangling slim hips. Paris Brown proceeded to work the room.

Taffy had to give it to her. A preening predator, the woman oozed appeal, advertising availability with swishing hips and a slow-cooked laugh. Testing waters, slinking from man to man, Paris was never long in one place or face, as if none merited her time, until darting eyes settled on a covetable conquest.

Taffy's brow arched as Paris sidled up against her target heavily engrossed in a card game, cigar tucked behind one ear. Offering a smile real as a six-dollar-bill, she leaned in, ostensibly to better view his cards, while rubbing his back and laughing huskily at something said.

Heads swiveled Taffy's way.

"Oh, devil-in-*hell no*! Can I cut her, Taf?"

Taffy turned a blasé eye on the bright whirlwind weaving womanly wiles about her heart's crave. "Dena, I have nothing on Roam."

"Don't mean he ain't tryna lay something on you," Dena countered, hopping up and snatching a shrimp off Taffy's plate. "I'mma handle that for you, Pretty City."

Taffy grabbed her cousin's arm. "Don't act the fool, Dena."

"Honey, I ain't acting." Dena moved off, loud talking as she went. "Sister Brown, how you doing? Where's *Brother* Brown? He lost in here somewhere?"

Taffy's laugh dissolved. Roam sat looking past Dena, eyes locked on Taffy, smug amusement lighting his marvelous face. Ignoring him, Taffy watched Dena skillfully extract Paris Brown so that the woman fell off Roam like rotten fruit from a tree.

"Anybody need anything from the kitchen?" Taffy suddenly questioned.

"I'll clear space in the dining room if you don't mind bringing out some sweets."

Acknowledging Chloe's request, Taffy sauntered off, playing impervious to her own jealousy and Roam's stare burning her back.

CHAPTER TWENTY-FOUR

He found her in the kitchen softly humming in sync with the parlor phonograph, her back to him. He preferred sitting and watching the sultry sea of her movements, but Roam couldn't resist the opportunity to sneak up unawares.

His breath was a feathery stroke against her neck. "You running from me?"

Taffy whirled, stumbling back against the counter. "Doggone it, Roam!" She slapped his arm. "You can't think of nothing to do besides sneaking up on folks?"

"I can," Roam replied, licking lips and salaciously roving Taffy's physique. "Can you?"

Ignoring the heat of Roam's suggestive scrutiny, Taffy maneuvered past him. "Can I get you anything? Potato salad? Greens? A cowbell to announce your coming?"

Roam chuckled heartily. "I'll take some of your cornbread and buttermilk."

"Talk about country! City folks don't eat cornbread and clabber."

"*City* folks don't *say* 'clabber'," Roam countered. "So who's country now?"

Smiling, Taffy scraped food remnants into a pan for Boss. "No matter. Cornbread's gone. I'm dishing up dessert in a moment if interested."

"Dollbaby, you're all the sweet I need."

Weariness and want clouded Taffy's tone. "Let's not pick up where we ended."

"Which was…?"

"I'm not sure," Taffy ventured, washing hands, "somewhere ambiguous."

Roam straddled a chair. "I'll clarify if I was in any way vague—"

"Thank you, Mr. Ellis, but your viewpoint's clearer than crystal."

"Then the ambivalence rests with you."

Approaching a parade of desserts lining the kitchen table, quietly Taffy admitted, "It rests with me."

Roam sat back watching Taffy ruthlessly cut a pound cake, hacking slices unevenly. He laid a hand on her wrist. "Sweetheart, you 'bout to kill that cake. You alright?" Roam inquired solicitously.

Inhaling, Taffy swallowed laughter and tears. She didn't feel like wrestling, had done nothing but these past seven years. Taffy wanted the freedom of being, living, loving however her heart chose. Consumed by his nearness, heart and body chose Roam. "I will be."

"When?"

Taffy couldn't answer. All day she'd confronted notions of death. Flashes of the red-drenched dream melded with the cemetery's white-clad phantom beckoning her near a headstone bearing Taffy's name as *You're already dying inside* warped the phonograph of her mind.

Having made definitive decisions for freedom, the vision was disconcerting.

Choose wisely, Knowing had cautioned. Didn't Taffy's choices lead to life? She chose not to return to Alfredo and his household of cadavers. That morbid existence wouldn't be the limit of her life's experiences. Now here was Roam. Was wanting him a contrary thing God couldn't cosign?

Then, Lord, why'd You have me stay? I coulda been in Chicago by now!

Roam's voice was smooth balm, interrupting. "Lemme say something." Putting the cake cutter down, Taffy peered into the liquid vulnerability of his eyes. "I don't pursue attached women, especially married ones. I'm flawed, but a god-fearing preacher's boy. I refrain from *some* vices..." Shrugging strong shoulders, Roam's hand completely covered hers. "So, Dollbaby, I know wanting you isn't gaining me points in heaven."

"Then why bother?"

"You're worth the brimstone," Roam decided, grin at half-mast. Sobering, he sat, unconsciously thumbing her hand. "And it is what it is."

Taffy's voice was stronger than she felt. "So your affection's genuine and not some short-lived fickleness?"

"You saying you don't trust me?"

Taffy studied Roam a while. "I can't trust a man with milk about his mouth."

"Woman, what're you talking about?"

Taffy smiled, mischievously. "Carrying your mama's packages downtown this afternoon like a good lil' something," Taffy teased. Swiping a finger over Roam's mouth, she added, "Might still have a lil' mama milk in your moustache."

Grabbing Taffy's hand, Roam slipped her finger in his mouth, tongue encircling, gently sucking. "Always did enjoy my milk with a little chocolate," Roam droned, grinning impishly.

Senses tilting, Taffy couldn't reply for the whirlwind entering. Paris Brown blew into the kitchen, mouth falling into a perfect "O" when assessing a sensuous situation. Too late, Taffy pulled her hand from Roam's, pressing it against her belly.

Something dark flashed through Mrs. Brown's eyes before her smooth recovery. "Brother Roam, I wondered where you'd gone off to," Paris Brown drawled, true southerner, make-believe belle. She took a dainty, uninvited seat. "You were doing so nicely at cards." She caressed Roam's knee. "You quit to come sit with nothing? I need a glass of water," she tossed over her shoulder. "With ice."

Rocking back on one leg, hip jutting, Taffy grabbed the cake cutter.

Roam was quick to intervene. "I believe there's ice water on the sideboard, Miss Paris." He moved his leg from beneath her grip.

"*Miss*? Honey, you make me sound old, when I'm anything but."

"Old enough for manners, so you might wanna *ask*, not tell Miz Freeman about your water needs. And if she does bring some, pray first." Leaning forward, Roam whispered conspiratorially. "She's evil *and* mean."

Paris was the only one laughing. Pitching an over-the-shoulder-glance at the knife-clutching younger woman, she patted Roam's cheek, promising to find him later, before exiting, switching unnecessarily.

"Lord!" Taffy *tsked*, returning to task, cake-cutting worse than before. "Rude *and* unsubtle."

"No home-training," Roam teasingly agreed.

"You hush! You're the thing she's 'finding later'."

Roam's booming laughter rolled over her back as Taffy created her own storm, moving about the kitchen, checking pots and slamming lids. "Darlin', you believe that you'll believe anything."

Roam pulled an ever-ready cigar from behind an ear, only to remember no smoking in Chloe's abode. Rolling the stogie between fingers, he watched Taffy vent her ire on innocent pots a while before rising to reach her in two strides. "Slow down and breathe," Roam advised, placing a firm hand at her waist.

Embarrassed, Taffy complied.

Amused, Roam ran a finger down her face. "These gray eyes turning green?"

"Jealousy requires a level of care I don't currently possess."

"So says you," Roam murmured, admiring Miss Marva's handiwork. "You clean up good, Taffy Lou, green-eyed and all."

Up in-arms over Roam when she'd serve Al on a platter to any woman of his picking, Taffy's tone was terse. "Was I walking 'round looking like something a half-dead cat coughed up?"

"Come on," Roam coaxed, "those braids were beat." Taffy had to laugh. NuNu's hairdos were functional, not fancy. "So just say thanks."

"Why? 'You clean up good' isn't a compliment," Taffy contended, moving away.

Roam blocked her path. "I'll rephrase that, tempestuous one. You Miss Bledsoe, being my quintessential epitome of female pulchritude, are the *only* woman *I* need to 'find' now or ever. Bet on it."

Taffy stared a moment before venturing mockingly, "Pulchritude, Roam?"

"Look it up."

"I know the meaning."

"Sure you don't."

Taffy sucked her teeth. "I'm not studying you."

Roam's baritone was decidedly low. "You should. Maybe then you'd see I'm true to mine, and wanting you exceeds temporary greed."

Taffy returned Roam's stare, daring self to take a page from The Book of Paris Brown. She should be so bold with what she wanted when, where and how. Let the Devil bother with 'why'. But Taffy loved something Paris didn't: an Angel Baby Boy. Until 'unmarried,' Taffy would tread lightly. Alfredo didn't love the child, but he'd use any unfaithfulness against her, taking Angel permanently, legally. *If* he ever found her! With Alfredo's knack for cunning, the mountain would stack against her, and Taffy—a young Colored woman—would most certainly lose in this world of race and men.

She couldn't step out with Roam. Not now. Winning her freedom meant keeping clean hands. Perhaps, once settled in the Windy City Roam would come. *And do what?* Taffy wondered. *Frolic sinfully?* Adultery wasn't her cup of tea.

Feeling as if she were dodging missiles before the battle began, Taffy left Roam in the middle of the floor to busy herself searching for a serving tray for the cake she'd ruthlessly carved. Spotting a tray on a shelf high overhead, Taffy vainly grasped at it, frustration flaring at another something out of reach.

She felt him behind her as Roam effortlessly retrieved what Taffy needed. Their bodies briefly connected in the process. Roam's firm torso at her back, Taffy's body flashed fire. She swiveled. Roam stood close enough to sync their heartbeats. Taking the tray, Taffy positioned it like a shield between.

Gripping the countertop, locking Taffy between his arms, Roam's words sent ice down Taffy's spine. "Who did you wrong?"

Unnerved, Taffy's "excuse me, please," was a soft, plaintive plea.

Roam stepped back, allowing Taffy to seek safety.

⸎

Music from a portable radio coated the night with smooth, blue notes. Out back, fancy-footing, finger-snapping women swayed in sync with Fats Waller's wailing.

"Whatchu got on this, Pretty City?" Cousin Dena dared, beneath a starlit sky.

"More than what you giving," Taffy volleyed, descending the porch ready to out-dance demons. Yes, she'd been done wrong. Anything living had. She'd tried not to keep score, had learned to note the offense and move on. Noting not for vengeance, but to know the enemy's face and ward-off his coming again. Still, Roam's query dug deep.

Dodging self-pity, Taffy inhaled the festive vibe. Flanked on either side, Taffy danced up the center, working that middle passage like she'd been paid. There was a howl and a holler when she finished with a saucy dip and vibration of blessed hips.

"Taffy Bledsoe, you're going to hell come Sunday!" Dena hollered.

"Been there and back and taking you next time." Taffy grabbed the nearest woman urging her then others up the center, crowding it with women whirling like brilliant, unfettered butterflies. Before long, menfolk were drawn outdoors to witness the devilment, adding their own brand of bold to the dazzling din.

"Make the goods slip where your backbone dips!"

"That's all jelly and no jam, so gon' and shake it 'til you make it, baby!"

"If I wasn't already married to you, gal, I'd pack you up and take you home."

Laughing, Taffy stood aside catching her breath as men entered, some pausing to perch on the steps, others joining so that couples paired up, leaning into love.

"Lemme fetch my wife 'fore she hurts something," Drew mumbled descending the steps, humored by Chloe's awkward antics.

"Handle it," Roam chuckled, leaning against the doorframe and lighting his clipped cigar. Through a haze of smoke, Roam locked onto what he wanted to tempt and taste. Caught in his greedy stare, she turned his way. Even in night her eyes glowed gray.

Taffy knew better. She couldn't couple up, and hunger couldn't be conveyed. Still, it percolated, leaving Taffy desperately wanting to know Roam in sinfully intimate ways...

Lord, deliver me from greed and need! Repentant, Taffy picked her way through the crowd, intentionally skirting the back stoop. Chloe interrupted her great escape.

"Taf, you were looking good out there," Chloe called from the porch swing where Drew had deposited her. "But you best save some of that gyrating for tomorrow."

"Why?" Taffy questioned, reluctantly mounting the porch stairs.

"Because." Chloe yelled for Dena. "You and Hamp still headed to JoJo's tomorrow night?"

"Hamp's working overtime, so we'll meet y'all there. Roam, that horn man you like is passing through," Dena announced before her husband pulled her back to dancing.

Chloe looked to Drew. "Want to, Babe?"

"I don't think you should be—"

"I'm fine," Chloe quickly asserted, near giddy. "Taffy? Roam?"

Drew looked sharply at his wife, wondering what she was up to. "Baby, listen—"

"Honey, it's just good company," Chloe whispered, stroking

Drew's thigh. "Plus, Roam knows the owner."

"Babe, don't egg that on."

"Honey, I'm not," Chloe quietly reassured. "Taf, you in?"

"I don't know…"

"Like you got something to do on a Saturday except say your prayers," Roam jested.

Ignoring Drew's loud laughter, Taffy stopped thinking her way through. "Lord willing and the creek don't rise." Needing distance from impulsiveness, Taffy turned towards the backdoor.

"Where're you going?" Roam asked, grabbing Taffy's arm.

"Anywhere you're not." Smiling, Taffy slid indoors, Chloe on her heels, leaving Roam and Drew outside.

Eyes still locked on the door through which Taffy disappeared, Roam offered, "Pick y'all up at eight?"

"Yeah," Drew replied. Stretching the length of the swing, Drew folded arms beneath head, relaxing. Still, his voice held a camouflaged warning. "'Ey, Ellis, don't get sweet on my cousin again."

Savoring its richness, Roam watched a red glow spread about the cigar's tip. His reply would have been simple, light as ash drifting on air, warm as the heat the stogie produced. *Always was, always will be.* But some truths weren't for mixed company.

CHAPTER TWENTY-FIVE

Saturday morning, two seasoned women sat in the company of a younger man, prattling, pining for times past while the man remained silent, removed and indifferent. Women's talk was a weary waste, but he'd chosen these two because they were his best link. If he sat smoking his cigarette and enduring their insipid chatter, sooner or later they'd say something worthwhile.

Unexpectedly, the butterscotch one he liked least turned her attention on him.

"Dempsey, I ain't heard from your mama in a while. How's Big Baby?"

Hopefully dead. "Just fine," Dempsey lied.

"She still looking to pastor?" The butterscotch one turned to the colorless woman of wicker baskets and daffodils. "Big Baby's feeling a call to shepherd wayward girls. That's what hussies need, a lady pastor who can smell their stank."

"Oh, now, 'Gene,'" twittered the pale one, delicately waving away Dempsey's obnoxious cigarette smoke. "That's so uncharitable."

"But true! Takes a sanctified woman to convert a 'ho. Speaking of...you heard? Taffy's back."

"No, I hadn't."

"Be glad when she's gone. Her presence don't do nothing good for her mama. Got Rachel walking 'bout all pitiful and pathetic."

"Still at odds?"

Imogene snorted. "That's how it is with this young generation, thinking they can stand toe-to-toe with their parents. In my day, mamas made decisions and liking it or not, you did what your ma said do! No such animal as being at odds."

"I'm sure they'll work it out."

"If I had my druthers, she'd take her nappy head outta here for good."

"Rachel would be heartbroken," posited the pale one.

"Rachel has Lacy in her. She'd heal. Me? I'd send that girl off with her little black bastard. Don't make sense Rachel raising that boy! Then again, that gal ain't fit to raise corn."

Finally, his attention was earned. Dragging deeply on his cigarette, Dempsey waited out the stormcloud obscuring his soul. A poor mother was the greatest sin of all, and his own—Big Baby—was the essence of neglect, abuse, and misuse. If Alfredo's wife was the same such, then she deserved whatever fate Dempsey devised.

Bad mothering. Illicit trysts. He'd never thought his sweet gray-eyed girl capable of such shenanigans, but he saw her yesterday accompanying that big penny-red in town. Something thick, unnatural brewed between them, and his mama had beat it into his head, literally: God hated unnatural things!

Dempsey's body bore permanent proof of Big Baby's corrective cleansing. Of all her attempts to save him from hell, Dempsey hated kneeling most. But realizing his tears merely refueled her rage, a young Dempsey had learned to endure dry-eyed and stoic.

Bare-legged, he'd kneel on raw, uncooked rice—hard grains cutting knees until tender skin burst and bled. When Mother indicated an hour of penance had ended, the boy simply got up and went outdoors, peeling bloodied rice from his torn flesh and swallowing the grains. Just like he swallowed life: detached, without feeling.

Didn't feel a thing at that odd temple-school, where lizards scrambled in boxes beneath an altar bearing marigolds and roosters' blood, governed by a principal-teacher who daily doled out funny-smelling cigarettes and touches that teased, pleased. Didn't feel a thing until the gray-eyed girl came for purging.

She'd been wicked, opened her womanhood too soon, and now she had nothing to offer the husband at home. He knew he was banned; still, Dempsey couldn't help peeking through the keyhole into a room filled with women in white and the stinging scent of lye. Chanting, mysteriously humming, his mother proceeded—parting, purifying.

His body sprang to life at his first sight of female iniquity. Strange, lovely. But then the naked gray-eyed girl awakened screaming, viciously fighting. Dempsey's blood raced and his body remained rigid, breathing increasing until an explosion flooded his underpants. Bewildered, he escaped to his private space beneath the porch to admire the dampness. Reaching inside, he pulled forth a viscous pool of maleness. Unlike rice grains on which he knelt, this essence came from his body, was part of who he was. Like the rice that slashed his knees, he swallowed the thickness in part, pushing his seed down his throat, preserving its pleasure and purity.

Now his lovely one was a filthy whoremonger and, abjectly worse, a miserable mother. Confident God had called him to this, Dempsey blew smoke rings. He'd accepted Alfredo's money because a workman was worthy of his hire, but purging the world of her wickedness was Dempsey's reward.

CHAPTER TWENTY-SIX

Tonight was for good music. Nothing more. Yet, she was giddy as a girl in route to her first dance.

Up North she'd been censored, her 'goings-on' winding their way to Alfredo's ears. Taffy remained respectful towards the wives of Alfredo's dull gaggle of friends, spying like one-eyed cats peeping in a seafood store. Fault-finders, they jawed her offenses in Alfredo's ears. Moving pictures with girlfriends. Dancing at community socials. Wearing red past Valentine's. Un-girdled hips sashaying like diamonds decorated the apex of her thick thighs. Freeman needed to handle that too young wife!

"A married woman ought not do such deviltry," Alfredo hurled time and again. When weary of his haranguing, Taffy retired to her room. Turning radio on as loud as volume allowed, Taffy danced alone, letting rhythm rule her until exhausting herself and her needs. Tonight, neither would be confined. Tonight, she simply was, simply being.

Freedom feels good, Taffy decided as a thud sounded on the hardwood floor. Retrieving the rolling ball, Taffy tossed it to the child sprawled in the center of her bed.

"Told Willie Ray don't mess with no stray hound, 'specially one looking all mangy-mouthed," Angel chattered, on his back in a careless cocoon, playing a solitary game of catch.

"Did he?" Taffy absentmindedly questioned. Intent on not looking like a painted lady wearing a welcome, she beautified face with *a lil' dab'll do you* in mind. Lightly applying perfume behind ears and knees, on wrists and throat, between her breasts, Taffy twisted and turned ensuring her dress wasn't advertising.

"Yep! Only a fool-headed fool would." Angel barreled on before Taffy could correct his name-calling. "Guess what happened? Willie Ray took to bothering that dog, and that dog turned 'round and bit

Willie Ray plumb on his ass."

Taffy spun. "Merciful Savior, this child's eating soap for supper! Angel, honey, don't use foul language."

"Huh?" Angel sat upright, genuinely puzzled. "Taf, even God says 'ass' in the Bible."

"Baby, God's talking about a donkey, not Willie Ray's backside and you know it," Taffy chastised, fastening rhinestones at her ears and curbing a smile.

"Oh." Angel seemed crestfallen that God hadn't sanctioned his verbiage.

"Is Willie Ray alright?"

"Dr. Blue gave 'im a shot in the," Angel paused and looked sheepishly at Taffy, "rear, but the fool-headed fool'll live."

"Angel Baby, enough name-calling."

"But, Taffy, yesterday Papa called Mr. Charles a 'fool-headed drunk-of-a-skunk swilling moonshine like milk'!"

"First of all, you were probably eavesdropping on grown folks' business. Secondly, you can't repeat everything adults say."

"Well, why grown folks say things they don't want repeated?"

"Because adults can be ignorant." Taffy pinched Angel's nose. "And you're too smart for your own good."

"PaPa's not ignorant!"

"Your papa's one of the smartest men God made. That still doesn't license *you* to call folks 'fool-headed'."

"Wish it did," Angel mumbled, returning to ball-tossing.

Taffy turned back to the mirror, head shaking. *Too much!* She looked forward to having Angel to herself again. Just as soon as whatever kept her here loosed its hold...

"Taf?"

"Hmmm?"

"Do you like M'Dear?" Angel sat up. "You don't spend much time with her, and she gets real sad like she's 'bout to cry."

Taffy watched Angel, wondering what else he perceived. "Baby, M'Dear's my mother. I'll love her always. But truth is we have some things to work out."

"What things? And when you working on 'em?"

"Adult things and sooner than soon," Taffy promised Angel as well as herself. "How's the poem?"

The staff and students of Bledsoe Normal School were preparing a special presentation for the Founders' Day opening ceremony that coincided with the end of the school year, replacing this year's Juneteenth celebration. Busy smoothing the upswept hair at the nape of her neck, Taffy missed Angel's unenthusiastic expression.

"It's okay."

"Care to practice on me?"

"Umm…sure." Angel dragged himself off Taffy's bed, stood in the center of the room, and with uncommon meekness began. "Tonight I recite 'Dream Variations' by Langston Hughes." Angel cleared his throat dramatically before proceeding, barely completing the four lines of the first stanza.

Taffy waited, expectantly. "Yes…," she encouraged with a smile.

Angel shrugged. "That's it."

"That's the poem in its entirety?" The child looked at the floor. "Angel?"

"There're a few more lines," he mumbled.

"How many?" Taffy asked, latching hands on hips.

"Twice as much or more…more." At Taffy's expression, Angel took off talking in a hurry. "I do all my schoolwork. I act right in class and get good marks, and I learn quick. I'll know the whole poem by Founders' Festival. Promise!"

"Honey, it's less than a week away. What've you been doing instead of practicing?"

"Playing ball, I guess. It's better than poetry."

"You think so, huh?"

"Yep."

"Hmm… I'mma give you a choice. My poem or Mr. Hughes'?"

Angel's eyes widened in surprise. "You write poetry?"

"I'm about to. Think I'll call it 'Beat that Bottom'." Folding hands Taffy set forth demurely.

> Young child, young child, best learn Langston's rhyme,
> If you don't memorize his poem I'mma beat that behind.

"Wait, now, there's more," Taffy warned as Angel snickered.

> Young child, young child, don't try me for its true,
> Learn Langston's poem or that bottom'll need Dr. Blue.
> Beat that Bottom.

Taffy bowed as Angel wildly applauded, before wailing, "Beat that bottom, baby," like he felt the Blues a beat bottom might bring.

"You're silly." Giving self a final once-over, Taffy asked, "Can you learn four more lines by morning?"

"It's Saturday!"

"You wanna be able to sit on your hinny come Sunday?" Taffy joked, grabbing her silver-threaded wrap and tiny beaded clutch. She doused the bedroom light and headed down the hall with a pouting Angel in tow. Taffy knocked on Chloe's open door before peeking inside. "Chloe, you look lovely."

"Don't feel that way," Chloe complained, kneading her lower back. "This baby's getting heavier by the day, and I still have four weeks to go."

Taffy's concern was immediate. "We'll cancel. I can do with-out—"

"No, you can't, and no we won't. Zip me up." Chloe looked over her shoulder. "Angel, you coming?"

"Yuck, no! I have better things to do, like—"

"Learning lines," Taffy interjected to Angel's dismay. "Pull up that lip before I recite more 'Beat that Bottom'."

The stubborn set of Angel's jaw relaxed into a grudging smile.

"What's that?" Chloe asked.

"Angel knows," was Taffy's laughing reply. "Grab a wrap, Chloe, just in case this breeze cools down."

"I will, but lemme see you first." Stepping back, Taffy executed a slow, dramatic turn, hands splayed at her side, face set like a manne-quin's. "Girl, you're pretty as a new penny," Chloe chimed. "Is that one of yours?"

Taffy nodded, pulling on lacy gloves matching the pale rose of the dress she'd taken from mere sketch to frothy vision. "You like," she asked, smoothing a hand over the satin bodice hugging her small waist. The dress flowed into chiffon layers falling mid-calf, inches above pale silver *poi de soi* sling-backs.

"Gorgeous! *Please* move on back here and open your own shop, instead of hopping to the Windy—"

"Angel Baby, gon' down and tell Cousin Drew we're coming," Taffy interrupted, "then wrap up that last slice of Cousin Dena's pound cake. You can have it *after* you learn your lines."

"Yippee!" Angel raced from the room.

"Sorry, Taf, I didn't mean to say nothing in front of Angel," Chloe apologized.

"It's okay, Chloe, but Angel doesn't know yet, and *I* need to be the one to tell him. I forgot my handkerchief. I'll meet you downstairs."

Taffy returned to her room, in search of a handkerchief and God's release. The more she prayed, the more the Lord said "*Stay.*" Made no sense, but Taffy decided to trust and believe. Finding what she needed, Taffy headed out, pausing at the stairwell and the sound of rising voices.

"*Wow, Mr. Roam!*" she heard Angel yell.

Taffy tensed, concerned Angel might look on Roam's presence as objectionable. She prayed Chloe and Drew's inclusion would dispel notions of impropriety. Descending the stairs, Taffy found her concerns unfounded. Angel was too smitten with a wooden cylinder to care.

Angel's rapid-fire excitement ricocheted about the room. "It really sounds like a train?"

"Try it and see," Roam suggested on his haunches, eye-level with Angel, the deep, buttery resonance of his voice spreading over Taffy.

A train's whistle filled the room. "Whoa, *man*! Wait 'til the guys see this. Willie Ray's gonna piss his—"

"Angel." He turned to find Taffy at the foot of the stairs, mildly displeased. "Oops, sorry. Taffy, Mr. Roam gave me a whistle that sounds like a real live train! Listen." Ebullient, Angel demonstrated for Taffy's benefit.

"Sure does," Taffy agreed, the softness of her face restored. "What do you say?"

"Thanks a bunch, Mr. Roam!"

Standing, hat in hand, Roam pried his eyes from Taffy long enough to enjoy Angel's delight. "My pleasure, little man."

"Wait 'til Papa hears it!" Angel yelled, racing towards the kitchen for his cake. He slid to a halt, hugging Taffy long enough to say, "You look real, real pretty, Taf, like a princess," before hurtling on.

"Man, I remember the days," Drew reminisced.

"Yeah," was all Roam managed. "Evening, Miss Taffy." His baritone was smooth velvet, calm water despite blood's thickening.

"Mr. Ellis," Taffy returned, ignoring Roam's visually feasting on her form. Had to admit she liked filling the man's mind with nothing save herself. Admittedly, she liked what *she* saw. From the cut of his dark suit to the shine of his black-on-white wingtips, Roam was debonair, what her Up North girlfriends called Too Clean.

Roam approached with uncharacteristic humility. "I brought you something...if that's alright."

Taffy's breath caught at the delicate unveiling of miniature tea roses. "You remembered."

"Always do," Roam stated, extracting the fragrant corsage from its container.

Taffy bit her bottom lip, reminiscing. They were to attend his senior dance. She promised to wear Roam's favorite color, blue, and Roam asked what she preferred: a garden on her bosom or corsage at her wrist? Laughing, Taffy elected a corsage. She wanted white. He vowed that and more, but life threw curves, and they never had their dance.

Swallowing tears, Taffy watched Roam situate roses at her wrist. "Thank you."

"My pleasure." He kissed her hand tenderly, his words warm breath against skin.

Taffy wobbled. Angel, in route upstairs for forgotten baseball, barreled through, shoving wrapped caked in Taffy's hands, keeping her from acting a smitten fool.

"Ready, Babe?" Drew questioned, disliking the obvious, still-existent energy between his cousin and Roam. "Sure you're up to this?"

"Absolutely," Chloe assured, hiding discomfort for everyone's sake.

"Anybody listen to the radio today?" Roam questioned, smoothly navigating his father's automobile. "Jesse broke three world records at the Big Ten meet!"

"And tied a fourth," Drew crowed. "That Owens is a running gun!"

"A hundred-yard dash in 9.4 seconds? *Lord*!"

"He's on his way to the Olympics," Taffy commented.

Roam glanced at Taffy's image in the rearview mirror. "You think so?"

She sat behind him, nodding. "He's too good not to let in."

"I don't know." Roam was skeptical. "White folks'll find a way."

"Not just regular white folks on Olympic committees," Drew elucidated. "There're them crazy Europeans, too." The vehicle filled with laughter. "Speaking of, those commies making any headway in the Scottsboro case?"

Roam sighed. "Some of the nine were acquitted."

"You think those boys were wrong?" Drew wondered, trying to make sense of the senseless.

"For what? Hoboing?" Roam sucked his teeth. "White boys do it all the time; hopping freights, traveling 'cross country fare-free. Colored kids do it in search of work, and they go to jail. For life! Some things are wrong beyond belief."

"Those boys did nothing terrible," Taffy muttered, "now they're looking at death."

Roam calmed his ire, saliently inserting, "Don't forget the larger issue: white females were involved," at which Chloe snorted indignantly. "I'm thankful it went to trial instead of a tree," Roam mused, thinking on the nine Colored boys who'd boarded a freight train and fallen into an altercation with a group of white peers, only to discover two were females in disguise, who later claimed they'd been intimately abused. Thanks to communist intervention, the death sentences of the convicted were reduced to life, which Colored folks knew was one and the same. "God willing, we'll see something other than southern justice with the CPUSA's ILD involved." Roam glanced back at Taffy. "Sorry, that stands for—"

"The International Legal Defense which is the civil rights arm of the Communist Party of the U.S.A.," Taffy supplied. Roam whistled.

Up front beside Roam, Drew turned in his seat. "Well, look who's been doing something other than painting her nails!"

"We can't all be dumb as donkeys," Taffy parried, returning attention to Roam. "Something in your tone says the ILD's involvement bothers you."

Roam weighed his words before responding. "I appreciate them, but the Reds can be just like any other political entity exploiting a Colored man's cares for its own cause."

"If the Communist Party's legal team saves those young men's lives, then the end justifies the means," Taffy decided. "But if it's any consolation, the NAACP's in there with them."

"Let me ask you something. Do you think we're capable of fighting injustices and securing favorable verdicts without the outside aid of *others*?"

"As a Colored woman, I prefer Colored people exercising power to affect change, legal or otherwise. But if outside aid produces a desired outcome, then I welcome it."

"Amen," Chloe concurred.

"I agree to an extent," Roam conceded, "still I'd rather see Negroes empowered and *permitted* to protect and provide for ourselves, especially in the courtroom."

"Then it's time for law school," Taffy pronounced.

Roam stared at Taffy's mirrored self, amazed that she'd remembered his dreams.

"Did the Scottsboro incident change life on the rails?" Chloe asked.

"It was tense for a while." Roam laughed. "White folks were testier than normal. Porters were banned from white ladies' berths, which was fine by me," Roam stated, thinking, *White women can't do me nothing.* "Things're as alright now as possible in a racist society. Still, I'm grateful I'm employed."

Sounds of agreement faded beneath the big band swinging from the car radio so that the remainder of the journey was carefree. Taffy almost hated to have it end, but as Roam pulled onto JoJo's unpaved lot, she experienced resurging excitement as Roam opened her door, ushering her from the car. Together with Chloe and Drew, they headed towards the unassuming structure flanked by a long line of eager patrons praying JoJo's had room.

Taffy's anticipation grew at the sight of the lively throng. His hand at the small of her back as Roam guided Taffy forward sent warmth through her core. Warmth became a low pulsing tremor as she traversed hard-packed ground.

She teetered. Roam caught her arm. Taffy peered about—cautiously observing her surroundings. Her stumble wasn't due to uneven earth, a precarious perch on high heels, or the delicious pressure of Roam's hand at her back. Cold shocked her skin, tumbling with the warmth Roam generated until her body was a swirling feud of fire and ice. Taffy calmed her racing heart as best she could. Thankful for Roam's presence so like a fortress, Taffy pressed forward, observant eyes open wide. Her prayer for divine safety was silent but earnest. Something hellish and unholy waited here.

CHAPTER TWENTY-SEVEN

JoJo's Place was small by big city standards, but for the town of Trenton—twice the size and east of Bledsoe—JoJo's Place was the good-timing spot of choice.

It was a simple, sizeable establishment with bar at back and stage up front opposite a small dance floor. Globe-encased candles atop cloth-covered tables cast prisms across walls boasting autographed photos of the day's latest and greatest. Whatever JoJo's lacked in elegance was made up in vibe.

JoJo's could be relaxed and cozy or wild and wicked, depending on who was doing what on stage. Just then, a three-piece ensemble wrapped the place with an eclectic but infectious blend of ragtime and swing. JoJo's Place was pumping. But for Roam, they might've been outdoors, lined up hoping for entry.

"Looks like Prohibition didn't hurt you any, Jo," Roam remarked as they trailed the owner, inching his way through a near-capacity crowd.

"Long as Colored folks got cares and quarters I'mma be in business. I'll do the best I can, Red, on account you didn't warn a body you were coming," the proprietor apologized in a gravelly voice decorated by decades of nicotine. He was a medium-sized man of indeterminate age, with shaven pate and a wheat-colored, pockmarked face.

"We appreciate whatever you have," Roam assured, a possessive, guiding hand at Taffy's back.

"Here you go," JoJo stopped at a table left of center stage. "Ain't straight center but it's still a good view." Casting Taffy an appreciative look, he added, "Knowing you, Red, you ain't gonna be heeding the music no how."

"Ladies…how's this?" Roam inquired, solicitous and attentive.

"It's perfect." Taffy accepted a proffered chair. Chloe concurred. Turning a smile JoJo's way, Taffy thanked him.

"Ain't no way I'd let lovely flowers stand outside with the weeds," JoJo flirted. Bending, he advised in a stage whisper, "If this cat don't mind his manners, holla. I'll fix him." He smiled at Taffy's conspiratorial laughter. "I'mma send y'all some of my famous fried wings. And just 'cause you ladies is too pretty for patience, tell me your drinks now. First round's on the house."

Chloe ordered root beer, Taffy a ginger ale.

"*Ginger ale*?! Lawd, Red, you done changed up and got yourself a church girl," the smaller man tittered, taking Drew's order before departing with a promise to send the drinks, including Roam's usual—a cold one, bottled not tap.

"What kinda females you usually bring here? Drunks?" Drew asked, arm draped across the back of Chloe's chair, not liking JoJo referring to Taffy as one of Roam's. He didn't know what all was going on between the two, but it wouldn't happen on his watch.

Unbuttoning his suit jacket, Roam sat back, using the opportunity to observe Taffy casually draping her wrap. Placing gloves atop her tiny evening bag, she gently readjusted her corsage before smoothing the layers of her dress. Humor lifted Roam's sculpted lips. "I'm entertaining a better class of people."

"The ginger ale drinking kind?" Chloe teased.

"There're exceptions to all rules."

"And as that exception, I'll be leaving sober," Taffy advised, mouth tight, gray eyes on the way to green.

Roam's laughter was booming. He was more than tickled and immensely pleased.

By the time Dena and Hamp arrived, extra seating had been brought onto the floor, requiring that existing patrons resituate themselves to accommodate the swelling crowd. Taffy and Roam wound up thigh-to-thigh.

Taffy forced her mind on the music and away from his warm press of muscle.

Roam thought to apologize. But he wasn't sorry. Not for his leg against hers, or the steady inferno burning between. This little leg-on-leg was a butterfly's caress, mild in comparison to the touches he intended. Roam let his thigh linger, enjoying its teasing, intentional press against Taffy's.

Taffy shifted, trying to escape Roam's heat only to realize the heat was hers.

I'mma need a chastening and a chastity belt, messing with this man.
She tossed Roam a warning glance. Innocent enjoyment rode his
strong features. She tried moving subtly, only to be hemmed in by
Chloe on her opposite side.

Roam leaned in whispering. "Dollbaby, any way you wiggle
I'mma feel these homegrown, grits-eating hips. Let 'em rest. Pleasure's
mine."

Taffy reached beneath the table, pinching Roam. Hard.

He bolted backwards, thigh smarting, claiming a need to dance
for Drew and Chloe's benefit. Grabbing Taffy's hand, Roam forged
a path to the dance floor where Dena and Hamp were cutting a rug.
"Violent thing," Roam scolded. "If I'm bruised come morning, you
gonna work your hoodoo and heal it."

Taffy's laughter was soft, nearly lost beneath the music. "Serves
you right."

"How 'bout you pinch, I stroke?"

Taffy's brows lifted. "My daddy always warned me not to start
what I can't finish."

"Can you?"

"What?"

"Finish this thing you started?" Roam twirled her about.

Taffy's face lost some of its playfulness. "There's a first time for
everything."

Confused, Roam's clarifying question remained unspoken as vig-
orous applause erupted, punctuating the song's end. The trio's leader
announced their last number for the night, one a bit less bouncy.
Roam made to pull Taffy near, but she stepped away.

"I need to excuse myself to the powder room."

"You tryna back outta slowing dragging with me?"

Taffy's laugh was a bell's chime. "We'll have our dance. I promise."

"I'm holding you to it," Roam forewarned, escorting Taffy off the
floor.

She wasn't sure what she'd started or if indeed she had. The
sweetness flowing between them was timeless and without origin—no
beginning, and prayerfully, no end. It simply was. For Taffy that truth
was liberating.

She'd lain awake last night, unsuccessfully seeking justification more than understanding. Taffy wasn't sure she had the right to feel what she felt, not after a seven-year lull. Not after a re-acquaintance of mere days, offering little more than a kiss that burned lips, a nocturnal call that left her reeling, and a walk and talk. Were her feelings merited, meaningful?

Taffy prayed. She called on Knowing, hoping her Gift would illuminate her way and cosign her craving. But heaven kept quiet. She wouldn't have answers always.

Left to her own designs, Taffy was forced to accept some things moved independent of her control. What she undoubtedly knew was Roam had grown into a good man. He was still *her* Roam—humorous, irritating and challenging to no end—a southern gentleman who effortlessly charmed his way into her good graces time and again. She intuited that he was yet rock solid and trustworthy. It was Roam's grown masculinity that left Taffy's flesh fluttering.

Washing hands, Taffy confronted herself in the bathroom mirror, wondering if she could ride the force of Roam's nature. Roam could penetrate her walls and disintegrate her guard one brick at a time. But perhaps, now, she could eradicate the very *need* for barriers.

Taffy craved openness, to offer her honest and intrinsic self. She considered Miss Marva wanting a contrary thing. Even Paris Brown and Miss Goldie, brazen enough to pursue desire despite outcome or impact. After an honest assessment, Taffy concluded she *was* willing to struggle for love. She wanted Roam enough to change her world. And his.

He deserves better this time.

Turning the water to cold, Taffy let the frigid flow soothe a sudden consternation.

She couldn't retrieve lost years or deny what was. But she could make things right. When her Daddy went to Winter Cove on business come Monday, Taffy would be along for the ride and a sit-down with Harold Jenkins, attorney at law. She wouldn't come to Roam with another man's name about her neck. Contrary to societal norms, Taffy would exert a right to a free life. Might not be easy, but it was time.

Taffy jumped at the sound of knuckles rapping against the closed door.

"Sugar, you finishing anytime soon?" a woman's voice slurred. "Gotta whole lotta beer on the bladder out here."

Taffy hurriedly dried her hands and opened the door. With an apologetic smile, she exchanged places with a liquored-up woman on wobbly feet. Taffy entered the ill-lit hall, high heels clacking against a cement floor as the jubilant clamor of JoJo's drew Taffy away from the coolness creeping up behind.

A chill claimed her. She stopped. Glancing back, Taffy searched the corridor, finding the hovering glow of a burning cigarette amid deep brooding.

She faced the being disassembling itself from the far wall where he'd merged with darkness. With a final drag, he tossed his cigarette and smashed it underfoot.

Taffy marveled at his absolute lack of light. Even Cousin Imogene, as malevolent as she could be, stirred the spirit world enough to create chaotic colors. But the man moving towards Taffy was colorless as if walking dead.

Taffy heard The Gift. *Remember this one.* Old stench and memory raked Taffy's nostrils. He was one she should know but couldn't name.

"How you doing, Black Beauty?" he rasped, gold tooth flashing as he passed beneath the single dangling bulb that cast his face in sharp, hazardous slants. No good flashed about him like a blazing menace. He even smelled wrong. Metal and sweat.

Caution gripped Taffy's neck. "Do I know you?" NuNu taught fearlessness when confronting evil. *Evil don't own your tongue. Call it out when you can.*

"No matter if you do or don't," the man answered, gold-capped tooth glinting, "I been after you." Recognizing his error, the man cleaned it fast. "Or something like you. Lemme spot you a drink."

Sight locked on present threat, Taffy searched inwardly. Post-Harlem haunts merged with this stranger, creating a canvas called 'nightmares'. Foreboding sprouted wings, perching on his shoulder like a predatory bird. The sleep stalker had come.

Taffy was mesmerized. She'd never observed such manifested malice, and was too fascinated to be afraid. Still she had the good sense God gave, and turned away.

He grabbed her, touch and voice sharp as glass. "I don't take to being ignored."

"I don't take to being touched without invitation," Taffy returned, yanking her arm free, as shadows slithered about him.

A ready threat lodged in his throat when glancing over Taffy's head.

Red warmth rushed Taffy's veins, dispelling the hallway's brittle chill.

"Everything's okay here?"

Changing faces, the stranger extended a hand to the large man who'd aborted his quest. "Dempsey Dupre. Folks call me Double-D."

Focused on Taffy, Roam ignored the gesture. "You alright?"

Taffy assured him she was.

"Sorry, Slick, wouldn't've messed with this had I known it was yours," the man stated, looking Taffy over. "But, *damn*, there's plenty to go 'round! Lemme get one dance."

Taffy decided the man was dimwitted or didn't care that Roam's jaw was flexing, teeth grinding like stone on dry corn, or that the height and weight advantage weren't his. Even so, Taffy noted the dead heat in the smaller man's eyes was nearly as fierce as the fire in Roam's. The malice driving this Dempsey Dupre was hungry for havoc.

Feeling his tension, Taffy gripped Roam's arm, sent a silent warning. Mr. Dupre wasn't worth trouble's stirring.

A toilet flushed. The door to the ladies' room flew open and the beer imbiber lurched forward.

"Nothing like a good tinkle to put you right." Cackling merrily, her eyes did a jig over the curious gathering, lustily lingering on the big redbone before considering the rose-gown girl and concluding her chances there were slim-to-none. "What we got here, a party?" the woman asked, bending and plunging a hand beneath the hem of her purple beaded dress. Extracting a pack of gum, she offered, "Piece anyone?"

Roam turned, escorting Taffy ahead of him.

Be seeing you, Miz Freeman, Dempsey Dupre inwardly raged, eyes locked on escaping prey.

Exiting the hallway, Roam stopped Taffy before reentering JoJo's central domain. "My granddaddy likes to say 'a two-legged snake's the worst kind'." Roam pointed over his shoulder at what they'd left behind. "That there qualifies. Be careful if you know him, if you don't keep it that way."

How to tell Roam that providence had decided and that reencountering Dupre was an inevitable part of her evolution? Taffy withheld foresight, simply promising Roam she'd remain safe with a conviction she couldn't guarantee.

Self-concern faded the moment Taffy reentered JoJo's central hub to see Chloe, face pinched, skin sallow, discomfort clear. Taffy rushed to her side. "What's wrong?"

"She overheated," Drew explained, rubbing his wife's hand, clearly worried.

"Told you not to be shaking those expectant hips," Dena fussed, fanning Chloe's brow. "Ever see a pregnant woman dance? It's far from pretty."

Chloe laughed despite herself. "Hush, Dena, and y'all back up. I'm okay. Just too much shimmying, too many root beers, and Tabasco on fried wings." Chloe felt queasy.

"Pains anywhere?" Taffy asked.

"No...just nauseous...and the room's spinning."

"And you're green."

"I'll get some water," Hamp offered.

"No, y'all, really, I'm fine," Chloe protested.

"No, you're not," Drew countered. He stood, helping Chloe to her feet. Hamp braced her on the other side. "We're going home."

"Honey, no," Chloe whined, watching Dena and Taffy gather up their things. "I can't ruin everyone's evening."

"Already did," Drew joked, kissing her cheek.

"'Ey, I worked a near-double, danced with my darling," Hamp managed around a wide-mouthed yawn. "So we're good. Right, Sweet Thang?"

Dena agreed instead of hurting Chloe's feelings.

"Taffy didn't get but half-a-dance, and Roam's horn man hasn't even played," Chloe protested, slowly waddling, aided on either side. "Taf, you stay. We'll go on with Hamp and Dena. Roam'll bring you home."

Taffy ignored the suggestion as they navigated the crowd.

Roam grabbed her hand. "Lemme thank Jo. I'll meet y'all outside."

"Thank him for us as well."

Outdoors, Chloe gulped clean night air. "Taf, I'm telling you, stay. No sense in everybody suffering."

"Do I look like I'm suffering?"

"Yes."

Taffy laughed. "Chloe, you and this baby mean more than some trombone."

"Saxophone," Roam corrected, coming up behind.

"Oh…well, now…" Taffy vacillated. "I'm only funning! Let's go."

"Hamp, where're you parked?" Chloe asked, ignoring Taffy and following Hamp's directions.

"What is she doing?" Taffy mused.

"Only crazy pregnant women would know," Dena answered.

Ignoring their laughter, Chloe waddled to the car, waited for Hamp to open the back door, then climbed in. "Let's go."

"Chloe," Taffy started only to have Chloe close and lock the door.

"Well, amen and pass the peaches," Dena muttered, sliding onto the front seat. "Guess you staying to hear a little horn, Pretty City." Rolling down her window Dena added, "Come home the same way you left. And you *know* what I mean!"

A yawning Hamp said his farewells and got behind the wheel.

Uncertain, Taffy turned to Roam. He shrugged. "It's your call."

Taffy motioned for Chloe to roll her window down. Leaning in, Taffy whispered, "Conniving wench."

Rubbing her belly, Chloe managed a smile. A party of six was down to two, leaving Taffy in the company of one.

Obviously perturbed, Drew's jaw clenched. "Get yourself home long before the cock crows," he instructed, pulling Roam aside. Voice lowered he warned, "Ellis, you been my brother since fatback was greasy, but that there's blood. I'll shoot first and ask questions later. Hear me?"

"With both ears," Roam answered, grin-free and eyes like steel.

CHAPTER TWENTY-EIGHT

JoJo's featured artist could smoke a horn. He was a maestro, working a trumpet on his upbeats, a saxophone when "toning it low." Taffy felt sublimely seduced. Melting beneath masterful melodies, she slid down a velvet slope that led to Roam. It was hypnotic, erotic, the maestro's magic and this man. She'd dissolve into a molten mess if it didn't end soon. Citing aching feet, Taffy begged off the next dance, allowing them both the chance to catch their breath. Music became the backdrop as, reseated, Taffy and Roam took a break to fill in the missing pages of their lives.

Roam proved an engaged audience. Ingesting the bulk of Taffy's years, savoring the rich syrup of her voice, Roam reclined in the radius of Taffy's joy. The longer he listened the more Roam realized how little he knew. Hearing how she'd carved a niche for herself Up North, Roam's admiration increased exponentially.

"You were always doodling. But you took it and made something for yourself. That's real good."

Taffy's smile bordered on shy. She hadn't done more than she had to. As the years progressed and his contempt increased, Alfredo withheld money meant for household needs. Innovation was necessary. Finding clothing not quite cut for Colored women's curvature—waists too big, back skirt hems hiked up high—Taffy had long learned to alter, then create her own garments with precision and artistic flare that proved eye-catching. So, she bartered her skills.

"I'd mend or make clothes in exchange for a few dollars off here and there." Taffy laughed. "I liked haggling. Especially with my butcher. 'Mr. Pearson, I mended six pairs of your pants last week. That's worth a pot roast'." She liked the way Roam's mouth curved when he laughed. "I'd rip the seams on anything. Old clothes. Linens. Draperies. Didn't matter. If I could remake it into something, I did." Some folks were still proud even though The Depression had many doing without. "I'd "accidentally" make too much of one thing or another and give the extra to neighbors in need. So," Taffy shrugged, "that's how I started. I kept sewing, designing really, and if folks could pay they did." Even with this new income, Taffy kept bartering. Living lean and bartering prices earned the pin money inside her brassiere. She'd parlayed sewing skills learned in preparation for domestic duty into liberty, and redesigned her life.

Thinking on Miss Marva's improvements to her shop, Taffy added, "More than all that, it's about creating clothes for us Colored women that make us feel pretty." Taffy's voice quieted. "I wanna open a dress salon where Colored women can walk in the front door and not the back, and be allowed to try on clothing and be referred to as 'ma'am'. Where we're customers treated with dignity."

"Impressive," Roam remarked when Taffy fell silent. Resting an arm at the back of her chair, Roam leaned in. "So, is this before or after you get to Savage's Art Studio like you wanted?"

Taffy's mouth parted in surprise. "How do you remember that?"

Roam grinned. "Told you I don't forget."

"Apparently." Taffy sipped ginger ale, remembering a time when they believed in each other's dreams. "I used to feel torn between wanting my art and being a nurse, because nursing was something my Daddy wanted for me." Taffy drew patterns in the condensation on her glass. "It made sense seeing as how I was always trailing behind NuNu learning her herbs and helping. But nursing's not my calling." Taffy studied Roam a moment before admitting, "And as much as I love 'doodling', studying art's a dream I don't mind deferring."

"Why? You got other plans?"

Yes. Disappearing Up North. Surviving with Angel. Finding someone like you to love. That last, unbidden thought had Taffy blurting, "I prefer dress-making, and Alfredo and I are going our separate ways."

Roam paused before asking, "Why?"

"I'm tired of living with less."

Roam leaned back, stroking his gold-shot moustache. Moments passed before he sat forward again, elbows on table, hands folded beneath cleft chin. "How long's this been in the making?"

"More than a minute. And it's my doing, not his." Taffy played with the tea roses at her wrist. "I'm telling without you asking. My leaving Alfredo was in motion before you... before...*this.*"

"Glad you finally admitting something's still real between us. But much as I wish you weren't with Freeman, I won't ever send a woman away from her husband. Whatever gets done, Dollbaby, do it for you."

Watching the genius on stage, Taffy soaked up soothing sounds before putting her heart on the table. "We lost us because of me." She had to breathe deep before boldly revealing, "I miss you and I want 'us' again. But I have to fix my business." Tentatively, Taffy touched Roam's face. "Can you wait for me?"

Thoughts taking a peculiar turn, Roam flashed on that biblical story of Jacob—Abraham's grandson, member of that Hebrew patriarchal triumvirate. Jacob labored seven years for the hand of his beloved but, tricked on his wedding night, he erroneously wed his beloved's older sister and was forced into seven more years laboring for his father-in-law in order to earn his true bride. Fourteen years working for one woman? Roam didn't have it in him. "Take your pick. Seven days *maybe* weeks. Won't guarantee months. Forget years." Taffy was clearly confused. "Never mind." Rising, Roam pulled back Taffy's chair as the horn man announced,

"I'm slowing it down for the lovers who ain't afraid to lean."

"Wait, now, you haven't shared yourself," Taffy protested.

"We'll get to me," Roam countered. "Right now, I need to dance with the loveliest lady in this place. Can you handle more than a two-step?" Roam goaded as a slow, lavish rendition of The Duke's "Sophisticated Lady" showered listeners with lyrical rain.

Taffy sparkled. "Try me."

Roam did. Claiming floor space, Roam pulled Taffy into a private rhythm. And they had *The Dance*.

In the circumference of his arms, Taffy closed her eyes and bathed her senses. She frolicked in strength, warmth, peace and belonging.

Enticed by her clash of innocence and allure, Roam embraced a desirable mystery. He knew how to satiate physical hunger, but Taffy stimulated much more. Her honey-and-summer scent invading his nostrils, Roam craved Taffy from top to bottom, inside and out, in body *and* spirit, intimately deep as deep could be.

Roam's breath against her ear was shiver-inducing. "Drew couldn't say your name when you were born, huh?" His voice was lazy, languid.

Wrapping arms about Roam's neck, Taffy held fast. "Donkey Head's 'Octavia' came out 'Taffia'. Family shortened that to Taffy and it stuck."

"Like something sweet," Roam droned, pulling her near. Space evaporated. Their bodies brushed and fanned a blaze that swept Taffy like a storm. She shivered at the heat of Roam's fingers drawing circles on her bare back, where her dress created an attractive "V." His hand strayed lower, pausing at the soft dip of her spine, where the slightest fraction of downward motion would land Roam's hand firmly against her backside.

Roam reeled in want. An accidental encounter would merely exacerbate his need to indulge in the temple Roam embraced as if Taffy was already his. "We have some conversing ahead. I have questions—"

"I have answers," Taffy instantly assured, fighting the urge to rid herself of deception right then and there. "I promise you'll know what I know over time."

There it was again. Time.

Too much could lead to idle living, too little to desperate deeds. Roam had to strike a balance. He'd give what he could, like a gift, allowing Taffy to set her affairs in order. He wouldn't rush her; neither would he wait in vain. Roam took a risk putting his whole self into loving her again, but he was greedy enough to want the rewards. For now Roam would cool his heels and let this engine idle. Vexed him to hell, but perhaps the lesson was: he couldn't hurry time.

With an ironic chuckle, Roam realized that like Jacob, he'd already waited seven years. Resting his jaw against Taffy's, Roam whispered a promise he prayed to keep. "I'll wait long's I know you're coming to me."

CHAPTER TWENTY-NINE

Silver moonlight splashed a gleaming embrace about thick night. Cool seeped into the car through wide-open windows, massaging Taffy's face, further mellowing her mood. Wrapped in Roam's suit jacket, she floated on peace, serene.

Roam's voice nudged her gently, but his words were lost on the breeze. Glancing from the road to her near-sleeping form, Roam grinned. "That's what I get for messing with lightweights. Barely midnight and you're out for the count."

Taffy stirred enough to look his way. JoJo's was still in full swing when they said their 'good nights' to head back to Bledsoe, away from the mad passion of jazz and the pleasure of privacy, of Roam's regaling her with stories of the rail.

Taffy had savored his adventures and his resonant voice painting pictures of his Pullman experiences until she felt as if she rode the iron horse as well. Roam enjoyed his living. Now, thank the Lord, *she'd* been granted another chance to enjoy him. She would fiercely cherish and protect the opportunity.

Taffy struggled to see her wristwatch before answering Roam's taunt. "It's one-forty-two...*A.M.!*" Taffy eased her head down against the seat, finding Roam's shoulder instead. "I'm allowed to be sleepy."

His baritone was a tempting tease. "My bed sleeps two."

"Maybe, but tonight that bed's hosting your lonesome and you."

Roam's laughter was something Taffy couldn't leash. "Dollbaby, you might as well admit my bed is where we're headed. But won't be much sleeping." Taffy sat up, staring at Roam, face amazed. "I'm just warning you."

"It's that bad I need a warning?"

Roam snorted. "Woman, you don't even know."

"Let's keep it that way." Taffy redirected the conversation. "You promised to tell me your plans."

"Don't get skittish. We're gonna get that loving even if it's not tonight."

"Your plans...?"

"Tasting you."

"Roam!"

Laughing and lowering the radio's volume on Chick Webb's "Stompin' at the Savoy", Roam announced without preamble, "Your comment on the way to JoJo's was on the money. It's time for law school." After years of traveling, witnessing inequities endured by Negro people coast-to-coast, Roam had tired of sitting on the sidelines engaged in armchair sermons and front parlor rallies composed of a handful of discontents. With God's grace, it was time to make a difference.

Wide-eyed and silent, Taffy turned towards Roam, flashing back on bygone conversations, Roam's passionate responses to the injustices their race endured, and his long exchanges with her uncle, Augustine, trying to understand the unjust laws of the land. She remembered, when courting, Roam's refusing Taffy's pleas to join their friends for picture shows at Richland's segregated movie house. *No, ma'am, I ain't sitting in nobody's buzzards' roost balcony, and neither are you!* Jim Crow wasn't worth his pride.

Her tone was quiet with awe. "How're you going about it?" Taffy's excitement swelled as Roam recounted meeting with a university's admissions administrator and, due to high graduation marks, being offered in addition to the entrance exam, the opportunity to test out of several introductory courses. "So...?"

"Took the entry exam and the opt-out tests, and Miss Lady, God be praised, this ol' brain's still worth its weight."

Exuding delight, Taffy tossed her arms about Roam's neck, kissed his cheek before sitting back. "So, why haven't you started?"

He was squirreling money away for college and life. Needed another three years on the rails to qualify for full pension. "When I'm in, I'm in, and wanna focus solely on studying. But if I have to ride that iron horse with a book in one hand..." Roam shrugged thick shoulders. "Plenty porters working those rails to put self or children through school. I'd be in good company."

Taffy made a sound of agreement while studying the silky night. Roam looked away from the road when she sat silent too long. "Whatchu thinking?"

"All-white judges and juries won't make lawyering easy, but some battles are fought and won from the inside out." Her voice rippled with something sweet. "Always believed you'd make an excellent attorney. You're articulate…when you wanna be—"

"When I'm not downhome with you backwoods Bamas, butchering English?"

"Mmm-hmmm. You're civic-minded, bullheaded, all-knowing, confrontational, and argumentative," Taffy offered, eyes shining. "Noble qualities of a legal advocate."

"Yeah…well…Lord willing," Roam modestly replied.

"Oh, He wills.

"How you know? You and your Grandmama been playing with tea leaves and cat bones?"

"Of course," Taffy jested, nestling against Roam's shoulder, dreaming a place for him where law and real justice reigned. "I'm thrilled you're gonna get what you want in life."

"You talking law school, a good cigar, or us living in the woods making namesakes?" Spooned against him, the lushness of her body potent against his, Roam lightly traced Taffy's arm as she laughed. "So how thrilled are you?"

"Hmmm?"

"Thrilled enough to let me taste you?"

Taffy scooted to the opposite side of the car. "You'd better bypass your house on the edge of town and hightail it to the parsonage where your parents live, 'cause you need all the God you can get."

A volley of good-natured ribbing about whose righteousness was worse than whose erupted. Seated sideways, Taffy paid little attention to car lights approaching from behind. "Roam Ellis, I'm finished with you tonight. Take me home."

Taffy missed Roam's reply. The vehicle barreling recklessly towards them gained Taffy's apt attention.

Following her gaze, Roam glanced over his shoulder before honing in on the rearview mirror. "What the hell's wrong with this fool?" Roam steered right, allowing the impatient driver to pass. But trailing lights followed suit. When Roam reclaimed the lane, the other vehicle did likewise. Roam's every move was mirrored.

Roam's voice was far calmer than Taffy felt. "Dollbaby, do me a favor. Open the glove compartment."

Taffy sat frozen as the pursuing vehicle increased speed, drawing so near Taffy imagined the warmth of its head beams.

Roam did a wild thing. Punching brakes, Roam forced the tailing auto to a screeching halt before gunning his engine and lurching ahead, leaving a stench of burning rubber and raised voices behind.

Taffy couldn't move for watching the pursuer regain position. Heart racing, she stiffened against a pending and unavoidable impact. But before impact occurred, the other vehicle swooped to the left side of the two-lane country road. It approached, parallel—a green pick-up filled with three white faces distorted by hurled obscenities and unmerited hate.

Roam called her name. Taffy shook herself.

"Slowly," Roam cautioned. "Look straight ahead and open the glove box." Taffy complied. The inner dome light glinted smoothly against Roam's pearl-handle revolver. "Ease it onto the seat."

The lightweight pistol felt sleek yet powerful in Taffy's grasp. She relinquished it just as the green pick-up swerved wildly towards them.

Roam spun the wheel right. A jarring thump and shattering glass ripped the night. Roam braked, narrowly preventing them from careening into an open ditch. Instinctively, he threw an anchoring arm across Taffy.

The vehicle rocked to a halt as the pickup sped off, leaving the dissonance of raucous amusement behind. Hearts pounding, Taffy and Roam recovered in silence.

"Are you hurt?"

"I'm fine," Taffy breathed, slowly plucking the fallen pistol from the floor.

Roam removed the weapon from her hands and reached for the glove box. Reconsidering, he tucked the gun into the waistband at the small of his back. Retrieving a flashlight, Roam exited the car, stepping into the night.

Taffy took time gathering herself before sliding across the seat and joining Roam on a moonlit road. Shaken, she watched him inspect the damage.

Minimal though it was, the rear door was dented where it hadn't been before. A heated curse left Roam's lips. He asked her pardon. Taffy touched his arm, conveying his fury was understood. Roam glared down the road towards taillights that were no more before angrily scouring the ground, honing in on a whiskey bottle splayed in broken disarray.

"A bunch of drunk hoodlums," he growled, tossing the flashlight onto the backseat before returning the pistol to its confines. Thunder knotting his bones, Roam leaned against the hood of the car, head wagging. "Oughta get my shotgun and *my* posse and doing some white boy head-bashing."

"Roam, they were kids probably out joyriding."

"'Kids' like that do more damage to Colored folks than we care to tell."

"Amen," Taffy offered softly, stroking Roam's arm, attempting to dissipate rage.

Eyes on the night, Roam steeped in anger. "I may play cocky and crazy, but don't *ever* doubt me when I tell you I won't let *anybody* hurt me or mine. A Colored man has the right to protect hearth and home, because the law sure as hell won't."

Squeezing his hand, Taffy somberly acknowledged his point.

"And I'm not being prideful when I tell you my Daddy taught me to defend myself." Roam yanked ever-present peppermints from pant pocket and slapped them in his mouth. "Hell, your daddy and most men in Bledsoe taught me that! And you damn sure won't find me sleeping on the job."

Taffy need not ask for details. They lived in a time where Colored men were forced to fight or die for even the most basic rights and sometimes, indeed, die they did. She shuddered at the thought of Roam ever coming to harm.

Roam came up and out of his vengeful place. "You sure you alright?" he asked, studying her beneath an illuminating moon.

Taffy offered a slight, reassuring smile. "I've survived worse."

"Tell me."

The turn of his words caught Taffy off-guard, seducing her to open self and let Roam in.

This one needs to know. Knowing's counsel came unbidden. Taffy might have questioned the wisdom of Knowing's instruction, but the thin stream coursing down Roam's cheek overrode everything.

Lightly, Taffy fingered Roam's face above an open wound. "You're cut."

Roam touched his skin, pulling away red, wet fingers. "Whiskey bottle must've ricocheted," he surmised, silently thanking God that worse hadn't transpired.

Returning to the car for the discarded flashlight, Taffy located the lace-trimmed handkerchief tucked in her tiny clutch.

"Don't mess up that pretty thing," Roam objected. "There's one in my jacket."

"Shhh," Taffy silenced, ordering Roam onto the driver's seat, legs sprawled outside. He complied, spirit mellowing beneath her tenderness as Taffy touched the cloth to her tongue before gently dabbing his face. "It's the best I can do for now."

"No complaints here," Roam muttered as Taffy pushed the flashlight into his hand. Standing between his legs, tilting his chin, Taffy cleaned the cut as best she could. She was gentle, thorough. Her closeness was a welcome balm, her scent like honey and soap. Inhaling her sweetness, Roam relaxed, becoming mindful of little else.

"Hold this to stop the bleeding." Taffy positioned Roam's fingers atop the cloth, indicating appropriate pressure. "It'll heal without stitches. Chloe has salve at home."

The salve Roam needed, he already had. Wiping fingers, he laid the handkerchief and flashlight on the seat before palming Taffy's waist. Standing, Roam locked arms about her, asking the invasive and unanticipated. "Why doesn't he touch you?"

Eyes wide with blunt amazement, Taffy tried moving away. But Roam's hold was sure. "Taffy, look at me. Answer—"

"It doesn't deserve discussing," Taffy rasped, voice splintering.

He didn't mean to wound. Simply couldn't comprehend her untouched, hidden places. "Can I touch you," Roam pressed against her, "for your pleasure and mine?" Meshing the fullness of his mouth with hers, Roam didn't await a reply. He poured himself into a kiss that invited Taffy to forget.

Like a healing river, Roam's ardor flowed. Taffy was caught-up by his craving. Slowly, she opened, she welcomed, fully reciprocating. She was soft fire, voluptuous heat, consuming easily. Fingers riding the broad expanse of Roam's back, Taffy licked his peppermint-coated lips, gorged herself with him. Roam's ready arousal bore witness: what Taffy gave was good.

He felt her reeling. "That's it, Baby," Roam groaned, lapping up every ounce of Taffy's offering—parting her lips with his tongue, testing, tasting. A soft purr danced at the back of Taffy's throat. Roam plunged deeper and found more waiting. The deeper he probed the more Taffy opened, until Roam was drunk. And like a drunkard he wanted more.

Maintaining a relentless hold, Roam swiveled, shifting Taffy backwards against the car. Cool metal met her backside. Pure heat provoked her front when, without warning, Roam lifted Taffy atop the hood. Gripping her hips, holding her firmly in place—Roam pushed against her, overwhelming Taffy with her effect on his flesh. Something unlatched deep inside her body. Barely conscious of Roam's hands stroking her legs, wandering beneath the hem of her dress and up her thighs, Taffy violently trembled as Roam slowly, sensuously ground his pelvis into hers. Taffy's world tilted, nearly wilted. She was lost and spinning—in need of terra firma for her feet.

"No." Taffy broke a ravenous kiss. "Roam...stop..." Struggling for even breathing, Taffy pushed against the wall of Roam's chest, intent on ending contact below the waistline. "*Now*," she panted, finding Roam unwilling to terminate this far too silky slide.

Cool air flowed between them, disrupting combustible heat when Roam finally, reluctantly complied.

Chests heaving in sync, they eyed each other, locked in aborted bliss.

"I want to be with you," Taffy slowly rasped, throat thick, "but not like this." Her fingers gently traced his lips. "Let's get me home." Roam helped her down, back onto solid ground. Rearranging her clothing, Taffy focused on the art of breathing life in, life out until the hurricane of heart and body were tolerable. Barely.

A lopsided grin tilted Roam's mouth despite his displeasure at being denied. "Be glad you got good sense, Dollbaby, or we'd be flat on that backseat," Roam taunted, liking the newborn smokiness of Taffy's eyes.

"That's what I'm afraid of."

"No, Baby, you're afraid of yourself and for good cause. You gotta whole lotta honey waiting on me."

Taffy blushed, suddenly feeling like a contradiction. "I didn't intend all this..."

Roam wanted to laugh. The woman was bashful? "Don't apologize for what comes natural. God gave it. Nothing wrong with it," Roam posited before stealing a kiss—quick and deep—that conveyed unfinished business. "Mark my word: we getting to the good stuff and when we do you gonna see this here wasn't but a touch and a taste." Roam waved a hand towards the car. "After you."

Seeing Taffy safely seated, Roam stood outside, collecting night air.

Body overloaded, Roam told himself to act like he had good sense, to stop responding to Taffy's heat like he was little more than an adolescent mess. Roam chuckled quietly. Shy about it or not, that woman had some good stuff percolating that he might be hard-pressed to handle. "I'll give it my damnedest." Still. Not here. Not like this. Thank God Taffy had better control and sense. Tempted as he was to lay her out on that backseat and handle business, Roam would never treat her like something cheap. Long-desired loving deserved better than best. And before he left Bledsoe, Roam would lavish that best on every inch of her flesh. As soon as he talked Taffy into his bed.

CHAPTER THIRTY

She treasured Sunday's dawning. A new week. Fresh beginnings. Those first moments when Sunday tugged off darkness and put on light were most precious. She sat aside Chloe's bed, quietly absorbing a Sabbath sunrise, her thoughts instinctively ascending upward towards the Most High.

"Welcome, Mighty One," NuNu whispered, soaking self in God's rest.

Chloe stirred. NuNu's attention swung to her grandson's wife finally sleeping soundly.

Fool-headed younguns! Fancy-footing in some juke joint at this phase of creation. Chloe was slight and the child great, pulling on her spine, stirring NuNu's concern. Baby wasn't waiting another four weeks but was already shifting, coming sooner than due. This was readying, not reveling time. Outdone, NuNu had banished Drew, sending him to sleep downstairs with himself. *Youth is wasted on the young...*

NuNu shooed vexation away.

She'd been young once, worlds ago. Hadn't done all this happy hopping. Was too busy working the earth alongside her man to give their family a surviving chance, but she had been young. Perhaps playtime was part of progress and these children were simply enjoying the fruits of their forebears' labor. Smoothing covers about Chloe's middle, NuNu's thoughts shot down the hall to that other fruit of her tree. Annoyance peaked.

Creeping in the house, smelling like hot need!

At the top of Drew's dark landing, she'd watched Taffy tiptoe up the stairs, guilty pleasure padding her feet in the dark of morning. To her credit, her Little One didn't cower when finding NuNu there. She stood tall without a hiding place, unlike back when...

Binding her belly, running off to the unknown and coming home with child.

She'd promised God she'd look after her namesake. She should've done better, but she'd given her best. NuNu no longer blamed herself for not seeing, for being distracted to the point of Taffy's downfall. Still, things might've differed had she…

We don't walk in the land of make-believe.

Even NuNu couldn't reconstruct time.

Back then, she'd been mightily distracted journeying back and forth and back again until finally staying in Drexel, tending Pastor Hollins' boy who liked to get himself killed for preaching voting rights. Child was burned so bad NuNu thought it best to let him slip to the other side, but that young man hung on. His fight became NuNu's and she stayed at his bedside for weeks that stretched into months that saw Taffy with child.

NuNu remembered coming home, wearily dragging a world about her back when meeting her newest great grand. She took Angel from Taffy's arms, placed a hand on his heart and knew: *he didn't come here the right way.*

NuNu never could gather the fragments into any kind of order with Taffy locking truth beneath falsehoods. And when Al Freeman came skulking around, looking like a cretin lapping spilled cream, NuNu wanted to hurl the universe into the sea. Wanted to misuse her gift and destroy like she'd misused and destroyed before. But it was that abuse that dimmed NuNu's gift, letting Taffy's trials pass unseen. It was like putting a cup over a candle. So NuNu bowed to destiny, knowing justice would happen in her own sweet time.

Readjusting a shawl about her shoulders, NuNu resituated herself in the chair beside Chloe's bed and faced sunrise, in need of the cleansing and the calm.

NuNu awoke, finding a child at her side. Smiling big, she opened her arms. "Well, if it ain't Mr. Man." Scampering onto his great grandmother's lap, Angel planted kisses on her smooth, dark cheek. "That's the best morning sugar ever. Where're you headed?"

"Sunday School."

"You lost? Church house is the other way," NuNu teased.

"I came for Taffy, but she's snoring like a dinosaur, so I stopped to see you."

"And, I'm right glad. You looking mighty handsome and smelling good, too."

"Taffy told me I have to take baths if I don't wanna smell like fried polecat."

"Ooh, now, that's enough to turn your hair green."

Angel giggled. Chloe stirred. NuNu raised a finger to her lips. "We best stop jawing 'fore we wake Little Mama. You gon' off to church and Poppy and I'll see you afterwards at Second Sunday dinner."

"But you and Poppy don't like 'disorganized religion'."

"We like organized eats," NuNu answered with a wink.

Smiling, Angel slid off his great grandmother's lap. "Don't forget it's ball day. You can sit with the other womenfolk and cheer us men on."

NuNu grunted. "What if I wanna get in the game?"

Stumped, Angel cocked his head sideways. "You're too old, NuNu. You might break something." NuNu chortled quietly, stretched cramped legs. Glancing down at his NuNu's bare feet, Angel asked, "NuNu, what happened to your baby toe?"

Raising the hem of her old-timey, floor-length skirt, NuNu lifted her left foot and wiggled the remaining four digits. "You know the story."

"Yes, ma'am, but I like it."

"Then you tell it."

"When you were born your mother, the African Octavia, tied thread 'round it 'til it dried up and fell off so, if she lost you in slavery, she could find you again." NuNu smiled proudly, knowing the fine details were missing, but it was her story in its nutshell. "She must've loved you lots and lots. Almost as much as me."

Kissing his head, NuNu shooed Angel out the room. Long after he'd gone, NuNu stared at the empty doorway, studying the thin veil Angel left behind.

She'd carried suspicion and disjointed truth his whole life, but for the first time, fragmented pieces and clarity shifted. The veil lifted and NuNu glimpsed a thing unseen.

The weight of truth pressed NuNu back in her chair. Something, no some*one*, wavered indeterminately at the edge of revelation. Still, what NuNu managed to grasp left her whispering, "Lord be praised."

Angel wasn't a bit more Al Freeman's than a cat was a coon.

CHAPTER THIRTY-ONE

Taffy awoke to sunshine and shadows. She awoke with pleasure on her lips and pressure between her hips. She was warm yet cool, a jumble of sense and sensation. Stretching like a lioness in the sun, Taffy lay in bed, gazing out the open window at the wealth of God's hands. The day was clear and welcoming—a blessed continuance from the prior night still bombarding her flesh. "Get your mind right," Taffy told herself, but self wasn't listening as she lay reliving.

Taffy itched and ached with unconsummated loving. Caught in an unfamiliar tailspin, Taffy felt Roam everywhere he'd been. She was a furnace trapping heat, needing dire release. "Stop acting like a juiced-up Jezebel!" she told herself, springing from bed as if the bed were to blame.

Gathering toiletries, Taffy padded to the bathroom. Filling tub with tepid water and NuNu's homemade bath salts, she sank into the fragrant liquid with a sigh. A craving had come calling and she meant to tame it, if not wash it away.

According to Roam, God gave it. It was good. No need to apologize for a natural thing. But was she? Natural? With 'female issues' courtesy of Big Baby?

Taffy reclined in warm water, letting doubt fade. "I'm a woman, not a wounded child." She willed herself forward. Her future *would* be filled with Roam, in all his capacities. His raw virility, the length and strength of him…

Aching with appetite, Taffy slipped lower into the tub. Splashing water over hot skin, Taffy soaped a body tingling with memory, knowing she couldn't do a thing to satisfy self in a small town where private business often made the church bulletin. Lord, help her to hold out until making it Up North. Bledsoe wasn't big enough for this kind of crave.

Laughing aloud, Taffy instantly sobered. She leaned her head back against the tub, and examined the ceiling. Before ever indulging in the ocean of his intimacy, she owed Roam a truth not easily conveyed.

Dressed for service and finding Chloe asleep, Taffy tipped down the stairs much as she'd tipped up the night before. And like last night, she found NuNu waiting.

Her grandmother sat at the kitchen table drinking strong coffee, coal black eyes peering intensely. "Morning, Little One. You sleep well?"

Taffy kissed NuNu's forehead. "Yes, ma'am. You?"

"No, indeed, these old bones are protesting dozing in a chair. But I'll be fine soon's I get to my own bed." NuNu chuckled lightly. "You shoulda seen Drew last night. That crazy boy come tearing up the porch, waking me and your Poppy, hollering like the baby was 'near bout born. Told him folks with good sense wouldn't've had a woman near her due out fancy-footing in the first place."

Sidestepping NuNu's rebuke, Taffy busied herself finding breakfast only to discover she was full. It was a strange awareness—her belly and body being preoccupied. As was, apparently, her mind.

"Octavia!"

Taffy turned quickly at the sternness of NuNu's voice. "Ma'am?"

The namesakes considered each other across new distance. In the afterglow of a favored dawn, NuNu saw her granddaughter in ways not previously viewed. Taffy had lushness about her. The kind that accompanied loving? But amid Taffy's opulence was chaos. "You hiding something in your back pocket other than your behind. Whatchu got yo'self into?"

Taffy could count the times her grandmother had entered a house of worship. NuNu's God didn't dwell in a brick and mortar edifice made by mortal man. The earth was His temple, and He didn't need Sunday service to commission His praise. Besides, according to NuNu, sitting in service with folks who'd raised Cain all week only to jump saved come Sunday was more burden than she need bear. Still, NuNu treasured decency in ways church folk couldn't comprehend. NuNu's need for rightness didn't flow from a sanctimonious spring. Her cosmos was Spirit-driven. Spirit desired truth, and truth order.

"Nothing I can't get myself out of," Taffy assured, anticipating tomorrow's meeting with Harold Jenkins, attorney at law.

NuNu shook her head. "You making your own way now?" Her Little One was misaligned. "You asking The Gift to lead, but ain't willing to follow."

Taffy opened her mouth only to pause, recalling Knowing's dismissed admonition. *This one needs to know.*

There was too much to tell. Chloe was her most intimate friend, and even Chloe didn't know all. Now Knowing wanted Taffy to divulge truths to Roam that could rip a world in two? Pulling a chair beside her grandmother, Taffy sat. "NuNu, I'm trying not to fail." Failure spawned ambivalence and ambivalence uncertainty of her connection to The Gift and Taffy's very right to host God's gem.

"Carting lies ain't easy, Little One. But God's gifts got more to do with willingness than worth."

"NuNu, what do you know?" Taffy asked, closely studying her grandmother.

"Freeman ain't the father." Taffy's silence neither confirmed nor denied. "So why you with him?"

Breathing deeply, Taffy sighed. "It was the only given choice at the time."

NuNu was caught between rejoicing that Freeman hadn't fouled her bloodline and wanting to strike her Little One for authorizing lies. "Freeman knows he ain't the pa, so why's he with *you*?"

A world deluged Taffy's soul and her eyes welled as years of humiliation and deprivation came calling. NuNu gripped Taffy's hand. "I ever taught you to live bound?"

Weeping inwardly, Taffy could only shake her head.

"Then why you tied yourself up so?" Not waiting on a nonexistent answer, NuNu yanked her blouse free from her skirt and lifted binding bands. Pivoting in her chair, she presented her back to Taffy. "Look on it!" she ordered at Taffy's sharp gasp. "This tree's planted on my back 'cause I tried to keep my baby brother from hanging." NuNu's voice broke. "It's Elias' tree, but it best not ever bear fruit."

Gingerly, Taffy traced the raised scars, thick as snakes, looking as if they might burst and bleed.

Voice husky, NuNu explained, "I saved your Poppy, but my Elias—"

"Poppy?" Taffy interrupted, confused. "Poppy was almost killed along with your brother?"

Memories tripped over NuNu's face, leaving it like stone. "You

younguns grew up hearing Bledsoe was bought with blood." Her fist
hit the table. "Wasn't no family lore to make y'all stand tall. Blood
requires blood, and every drop your Poppy shed, I took it back by the
pound! It's where your name comes from!"

Here is where I bled. I bled so here.

The distant echo haunted Taffy's hearing. Poppy had cast off his
slave master's moniker, renaming himself: this Taffy already knew.
But a buried treasure of truth rang like an echo. *I Bled So.* Poppy had
been harmed and NuNu had atoned? The echo hinted that whatever
their scope, NuNu's deeds *were* the reason for white folks staying out
of Bledsoe. *I Bledsoe.* The Dream reemerged, a forebear sowing blood,
sprinkled like seed, Taffy racing for a train, 'Blood has Memory'…
Taffy flashed on the long scar on Poppy's left temple, but NuNu barreled on, erasing room for questioning.

"When that tree got planted, I swore Elias would be the last
one I lost that way. Did all in my power, sometimes right sometimes
wrong." NuNu covered her head in shame. "Now here you are, my
heart-child, hanging by the knees." NuNu's tone sharpened, voicing
words without warning. "Too much blood's been shed for you to be
tangled up at Lacy's feet! Set yourself free!"

Taffy's voice was a raw hollow. "NuNu, I've been fighting seven
years for my freedom. I can't quit now…but I'm tired."

"That's 'cause a bent body gets weary walking 'round looking
down at the ground. Get all these lies off your back! Tell that Ellis boy
your truth, *whatever that truth is*, so you can stand up straight and
stop shaming your legacy! *You hear?!*"

Kneeling, pressing her face against NuNu's back, Taffy answered
by watering a tree with tears.

Sunday School was long over by the time Taffy headed down the
back steps trying to make service before Reverend Ellis took to the
podium with the morning's sermon. She needed solace and God's
sanctuary.

Drew was gone, but his old Ford sat vacant in the drive. It was
her best bet if she was to make church in time. Intent on locating
keys, Taffy turned towards the house and froze.

Something lay piled beneath the raised porch, a curious, uniden-
tifiable mass.

Taffy approached, stooping to better see. Shadows obscured clarity.

Cautiously, Taffy prodded the soft mound with the tip of her shoe, encountering something soft and slippery. Running shoe across grass, Taffy watched blades turn crimson. Heart thumping, Taffy found a stick and used it like a shovel. The mass tumbled forward and Taffy lost what little breakfast she'd consumed.

Hearing frantic calls, NuNu rushed outdoors, stopping cold at the sight of carcasses at Taffy's feet.

An animal corpse in the country was no rarity. Foxes, coyotes, and raptors often left evidence of a hunt. But this differed. Rabbit carcasses littered the ground, decapitated, mutilated, the clear evidence of a depraved human hunter.

NuNu hailed the ancestors. Only ancient strength and wisdom could intercept this evil hell had unleashed.

CHAPTER THIRTY-TWO

For the first time in Bledsoe history, crumbled cornbread stood proxy in place of the Lord's body and buttermilk in lieu of his blood. The servers of the sacrament, caught up in Founders' Festival preparations, failed to properly restock sacred elements. First Lady Ellis and the Women's Willing Workers were beyond mortified. First Lady was forced to run out back to the parsonage while Rachel Bledsoe corralled auxiliary members into the church's basement kitchen, seeking to make-do.

Reverend Ellis' scowl was enough to crucify. Yet with no other alternative, cornbread and clabber were served in honor of the Savior's death, burial, and resurrection that Sunday after Taffy's return.

The choir sang two beats behind the music.

Deacon Ashton stumbled over Papa Nash's cane left jutting in the aisle, subsequently dropping the offering plate atop Mother Wheatley's head. Mother woke up swinging. The rhythm of life was obviously out-of-sync.

Despite his father's being hot under his clerical collar, Roam sat swallowing laughter, grateful and amused. The unprecedented comical goings-on kept his thoughts from straying where they willed. To juicy lips, and abundant hips. Last night she'd been lush in his arms—opening, purring like she tasted something good…

Shut it down, Roam!

Roam resituated himself in his seat. He'd experienced trouble enough getting his body to behave. Tossed his way to sleep, only to awaken this morning right where he'd left off, with Taffy on his manhood and his mind. Roam need not borrow trouble sitting in First Zion under God's watchful eye. Still…

He'd been seduced and beguiled before. He'd enjoyed painted lips and gyrating hips, *double entendres* or blatant beckoning; tantalizing traps camouflaged with womanly wares. Women were masters of intrigue, maneuvering matters so that the hunter became the hunted. Roam was game for the sport. But this here? Ridiculous! Taffy's unsullied seduction had him entangled, belly hard with hunger. And impatience. And she did it without fully recognizing her power.

Taffy drew Roam deeper, had his mind refastened on a forsaken notion called matrimony. The rails wouldn't hold him always. When he walked, Roam preferred it be into the arms of the woman he'd call wife. He'd only imagined crowning one with that title. But Freeman got to her first.

Wasn't right to envy another man's blessings, but he did. *It'll be rectified.*

He was unsure the protocol, the amount of time a woman need wait between leaving one husband and taking another, or even a lover. Until then? He had to step back and stand clear. Let Taffy 'fix her business' and exercise restraint in the interim.

She'd asked him to wait. He trusted her to find her way. And when she did? Roam would be ready. For what? A casual consort or a commitment? What, precisely, did Taffy want? And what of Angel? *Woman's packing bullets in both barrels*, Roam mused, trying to focus on the reading of this week's announcements.

Bearing a child out-of-wedlock was one woe. A woman leaving her husband? That was an abominable atrocity in the minds of many.

Folks, his parents included, believed in keeping what God connected. Roam agreed. But what happened when folks were united who ought not be?

Rising with the rest of the congregation for a final, pre-sermon hymn, Roam was soothed by his father's deep, mellifluous voice. Roam had his mother's coloring, but—from build to behavior—he was his father's child. Years, experience, and a good woman had mellowed the Reverend's raw edges and rounded his being. Roam didn't know the years or experiences ahead, but he'd found his woman and, *Lord!*, he'd tasted but enough to know she was yeah good. Just scratching a heated surface. Hadn't dipped down deep. But when they did! Roam had it ready and waiting...

Roam snapped to attention as the hymn ended and his father, the right Reverend, announced his sermonic topic for the day, "*The Devil You'll Find in an Idle Mind!*" Roam dropped his head and repented. The Lord need not tell him twice.

⊂∂℮⊃

The grassy lot behind First Zion was packed with picnic tables, food, folks, and bright fellowship. Summer tipped into the temperature. Tie and jacket removed, Roam rolled up shirt sleeves, ready to do a chicken leg some harm.

"Man, you still single?" Mouth full of good, Roam looked up to find a smirking Drew. Drew plopped onto the opposite bench before lowering his voice. "Thought I saw some swooning sisters cutting eyes at you."

Roam rolled his. "I'm not messing in that."

"Why not? They're putting it on a platter."

"You want me popping off all over the place?"

"No, indeed! Can't have your seed springing up so the whole town's looking like you."

Roam made a scoffing sound before scooping up a mound of potato salad. "I don't fertilize fields."

"Good…but if you change your mind, that Paris Brown was staring like she wanna reproduce you."

Dropping fork on plate, Roam studied Drew. "Why you putting me off on other women, the married included?"

"So I won't have to shoot you," Drew replied, tearing into an ear of corn. "Speaking of, what time you bring my cousin home last night?"

"Ask Taffy."

"I'm asking you since she ain't here."

"I noticed," Roam commented, looking around as if willing her to appear.

"Must've overslept. Got anything to do with that?"

"I'm the god of slumber now, huh?" Roam remarked, snorting.

"You know what I mean," Drew countered.

"I'mma act like I don't, Drew, 'cause you talking cheap. How's Chloe?"

"'Bout to get up and go check." Drew chugged sweet tea. "*If* NuNu lets me in. She's mad as three cats in a bag."

"Why?"

"Told me I didn't have the sense in a penny, letting my expectant wife hoochie-coo at a juke joint. I tried telling NuNu it wasn't a juke joint, it was a speakeasy."

"And?"

"She cracked me in the back of the head." Their laughter boomed across air, relieving uncommon tension between friends. "Tell the brothers I'm outta today's game. Going home to see 'bout my baby," Drew said, rising.

"As you should," Roam agreed, admiring Drew's devotion to Chloe.

"So…what time did Taffy get in?"

Sucking on a chicken bone, Roam granted Drew a hard-eyed stare.

"Alright, man, no offense meant. You're my brother, but I gotta take care of kin." Looking up, Drew smiled. "Speaking of, looka this here ragamuffin."

Angel and a pack of boys raced their way.

"Hey, Cousin Drew!" Angel slowed enough to hop onto Drew's back. "Hi, Mr. Roam! Y'all playing ball today? The teams are heading to the field." Angel pointed out a group heading towards the acreage further back of the church. It was second Sunday, after-church-ball game day.

"Not today. Gotta get home and tend to Chloe," Drew answered, bouncing Angel on his back.

"Is that what married men do?" Angel asked.

"They should," Drew replied.

"Then I'mma stay a batch of lard."

"You mean 'bachelor'?" Roam offered, grinning.

"Oh." Angel giggled along with friends. "Is Cousin Chloe sick 'cause of the baby?"

"In a way," Drew answered.

"Can she take the baby out 'til she feels better, then put the baby back in? How'd a baby get in her belly in the first place?"

Drew coughed.

"Grandmama Olivette says if you swallow seeds when drinking lemonade a tree'll grow on your insides," Angel's best friend, Willie Ray Williams III, offered.

"Cousin Drew, you and Cousin Chloe gotta be more careful 'bout the lemonade you drink next time," Angel advised.

Roam laughed like he'd lost his mind.

"On that note, I'm heading home." Drew lowered Angel to the ground.

"But we wanna watch you play," Angel whined.

"Mr. Roam's playing. Go watch him."

An excited chorus erupted.

"Gotta change outta these Sunday silks first," Roam commented, tossing a balled up napkin atop his empty plate.

"You need me to be your caddy?" Angel kidded, happy to oblige.

"Yeah, Champ. Help me get my change of clothes from the choir room."

Angel grabbed Roam's hand, leading the way.

"I'll ask the other team to take it easy on you, Ellis," Drew called after the departing cluster. "Rail-riding'll make a man weak and you looking like you need more time in the fields to get you hard."

Surrounded by a cloud of children, Roam simply grinned. *If Drew only knew.*

CHAPTER THIRTY-THREE

Agitated and angry, she'd moved like a cyclone, eradicating the blood-soaked calling card left by some impudent fool. Following instructions, she'd helped her grandmother burn mutilated carcasses on a pile of cypress leaves to cancel blood-letting. *When evil plots, you contain it 'fore it strangles you*, NuNu explained, collecting a portion of the ashes in a small box. Taffy didn't want ashes. She preferred emptying a shotgun in somebody's back-side. Yet, she'd carried out the ritual cleansing, somewhat soothed by NuNu's singsong prayer in an ancient tongue Taffy couldn't compre-hend.

Now, having swallowed nothing but trouble, she tried enjoying the bounty of church ladies' cooking, but her stomach rebelled. Taffy discarded her untouched plate, thinking it sinful doing so as a crew of cousins caught her attention, waving.

By the expressions on their faces, they were chomping at the bit to be in her business; thanks, no doubt, to Dena sitting in the mix. In no mood to be put on parade, Taffy stuck out her tongue and walked right into Aunt Vesta. Vesta Jo Bledsoe wasted no time linking arms with Taffy and turning her in the direction Vesta chose.

"Get her, Aunt Vesta!" Dena yelled. The crew cracked up, earning them a menacing look from Taffy.

"Don't pay them nosey heffas no mind. You eat yet, baby?"

"No, ma'am. I'm not hungry." Taffy answered, belly occupied.

"Had a big breakfast?"

"Not really," Taffy replied, recalling the sight of dead animals pulling her stomach out from the inside.

"You ain't had much and you still not hungry?" Aunt Vesta peered at Taffy, waiting on something that sounded like good sense. "Ever hear that when a woman's belly is full of nothing, it's full of *some-thing*? Must be that Little Mr. Ellis," Aunt Vesta instigated, using the name by which her late husband called Roam. "He's a big one."

"Dena!" Taffy spewed, whirling about.

Aunt Vesta pulled Taffy forward. "Baby, one Bledsoe knows we all know. You went out and had yourself an evening and—"

"It wasn't *my* evening, Aunt Vesta. Dena and Hamp and—"

"Everybody came back 'cept you. That constitutes 'an evening'. How was it? And what'd you do to that Paris Brown?" Aunt Vesta suddenly questioned. "She's looking like you got something she wants."

Following Aunt Vesta's gaze, Taffy was grateful for Paris Brown's glaring that sidetracked Aunt Vesta, if only momentarily. The less Taffy's family knew of her relationship with Roam the better. Taffy snorted. "If it was hers I wouldn't have it."

Aunt Vesta snickered, picking up where she left off. "So, how fine was he...I mean it...your evening? Was he...*it*...this fine," gradually increasing distance, Aunt Vesta's hands indicated length, "this fine... or *this*?"

Taffy's mouth dropped open, grasping Aunt Vesta's intimations. "Lord, let me outta this town full of repressed women, always talking up under somebody's business."

Aunt Vesta's big laugh attacked the day. "Honeybear, don't be too sweet to measure. But he remained a gentleman?"

Taffy missed a step, recalling how gentle Roam truly was—warm lips, soft tongue. It was the powerful firmness of him that had Taffy unhinged. "Absolutely," was all Taffy offered.

"Good, 'cause you in a predicament that don't need no added problems. I'mma tell you something you youngsters probably don't know," Aunt Vesta said, sobering. "I was married before your Uncle Auggie."

Stopping to look at her aunt, Taffy dredged family history. Poppy and NuNu's firstborn, Augustine, graduated Fisk University, couldn't get a decent job in the white man's world, so he enlisted in the army. He came home from the Spanish American war with shrapnel in his left hip and a bride on his arm. She was as lovable as she was loud, and when they repeatedly tried but failed to conceive, the couple questioned if failure was due to the metal floating in Augustine's war-injured hip or a problem with Vesta's baby-making mechanisms. Whatever the issue, NuNu and Dr. Blue couldn't solve it, so the couple resolved themselves to spoiling the passel of nieces and nephews

Bledsoes eventually bore. Yet, for Taffy, Aunt Vesta's prior marriage was a family mystery.

Their ambling walk led them behind the church to a place of quiet privacy. On rear steps they sat.

"I'm telling you this 'cause I've watched you struggle too long," Aunt Vesta began, voice softer than Taffy knew her aunt's voice could be. "Seems you're wrestling harder now than before." Aunt Vesta looked down at her lap, smoothed her dress. "My hell-of-a-marriage was going on its second year when I left that first husband 'cause I couldn't take it no more."

Aunt Vesta breathed deeply, voice turning bright again. "I was on my own and making my way laundering clothes for white women in between working shifts at a candy store. Well, one day I'm at the store when in walks this tall...*pretty*...ebony-black soldier on his way home from the war. He told me I was the sweetest thing he'd ever seen and asked me to marry him. I laughed. He didn't. Next thing I know we're courting all of two weeks and I'm married again and riding into Bledsoe." Vesta considered her niece. "Your Uncle Auggie was direct that way."

Taffy nodded, unwilling to think on Augustine. "What put hell in your first marriage?"

"That man's fists."

Taffy stilled instantly.

"That man beat whenever, however he felt like it. Sun too hot? I got hit. Snow too cold? Hit me again." Aunt Vesta shuddered with memory. "I was young enough to listen to folks counseling that a wife's place was at her husband's side, heeding his beck and call, no matter her suffering. But the last beating I took was the one that made me say to hell with other people's opinions."

Slowly, mechanically, Aunt Vesta related her first husband's coming home to find a salesman sitting in their tiny front parlor. When business was concluded and the salesman left, Vesta was falsely accused of being unfaithful with him. Her husband beat her within an inch of her life.

Her chuckle was mirthless and heavy. "Crazy thing is *he's* the one asked that man over. But I caught blame." Without warning, Aunt Vesta grabbed Taffy's hand and positioned it atop her thick abdomen. Aunt Vesta manipulated her clothing until Taffy felt long, jagged keloids. "I'm convinced this is why I couldn't give your Uncle Auggie a child. That first man cut me so bad that last beating, you could've painted a wall with the blood coming out of me."

Teary-eyed, Taffy held her aunt's hand. "Aunt Vesta, I'm so sorry you endured that."

"And I'm sorry you living what you living," Vesta replied, squeezing Taffy's hand before adjusting her clothing. "I know we're existing in a time when women ain't supposed to want nothing other than what we have. We're supposed to be satisfied. And Colored women ain't but a womb away from slavery, so what we have is sho' 'nuff more than what our mothers owned. We're blessed but, Taffylove, I'mma tell you." Aunt Vesta laid a hand on Taffy's back. "Loving your Uncle Auggie taught me I could have more than crumbs."

Pushing against the steps for leverage, Vesta stood and stretched kinks away. She smiled at the bright sapphire sky, the warm country air thick with nature's perfume. "I was scared to marry Augustine after what I went through with the first, but Lord I'm glad I took a chance." Vesta looked down at Taffy. "That man knew something about loving!" Vesta shimmied happily. "With the heart *and* other parts." Aunt Vesta laughed at Taffy's eye-rolling before growing serious.

"Buttercup, life's too precious for you to be bleeding it out on Al Freeman's floor. Do what you need to handle that sticky icky. And while you at, do something 'bout whatever the mess is between you and your mama. Sick of that, too." Aunt Vesta made as if to leave, only to stop suddenly. "Let me learn you this from my experiences. Al mighta been your first man, but he ain't gotta be your last."

CHAPTER THIRTY-FOUR

She headed for the ballfield, reflecting on testimonies.
Aunt Vesta and Miss Marva—and even NuNu in baring
her back—had relaxed generational barriers to take her into
their confidences, shedding light and sharing power. What Taffy had
to do was far from easy, but now her road was paved with aid.

Trash-talking was in full effect by the time Taffy arrived at the
ballfield to catch the last inning-and-a-half of the game. It was fast
and furious, like bets were made and money laid.

"Man, my grandmama hits better than you!"

"That's 'cause she *is* a man! Pick up the ball, Negro, and stop
scratching yours!"

"Grab that little bat! You know you ain't used to handling nothing
big."

Humor and insults flew like fastballs, forcing the umpire to call
for temperance in the presence of women and children.

"Don't you dare repeat a word," Taffy warned Angel. Giggling at
raunchy repartees, Angel promised he wouldn't even while storing
new insults for future use.

Summoned by friends, Angel trotted off to a group of huddled
boys exchanging whispers before running back to Taffy. "Can I go
frog-catching at the creek?"

"Yes, but be home by nightfall."

With Angel's departure, Taffy settled on planks nailed to overturned buckets serving as bleachers and got into the game.

They were deep in it, rolling up on the top of the eighth, sweating and playing like contenders for The Negro League. Taffy was
easily caught up, cheering from the sidelines, didn't matter the team.
If a good play was made, she cheered; a bad play, she snickered even
jeered with other spectators framing the field.

"Aw, watch it, Hamp's up!" a sweaty player warned, now at the bottom of the ninth. "Back up, outfielders. Ellis? You on it?"

"Best believe!" Roam assured, crouched and weaving side-to-side.

"Roam, you ain't on nothing but some slow feet," Dena countered from the sidelines. "Take your time, Hamp baby, and hit that thing!"

Positioned at home plate with runners on second and third, Dena's Hamp took his sweet, unhurried time. One ball. Two strikes. Then he laid into it like white on rice.

Roam took off, running after the high fly. Runner one, runner two came in. Hamp rounded second as Roam rocketed the ball to third. Third baseman dropped the heat. Hamp stole for home.

Shortstop recovered the dropped ball, sizzling it into the catcher's glove as Hamp slid. Ump called in Hamp's favor and the field erupted in celebration (and frustration) as the game ended ten-to-seven with Hamp the hero of the day.

Ruthless ribbing was inevitable as players straggled off the field—hot, tired, and satisfied.

Reverend Ellis was there in his shirtsleeves, like a proud father praising the players before clapping his own son on the back. Reverend Ellis' midsection had increased, hair decreased, and he needed spectacles to aid his reading. Still, he was a handsome man—same red-brown hair, chiseled features and cleft chin, broad build and extra-long frame as the one he called son.

Taffy's gaze couldn't help but stray Roam's way.

Lord had no business making a man like that, sweat-soaked shirt clinging to a magnificent build boasting strength. Took her a moment to harness memory of that strength pressed against her, but Taffy fixed her mind...even if her body refused to follow.

"Hey, Taf." Dena was beside her. "Didn't mean to make you mad, but I'm still the oldest grandchild. I'm responsible for y'all young-heads. So, yeah I put last night on the family vine and that got Aunt Vesta up in your chest—"

"I'm fine." Taffy ended Dena's torrent. When downhome, privacy was a myth.

"Might be disagreeable, but at least you know."

"Don't I," Taffy muttered, watching Dena hurry to her husband's side. Tipsy with victory, Hamp hugged Dena off her feet, whispering something in her ear that lit her face like a lamp and had them grabbing their children and saying quick goodbyes. Smiling, Taffy made to follow.

"Sister Freeman?" Reverend Ellis' ocean-of-a-voice halted her leaving. "I heard you were home, but didn't see you in service today."

"No, sir, we had an unfortunate family matter."

"All is well?"

"It is," Taffy assured, praying it was and would be. "So sorry I missed service. I always benefit from your teaching."

"That's very kind of you, Sister Freeman. Hope you join us before you leave."

Taffy merely smiled, praying she and Angel would be in Chicago before another Sunday rolled around.

Bidding her farewell, the Reverend watched his only child slipping a clean dress shirt atop his sweat-soaked A-shirt.

"Son?"

"I'll catch up, Pop," Roam assured, slowly rolling up shirtsleeves.

Looking between the two, the Reverend nodded, his misgivings bowing before the fact that he'd raised his son right. Still, for good measure, he shot Roam a wordless warning.

Sensing the disconnect, Taffy watched him go. Reverend Ellis was cordial but reserved since…Angel and Alfredo. Unlike First Lady, he withdrew fond embraces, kept Taffy at arms' length. Though she understood, separation didn't sit right on Taffy's soul.

"'Ey." Roam's voice slid over her thoughts. Taffy found Roam taking his time gathering gear, intentionally allowing spectators to collect belongings and head towards the church house in the distance, some throwing questioning glances while passing the two. "Don't go anywhere," Roam quietly ordered, discerning Taffy's intent.

"I shouldn't be out here with you."

"Gal, please," Roam countered, grinning rakishly beneath a setting sun, "I'm the one needing a chaperone seeing as how you don't know how to kiss a man without losing your mind every time."

"Shhh!" Taffy hissed, looking about, relieved no one was left to hear, only to grow cautious at their being alone. "And don't worry. I won't be kissing you tonight. I'd best get home," Taffy stated as Roam stepped into her private space.

"Yours or mine?" Roam slyly posited, earning himself a cutting, no-nonsense look. "What's wrong, Lightweight? You still tryna shake all that Saturday-sinning this Sunday?"

Taffy's laugh was light as the evening breeze. "I'm good."

"You taste even better." Roam pulled her near.

"Don't be inappropriate," Taffy cautioned, pushing Roam away.

"What's your problem?"

"I'm not giving folks nothing to talk about."

"Taffy Mae, these folks aren't judge or jury. So relax yourself. Besides, ain't nobody thinking 'bout you 'cept me," Roam teased.

Once a scandal always a scandal, Taffy thought, refusing to give the good folk of Bledsoe cause to resurrect her moral crimes.

"Everything's fine on the homefront?"

Scolding herself for her cynicism, Taffy exhaled. "Just a bit of unpleasantness."

Residual of last night's pickup chase brought edginess to Roam's tone. "What kind of unpleasantness?"

Loathe to push trouble off on another somebody, Taffy chose not to divulge. "Everything'll be fine."

"Truly?"

Taffy nodded, nostrils flaring with the earthy aroma of the root-filled sachet NuNu pinned inside Taffy's brassiere after the clearing of dead rabbits, pronouncing, *You gonna put on protection and keep this threat from falling on you.* Initial fear became anger. Now anger resurfaced, threatening to darken Taffy's mood. "I'd better get myself on home."

"You said that already, but you're still here." Roam reached for her hand.

"There'll be no touching," Taffy warned, voice smoky with memory.

Roam's trademark grin was in full effect. "Let me see your left hand." Successful in his quest this time, Roam studied Taffy's palm before turning her hand over. "Where's your wedding band?"

"I don't have one," Taffy responded, accustomed to Roam's blunt queries.

"Why not?"

"No sense binding my whole self. Let my finger be free."

Al Freeman was a fool. Couldn't pay Roam to have a wife living untouched, unloved, and without symbolic signification that she was his. Taffy might call it turf-marking, but a man needed to identify what was his somehow, some way—especially Colored men whose collective history was, by and large, "from nothing to something".

An odd thought slid about Roam's mind.

Maybe Freeman wasn't invested in the union because it was little more than smoke and mirrors. Or was that wishful thinking? Roam let the notion go. No sense juxtaposing another man's methods with what Roam deemed fitting. But if Freeman didn't want Taffy the way Roam did: it was all over but the shout.

"You looking like the cat that caught the canary," Taffy remarked at Roam's smug expression.

"Not yet, Dollbaby, but just about. Come on, I'll walk you home."

"No, thanks, I'm fine."

"Fine. You walk *me* home...the long way." Laughing, they strolled towards the backend of the field preceding a gently sloping descent. "Enjoy yourself last night?" Roam taunted, voice dripping with ardent memories.

"Music, yes. Present company? Not necessarily."

"Baby, you woulda enjoyed a whole lot more than you could handle if I didn't have the good sense to get you off me."

Taffy slapped Roam's arm. "I wish you'd gon' somewhere!"

"I am. And you gonna be sitting up here weeping when I hop on that iron horse this week," Roam reminded, taking the sloping decline. He reached back for Taffy to help her do likewise, but found her rooted and unmoving. Evening's descent muted its full force; still, Taffy's face was a kaleidoscope of emotions.

She'd fallen prey to pretense, and the fantastical comfort of down-home. And Roam. In the beginning obligation slithered about her ankles, keeping Taffy here knowing she owed Roam an explanation, face-to-face. But truth was, love prevented leaving.

Watching this man, hand extended waiting on her descent, Taffy loved him like life. Couldn't recall a time before she did. Leaving would be more bitter than sweet. Their worlds were distinct, not bound—unable to converge until she was free. Parting was inevitable and deflating.

The sound of a late train rolling along the backside of Bledsoe rumbled across the distance, emphasizing the unavoidable and sending an ominous shiver down Taffy's spine. Determined to soak up whatever enjoyment remained, Taffy accepted Roam's hand, savoring his touch, determined to take remembrance with her when he'd gone.

"You looking funny 'bout the face," Roam commented. "Missing me already?"

"No."

Roam's chuckle was melted butter in warm air. "You can't lie worth nothing." Roam erased distance between. "Stop your worrying, Dollbaby. We'll be together. I promise you that." Gently, he stroked her jaw. "Told myself I could go without touching you again until." Tilting Taffy's chin Roam rumbled, "That was my lie," before helping himself to provocative lips.

The kiss was tender and restrained yet immense with longing.

That full sensation in Taffy's belly dissipated as if mere marker holding place for this man. Familiar thawing beneath her skin set off a volley of chills, rousing hunger like a river ever-ready for Roam. Taffy broke contact before she flowed over the edge.

She pulled back, distracting self with last night's injury to Roam's cheek. A clean cut, the wound had already closed. She touched his face gently. "How's it feel?"

Roam's baritone was deeply suggestive. "Tell me when we finish."

"Lord...Roam..." Taffy unsuccessfully tried to wiggle out of his hold. "Walk me home, heathen."

"Yeah, I'd better. My virtue's not safe around you. But you best believe we gonna finish what you started last night."

"What *I* started?"

"Yes, ma'am, *you*! I was minding my business 'til you come 'round, floating all this silk and sugar in my face. Got me all deprived and needy. "

"Sorry for you, sir, but what you got is all you get. Your needs'll keep."

"Like hell," Roam grunted, nuzzling Taffy's throat, hands straying towards her hips—his baritone raw. "I need you in my bed like I need my next breath." Slowly, Roam licked her neck. "Come with me when I leave."

Shivering with need, Taffy's would-be response was swallowed by a furious blast of internal heat, and a child's frenzied screams.

"Miss Taffy!" Bus-driving Deacon Williams' grandson and namesake, Willie Ray, raced their way. The boy was panting, running hard, his words flinging across the night like knives. "Miss Taffy...Mr. Roam...Angel's stuck...and he's hurt...real bad!"

Heart constricting, Taffy's voice rattled. "Where?"

Bending over, clutching knees, Willie Ray gasped, "Bottom...of the ravine."

CHAPTER THIRTY-FIVE

Prostrate on his tummy, aching in head and hinny, Angel dripped big tears. "It hurts, NuNu."

"Pain works that way, Mr. Man. You traipse across a train trellis and tumble into a ravine you can't get yourself free of. Now you're feeling poorly," NuNu commiserated, expertly bathing Angel's injuries with a warm, medicinal concoction from the basin at her feet. "Gonna take a while, but we'll get all these briars and thorns out your bottom. You'll be right as rain come morning."

"Will I have to stay home from school?"

"You want to?"

"Yes, ma'am," Angel answered, sniffling.

NuNu's smile stretched wide. "Then you got the wrong one tending you, 'cause when I finish, this bottom'll be newborn pretty. But you gonna have to take these skivvies all the way off for me to dig out the rest of these brambles."

"*You gonna see all my business?*" Angel shrieked.

"Mr. Man, who you think helped keep your baby behind clean? You ain't got no business I ain't already seen."

"I'm not a baby no more, NuNu. Ladies can't be looking on men's nakedness." Angel wiped tears from his face, bristling.

"Angel, stop all that and lie down," Taffy ordered. She'd been quiet since their return, vacillating between anger, relief, and flashbacks of Angel at the bottom of that ravine.

Compliant, she'd waited aboveground, barely breathing, as Roam skidded down uneven earth. Angel, hurt and crying, was unsuccessfully trying to hop his way up treacherous terrain with the aid of friends not much bigger than he. Injury to his left leg prevented it from being weight-bearing. Hoisting Angel onto her back, Roam managed the incline, carrying him to her grandparents' at Taffy's request. The Place was closer than Dr. Blue's, and NuNu possessed knowledge medical annals had yet to see.

Now here they were, Angel sprawled face-down on his great-grandparents' bed, Taffy mixing a thick paste in a small bowl as NuNu tweezed debris from Angel's lacerations with surgical precision. "What happened to frog-catching? And why didn't those dungarees protect his backside?" Taffy vented, watching NuNu work.

"That ravine's steep, Little One. We oughta be thanking the Master we ain't crying over more."

Taffy conceded NuNu's point. Other than lacerations in varying degrees, a twisted and swollen ankle, multiple bruises and aching behind, Angel was intact.

"What *I* don't see is why this child was running across a train trellis in the first place," NuNu voiced.

"It was on a dare," Taffy supplied as Angel buried his face in a pillow. Bragging he could cross the trellis, Angel accepted a dare to prove a point. He was half-way across when the train sounded its approach. Panicked, Angel ran towards safety and fell.

"Now, that makes perfect sense seeing as how another somebody in here wrecked her Daddy's car driving behind a dare at the old age of twelve."

"Twelve?" Angel parroted, raising head and wiping tears. "You crashed PaPa's car, Taf?"

Taffy wore a stingy smile.

"Gon' and tell the child," NuNu instigated, continuing when Taffy kept quiet. "We've all fallen short of good sense and God's glory." Angel giggled. "But try crossing that trellis again and I'mma chop you to pieces and glue you together again. *Maybe.*"

Taffy laughed for the first time since Angel's fall. "NuNu."

Seeing Angel's dejected face, NuNu softened. "Alright." She dabbed Angel's back with a thick, dry cloth. "Let's get these undies off so I can see the true damage."

"No, NuNu," Angel wailed.

"Honey, we have to clean your bottom to avoid infection," Taffy explained, still stirring the paste NuNu instructed her to make.

"I don't want women looking at my man-ness," Angel blubbered. "Let Poppy or PaPa do it, *please...*"

"Fine, let the menfolk have at it," Taffy agreed.

"This new generation's some kind of crazy," NuNu muttered, exiting.

Poppy *and* PaPa lasted all of five seconds, Angel was hollering and cutting up so. "What's the problem?" NuNu demanded as she and Taffy returned in a rush.

Thaddeus chortled as Poppy sighed and confessed, "My hands and T.'s are too big and clumsy to get these thorns without hurting this boy more. One of y'all finish up."

"Who you want, Mr. Man?" NuNu asked.

"Taffy," Angel whimpered.

Taking the tweezers from her grandfather, Taffy sat beside the bed waiting while everyone exited before lifting the sheet shielding Angel's backside.

Cuts and thorns mingled with caked blood and bruises caused her breath to catch.

Lord, I do thank You it isn't more, Taffy praised before speaking soothingly. "I'll be gentle as I can, Angel Baby. Take this rag. Ball it up and bite on it when it hurts." Angel accepted the cloth, squeezing his eyes tight. "Enjoy the ballgame?" Taffy questioned, intentionally distracting Angel from pain.

"Yes."

"Like the way Cousin Hamp hit those runners in and won the day?"

"Didn't get to see it."

"Why not?"

Angel mumbled sheepishly. "I was over at the trellis."

"Well, you sure missed a good play."

"Mr. Roam plays good, too. Can you thank him for giving me a piggyback ride?"

"The thanks'll sound better coming from you."

"Yes, ma'am. Sorry for going off like that and getting hurt."

Taffy exhaled, upset with herself for getting caught up in personal pleasures. "Like NuNu, said we all fall short of good sense sometimes. But you won't do this again, will you?"

"No, ma'am, 'cause...*ouch*!" Angel yelped.

"Ooo, Honey, I'm sorry. That's a stubborn one." Defying progress, Taffy's grandparents kept their dwelling electricity-free. She was forced to work by lantern light. Using the antiseptic water NuNu prepared, Taffy cleaned Angel's buttocks before pulling the lantern closer. She laughed. "I'm plucking at your skin, thinking it's a thorn." Taffy leaned forward, questioning a triangular pattern of dark marks.

Angel glanced over his left shoulder, puzzled by Taffy's unawareness. "They're birthmarks, Taf."

"Baby, I know that, but you didn't have them—"

"M'Dear calls 'em 'latecomers.' She says some birthmarks don't show at birth. Some come later. Or maybe they're pale 'til they get their color down the line."

"True but…" Taffy pulled on recall hoping to understand what she saw only to come up empty. "You sure they're not old scars?"

"Nope."

Further questioning faded as The Gift intervened. *See what you know and know what you see.*

Yet, again, her Gift asked strenuous things. Taffy's senses felt opaque, cloudy. Sight wasn't easy. Perhaps as she lay alone in the quiet of night, revelation would uncover this hidden thing.

Mind itching with the concealed, Taffy finished her task. "I believe someone's briar-free."

"Yeah!" Angel celebrated, ready to scoot from the bed.

"Hold your horses, Bill Pickett. Let's put that sticky paste and a warm compress on, then have you drink some of NuNu's tea."

"*Ewww*! NuNu's teas taste like mud and mildew."

"I'll add a dash of sugar for the stomach's sake. You hungry?"

"Yes, ma'am."

"I'll bring you something to eat and then its bedtime."

"I'm staying here tonight?"

"Yes, Sweetie, I don't want you walking on that ankle, plus you need to stay on your stomach so the medicine can work on that hinny."

"Can you stay with me?"

"Why? You scared?" Taffy questioned, stroking Angel's head.

"No, but have you heard Poppy snore?"

"Ooo, yeah! Sounds like a cave of bears!" Angel giggled around a yawn. Taffy kissed his cheek. "Guess Willie Ray's not the only one needing a pillow—"

Taffy failed to finish for the commotion outside. Raised voices and rushing feet preceded the bedroom door flying open to reveal Rachel, nervous and wide-eyed. "Dear Father!" She dashed across the room, lifting the blanket from Angel's prone form, freezing when seeing his cloth-covered posterior. "Oh my, Lord. Angel, are you okay?"

Angel nodded as Taffy answered, "It may look worse than—"

"What in the world happened?!" Rachel whirled. "Wasn't Angel watching the game with everyone else? And weren't *you* watching Angel?"

"It's not Taffy's fault, M'Dear," Angel weakly mediated, unaccustomed to Rachel's ire. "I was supposed to be frog-catching but me and Willie Ray and—"

"Willie Ray and I," Rachel corrected, returning wrath towards Taffy. "This child could've been killed because of your shirking responsibility. *Again*! And why isn't Angel at Dr. Blue's? He needs proper treatment, not some backwoods...*hoodoo*!"

Taffy went rigid, ignoring one insult, focused on another. "Hoodoo, Mama?"

"Yes, hoodoo!" Rachel shrilled, hands flailing angrily. "Backwater, backwoods, heathenish hoodoo!" Uncensored, ancient wounds bubbled up like hot pus. "I *never* wanted you to be sighted. I wanted you to live like a normal child. But who am I to tell heaven—or whatever the source—to take it away?" Trauma warped Rachel into an unrecognizable being. "It wasn't enough that you were gifted; your Daddy went and put 'Octavia' on you, too. I did what I could to balance the scale with my 'Marie', but it was never enough. You always belonged to them!"

Voice quiet, controlled, Taffy struggled to find her mother beneath the livid façade. "I'm sorry you feel that way, Mama, but I don't regret my gifting. Knowing walked me through the dark parts of life when *you* didn't. But then again, you caused that darkness, didn't you?"

"I promised to set things right—"

"Mama, you're controlled by the dead. You can't free me until you free *you*!"

"Don't tell me my capabilities," Rachel stormed. "I have more strength than you think!"

"Fine, Mama. Free us all. Right here, right now—"

"Hush it up!" NuNu's six-foot frame filled the doorway, countenance thundering. "You two gonna reckon with each other yet, but it won't be here in front of that child!"

Mother and daughter silently regarded each other, gray eyes flaming, neither foolish enough to defy NuNu.

Ignoring Taffy, Rachel turned to Angel. "Look at these jeans," she sighed, picking up pants that were cut from his body to spare unnecessary pain. "Let's get you home."

"I don't think he should be moved," Taffy began but her mother cut her short.

"I didn't solicit your opinion, *Octavia*. Angel's coming home where he belongs."

"Rachel, let that boy rest the night," NuNu commanded. "I understand this child's hurting himself has y'all in a tizzy, but Rachel, you sounding too much like Lacy to be welcome here right now. Gon' home and collect yourself."

Rachel looked from NuNu to her daughter. Dark shadows played across Taffy's face. Her eyes were devoid of mercy.

Rachel wilted, barely managing, "I'll come for him in the morning."

CHAPTER THIRTY-SIX

Imogene made strong coffee. Sipping quietly, she suffered Rachel's sorrow until she'd had enough sniveling. "You made a choice, honey. Now you choosing differently?"

Rachel dabbed red-rimmed eyes. "What else can I do, Cousin?"

"What you been doing: living without apology."

Rachel shook her head, fresh tears flowing. "It's wrong now. It was wrong then."

Imogene leaned forward in her seat. "Taffy did what Taffy did—"

"You know that's not so!"

"She chose Freeman," Imogene continued, undeterred.

"*We* chose Alfredo because 'bastard-bearing' was unthinkable in Mother's legacy and line. We forced Taffy to say 'I do', when she never did! She was barely sixteen!"

"That's old enough to know! Weren't you married at that age, Rachel Marie? Wasn't your Mama? I'd had multiple lifetimes by then, so I can't put pity on it." Emphasizing each word with a tap against the tabletop, Imogene insisted, "Taffy was old enough to know." Watching Rachel wrestling with conscience, Imogene was momentarily shaken by the strange resistance flickering across Rachel's face.

Lacy had been her most cherished kin. The affection she had for Lacy, Imogene passed onto Rachel, loving Rachel like her own. But she'd be damned if she'd sit and watch Rachel discard Lacy's gains.

Imogene's tone overflowed with sarcasm. "Whatchu wanna do, Rachel, tell the pa?" Rachel was instantly malleable. Taking advantage of her silence, Imogene wiped the guilty pages of Rachel's mind. "We ain't walking this road no more. Your mama worked too hard to get you a good life. So keep it! Tighten yourself up—"

"Taffy's my daughter, Cousin," Rachel softly implored. "You'd do the same for your child."

"I *did* the same! Married some no 'count when I wasn't ready to quit living," Imogene hotly recounted. "Was in a family way one day and hitched up the next. Should've kept walking when he started talking love. What I need with some nigga's notions about loving me?" Imogene sighed heavily. "But there ain't no going back and examining options all over again."

Rachel long ago learned to turn a deaf ear on Imogene's tirades against Rayford—a hardworking and honest man. Never could understand Imogene's aversion. But hearing Imogene now, Rachel detected a desolation unheard before. Rachel placed a gentle hand on Imogene's arm. "You have regrets, as do I, but I intend to right my wrongs."

Sadness fled. Imogene flared. "You doing it over my dust and bones. I won't watch you wreck what your Mama built! You don't know the half of what that woman did for you, Rachel, but you gonna appreciate her. You hear?"

"I'm very appreciative but—"

"*But dick*! Lacy stayed on, helping her parents sharecrop, despite winning a scholarship to that fancy Colored girls' college. Did you know that?"

"Yes, ma'am," Rachel dutifully replied, "Oberlin."

"Yeah, that! Lacy's parents fell down deeper into debt every passing year. Still she did right by them. Do right by yours. Your daddy licked all kinda white ass getting that school superintendent position, so he could set your mama up in a pretty house and keep her the way she deserved to be kept. She was refined. Good. And she poured all that refined goodness into you, and you gonna keep it and not make a mockery of my cousin's memory. Act like you got good uncommon sense and leave yesterday alone. Ain't gonna be no 'mends made if that constitutes upsetting Lacy's soul. I mean it, Rachel! Test me and see."

Rachel clutched at strength, yet she felt herself deflating. They'd always held power to puncture her will, these matriarchs of her line. Rachel hated her spinelessness, but she'd yet to find strength to refuse their whims. Besides, she understood to bury lies was to excavate truth, and truth would leave Rachel shackle-bound. So, capitulating, Rachel let Cousin Imogene lead in Lacy's absence.

Rachel sighed. Her mother had meant well, wanting Rachel to have the finery Lacy'd lost. Father dead, mother remarried to a sharecropper, Lacy had little. Marrying a successful educator, she pulled herself up from penury and crowned herself a lady, bestowing lady-ship on her child. She'd designated Rachel a refined young Colored woman of class and distinction. Rachel spoke a language other than English. Graduated college Up North. Used jelly jars for jelly, not juice. All at Lacy's insistence.

I was her marionette, Rachel admitted. Propped and placed. A controlled, decorated trophy. She preferred cello, but played violin, because no child of Lacy's would 'sit legs gapped, something stuck in between'. *Sit straight…lift your chin…enunciate when speaking…smile politely despite a fool's being in your face…*and direly important…*don't marry a dark man.*

Told what to wear, who to befriend, how to live, Rachel obeyed Lacy's every command except the last. Rachel chose who to love.

> *She hadn't meant to spy.*
> *Fifteen and fanciful, Rachel ran to Lake Forest—the usual meeting place with her like-a-sister friend, Corrine—where they'd swap secrets while gorging on pickings from the berry bushes in a most unladylike way.*
> *Rachel arrived first that day, bubbling to tell Corrine that Henry Haynes kissed her behind the schoolhouse. But sighting a fully-grown man swimming in the lake Rachel forgot every other male God ever made when Thaddeus Bledsoe came up for air in the shallows, clothed only in skin, sable-deep and opulent.*
> *Shaken, Rachel didn't stop running until reaching the safety of her room, where she fell on her knees begging God's forgiveness for her indecency—for wanting to know the texture, taste, and weight of that grown man's nudity.*

Well-bred ladies despise wifely transactions. Simply do what the Lord's required.

So her mother incessantly preached until a psalm-like litany.

The Lord is my shepherd; your duty only do…

Mother-be-damned, Rachel entered her marriage bed hungry for the pleasure that long-ago glimpse of Thaddeus Bledsoe foretold. Thaddeus, Rachel's fantasy, became her defining act of defiance.

Lacy was outraged.

Their shy and sheltered child—with her proud father and quasi-white mother—was earmarked for greatness. Superintendent Marchand was a dignified man making a good enough living so that, while many Colored women worked in white folks' homes, Lacy Marchand tended her own—

too proud to work for the pale folks she resembled. It was that dangerously inflated glory of pale skin that made Lacy declare Thaddeus Bledsoe unfit for her precious cream-and-honey-colored child.

"He's too black!" *Lacy unapologetically objected when her husband named the man interested in "keeping company" with their daughter.* "You can't find Thaddeus Bledsoe on a moonless night unless he smiles. My child's not mixing tar in her tan."

Rachel deserved a man of impeccable social standing, reasonable wealth and bright skin. Bledsoes were the wealthiest family in town, but they were the darkest, too.

Dark, backward, land-tillers. No socialites hosting china-cupped tea parties, pinkies extended. They were unpretentious, earthy people calling Rachel's violin a 'fiddle' and consuming fried fish eggs as if caviar. When Thaddeus' intentions were proclaimed, those "simple" Bledsoes opened pure hearts as if Rachel was their own.

Lacy tried maneuvering Rachel into the dry arms of a middle-aged, stone-eyed, wealthy widower in nearby Winter Cove. Rachel rebelled, refusing to eat, plotted worse if her mother denied her her dream.

"But he's ten years Rachel's senior," *Lacy Marchand lamented, conveniently forgetting she was a topsy-turvy four years older than Superintendent Marchand.*

In the end, the lure of Bledsoe bankroll reduced Lacy's blatant hostility to minor disdain. Blood connections to the founding family could be a prestigious feather in Lacy's social-climbing cap. Pride salvaged, Lacy focused on making Rachel's wedding the finest thing in Progress County. Even more than Lacy's winning a scholarship to Oberlin College and marrying an educated, fair-skinned, "good"-haired man, an end-all-be-all wedding would boost Lacy's reign in Bledsoe society. Lacy was appeased.

It was Rachel's fiercest, most important battle won. Thaddeus was her prize. Yet Rachel had abdicated her maternal role, sacrificing their child on the altar of Lacy's obsessions.

Didn't fight then, have no ground to stand on now. She surrendered with a sigh.

Satisfied that Rachel was once more under control, Imogene refreshed their coffee before slicing layer cake kept fresh beneath a glass dome and sold a dime a slice. Cake served, Imogene glanced about her dimly lit store. Indeed, they'd worked too hard for Rachel to upset progress. Still, Imogene could afford generosity.

"Dry your eyes, Baby." She patted Rachel's cheeks. "Fix your face and gon' home. Everything'll be alright." Imogene made a silent promise. *Lacy, on my life it will be!*

After wrapping Rachel's strange purchase and listing it on her account, Imogene doused the lights and returned to her house in back of the store to check on her child.

R.J. slept soundly, calico kitten a furry ball against his head. No need to check on Rayford. Buzzsaw snoring signaled his slumber. Still, Imogene did what she did quietly.

Lifting floorboards, she retrieved a box wrapped in burlap. Its interior was musty, relics and memories. Outdated Smith & Wesson. Brown bottle of liquid death. A money-stuffed envelope and telephone numbers rarely used.

She found Mr. Hill...

"*Mister?*" Imogene laughed. More like high-toned slickster and two-bit gangster hustling one step ahead of the law. But he could reach Dempsey. Despite the lie, Imogene knew Dempsey had broken off with Big Baby long ago. His mama couldn't find him, but Hill could. Hill used men like Dempsey to do his business while keeping his hands clean. Imogene found no fault. Sometimes you had to transfer your sins in order to live.

Imogene thumbed the envelope holding upwards of eight-hundred dollars. Money apportioned for Alfredo's monthly stipend kept the man quiet and in comfort. But Rachel was coming apart at the seams and Imogene needed to put said money to better use.

Dempsey was greedy, would probably empty that envelope and want more. Thankfully, Lacy had left an account in Imogene's name over at Richland Bank, where xenophobic white folks accepted Colored cash.

Imogene placed the call.

Hill was too big a man to bother with Imogene, despite familiarity. A lackey served as mouthpiece. Dempsey was somewhere down south near some place called Bloodsow.

"Bledsoe?" Imogene suggested.

"Yeah...that. Been there a long minute, plans to stay a few more." Slowly, Imogene disconnected.

He'd sat with her yesterday morning, claiming he'd only stopped for a quick visit instead of sitting in Richland's depot, waiting for a connecting train. But he'd *been* in Bledsoe and was still holed up near here? Why? And for whom?

Dempsey. Posted up in a place he called 'the crust 'tween God's toes'? Because of Hill? Or was Dempsey's business his own?

She sat, mulling, straining. Then one name came. *Alfredo.* Dempsey was Imogene's kin. But Alfredo was his kind. Mercenary. Ruthless. Anything for money. Alfredo needed Dempsey? Why?

Their last conversation came to mind. He'd wanted Dempsey's contact. Imogene lied, claiming she didn't have it. Obviously, Alfredo found it. Why?

Because she'd refused further extortion. The amount she gave was the amount he'd get. But he demanded more. He was sick of sacrificing, giving his name in exchange for...

One frigid wife too many. Eyes wide, mouth dropped, Imogene sat disbelieving. Would he really?

She cackled a rusty laugh. "Well, oh well, oh my." Dempsey was deadly and working on Alfredo's dime? Bless God, Imogene wouldn't have to cash-out for risk removal after all.

She'd decided the gal was back for no good, could cause the kingdom to crumble beneath her lies. Wasn't much to prevent Taffy's blabbing in Lacy's absence. She deserved to be removed. That husband, too. Maliciousness of mind went into overdrive.

Alfredo knew too much. Was as much threat as Taffy. Imogene had tired of him, palm out, collecting income unearned. He was bad as Madame. And Madame had been monstrous...

Eleven was old enough to know she'd been offered up. I'll be back for you, Mama lied, tucking Madame's greenbacks in the security of her one-and-only brassiere. Pecking little Imogene's forehead in a final farewell, Mama boarded her lover's waiting wagon and faced forward, ignoring Imogene's wailing on the doorstep of the ramshackle brothel that became home.

Maid to broke-down whores dispensing pleasure for pennies, Imogene spent a year as apprentice relegated to musty shadows, learning, until Madame deemed Little Imogene ready to recoup her investment. She was repeatedly beaten for refusing. Overriding the child's terror at the prospect of a man riding her pubescent body like a bull, Madame first rented Little Imogene to an itinerant preacher in route to revival. The un-right

Reverend Odysseus Jenkins defiled innocence, leaving Imogene a victim of flesh dead to the wonders of love.

    Ten years Imogene lay on her back for Madame's benefit, accumulating scars of bamboo beatings. Debt paid-in-full, Imogene vanished after serving Madame a drink to remember. Searching out Cousin Lacy, Imogene found refuge, if not redemption. But seeking salvation one night in the arms of God, Imogene encountered revival-running Odysseus Jenkins sweating in the pulpit, that same bull that broke her temple. Benediction said, she trailed him down a dark boardinghouse road. He was found next morning propped atop the porch, green about the gills. Dead eyes as wide as the sharecropping stepfather's who was served deep tea for prohibiting Lacy's accepting her college scholarship because the fields had needs. After Jenkins, Imogene and Lacy left town and corpse behind.

    Imogene faulted others for her deficits. Mama. Madame. Reverend Jenkins. Customers renting her bodily wares before turning to hearth and home, because she couldn't hold a man once pleasure passed. Too viperous in spirit, like the world had done her wrong. And it had. But what did men care that she'd acquired boudoir skills and an acidic disposition in the house of ill-repute her mama sold her to?

    Rayford cared. He held her as Imogene shed memory's tears. She told him her story because his open face indicated he was without secrets and had room enough for hers. She married him for his cleansing, quiet affection. But unaccustomed to gentleness, Imogene deemed him weak, deriving a sense of power believing she'd made him that way. But that was the worthless past.

    They'd come too far, seen and done too much, to allow Rachel's hussy and that husband to ruin it all. "This is Lacy's inheritance," Imogene growled, fingering the cash-stuffed envelope. "Proof she was her Pa's."

    Gently handling the brown bottle, Imogene rehearsed Lacy's lessons of how to rid herself of unwanted things. Would Dempsey mind killing two birds with one stone?

    She'd have to pay. Imogene could. And gladly would.

CHAPTER THIRTY-SEVEN

She fetched Angel the next day, meekness restored, tongue in proper place, and a peace offering in the crook of her arm. "Good morning."

Taffy and Angel paused their conversation, finding Rachel at the open door. Both looked on silent and uncertain.

Rachel approached the rough-hewn table Poppy made, where Angel and Taffy sat breakfasting. "How're you feeling, Sweetheart?"

"My ankle doesn't hurt no more...I mean *any*more but my hinny still does." Angel pointed out the pillow beneath his bottom.

Rachel ruffled his hair and offered the unthinkable. "You might need to stay home today."

Angel beamed like a morning star. "Can I?"

"A full day's recuperation's probably best. I'll go by the schoolhouse and discuss assignments with Ms. Statum so you don't fall behind."

Angel dimmed slightly. "Can I skip math?"

"Yes, if you don't mind being ignorant."

"I don't."

Snickering, Taffy turned her attention to her plate.

"I do, so we'll finish math first," Rachel instructed.

"Yes, ma'am." Scooping up the last of his breakfast, Angel scooted from his chair. "I'mma go help Poppy and NuNu de-worm the tomato plants."

"Worms?" Rachel feigned disgust. "Oh my!"

"If I collect a whole bunch maybe Papa'll take me fishing," Angel excitedly decided, heading towards the door.

"Angel." He turned at the sound of Taffy's voice. "Did you clear your place?"

"Oops." Angel hobbled back to the table as fast as his wrapped ankle allowed, stopping to hug Rachel. "Thanks for giving me the day off, M'Dear. Men need rest after injuries."

Rachel's musical laughter filled the room as she watched him go. "That boy," she muttered, turning attention on the room's remaining occupant. "Alfredo was Mother's choice not mine."

Taffy sat in silence, shocked at her mother's sudden plunge into the murky pool of their past. "Doesn't matter whose choice he was, Mama, the end result's the same."

"I didn't want you stigmatized. A husband was best," Rachel insisted.

"I had better."

"Baby, a wounded man never understands no matter how much you explain. Besides, your way would've left you alone with a newborn weeks on end. Porters' wives live with loneliness, and loneliness leads to no good. You would've been vulnerable with a husband away from home for such long stretches. Other men would've wanted your company and persuaded you to break your vows. Once vows are broken…"

Eyes glittering dangerously, Taffy was sickened by Rachel's warped reconstruction. Yet finally, completely, Taffy understood. "Is *that* the story you've written for yourself, Mama?"

"I spared your reputation—"

"No, ma'am, you didn't. Ostracism happened just the same. Friends were pulled. Men looked at me like something they regretted not tasting. I wasn't spared a thing."

Rachel sat in the chair Angel abandoned. "Mother told me to get you married right away, but I didn't share her viewpoint until too late, until after Angel was already weeks old. I'm sorry I waited and you experienced such backlash."

"I'm sorry, too," Taffy agreed, leaving table for the open window where she could breathe.

Rachel watched her daughter mere steps away, knowing the distance between them couldn't be measured in feet. "Taffy, honey, we did what was best."

"*For whom?*" Taffy shrilled. "I complied with *every* demand. I vowed silence on my life, still you put Alfredo on me. *Why?!*"

Rachel couldn't answer. "Your Daddy asked me to tell you he'll hold off going to Winter Cove until tomorrow so you can tend Angel today. You have business there?"

Taffy didn't respond.

Sighing, Rachel removed the package tucked beneath her arm and placed it atop the table. "I trust it fits. If it doesn't we'll exchange for one that does." The tremor in Rachel's voice contradicted her apparent calm. Nervously, she sat in anxious anticipation.

Eyeing the brown paper-wrapped parcel tied with hope, Taffy wondered when Rachel had learned to beg love. Disinclined to accept the paper-wrapped olive branch, Taffy forced herself not to scream insults for every injury, to act charitably. Woodenly, Taffy opened the parcel. Peeling back paper, Taffy stared.

"I noticed you didn't have one," Rachel rushed. "I thought it might help."

Speechless, Taffy could only emit a feral laugh that caused Rachel to cringe.

Taffy pushed the parcel back across the table. "It's too little, too late, Mama. You can't bind me." Taffy left before saying or doing a regrettable thing.

Rachel sat gingerly fingering the gift purchased last night at Cousin Imogene's: a girdle…designed to bind, constrain and contain.

Already there were whispers. It was inevitable, still Rachel feared it happening. And it had the moment Taffy and Roam both landed back in Bledsoe. Town folks resurrected speculations and dusted off rumors. She didn't want her daughter cast about by crooked tongues. More importantly, Rachel couldn't let dead things rise. She thought to call Alfredo. His presence would dispel gossip and shift focus, keeping folks from looking too closely. Perhaps he'd come to their rescue. A second time.

⌘

"You sure this is what you need to do?"

Taffy looked away from the office building to her father seated on the driver's side. "Daddy, it's my only hope."

"He's given just cause?"

Taffy mentally scrolled a list of nameless consorts, liquored-up nights and brothel support; years of verbal barrages and the vindictive cruelty that sent Angel home. She thought of Miss Truly Earl's girls and resolve thickened. "More than enough."

Thaddeus studied his child. "Sure you don't want me to sit with you?" His pride rose at Taffy's decline. "I'll go handle my affairs and be back for you in an hour. Walk cautiously, Taffy Sweet."

Attorneys Augustine Bledsoe and Harold Jenkins once formed an alliance, providing legal services to Colored citizens in the tri-towns of Bledsoe, Winter Cove and Drexel. With Uncle Auggie's passing, Mr. Jenkins became lead esquire, maintaining a thriving practice in Winter Cove. He was welcoming, affording Taffy extra consideration in light of her relation to his deceased comrade. Yet, he couldn't extend legal help. Wrong jurisdiction aside, he was of an opposing opinion.

Alfredo's immorality notwithstanding, Taffy should maintain her marriage. No physical abuse. No absence of resources or denying a proper welfare. She had clothes, food, shelter, and had taken sacred vows. Not to mention a child had already been removed from the home because of her alleged shortcomings. She could lose him permanently if Mr. Freeman countered. Perhaps she should focus on restoring her family.

Dispassionately, Harold Jenkins listened as the young lady persisted. He questioned her motives. Why so resolute? Had she alienated her affection and involved herself elsewhere? When his questions remained unanswered, Harold Jenkins apologized, but Taffy Bledsoe Freeman would need to seek legal counsel elsewhere.

～

Riding his favorite stallion, Drew made his rounds about the ranch, mind roiling with vicious rumors. He'd heard most before, back when Angel was born, but new sins joined the brew. So he went in search of Roam.

Bent over his task, Roam heard the soft clod of hoofs coming up behind. Glancing back, Roam found Drew astride that chestnut stallion he loved. "'Ey!" Roam called, busy securing new fence posts on Bledsoe land.

"You still ain't finished?"

Amused, Roam wiped sweat from his neck. He'd been at the mile-long fence since daybreak, removing decayed posts, reaffixing new. "Who's working and whose lazy ass is riding?"

"Overseer has its privileges," Drew jested.

"Been slaving for y'all since we were kids. No use stopping now,"

Roam boomeranged, task resumed. "Just make sure I have my pay come Friday."

"You will," Drew chuckled, sobering instantly. "Need to talk to you." He looked down the line ensuring the nearest workman was well beyond earshot. "Folks got you and Taffy on the tongue, and stories are circulating. They're saying Angel's not Freeman's. He's yours. Know anything about that?"

Like one stunned, Roam was slow in rising from his crouched position. Fully erect, he was even slower in turning Drew's way. Face reflecting the blunt impact of Drew's disclosure, Roam looked like a man who'd been sucker-punched and was set to fall.

CHAPTER THIRTY-EIGHT

Angel had enjoyed playing patient. Thanks to NuNu's healing ways, his hind parts recovered nicely. Still Angel milked his role yesterday, enjoying being waited on and indulged while missing school. Come Monday night, Angel was bored and ready to return. But when Tuesday afternoon rolled around, Angel couldn't wait to jump off the school bus wanting to see his best friend never again.

Taffy leaned against a tree, awaiting Angel's return. Denied the legal aid she needed, Taffy was despondent, wondering if heaven had aligned against her. She didn't want to be contrary, but if forced to, could Taffy defy the divine and take matters into her own hands? Perhaps, she'd already done too much. Leaving abruptly. Purchasing a round trip ticket to Bledsoe just to throw Alfredo off, falsely indicating her return after Founders' Festival next week. Once Alfredo realized she'd gone, he'd find the series of twisted clues Taffy left, multiple cities. After chasing rabbit trails, if ever Chicago surfaced in his mind, Taffy would be well-armed and ready to face his fury...if she could only decipher Greenville and whatever scandalous shadows Alfredo had left behind. Greenville was her leverage. It held power to make Alfredo cave. But its meaning remained opaque. Even so, Taffy couldn't stay. Harold Jenkins wasn't God's only attorney on earth.

Mind searching other remedies, Taffy mechanically waved as the bus stopped with a *whoosh* yards from where Taffy waited. Door opening, she was greeted by Deacon Williams' somber face.

"Sister Taffy, there was a bit of trouble on the way home. Had to break them boys apart, they was scrapping so, but don't you worry. I'mma rip Willie Ray's behind soon's I get 'im home." Deacon Williams sighed wearily. "Just thought you should know."

Taffy watched Angel hurry towards the door, sulking and bleeding. "Angel?" He raced down the steps, ignoring her. Taffy reached for him but, yanking free, Angel took off running.

"Sorry 'bout all this, Sister Taffy, but like I said I'mma deal with my grandson. Y'all enjoy the day."

Taffy rushed to catch up with Angel's hard pace. "Angel, what happened?" The child studied the ground, walking fast, blood beneath his nose. "Angel?" When he refused to answer, Taffy restrained him.

"Let go of me!"

"Angel Baby, what's going on?"

"I'm not your baby. I'm not *anybody's* baby!"

"Fine. Talk to me, young man. *What happened?*"

His eyes were filled with fury, but beneath the venom was a child's pain. "Willie Ray and I had a fight."

"Over?"

Angel studied the ground, chest heaving, eyes aflame, sulking until barking, "You!" Taffy held her tongue and let Angel find his way. "Our friends made a big deal 'bout me running 'cross the trellis and I guess Willie Ray got tired of the attention I was getting on account it kept us from playing." Angel took a deep breath like he'd run out of air. "He's just jealous 'cause I was braver than him. He coulda run 'cross too but he chickened out. So on the way home he said I sounded like a broke record needing a new tune. Told him at least I had a tune to play, and all he could do was cluck like the scaredy-butt-baby he was."

Taffy held her tongue. Now was not the time to chastise.

"Willie Ray got mad when the kids laughed, and said 'at least my Mama don't let men feel her up'. I told that slewfoot lie to take it back! But he said he saw you. Said when he went running for help after I fell, you and Mr. Roam were hugged up kissing," Angel paused, tears and shame tainting beautiful eyes, "and that Mr. Roam was feeling up under your personals, so I punched him. Deacon Williams stopped the bus and broke it up. I quit fighting, but Willie Ray kept talking flip."

"Saying?" Taffy softly inquired.

Angel looked away as stored-up tears trickled down chocolate cheeks. "'At least I know my real daddy, and my mama ain't no whore!'"

Dear Lord, do deliver...

Taffy reached for Angel standing stiff and resistant. "Honey, I'm sorry you encountered that." Angel tried to shake her off, but Taffy held on. "Come on, Sweetie." Unwillingly, Angel let himself be held. "It's okay," Taffy soothed. His shoulders slumped and he cried in Taffy's arms. She stroked his head, rocking gently until Angel's sobs subsided.

"I don't know what a whore is, but Willie Ray made it sound *real* bad," Angel sniffled. "And I don't think you're bad, Taffy, 'cept when you leave me behind. How come you never take me with you?"

Taffy cradled Angel's face and stared into wet eyes. "Honey, we've talked this out before—"

"Still don't make sense!" Angel wailed. "You want me down here so I can have family and not be running big city streets while you're sewing and working, but I can take care of myself. I like it when you let me visit, Taffy! I wanna be with you."

"Angel Baby—"

He cut her off again. "You're like Mr. Al. You don't want me!"

Taffy's heart crumbled. "Honey, I love you more than life. Shhh, and listen," Taffy interjected, preventing Angel's ready response. Ignoring caution, she took a chance. "When I leave this time, you're coming with me. For good."

Angel's eyes narrowed. "For real?" Taffy nodded. Angel returned her gaze. "But Mr. Al won't want me there."

"We're going to Chicago, not back to Alfredo—" Angel interrupted, happily whooping until Taffy quieted him with, "That's between us. No running off at the mouth, understand?"

Angel happily nodded before firing suddenly, "Is Mr. Roam my daddy?"

Windless and reeling, Taffy stalled, wiping a lingering tear from Angel's chin. "Where'd you get that notion?"

Angel shrugged. "Willie Ray said Mr. Al's not my pa, Mr. Roam is. Is he?"

"You tell Willie Ray grown folks' business ain't none of his."

"But it's my business, right?" Angel's voice was desperate, aching.

Taffy bent so they were eye-to-eye. "Remember how we talked about adults saying things children shouldn't? Well, adults often do things they don't want children doing, and know things children can't."

"Is that a 'yes' or a 'no'?"

"That's enough, Angel."

"But, Taffy—"

"Baby boy, it's not the answer you deserve, but right now it's all I'm offering."

"That's not fair! You're treating me like a baby. I hate being a kid."

"Oh, come now, that's not true—"

"Yes, it is," Angel insisted.

"Well…I guess we'd best get you a job so you can be a man. You wanna work on the ranch with Papa and Drew, or at the lumber mill over in Drexel, or one of the factories Up North? You could be a carpenter or painter since you're good with your hands, or a politician because you talk so nice. How about a dentist, so folks can have pretty teeth like yours? Which do you prefer?" Angel scowled to keep from smiling. "And if you're gonna be a man, best throw away your toys and get a driver's license, a registered voter card, a house, a wife—"

"Girls are giggly and silly-looking and stink like flowers," Angel protested, pouting as Taffy laughed. Noting his blood marring her blouse, Angel apologized. "Sorry I messed up your shirt."

"Baby, that's nothing but a little life. And like NuNu says, it'll all come out in the wash," Taffy soothed, examining Angel's nose for damage. "Little boy, you're keeping me on my toes falling down hills and getting into fights." Shamefaced, Angel grinned. "Let's get you home and get us both cleaned up."

"Okay," Angel quietly agreed. They walked in silence, a silence broken by Angel's admission. "Taf, I like Mr. Roam, so if he is my real pa that's okay by me."

Refusing comment, Taffy took Angel's hand and headed home, conceding providence had moved matters beyond her control. Unnerved, Taffy knew truth and lies were surfacing, ready to come out in the wash sooner than soon.

Home was in sight when their paths intersected. His stride was predatory as he stalked their way. His thunderous expression altered only on seeing bloodstains.

"Hi, Mr. Roam!" Angel moved towards him until a sudden shyness stemming from his recent, wistful admission caused him to hesitate.

Roam approached, frowning at Angel's soiled shirt. "You been scrapping, Little Man?" Angel nodded. "Your blood or the other guy's?"

"Mine, but come morning Willie Ray's eye'll be black."

"Guess that evens the score," Roam offhandedly remarked, intently scrutinizing Angel. "What was the fight about?"

"Angel Baby, gon' home and have M'Dear fix an icepack for your nose," Taffy intercepted.

Angel reluctantly obeyed. Roam watched him double-time, trekking Angel until out of sight.

Taffy waited, discerning a near-violent simmer beneath Roam's surface. She made herself ready. Even so, the look he levied sent needles over her skin.

"You know why I'm here?"

"I have an inkling," Taffy confessed, realizing Willie Ray had merely repeated adult conversation. In a small town, rumors moved rapidly.

"You wanna tell me without my pulling it from you?"

Taffy couldn't fix an answer for watching a gradual manifestation of gossamer hands. Earth-brown fingers transparent as whispers covered Roam's heart and head, anointing and appointing Roam a chalice into which to pour all things. *This one needs to know.* Knowing's voice, like her appearing, was delicate yet undeniable. Still Taffy declined.

"Any answer I give won't satisfy," Taffy stated, praying Roam granted grace to share the whole in measured doses, doling out truth as smoothly as time allowed. "Whatever I did, it was for him."

"What precisely *did* you do?

"What I needed —"

"Let me ask you a question, and don't feed me the same damn half-cooked fairytales you've fed that child," Roam interrupted, voice a dangerous rumble. "Are you married to Angel's father?" A galloping pulse was Taffy's only reply. Roam inhaled a slow, calming breath before speculating, "You're leaving Freeman partly because Angel's not his. And Freeman knows. Am I right?"

Taffy nodded stiffly. The air between them thickened. Despite wanting to escape his ire, Taffy stood her ground. "Roam, I promised you'd know everything, and you will." Want and need hovered light and shapeless about him. She wanted to touch it, him. "The rest will come. Please, just give me time to—"

"Told you time is something I don't waste."

Taffy's voice acquired an otherworldly timbre, leaving Roam with the impression she addressed someone beyond his naked eye. "I won't do this here and now. Too many ghosts."

"You *won't?*" Roam growled, aware that Taffy's strangeness might be on her, and she'd gone somewhere he couldn't. "Or you can't? 'Won't' means you're mulish. 'Can't' means you've had more men than you can name. Which one should I believe?"

Taffy shivered. "Whichever you will."

Stuffing hands in pockets, Roam walked a short distance to spew hot air at the sun. Anything to avoid strangling her. At her approach, Roam shook off Taffy's gentle touch, "You'd do best to stay off me."

Hand falling stone-like at her side, Taffy stood quietly. "I didn't have power. Was too young to know front from back, but his survival was in my hands," she nearly whispered, as memory of Angel's birth—feet first, swimming an ocean of blood—soaked her mind. "I did what they dictated; still they took him from me..." Wedged between yesterday and today, Taffy couldn't evade memory. "And I let them. I stayed in a wrong place for right reasons."

Roam towered over her, wanting Taffy to remain in the here and now and stop trudging backward through time. "*Dammit, Taffy!* You saying a whole lot of nothing!" Roam bellowed, lost on Taffy's rollercoaster of recollection.

Taffy pushed away from yesterday into the nakedness of Roam's rage. "I let them," she repeated, heart breaking as heavy silence sloshed between them, pregnant with unshed history.

He grabbed her, shattering the silence. "*Who the hell is Angel's father*?!"

Taffy's sensation was that of falling. Roam was pulling, pressing, when she'd vowed silence on Angel's life. Her response would seem senseless. Still it was all Taffy had. "I'm not what you think I am, and I haven't done what you think I have."

Releasing her gruffly, Roam avoided Taffy's words so like scattered dissonance and broken glass. Taffy grasped for him. "Roam, Sweetness, *please*...not here...once we're gone..."

Flinging off her hands, abject disgust distorting his features, Roam stalked away—heart lacerated—beyond mercy and impervious to Taffy's crying his name.

CHAPTER THIRTY-NINE

Nightmares returned. Intense, detailed and disorienting. In a smoky room surrounded by women in white, she brought a child into the world, unaided and isolated. Blood thick in nostrils and on hands. Blood and pain and life fading with every grunt and rip. A man. Enemy. Hungry for soul. Waiting in the wings of her demise. A girl twirling. Smiling. Wrapped in blankets weighted by bricks and water. Dying...

Drenched in sweat and fear, Taffy flung herself awake. Fumbling with the bedside lamp, mind abused, she stumbled from bed to the middle of the floor as dream demons receded to the corners of the room. Yet, her head whirled with bloodied sleep and an assailant unseen.

She staggered to the chifforobe, unceremoniously cramming belongings into her luggage before descending backstairs like a thief in the night. Needing to alert Cousin Gracie that they were in route, she turned towards the telephone tucked in the hallway niche only to freeze.

He filled the parlor doorway, menacing in the shadows of first light. Eying her luggage, the hastily donned attire, he knew. In three strides he confronted her where she stood. Furious, he glowered at her premeditated desertion, this slinking away before daylight. Incensed, Alfredo Freeman hauled back and savagely struck his wife.

CHAPTER FORTY

Thaddeus put him out and saved Alfredo's life.

A ruckus hastening his morning descent, Thaddeus found Al Freeman backed into a corner, Rachel's letter opener piercing his throat. His daughter's hand shook with fury, but her aim was true, like Taffy meant to open Alfredo and read his insides.

"You wanna be your own customer?!" she snarled.

"*Taffy!*" Thaddeus reached Taffy before murder and mayhem could.

Grabbing the letter opener, Thaddeus pulled his child away as Rachel joined the melee, wrapped in a robe. The bright, angry patch marring Taffy's jaw answered Rachel's frantic queries. Freeman had laid a violent hand on their child.

Thaddeus' hands were full keeping Taffy from assaulting Alfredo as Rachel pushed the offender towards the door.

"That red nigga don't want you!" Refusing to leave silently, Alfredo paved his way with poison. "He got ghost quick-as-you-can." Taffy loathed the delight on Alfredo's face. He was too pleased telling how he'd exited one end of the morning express while Roam boarded the opposite. "Guess he got sense enough to know you can't please a man." Alfredo wiped his wounded neck. "Sorry, Miss Rachel, but I cain't help this time. I've had enough of your broken daughter! I'm through!"

Denying Alfredo the satisfaction of victory, Taffy waited for Alfredo to obey her father's profane demands to leave before crumbling. She didn't care that her mother had obviously summoned him. Taffy was too consumed by a need to know if Alfredo spoke truth. Was Roam gone?

Chloe didn't know a thing. Drew wouldn't or couldn't offer insight other than the location of his rooming house back East. First

Lady Ellis, sorrow making her less effusive than before, declined to inform, and the rooming house owner proved unknowledgeable. Drained of hope, Taffy choked on bitter consequences.

Life tumbled. A morose fog wouldn't lift.

She stumbled through her days, face brave when folks looked at her cross-eyed as she walked through whispers tying Roam to Angel, and Taffy to hell. She struggled for Angel's sake, hauling up vaporous smiles and a semblance of normalcy. Taffy's veneer collapsed when alone; she submitted to misery.

Alfredo camped out at Imogene's, multiplying Taffy's melancholy. He watched like a hawk from a distance—predacious, plotting. Taffy was forsaken, lover long gone. The physical extent of their affair was of no concern. Consummated or not, Taffy's heart had sufficiently sinned. Patiently, Alfredo awaited holy reckoning.

Her patience was imperfect, her hope utterly deferred. Couldn't escape prying eyes. Rachel. Alfredo. Watching, hindering. How and when could she leave? Hope was out-of-reach, and rebellion left Taffy reaping a pathetic return.

I was blatantly disobedient, Taffy repented, propped against that stump-of-a-plum tree, sketch pad in hand, absentmindedly doodling. She'd tried not to lay a hurricane at Roam's feet, but hindsight exposed her motives too clearly.

She'd tried keeping sweetness between them at all costs, no matter Roam's right to know. But the delineation between preservation and blatant disobedience was slim-to-none. Human will was what it was, and despite The Gift's guidance, she'd been contrary. She knew following The Gift was following God and had carefully done so. Until now.

Now Roam was gone, The Gift was silent, and Taffy was numb. Viciously, Taffy hurled sketch pad and pencil at receding dreams, self-chastening and berating. "Gotta be a real fool to lose the same good man twice in one life!"

Plopping back onto the grass, Taffy watched dusk descend through dripping tears. She lay anesthetized as night diamonds appeared. NuNu called them the eyes of the ancestors. Waltzing with self-pity along the edge of blasphemy, Taffy maliciously reduced them to nothing more than stars. She ignored the one that fell, etching a brilliant arc across the diamond-lit sky.

Falling stars ain't nothing but tears. Taffy covered her ears as NuNu's lessons cycled her skull. *Could be from joy or grief. Up to you to know what you pulling from the ancestors' eyes.*

Taffy chuckled drily. Joy was a distant concept. Grief was intimate. She'd made an insurmountable mess, disappointing all, herself included. Finding Roam was imperative. She'd wait until the week ended, allowing a cooling off period; then she was on a train bound for his rooming house, his local Porters' office. Whatever it took to find him. Whether or not he'd listen, she had to tell, disclosing every sordid bit. Truly, all secrets weren't best left sealed.

The ensuing days were a merciful blur. Only the mass family photograph beneath the shade of an ancient oak tree and Angel's recitation of 'Dream Variations' at the Founders' Day opening ceremony offered reprieve. Wearied by her futile attempts to locate Roam, Taffy was troubled by prospects of a forlorn future. By week's end, she desperately needed the distraction the Founders' Picnic provided.

Saturday rose with summer's kiss on her crown. Angel bounded from bed, finishing chores in record time. The fairgrounds—acreage on the other side of Lake Florence cleared by menfolk—waited beneath an amber sun.

There was much to celebrate, mainly sixty years.

Six decades before, Bledsoe began as a marshy patch unwanted by whites. Newlywed and slaves newly freed, Matthias and Octavia Bledsoe—now Poppy and NuNu to their brood—toiled for Preacherman Hale, Miss Goldie's pa, in exchange for six soggy acres and a poor-mouthed mule. Wasn't the rich highlands and team of oxen as promised; still, they took what was given, including ridicule. All because Poppy's blood soaked that soggy ground.

Couldn't settle elsewhere, leaving essence behind. Had to drain that swampland with Octavia at his side until little-by-little, the miracle emerged. Rich, loamy soil responded to Matthias' caress and call. Vegetation appeared. Wildlife returned. Each year, another unwanted adjacent acre was acquired, cultivated, leaving Matthias and Octavia with enough for themselves and others.

They opened heart and home. Weary travelers, displaced or dispirited, took to stopping by. Many seeking loves lost in slavery flooded roads 'in search of', posted petitions in "Lost Friends" columns of Colored newspapers, when simple word-of-mouth failed. Jubilant successes were outnumbered by paths that never crossed again.

Hope often shattered with mirages of Up North freedom reduced by restrictive covenants, governmental prejudices, and riotous pogroms leaving Black blood on northern shores. Trickles flowed back below the Mason-Dixon, preferring a familiar foe to peculiar adversaries in a failed Promise Land. Some made their home in Bledsoe.

Word spread. The land became a resting place for the weary, the worn, and those yet able to dream. They brought skills—blacksmithing, farming, carpentry, medicine and more. There were healers and dealers, cooks, scholars, preachers, poets, and an ousted pickpocket. A lively hodgepodge, they built a Colored Canaan on second-hand soil.

But soil said who built where.

Her cry was mournful, a sad wind wailing as blood called to blood, quieting only for Matthias. Where his substance soaked, feeding earth's needs, only Poppy and his could remain. But about her perimeter, land embraced others, serenely.

So folks built beyond the ring, blossoming into a township spread like a patchwork quilt, offering comfort beneath her covering. Thus a town began. By the time their firstborn was college-bound, Matthias' and Octavia's holdings had truly flourished. Herds of cattle grazed acre upon acre of fertile land in a town bearing their name.

Free of hooded, vigilante terrorism too often used to subdue and abuse Colored folks below the Mason-Dixon divide, Bledsoe had been spared lynchings, rapes, unjust trials by all-white juries, and the razing of Negro townships like Florida's Rosewood ten years before. Bledsoe outlived losses natural or not—drought, weevil infestation, and a long ago brush fire that guzzled farmland aplenty. Its Mutual Aid Society sustained many, keeping folks from desolation and soup lines. Bledsoe buried, birthed, and married many; said hello to newcomers, farewell to old. Its borders were protected, its insides vibrant with offspring, boasting a sense of obligation mixed with pride. Unlike many Colored establishments plunging from earth—be it at the hands of white outsiders or natural attrition as children grew up and moved on—Bledsoe survived.

"I'mma do everything, Taffy!" Angel chirped in anticipation of boundless fun: sack races, pie-eating contests and cakewalk, a ball-toss booth and dunk tank. Games, jugglers, fire-eaters, the bearded fat lady and contortionist courtesy of a traveling Colored carnival. And rumor had it a troop of Buffalo Soldiers might ride by!

"That's fine, Baby, have all the fun you can. Just make sure Papa, M'Dear, or I know your whereabouts."

"Okay. And I'mma get a stomachache," Angel announced, already salivating. Cotton candy, hot dogs, snow cones and popcorn. Barbeque. Links. Fried chicken and fish fresh from the lake. Sliced melon, feather-light rolls; deviled eggs, roasted corn, baked yams and potato salad for all. Sweet tea and lemonade. Dr. Blue's famous homemade ice cream and a mountain of desserts that could send the sugar-afflicted into a coma with one whiff.

"Bet my stomachache'll be worse," Taffy bragged, determined to breathe without defeat. Future was uncertain. But like Bledsoe, she was determined to survive.

"Naw, go enjoy old people stuff like that old timey jug and washboard band with the spoons. Leave the fun food to me."

"Guess I'd best add the blue ribbon contest for quilting and canning, huh?"

"Yep," Angel teased. Voice dropping, he earnestly informed, "I did like you said, Taf, and didn't tell nobody. But my suitcase's almost ready."

"Good, Baby," Taffy praised, taking Angel's hand, praying, *God help, God lead.*

With Bledsoe's population and visitors from Winter Cove and Drexel, the fairgrounds were swollen, leaving Deputy Newsome strolling about, a lone lawman hoping to prove a deterrent to devilment. Bledsoe didn't have a proper jail, just a holding tank for committers of minor disturbances—sleeping off drink, or cooling heels and head after a poker game gone south. Richland housed the real jail with the white sheriff, who rarely came across the dividing line. But by the time twilight rolled around, peace still reigned, leaving Deputy Newsome with nothing to do except enjoy.

Bellies were full, spirits free, laughter rich and pleasure pure. Evening's mellow magic stood at the ready, waiting for day to surrender to night's velvet potential. Anxious stars, too eager to sleep, made a premature appearance despite twilight lingering.

A group of girls too big for preschool games and too young to trail behind older sisters more interested in boys than babydolls clustered together, their singsong voices bouncing as two well-synchronized ropes tap-slapped the ground. A little brown beauty jumped in the center.

"Girl, when was the last time we double-dutched?" Chloe asked, spooning her third cherry snow cone of the day.

"Prior to these." Taffy discretely indicated full breasts while enjoying the antics of the little girl skipping herself into a sweat.

"And this," Chloe laughed, cupping the underside of her belly. "Join in, Taf."

"I'm not breaking my back!"

"Oh, hush. Excuse me," Chloe called, gaining the attention of the girls handling the ever-moving sphere of twine. "Can Miss Taffy have next?"

"Can she do doubles?"

"Pumpkin, please! We did triples way back when," Taffy bragged.

"Well…okay. Come on, Miss Taffy," a rope turner agreed, unenthusiastically.

Taffy hesitated until the jumping girl in the middle issued an invitation she couldn't refuse. "Yeah, Miss Taffy, show us how our grandmas used to do."

"*Grandma*?! Honey, move," Taffy admonished, adjusting the waistband of her denim capris and minding the rhythm, jumping in. A cheer went up as Taffy and her doubles partner set to making music with their feet.

"I know that's right!" Chloe encouraged. "Show these sass-talking young things."

Taffy's laughter was girlish and carefree. She executed a turn on one foot, eliciting a chorus of "oooohs." She beamed. "Uh-huh, who's old?"

"Not you," one rope-turner admitted.

"That's what I know," Taffy boasted, showboating until missing a beat.

She sensed the intrusion, an invasion of spice. Unexpected mint. Sienna mist. Deep notes of his being, like an upright bass strummed low. His essence danced on air.

She lost her rhythm. A rope snagged her ankle. Recovering balance, Taffy turned, searching. He was there. Watching. Waiting. Within reach.

Taffy's heart contracted with gratitude. Her God answered impossible prayers.

back?"

"Just now."

"Lord, I'm glad to see *you*," Chloe trilled, watching Taffy hugging herself as if to avoid touching Roam.

"Miss Taffy, you still roping?"

Taffy shook off paralysis. "I'm finished, honey. Thanks." Needing air, Taffy moved away.

Roam intercepted what he mistook as flight. Not extending a greeting or explaining an extended absence, he offered gift-wrapped grace. "I'm here 'til midnight. When I board that train, I want you with me."

The strain of days abated and her body breathed. Soaking up the sight of him, Taffy spoke softly. "My mother said a wounded man never understands. I don't expect you to." She refrained from touching, healing every hurt. "'I'm sorry' is too asinine and empty and—"

"We'll deal with it later. I'm on the midnight special out of Trenton. Am I going alone?"

"Angel—"

"You have two tickets." Extracting his billfold, Roam handed Taffy an envelope. "Porters ride free."

Humbled, Taffy gripped the envelope as if a lifeline. "Alfredo's here."

Roam nodded, jaw tightening. "Are you tied in any way other than by law?" Roam believed Taffy's union was a contrived illusion. Why? He wasn't sure, but notions had fomented and formulated, and he meant for her to address every one.

"A last name is the only thing we've ever shared."

"Then we're gone. *Now*. And when you end that thing with Freeman, I'll be on bended knee. Don't pack a thing from him. Whatever you need, my money'll buy."

"I've been self-supporting for years," Taffy reminded. "What *I* have *I've* earned."

Roam snorted, wondering what all she'd done without. "If you don't need it, leave it. Right now we're getting beyond the ghosts."

Taffy understood. She owed Roam *the rest*. "No Bledsoe, no baggage?"

Roam nodded, waiting, masking fear of her refusal as she stood too long silent. "You have a gift, Taffy. I have a gut. I trust mine.

Now, trust yours."

Taffy studied him, weighing the wisdom of Roam's proposal only to offer her own. "Why wait 'til midnight? Better to leave while the fair's in full gear." Taffy returned the envelope. "Keep it safe for me."

A lopsided grin was proof of Roam's relief. He delayed his response at another's approach. "Mr. R.J! Whatchu know good?"

Taffy turned to find Cousin Imogene's overgrown man-child, ever-present calico kitten in arms. "Hi, Honey. How're you?"

"Fine. Fine. Fine," R.J. answered in his fashion.

"Enjoying the fair?"

"It's fun. Fun. Fun." He pointed at the circle of girls. "I wanna jump, jump, jump."

"Let's see if these little women have sense enough to let handsome men in," Roam suggested, before whispering to Taffy, "Find Angel. I'll be here."

"I will, but I gotta see this to believe it."

After persuasive arguments on Roam's part, the jumping girls agreed. Passing off his kitten to Chloe, Taffy walked R.J. to the center and helped with his positioning. But when the ropes rounded, R.J. stood there, arms covering his head.

Taffy shot down giggles with a look before suggesting one rope only. This time R.J. hopped out of sync. He tried repeatedly, until eventually bouncing in time. Cheers erupted. Exhilarated, R.J. kept at it until Taffy noticed sweat on his brow. Whatever R.J.'s condition, it included being prone to convulsions if overheated.

"R.J., honey, I think that's enough," Taffy gently advised, leading him from the ring.

"I jumped!"

"You were good too!" Chloe praised, returning the calico kitten.

"Chloe, is your snow cone gone?" Taffy asked, wiping R.J.'s sweaty brow.

Chloe turned the empty cup upside down.

"Hot. Hot. Hot. Need snow connnnnnnnnnnnnnnnnnnnne!"

Taffy laughed, lighthearted again. "I'll find Angel," Taffy pointedly informed, dreaming of sweet love on the other side of a train ride, "after R.J. gets a cool drink—"

"Snow cone, cone, cone!" R.J. corrected.

"Fine, a snow cone," Taffy amended, amused.

"I'll stay here and teach these little ladies what real roping looks like," Roam preened.

"We'll be back," Taffy prematurely promised, sending love Roam's direction, before leading R.J. away.

CHAPTER FORTY-ONE

Mother said good things came to those who wait. For once, the bitch was right. Thanks to patience—his sole virtue—his gray-eyed, golden apple was his for the taking.

From his perch in the shadows, he watched her leave that rope-jumping gang, where that big penny-colored one was acting the idiot, playing foolish girls' games. He didn't fear him, but he was shrewd enough to know the redbone had a greedy stake in the girl. *He'll get dealt with*, Dempsey decided. Despite Freeman's only paying for one.

Formaldehyde-smelling Negro was chittlin' cheap, claiming one-hundred-fifty was all he had. He threw it back in Alfredo's face. *One-fifty!* It was chicken crap compared to what Dempsey earned running numbers for Hill. But in the end, Dempsey took it: crumpled bills and clinking coins, because this was a matter of principle, not price.

Learning of this foolhardy festival from Imogene, who would've gladly served Gray Eyes up for his consuming, Dempsey's principles dictated a patient wait. The Lord, not Dempsey, was orchestrator of all things. Jehovah had granted this massive crowd much like the cloud covering to His exodus-ing children. When she left that crazy-red to go off with that unhinged, unholy thing of Imogene's, Big Baby's boy took one final drag before crushing cigarette underfoot and making his move, confident the time had come to do heaven's bidding.

❧

R.J. wanted grape. Only strawberry remained. "Grape. Grape. Grape!" he shouted, startling the ladies manning the snow cone stand.

"R.J., there isn't any grape syrup left," Taffy soothed.

"Grape!" he roared, agitated and rocking on his heels.

"Taffy, maybe you best find his mama," suggested Miss Olivette, Willie Ray's grandmother.

Taffy agreed while diffusing R.J.'s anxiety, softly but firmly explaining, "Sweetie, your only choice is strawberry. It's that or nothing."

He became petulant, lips pouting, eyes welling. Suddenly his tirade ended and R.J. took off running, kitten in arms. "I find. I find. I find grape."

"Lord, now…" Willie Ray's grandmother guffawed. "That child's a notion. If you catch him, Taffy, take him to his parents."

Taffy went the direction R.J. fled. She saw Angel had finished his game of stickball and was with Poppy, encircled by a passel of boys ready for storytelling. In a matter of hours, Angel would be leaving all that he loved. Taffy prayed she'd made a right choice. Pushing second-guessing aside, Taffy continued, seeing R.J. in the distance at the edge of the clearing, his gait odd and agitated as if skipping and dancing simultaneously.

"R.J.!"

He turned long enough to holler, "I find grape!" before running past the clearing, away from the lake, and into uncut underbrush. Passing the Turners' old abandoned barn, R.J. headed west towards town.

Town was shut down with everyone at the fairgrounds. Taffy thought to let him go, he'd come to no harm. But R.J. could become disoriented and further agitated when finding downtown dark and vacated. He was already overheated.

"Lord, Jesus," Taffy sighed. "R.J., come back!"

R.J. was too far to hear and too intent on his quest to care. By the time she reached the abandoned barn, Taffy was winded. "Girl, you *are* getting old," she mocked, intending to catch her breath before heading on. But she felt him.

Stealthy. Stench of twisted evil and tobacco on the tongue. Metal and sweat. The one who'd waited in the wings, the demon of her dreams, had come. Reproach cramped Taffy's soul. She'd been too caught up in revelry to heed the sign of stars twinkling before nightfall—the ancestors offering extra so a body could see. Speaking. Warning.

Evil always announces its coming…

Was it past praying time?

Resolute, Taffy stepped away from the barn, fervently praying, intent on looking evil in its eye. Taffy was unprepared when evil snatched her from behind.

Slammed against the barn, his vileness in her face, Taffy was treated to the brunt force of his rage.

"Whores never listen or learn!" Insult curdled his breath. "You keep forsaking your vows!" His forearm savagely pressed against Taffy's throat, choking. "I tried bringing you back, but looks like rabbit blood ain't enough for your redemption." Madness carved his face into a bone-chilling mosaic. "You need deep saving."

His was an insanity seen before. Taffy choked out words from a place of knowledge Taffy couldn't claim. "You're Big Baby's boy."

Blood has memory…

Taffy's words stoked new rage. *"Dempsey Dupre!"* he bellowed, wrapping hands about her throat until a near-death grip. "I ain't *no* bitch's boy."

Taffy tried prying herself free of his iron hold, but panic softened her bones. Still resistance rose, fueling a guttural instinct to fight, until her Spirit cautioned stillness. Hands falling at her side, Taffy rasped, "Double-D.," the moniker provided that night of mad jazz. Why the wait? Could've tried at JoJo's what he thought to do now. Judging by the brutality of his gaze and grip, his delay wasn't due to softness.

His hold slackened. "Seems remembering's what you do best." He was a beast bloated with vengeance, and a more insidious intent. His voice turned wishful, pathetic. "You remember making me a man?"

His hands tight about her throat, Taffy barely managed a whisper. "No."

"You should!" he screamed, clutching at Taffy's clothing, her body.

His sour spittle sprinkling her face, Taffy took to praying, understanding this man meant to take more than her life.

Yea though I walk through the valley of death I won't fear…

Though his breathing was ragged with rage, his voice calmed. "You couldn't give your husband his due. But you gave me mine."

You are with me…

Surreptitiously, Taffy scoped her surroundings for what her Daddy called an equalizer. Something to turn the tide. She spotted the long, broken handle of a discarded farm implement not far from the barn door.

Your rod and staff comfort me...

"You remember?" His tone was pleading, needy. "You do. You got to!" He'd never touched her softness. Recalling being catapulted into manhood with a mere glimpse of her iniquity, he leaned in, sex stiffening. Distressed breathing pushed her breasts in a rapid inhalation, exhalation against his chest. He mistook it for excitement. "You remember," he moaned in satisfaction—grabbing, roughly fondling Taffy's breast. Bile clogged Taffy's throat, drowning out protest as she resisted Dempsey Dupre's intent. But fight was Dempsey's stimuli. Heaving sour air down her ear, he clutched her hand, maneuvering her palm onto his personals.

"*No!*" Taffy reacted, squeezing, twisting what he'd placed in her grasp. Heavily, her assailant fell to his knees in misery. Yet, cradling self, he managed to grab the hem of her capris as Taffy turned, fleeing.

Tripped, Taffy landed on her face, his pain-filled howls at her back. Taffy flipped herself over, kicking against his advance as—grip about her ankle—he cupped his wounded self while yanking Taffy towards him with the enraged strength of a madman. Taffy launched a vicious foot into his face. Something cracked, caved. Blood splattered. He staggered back, and Taffy scrambled for that wooden handle of a long abandoned farm implement.

You provide for me in the presence of my enemies...

Old, but sturdy it held when she stood, pivoted, crashing wood onto her assailant's bent back. The blow sprawled him into her. Both fell with a bone-jarring thud, the back of Taffy's head flashing fire on impact.

Taffy's eyes closed against raw pain. When she opened them, it was to find a firearm in her face.

Surely, goodness and mercy will follow me?

There was a ponderous blast, and Taffy's world went black.

CHAPTER FORTY-TWO

The moment the gun discharged, Miss Octavia fell away. Some say she sank into the ground searching for worlds gone by. Others claimed she flew like a bird before crashing to earth, allowing Dr. Blue to peer beneath her eyelids in search of living. But her eyes were stark white. Gone to a world from which none could hail her home. Miss Octavia was strange that way, seeing other worlds, walking other ways. Bound for the crazy house next opening. Her husband and sons carted her to a waiting car to take her home, where she could rest it away.

⌾⌾⌾

R.J. never reached his destination. He found Canaan instead. Thick vines, dark grapes, purple and sweet. Shifting Cocoa in arms, he snapped a cluster, giggling gleefully. "I found grapes. I tell Taffy. Get snow cone now." Pleased with his bounty, R.J. bounced away, anticipating Taffy's smile. Would she hug his neck like that man hugged hers, looking devil-dog mean?

R.J. didn't like the man's dragging Taffy, or her limpness. Like the sock dolls his mama made. R.J. never treated his dolls the way Big Baby's son treated Taffy, pulling her into that drafty, nasty barn, getting her filthy.

R.J. didn't want Cousin Rachel scolding Taffy like Mama did him when he messed himself. He'd help her get clean. And then they'd make snow cones. But only two. That mean boy of Big Baby's didn't deserve any.

⌾⌾⌾

She was a beautiful angel. Still and silent, obedient and compliant. Unavailable to this world and serene. She would be magnificent, wide open, redemption welcoming. He shuddered expectantly.

He'd spread many women, some resisting and unwilling. But this would be sacred. Holy for her, as his blissful virgin voyage through the sight of her iniquity had been for him. So like an opiate, the magnitude of that release was never matched again. But here she was—the pathway to first paradise. Flesh pounding at the prospect, Dempsey Dupre grappled with his pants. Too bad he'd had to crush her beyond breath. But she'd been brazen in battle. Now, he could anoint her, in her humbled, unmoving state. Their mating would resurrect her soul, if not her body. Dempsey delighted that God had chosen him to purify her this time.

❧

Something wasn't right. Taffy should've returned with Angel long ago.

Had Freeman caught wind of Roam's presence and hemmed her up somehow? Or was she somewhere negotiating R.J.'s needs? The fair offered plenty distractions for the soundest minds. No telling what might've mesmerized R.J. along the way. Still, Roam couldn't shake foreboding.

Ladies at the snow cone booth confirmed they'd passed ages ago. "Told Taffy to take R.J. to his mama," Miss Olivette supplied. "No telling where they got to."

Roam's unrest increased when discovering neither Tinsley could account for their son. Wasn't he with the boys, listening to Mr. Matthias' tall tales?

R.J. wasn't. Angel was. And Angel couldn't speak on Taffy's whereabouts.

Unable to scour the fairgrounds alone, Roam enlisted Drew and fellow Bledsoes. NuNu's grandsons were edgy after her episode and only too ready to aid. They split up, headed in various directions, searching.

An empty-handed search left Roam casting suspicion back on Freeman. How would a man who didn't love his wife handle the reappearance of one who did?

"I'll get Deputy Newsome," Drew concluded. They'd been discreet, not wanting to raise undue alarm. But it was beyond them now. Tight-jawed, scouring the horizon once again, Roam agreed. A lawman was needed. Taffy was missing.

Drew left Roam near Lake Florence, staring at the untamed clearing beyond Turner's old abandoned barn, willing the night to give her up. Night refused, offering nothing save that distant, dilapidated edifice.

Roam stilled, swearing the doors were closed when earlier reaching the clearing. Now they stood open to the night, oddly angled, flung back on worn hinges like broken wings.

"*Drew!*" Roam yelled, an icy hand walking his spine as he strode towards the barn. Swallowing ground, pace increasing, praying like his future wasn't finished. Full-out running when hearing distant, frenzied screams.

CHAPTER FORTY-THREE

She drifted weightless on a glassy sea.
You won't die but live and declare God's glory!
Knowing? A honeyed voice poured Psalms like breath into Taffy's still chest.

Warmth returned. Chill faded. Her skull throbbed. Her body seeped misery. Eyes burning and bleary, Taffy fought to comprehend lying in an enclosure reeking of forgotten animals, age, and decay. A roof riddled with holes showcased a sky where night met day. Decomposing hay bales littered a floor dotted with rodent droppings, a rusty pitchfork, and a blazing ring of feet.

Three sets in all. One: beautiful Africa black. Two: left foot missing a digit, ankles decorated with the imprint of slavery's chains. Three: tapping, restless Babygirl feet that never lived long enough to dance and run, now grown beneath a body rising higher than her mother's six feet.

The Octavias were come.

They gripped the shoulders of Knowing crouching, exhaling into Taffy's ear. *Our strength is yours.* Her voice was NuNu's, face like a woman not bound by time. *Live!*

Obeying the command, Taffy managed to gather herself enough to move. She couldn't die at the hands of the man jerking the barn doors closed.

Breath ragged, sweat raining, Taffy tried standing, but vision blurred and the barn spun, making her nauseous. She dropped to a crawl, edged her way towards a pitchfork in the hay. Equalizer an arm's length away, Taffy lunged in vain.

His weight crashed against her. He flung her onto her back, spewing stale tobacco and ripe brutality. Lowering his pants, he ripped at Taffy's clothing.

"*No!*" Taffy screamed repeatedly, skull throbbing with ache and memory. Outside the barn, she'd fought him with her everything. He'd fired a warning shot that failed to stop Taffy's struggling. So, he'd slammed the butt of his gun into her skull, painting her world opaque and unfeeling. Now, he meant to destroy her everything.

Clawing, screaming, Taffy returned insult for injury—despite the pistol's suddenly reappearing. "*Shoot me!*" she hissed. "You can't take it any other way!"

Incensed, Dempsey Dupre raised a fist, determined to strike fury from her face. But her eyes swam with uncanny images. Warrior women, large and strong? Startled, he glanced over his shoulder to see what Taffy saw. Instead, he was grabbed by meaty hands. Dempsey went airborne, flung aside like he weighed no more than the kitten licking its paws atop a bale of hay. He landed haphazardly against a wooden stall, pistol flying free.

"No hurt Taffy! No, no, no!" Imogene's 'aberration-of-a-son' bellowed like a bull, pacing, head between hands.

Taffy scrambled for the gun.

Dempsey reached it first and came up crazy, pistol wildly waving. "You wanna put your nasty hands on me, you brain-diseased mutha—?!"

He finished his tirade by aiming, firing.

Blood and fur exploded and R.J.'s kitten fell to the floor mangled, dismembered.

His unearthly cry tore the air as R.J. moved with unexpected grace and speed, ridding the earth of wickedness by horrifying means that would be forever imprinted on Taffy's memory.

⸒⸒⸒

Legs aching, lungs burning, Roam reached the barn, propelled by Taffy's terrifying screams. Roam burst inside only to stall in the doorway locked by the sight of death in the midst of life.

The no-good encountered at JoJo's lay on the ground, lifeless eyes bulging in shock that the hunted had overtaken the hunter. A pitchfork was planted deep in his chest. Bloody fountains oozed from mortal wounds, mixing and mingling with tufts of calico fur and what must have been an animal once upon a when.

Racing towards her feral screams, Roam avoided the carnage.

"R.J., no!" Frantically, she pushed against R.J. trying to undo what was done.

He grabbed her. Taffy whirled, reflexively swinging. Roam deflected the blow easily.

Her face filled with recognition and relief. *"My…God…Roam."* Adrenalin crashed and fight fled. Taffy sagged into him, weeping.

Roam held on tight. "Shhh, Baby, I've got you."

"What the hell!"

Roam glanced back, finding Drew at the doorway. He looked to Roam for answers. Cradling Taffy, Roam offered none. Chaos spoke for itself.

Dead man. R.J. kneeling, covered in blood, scooping scattered remains of a shattered pet. Patting a kitten's lifeless head.

Gut twisting, Drew leaned over a wooden stall, gagging.

"Drew, you alright, man?" Roam asked when the sounds of heaving ceased.

"Yeah," Drew rasped. *"What the devil happened here?!"*

"It's my fault," Taffy sobbed, babbling, "I didn't pay attention. I didn't heed. I saw signs. I ignored them. This happened because of me."

"Taffy's fault. Taffy's fault. Taffy's fault," R.J. parroted, faithfully recollecting his fragmented kitten.

"Drew, stop him," Roam appealed, nodding towards R.J.'s sickening attempts to reassemble dead parts as if a puzzle.

Breathing deeply, Drew approached, kicking something in the hay. Bending, he found a fallen firearm. Retrieving it he tucked it at his back while heading for R.J. "Come on, Mr. R.J., man, you gotta let that go. We'll find a good burying place," Drew promised, clasping R.J.'s shoulder.

R.J. screeched as if burned. "No. No. No," he moaned, hiding Cocoa's remnants beneath the hay.

Drew looked to Roam, who merely shook his head. "R.J., what happened?" Drew asked.

"He can't help," Roam determined. He turned to Taffy. She was disheveled, exposed, clothing blood-splattered and torn. "Here." Roam snatched the shirt from his body. Left wearing the simple A-shirt underneath, he averted his gaze, handing Taffy his button-down. "Fasten it."

Taffy covered herself, chilled by how close she'd come to…

"You're okay," Roam assured, suppressing her violent trembling with an iron embrace. "What happened?" Sobbing, head swinging side-to-side, she wouldn't speak. "Help us out here, Dollbaby. *What happened?*" Roam couldn't get past her wall of tears. Passing a hand over his head, Roam looked skyward and cursed before reassessing the violent scene.

His eyes scanned back and forth between R.J. and the dead, the dead and Taffy, the deceased with unclasped pants draping ankles, and Taffy—scratched and scraped, mouth split, clothes torn…

Roam's face hardened. "What did he do to you?!" Burrowed against his chest, Taffy offered nothing. Roam held her away enough to see her face. "Did he?" He waited. "*Taffy!*"

"No," she whispered.

"But he tried?" Evidence was its own reply. Incensed, Roam snatched the dead man's pistol from Drew's waistband and aimed.

"*Roam, don't!*" Taffy knocked his arm off-course. Misdirected bullets splintered a decaying beam. "He's already dead," Taffy breathed.

"A bullet won't hurt, then will it?" Roam snarled, stalking away. Sweltering with rage, Roam pulled the trigger until the chamber emptied. A precise pattern on a far wall left no question of his marksmanship. The corpse lay unmolested by choice.

Anger somewhat slaked, Roam tucked the pistol at the small of his back.

"Roam, come on, man. We need to do something other than shoot the night," Drew cautioned. "Light's fading fast, and we need to handle this and get R.J. out of here. R.J., think you can come with us?"

"I'm staying with Cocoa," R.J. announced, his lack of repetition as shocking as the clear and emphatic words that were formed.

"You can't—"

"I stay. I stay. I stay." He resumed rocking and humming. Humming became singing and R.J. crooned a lullaby. "Go to sleep…go to sleep…go to sleep little Cocoa…"

It was too much.

Taffy shook her head as if flinging the night from her mind. But she couldn't reverse time to a place where death and madness didn't reign and killing could be negated. Gingerly moving as if her whole self ached, Taffy approached, kneeling beside R.J. in the hay. "R.J., honey, Cocoa's asleep for eternity." Her voice was strained. "A horrible thing happened here and we have to go."

Refusing to leave his kitten behind, R.J. took refuge in a corner of the barn. "I stay!"

"R.J., we can come and get Cocoa another time," Taffy promised, moving towards him.

"No-no-no!" R.J. fled.

"R.J.!" Roam shouted, reaching.

R.J. dodged Roam. Running erratically, he tripped over Big Baby's boy. Flat on his face, R.J. twisted, saw Roam and Drew approaching. R.J. jumped up, grabbing the handle of the pitchfork buried deep in the dead man's chest. Frantically, he heaved, trying to release the waiting weapon. His pursuers stopped. Heartbroken, R.J. bawled. "Your fault, mean man! Your fault!" he bellowed, kicking Dempsey's corpse over and again.

"Alright, R.J., it's okay," Roam soothed. "Stay with your cat while we get Deputy—"

"Don't involve the law! There has to be another way."

Roam turned, found Taffy rushing at him. He eyed her warily. "What way, Taffy? I'm not sad for the loss, but there's a dead man here. That has to be handled."

"*We'll* handle it!"

"Taf, this isn't something to play with," added Drew.

"Neither is R.J.'s life!" Taffy spat. "If you bring in Deputy Newsome, R.J.'s as good as gone. I'm not letting him die! I'm not sacrificing another life."

Roam peered at her, wondering if Taffy were telling her story instead of R.J.'s. "This isn't about you or who you tryna save," Roam reasoned. "It's about the law—"

"Who's law, Roam, the lynch-happy white man's? You don't wanna help? I'll handle this."

"You're not thinking straight or doing a damn thing!" Roam stopped, inhaling deeply. "Listen…our judicial system doesn't care if one Colored man kills another."

"Only time the white court cares is when we're a threat to them," Drew supplied.

"R.J.'ll get a slap on the wrist and time in the tank. Regardless, this isn't for you to decide. We're staying on this side of right."

"Roam, its *R.J.!* If the law doesn't kill him an asylum will," Taffy contended, tears flooding her face. "This was an accident. We can help resolve—"

"It's out of your hands, Taffy. You're finished and so am I," Roam concluded. "Drew, take Taffy out of here. I'll get Newsome."

"Roam, no." Taffy clung to him, "turn him over to the law and R.J.'ll be just another Colored man gone."

"Dammit, Taffy!" Exhaustion choked Roam's neck. "You proposing we dispose of evidence?"

"Yes."

Roam kneaded the bridge of his nose, thinking, finally speaking so that meaning wasn't missed. "It was self-defense. The deceased…," Roam swallowed bitter gall, "attacked you…R.J. came to your aid. The assailant turned on him," Roam sighed heavily, his surmised reconstruction spot-on. "R.J. retaliated. Understand?"

Taffy nodded. "I'll stay with R.J. until you return with Deputy Newsome."

"No. The further away from here you are, the better."

Dread had Roam reconsidering. Taffy's presence in the barn with a dead body would incite a maelstrom. Old memories could morph alien. Townsfolk would pile new offenses on her back that didn't belong. Taffy's version of what occurred would be stacked against R.J.'s babbling inconsistencies. He'd become the victim, she the cruel victimizer, pinning her crime on an innocent unable to fend for himself. She'd be deemed a manipulative murderess. R.J. refused to leave? He could stay, but Taffy had to go.

The barn was empty when the two returned. Other than tufts of bloody fur and tracks indicating something or someone had been dragged away, there was no evidence of the slain. Flashlight sweeping the barn, Deputy Newsome noted glutinous liquid trailing towards the door, where it stopped at the threshold, suggesting the object had been lifted and carried from there. "We gotta find R.J. Tinsley."

Roam agreed, grateful to leave hungry rodents drawn by the smell of bloodshed.

CHAPTER FORTY-FOUR

The festival closed with a crash. Whispers spread. Someone was missing? *Murdered*? Folks packed quickly, trying to outrun death. Children were pulled along, not understanding the need to leave, parents offering no explanations, just hissing them into silence as they fled.

Thaddeus and Rachel gripped Angel between them, abandoning danger unseen. Rachel's heart ached. Bledsoe had never experienced such travesty. Minor squabbles and neighborly disagreements, an occasional outright Saturday night brawl? Certainly. But murder?! Unfathomable! So, too, was the conversation she stumbled over in their retreat.

"Who was it got killed?"

"Some Dempsey Duncan, Dupre Dempsey or some such."

Rachel faltered. Dempsey? In Bledsoe? Hadn't seen Cousin Big Baby's family since Taffy was born, but they'd spoken via telephone just the other day! Why hadn't Big Baby or Cousin Imogene mentioned Dempsey's visiting? Now he was dead? Dear, Jesus, poor thing. Imogene always hinted he was a bit unhinged. Said he'd even served time for forcing affections with excessive brutality on an unwilling woman. Rachel's skin turned cold. "Where's Taffy?"

"Don't know," Thaddeus admitted, opening their car doors, Angel scooting inside, lip poked out over interrupted fun.

"Thaddeus, honey, I need to know where Taffy is," Rachel shrilled.

"Maybe she's with Drew and Chloe," Thaddeus offered, concern knotting his limbs.

"She wouldn't leave with Angel still here. Where's my daughter?"

"Rachel, Baby, get in the car. I'll find her," Thaddeus promised, earnestly praying their daughter was safe in God's care.

❧

The Tinsleys huddled in the rear of Deputy Newsome's car, Roam Ellis up front riding shotgun, in search of their son. Wanting their cooperation, the deputy merely informed the Tinsleys of R.J.'s disappearance, withholding talk of crime. R.J.'s favorite hiding places proving futile, a lullaby led them. They found him curled beneath the family's front porch, singing Cocoa's so-long. Took all three men to extricate him, and when R.J. emerged he was caked with blood, innards, and earthly debris.

Imogene came undone.

Holding cards close to his chest until reporting to the sheriff over in Richland, Deputy Newsome assured the Tinsleys R.J. was uninjured. The blood was another man's, now dead, one Dempsey Dupre.

Demanding to know who killed her kin, Imogene wilted when her son was accused, only to spring to life, wildly refuting. But Rayford Sr. managed to silence his wife long enough for the lawman to do what he needed to.

"R.J., how'd your shirt get bloody?"

R.J. rocked side-to-side. "Cocoa. She's gone. Bad-bad hurt."

"Too much blood here for a little cat, R.J. Where's the man from the barn? Did he hurt you?" the deputy asked. R.J. shook his head. "Did you hurt him?"

R.J. stopped his restless rocking. "All gone, gone, gone," R.J. offered. "He hurt Taffy. He went away. Bye-bye, bad-bad man."

"Taffy?" Newsome turned a questioning look on Roam. Having omitted Taffy's presence, Roam elected silence over a lie.

"Bad man hurt Taffy to heaven Cocoa gone I jump rope get big grapes for snow-snow-snow cone," R.J. streamed in his increased aggravation.

Deputy Newsome looked pleadingly at Mr. Rayford stooped beside his son.

"Son, stop all that and answer the Deputy's questions," his father gently admonished, gloomy sorrow marring his brow. "Did you hurt somebody?"

R.J. answered by humming the lullaby that led them. Exasperated, Deputy Newsome detached handcuffs from his belt.

Planting self like a barricade before her son, Imogene set to wailing, declaring R.J.'s innocence, demanding a corpse as proof of his supposed sin.

The deputy had had enough for the night. "Move aside, please, Miss Imogene." Ignoring her tirade, he reached for the accused who babbled incoherently, as if understanding his fate.

"Take your hands off my child and go find that bitch who squatted her stank on this town! She's responsible! My child ain't never hurt *nobody*," Imogene keened within Rayford's restraints.

Deputy Newsome apologized for protocol, but R.J. had to be detained. Moved by the Tinsleys' distress, he compromised. "I'll give him supper and he'll have a good night's sleep. I won't notify Richland 'til morning."

Imogene's howls shredded air.

"Can it be done without the cuffs, Deputy?" Roam suggested. "Might be easier on them." Agreeing, Newsome led R.J. by the arm, away from his mother's dirge.

"He'll be alright, 'Gene," Rayford comforted despite his own heartbreak. "The deputy said he won't do nothing 'til morning. R.J.'s just sleeping over."

Pushing away from her husband, Imogene wiped her eyes. "My child's being carted off like a low-down criminal! For what? *Taffy*? God bless, I'll kill her dead before the sun shines!"

"Miss Imogene, it's best heaven don't answer that prayer. If it does, you'll be eating dinner with the devil," Roam solemnly warned before walking off into the night.

CHAPTER FORTY-FIVE

C urled in the dark in the chair beside Roam's bed, she couldn't rest for being haunted by the cadaver on the barn floor. His claws clutching her throat, clothing ripped and body bruised, she'd wished him harm. Now he was gone. A depraved soul grown fat with the blood of others, Dempsey Dupre was dead before he died.

She didn't relish a loss of life, yet her mourning was for R.J. alone. She felt accountable, that R.J.'s predicament was her doing. Even so, as much as she wanted to assume R.J.'s wrong she couldn't atone for anyone's sins ever again. Still, she needed to know his fate, but wouldn't until Roam arrived.

Taffy tightened his robe about her. Having relegated tattered and soiled, blood-splattered clothing to the trash bin, all Taffy had were Roam's robe and oversized shirt hanging loosely about her bare frame.

She'd scrubbed terror and chaos from her skin, scoured her body head-to-toe until she ached and bathwater turned cold. Craving grace, Taffy refilled the tub with near-scalding water, sanctifying herself again. Now, utterly exhausted, Taffy waited.

It was dangerous being here, heeding Roam's request. Said he needed her safe in his care. Taffy simply needed him. With Roam she had hope and a future, and the boarding of that midnight train in Trenton, love at her side. Destination didn't matter as long as the past stayed behind.

Restless, Taffy rose, pulling back window curtains above a bed with turned down linens and crisp sheets. Moonlight spilled into the unlit room. Taffy stood in its cascade, affirming her existence with slow, deliberate breaths.

Lord, my God, I'm ever grateful to You!

Words couldn't embody her praise. But for R.J., her fate might've been decidedly different. She'd narrowly escaped violation...and walking with the ancestors on the other side. Here she was whole and ever indebted to the God of her salvation, to R.J., and her warrior women who defied the grave. Cupping hands to mouth, Taffy blew a sacred kiss trusting God to find it amid the ancestors' eyes.

A knock sounded at the door. "Taf," Chloe entered, steaming cup in hand, "honey, you decent?"

Wiping tears before turning on the bedside lamp, Taffy quietly replied. "Yes, considering." Accepting fragrant tea, she blew steam before sipping the soothing brew.

"Should Drew bring your things?"

"Drew's clear about wanting no part of this. Hamp's bringing me something of Dena's. I'll get my clothes when collecting Angel on our way out."

Chloe perched on the bed's edge. "You're really leaving?"

Taffy's voice was husky, strained by the night. "You've always urged me to."

"Honey, I didn't mean run off with a man and give Al ammunition."

"Chloe, what can he do that hasn't already been done?," Taffy quietly seethed. "He's taken enough! I'm not losing another day chained."

Sighing, Chloe stroked Taffy's arm. "Taf, I want you with Roam as much as you wanna be with him. But is this the way?"

"Paths aren't always perfect."

"No, but I want better for you both."

"And I don't? I almost lost more than my life tonight, so I'm boarding that train, taking my pleasure however I decide."

"Taffy, honey, you're not one for dishonest living. Wait 'til you're free."

"When will that be, Chloe, seeing as how no one's taken my case?"

"There're other lawyers besides the two you've called."

"I'm finished pushing for now."

"Taf—"

"Chloe, stop, *please*! You have your first love. Let me have mine." Rattling her teacup onto the bedside table, Taffy returned to the window.

"He's okay, Taf," Chloe assured, terminating prolonged silence.

Taffy merely nodded, spirit uneasy.

Roam could handle himself. But Alfredo was out there some-where, vindictive and capable of anything. Taffy told herself her am-plified fears were a byproduct of the night. Al knew nothing of their plans. But if he did? Roam was armed and Drew—stationed on the front porch like a sentinel, despite his objections to Taffy's presence in Roam's home—was, as well. All would work out. *Had to!*

"I need to check on Angel."

"You already called," Chloe reminded. "Uncle T. told you he's sleeping. And NuNu is too, Taf, so come sit and rest your own self."

Reluctantly she did, curling up again in the wingback chair beside the bed.

"Why'd you tell Uncle T. you're with me and Drew?"

"Aren't I?"

"You know what I mean, Taf."

"So he won't worry."

"Mmm-hmm, so he won't get his shotgun and drag you home," countered Chloe. "Does it hurt?" she asked, reexamining Taffy's inju-ries.

"No more than life," Taffy answered, gingerly fingering cuts and abrasions sustained, glad to be alive to feel anything, including pain.

Chloe cautiously felt the knot on the side of Taffy's head. "Swell-ing's near 'bout gone, thanks to the ice. Headache powder helping?"

"Tremendously," Taffy assured, covering Chloe's hand resting against her temple. "Chloe, no, I'm not one for wrong but I'm step-ping away from right in order to re-collect me." Taffy resisted images of R.J.'s gathering the broken pieces of a beloved pet. "I mean dishon-or to no one, especially my God, but I can't live fragmented anymore. Understand?" Chloe did. Taffy relaxed. "Just say a prayer."

Chloe squeezed Taffy's hand. "We're cradle to crypt." Chloe gri-maced. "Right sentiment, wrong time?"

Taffy half-smiled for the first time since being snatched outside that barn. "Can't hold it against you," Taffy allowed as voices mingled outdoors.

"It's Hamp and Roam," Chloe needlessly announced.

Taffy's warmth already knew. She headed for the bedroom door, stopping suddenly at her state of undress. "Lord, I can't go out there wearing this."

Chloe struggled into a standing position, baby-belly leading the way. "Put your keepers back on and I'll get the things Hamp brought."

Taffy shivered as if the evening's malfeasance had imbedded discarded garments. "They're gone."

"You burned *everything* including your binders?" Taffy nodded. "Heavenly Father," Chloe mumbled. "Oh well, drape that robe over whatever Dena sent so you ain't walking 'round stuff all loosey goosey. You'll get your things before Hamp drives y'all to Trenton," Chloe concluded as a knock sounded at the door. Closest, Chloe answered.

He spoke in a near-whisper, thinking her asleep. "How is she?"

"Waiting on you," Chloe informed, pushing open the door.

Roam stood stock-still, soaking up relief.

He'd left and almost lost her. Enraged, broken, he'd abandoned Bledsoe, needing to find his mind and make sense of the insane. Impaled by the fresh wound of her deceit, he'd consoled self by declaring liberation from need. Want proved a nonnegotiable thing.

I can't outrun this woman. He stood intrigued by the damp mass of freshly washed curls tumbling about Taffy's face. No matter the scrapes and bruises she was all woman, all beauty. Taffy was here. Safe. But had he lost her...

Roam's expression hardened, refusing to fathom a world without Taffy, his one love lifeless instead of Dupre. *Dear God!* Roam was grateful. She'd escaped death and desecration. Still, Roam found himself hating a dead man. "You alright, Taffy Mae?"

"I am," was pure balm as Taffy poured into Roam's embrace.

Taffy reveled in the seductive safety of Roam's fierce grip. Time quietly passed, sealing a seemingly endless embrace until Roam bent to kiss.

Chloe coughed, reminding others she existed. "Hello, innocent eyes here," Chloe called, patting her stomach.

Taffy's hand in his, Roam approached Chloe. "I appreciate you staying."

"Anything for my bestest," Chloe assured. "How's R.J.?"

Roam updated them, concluding, "He's fine tonight. Tomorrow? Get a lawyer and say two prayers."

"Lord, today," Chloe uttered. "And R.J. won't say where Mr. Dupre's body is?"

"*Mister?*" Roam growled, murderously.

"Sweetness, don't," Taffy cautioned. Eyes housing a potpourri of emotions locked onto his. They couldn't afford harbored hate.

Roam acquiesced, honoring Taffy's need for peace. "Just so you know...I hear Freeman skipped town."

Taffy's joy rose like sunrise.

"Hallelujah, heaven worked that out," Chloe decided. "Taf, honey, we oughta get going—"

"Plans've changed, Chloe. Lemme talk to you." Roam led Chloe from the room, closing the door, leaving Taffy shaken, wondering if Roam's heart had changed.

Taffy leaned against the bed as if to sit only to decline its intimacy. Electing again the chair, Taffy retrieved her tea. Warm liquid soothed as her thoughts went on a warped ride. *R.J. Dupre. Blood, carnage, and the chance of Roam leaving.* "Stop it, Taffy." She grasped calm, willed the night's unrest to recede, vowing if Roam moved on without her she'd do what she knew to: live. Albeit, brokenheartedly.

Resisting morbidity, enticed by the novelty of a man's room, Taffy glanced about for clues of Roam's private self. Scant effects were proof of Roam's nomadic existence. After transient years rail-riding, could he adjust to permanence? She and Angel constituted family. Was Roam ready? Taffy thought to pray grace for transition, but she doubted a vow-breaker's petition would reach beyond the ceiling.

Lord, I don't *mean to offend...*

Head reclined against the chair, Taffy closed her eyes and sank towards rest until loud, agitated voices had her up at the window watching family drive off without her. Chloe hollered something unintelligible. Roam's chuckle was followed by the closing front door securing them within that small frame house on an isolated edge of town.

They reached the bedroom door simultaneously, Roam knocking, Taffy opening.

"What's wrong?" Taffy questioned. "I heard arguing."

"Chloe promised to bury me alive if I let anything harm you."

"I meant you and Drew."

Setting Dena's wrapped bundle of clothing in the bedside chair, Roam gingerly touched Taffy's injured lip. "I want you here 'til heading to Trenton in the morning—"

"Our train leaves at midnight."

Roam kissed Taffy's brow. "The train does." Kissed her jaw. "We don't." Proud about self-presentation, Roam thought to wash the night away. But need demanded. Postponing wasn't possible. He'd secured her here for safety's sake. Now, Roam needed something altogether different. Fingering the soft, loose mass of Taffy's hair, Roam skimmed Taffy's neck with one hand. "We leave come morning." The small of her back with the other. "You're here with me 'til then." He was deliberate, unapologetic. "Drew has a problem with that. Do you?"

"No," Taffy whispered, heart pounding at Roam's all-consuming nearness.

"Good," Roam rumbled, offering a deep and convincing, coaxing kiss.

Taffy easily fell into the grace and the greed. The horror of a tumultuous night melting beneath Roam's touch, Taffy coveted Roam's love and another opportunity. She *would* honor Roam's right to choice and knowledge. Reluctantly Taffy withdrew, breath unsteady. Aware Roam could refuse her once he knew, Taffy's voice fluttered with appetite and uncertainty. "Sweetness…there's a lot unspoken—"

"Words'll wait," Roam interrupted. "We won't." Roam unfastened the robe's belt at Taffy's waist. Night had nearly taken her from him. To hell with delay. "You love me?"

"Only you. Always. But you need to know what you don't."

Freeing Taffy from his robe, Roam let it fall unheeded, no longer a hindrance—terminating all discussion with, "You want *this*?"

"Desperately," Taffy admitted, electing the illicit.

"That's all the knowing I need," Roam decided, anchoring Taffy against him. Helping himself to the luxury of Taffy's lips, Roam kissed her with a raw fierceness, leaving Taffy nearly incoherent. Her mouth opened at the greedy flick of Roam's tongue, receiving the completeness of a kiss meant to satisfy their collective ocean of need.

Gripping Taffy's hips, Roam acquainted her softness with his growing solidity. Her responsive shivers were tantalizing, left Roam wanting more of her quivering. His hands strayed from her hips, beneath Taffy's shirttail, to the silk of naked skin.

"Damn, you feel good," Roam moaned, breaking their kiss to bury his face in the hollow of Taffy's throat, breathing heat. Teeth nipped. Tongue licked. His mouth sucked and savored her warm skin as Roam palmed the provocative expanse of Taffy's hips and thighs he craved open wide.

Taffy couldn't control the trembling or the sound of her erratic breathing. Or the soft burning in her body, the tender ache in her unbound, cloth-covered breasts against Roam's solid chest. Roam released Taffy enough to hastily remove dungarees. Clad only in underwear, Roam pulled his shirt overhead as words flowed from Taffy's lips like liquid. "You're beautiful."

Roam stalled at the awe in her voice and the gentleness of Taffy's caress.

Touch like butterfly wings, Taffy drew sensual circles up Roam's spine, over wide shoulders and strong arms, committing muscle to memory. Mesmerized, Taffy traced the powerful lines of Roam's bare chest, planting tender kisses everywhere her fingers led. Slowly, Taffy kissed a path back up to Roam's neck as her hands drifted below his waist on a downward exploration, until encountering substance and strength.

Taffy gasped. Roam quickened, body shocked by Taffy's firm caress that unleashed new need, dense to the point of pain.

Roam lifted her easily, wrapping Taffy's legs about his waist, so that they were locked in a voluptuous embrace, face-to-face. A relentless grip about Taffy's hips, Roam lowered her onto the bed, settled himself between her thighs, his underwear a teasing barrier between.

Taffy was hypnotized by the slow, teasing, serpentine-like undulations of Roam's pelvis. She felt that unfamiliar something seep hot between her legs.

His hungry, wolf-like grin told Taffy Roam felt it, too. "Hold on, Baby, we gonna get what you want and need," Roam promised, slowly undoing her shirt buttons only for Taffy to still his hand. Wanting the uncovering and discovering, Roam looked at her questioningly.

"It's mine to give." Taffy's words were an erotic jolt and elixir, pausing Roam enough to allow Taffy a deliberate unveiling. Buttons undone, Taffy took a steadying breath before revealing herself before the eyes of her one love.

Roam wasn't ready. What enticed while clothed was art in the raw. Wholly tantalizing. Hands wandering and riding, Roam shamelessly admired Taffy's lushness. She was smooth bounty beneath his meandering touch. Gently, he claimed one breast. Cupping, stroking, he liked her eyes closing. Her body quivering, back arching when he kissed, licked, tongue lavishly caressed.

Light danced up her legs, exploding in Taffy's belly, leaving her weak when Roam drew her into his mouth. Sinking in pleasure, she nearly whined when Roam moved away long enough to remove his unwanted underwear until as free as she.

Taffy's obvious admiration heightened Roam's hunger.

Fascinated, a silken sound oozed from Taffy's mouth as she slowly stroked Roam's length, caressed breadth. He throbbed in Taffy's gentle grip—his sharp inhalation a sensuous hiss. "Woman, you 'bout to kill me," Roam rasped. Ravenous for carnal mixing, and long-intended pleasuring, Taffy's touch made him near reckless.

Give pleasure before you get it.

Wise words calmed but couldn't dampen Roam's need to be altogether deep inside of Taffy. He struggled to clamp a stranglehold on hunger. Wanting Taffy's satisfaction first, Roam reluctantly extracted self from Taffy's lethal grip. Lacing fingers with Taffy, he secured their hands above her head against the bed only to resume an inebriating kiss.

Submitting wholeheartedly to the intoxication of him, of *them*, Taffy felt herself dissolving as Roam's mouth worked magic. Exploring. Intentionally, relentlessly.

Mindful of every injury, Roam's kisses turned languid, healing as he etched an agonizing course over Taffy's body, gorging self, finding Taffy's heat equal to her sweet. Learning and loving her copious contours, he discovered the treasure map of Taffy's temple—molding Taffy's flesh to his fit with a sculptor's diligence.

Foreign sounds escaping her lips, Taffy felt dizzy, as if Roam was in all places at all times. But when Roam walked a slow hand between her legs, sound momentarily ceased and Taffy was paralyzed by his pleasuring.

Thighs parted. Body shook as Roam's strong fingers found Eden's apex. Roam's unhurried, masterful manipulations turned Taffy into liquid fire. Taffy's voice returned—a symphony of whimpers and whines.

Hips moving slowly, rhythmically, her jagged breathing escalated as Roam's wide hand caressed her crown of paradise. He was possessive, his fingers steadily dispensing joy, as his mouth reclaimed her breast, simultaneously creating and increasing pleasures above and below, driving Taffy deeper into senselessness. She was helpless—her body Roam's instrument. Intent on her pleasure, Roam stroked her incessantly. Taffy responded deliciously.

A concentrated mass of sense and energy, Taffy's tortured moans deepened as her body bloomed wider. Hips undulated higher, frantically rising on a whirlwind until. Sky met Earth and flesh orbited. Her cry was feral, body spasmodic. Brilliant. Breathless. Spiraling sea waves, luminous and resplendent.

Taffy's bottomless ecstasy was an invitation opening, her body rippling, shimmering magnificently. Straining against a visceral need to simply fuse their flesh, plunge into Taffy's sweetest heat, Roam repositioned himself above her. Slowly, Roam entered Taffy but barely, only partially.

Lord, but yet and still...

Roam's errant expletive shot free at her sweetness. Residual shockwaves of Taffy's pleasure proved utterly welcoming. Paralyzing. Roam burrowed his face in the tumble of Taffy's hair. She became the oxygen he struggled to breathe. Her smooth velvet clenched about his tip, Roam abandoned fantasies of their bodies meeting mere measures at a time, of titillating her honey-love until Taffy once more lost her mind.

Captured, Roam gently, slowly eased towards paradise, struggling to keep something in reserve. But gripping his back, her passion demanding, Taffy's raw moans and still rolling hips were Roam's ruin.

Roam's rhythm increased, as did his entrance. Stroking deeper, fiercer until he could only give her everything. Clutching her buttocks, Roam raised Taffy's hips to meet him fully as he finally, thoroughly plunged—sinking in a full fusion that devastated his sanity.

The room erupted with Roam's stratospheric satisfaction and Taffy's strangled sob ricocheting equal parts pleasure...and pain.

Enthralled by absolute union, they lay gasping, satiated and entwined. Encased by Taffy's intimacy, Roam's body poured into hers. Recovery incomplete, Roam was caught between relishing or removal, contentment and confusion. Her warm velvet tight about him in a possessive embrace, he'd felt the concaving. Taffy's deflowering? Her shift from passion to pain...and the collapse of an untouched thing?

Mystified, Roam slowly retracted. Taffy winced, her jagged inhalation causing alarm, prompting Roam to carefully extract from the sole place he wanted to be.

Frowning, Roam lay a palm against the flat of Taffy's belly, looking the length of her glory. Roam stared in disbelief, vainly asserting alternate possibilities. But truth was indisputable. So, too, was Roam's essence mingled in the red fountain of Taffy's virginity.

CHAPTER FORTY-SIX

Roam Ellis stumbled along an opaque tunnel of obscure truths dotted with telltale droplets of disclosure. Words haunted. Prickly thoughts lost all thorns. Truth was unearthed, revealing herself where she'd waited all along.

I'm not what you think I am, and I haven't done what you think I have.

Angel's calling her by name…

If talking time comes you'll understand more craziness than you care to.

Enigma of shy innocence and outright intoxication…

A last name is the only thing we've ever shared.

Married but unconsummated…

There's a first time for everything.

Unmarked, untouched, unloved…

The rapturous, studious way she'd caressed and outlined his nakedness as if she'd never touched a man…

You need to know what you don't.

She'd spoken truth moments before the two became one, in answer to his question of love.

Only you. Always.

Gathering seeds sprinkled over time, Roam saw. Still, he understood nothing. Knew she hid behind secrets when convenient. He'd had suspicions. But not of *this*.

He'd abandoned Bledsoe days ago, knowing despite suspicions that Angel *wasn't* his, that years before, they'd vowed marriage, choosing honor and abstinence until 'I Do'. Days ago, he'd left incensed over the bitter thought that Angel wasn't Freeman's but *another* man's, that Taffy had betrayed him but again.

The past few days had cleared Roam's head, summoned memories of her loyalty and Taffy's promising him *everything*. How, many years past, she'd kept their bond, only to disappear three months running, returning with a newborn in arms—looking distraught and defeated—leaving Roam wondering on tonight's ride back to Bledsoe if she'd, back then, experienced a violating thing. Tonight, he'd returned unable to rip Taffy from his life, choosing to take them somewhere where she'd pour her secrets into him because Roam suspected much…but *never this.*

Roam staggered from bed, pulled on discarded underwear. He stood unblinking, stupefied by her red proof of purity. "Woman. What. Is. This?"

Taffy's amazement outstripped his. A supplicant at a shrine, Taffy knelt at a maiden pool of innocence presumably destroyed by Big Baby and an invasive instrument. Entranced, Taffy was stunned by her first flow. Not bright and crimson like the blood drawn by Big Baby's demented doings. This stream, red-brown like her lover's hair, provided proof that God preserved.

"Taffy!"

Like one waking, she looked Roam's way, exonerated from disgrace and shame. "Yes, Love?"

Voice a dangerous rumble, Roam asked the unnecessary. "Have you ever been with a man?"

Wrapping arms about herself, Taffy reverenced the sacred sight with an expression divine. "I kept my promise."

Numb, Roam stood, certain God played with his mind. His words stumbled. "You've…*never* been intimate…never had…?"

Taffy nearly whispered, "Only you. Only now."

Roam's gaze narrowed against Taffy's bliss. She was ripe and rounded, a satiated woman. Without question, he'd orchestrated Taffy's inward rupturing and first joy.

Disoriented, Roam called the only name he could. "Angel."

Taffy shivered as if cold.

Pulling robe from floor, Roam handed it to her, watched her slip into it.

Captivated by stains of innocence, Taffy leaned against the headboard, tucking her legs beneath her. Slowly, Taffy unleashed the weight of years. Words tumbled bittersweet until silence consumed the room as lies lay naked and unsealed.

Slumping onto the bedside chair, Roam spat a dry expletive that raked the atmosphere. He'd rather that place of oneness they'd achieved, moving deep inside of Taffy still. Instead, he sat legs sprawled wondering what in hell was going on, had gone on for seven long years?

Head bowed, Roam kneaded his brow. He could testify. Angel *wasn't* Taffy's. But Angel was clearly Bledsoe. Looked too much like Taffy not to be.

Scrolling back time, Roam couldn't recall a scandal other than hers. Who or what had the mind overlooked? Drew, Dena, one of the myriad cousins? Was Angel the result of an illicit coupling? And why the hell would Taffy take Angel on her back all this time? Roam couldn't fathom for figuring…

Understanding slowly dawned. She was protecting. "Who does Angel belong to?"

Roam watched Taffy climb from bed and reverently touch cool cotton before removing and meticulously folding love-soiled linen as if a cherished memento worth keeping. Bent by the ludicrousness of it all, Roam reacted, lunging, snatching the blood-soiled sheet. "*What the hell is this*?!" he thundered.

In her silence, Roam hurled the sheet against the wall.

"Taffy, damn! Who the hell are *you*? You're married but not. A mother but a virgin. Your realities are your opposites and, hell Sweet Baby, I'm damn-upside-down-and-confused!" Breathing like a bull, Roam caught the scent of himself radiating from Taffy's skin, was forced to ignore conjured sensual images. "*Whatever* you do don't insult my intelligence. Keep your half-assed explanations and spit the shi—" Roam caught himself in time. "Try the damn truth!"

"It's a long, sad story," Taffy barely breathed, mortified by her truth-concealing.

"I got all night!"

Searching Roam's face, Taffy found a storm. She closed her eyes and prayed truth flowed from her lips coherently.

⟨∂⟩

They made the drive in silence, hands clasped, Taffy's heart drumming. She'd unearthed every secret until lies fell away in layers. Now Roam knew.

Taffy was free. Release was exhilarating, diminshed only by the fact that loss was tied to liberty. Watching the dark night, Taffy feared the moments ahead that would determine just how great her loss would be.

My grace is sufficient.

Taffy desperately held to promise, assuring self the Father worked *all things* together for the good. Even this? Even now? Despite her disobedience, and an illicit loving that might've misaligned a pure thing?

Lord, forgive me. Wash me clean.

Might prove painful navigating the chasm and consequences of willful sin, still Taffy prayed to the God of mercy who was capable of all things...

Lost in thought, Taffy snapped to attention when the car jerked to a halt to avoid her father's vehicle barreling from her parents' driveway and into their path.

Stopping abruptly, Thaddeus Bledsoe's door flew open and he stepped from his idling vehicle, shotgun ready. "Dear God," Taffy groaned, scrambling from Roam's automobile and rounding the other side. "Daddy?"

Illuminated by high-beams, Thaddeus looked at his daughter long enough to know. Thaddeus stood ashamed, ears echoing their illicit intimacy. "Go inside, gal," Thaddeus growled, eyes boring into Roam Ellis cautiously exiting his automobile.

Approaching, Roam's tone was sober, even somber. "Mr. Thaddeus, sir, with all due respect—"

"*Respect*?!" Thaddeus roared. "Roam Ellis, you know hell about respect due or otherwise."

"Sir, I understand it might appear that way—"

"Might?! You come here after wiping your damn mouth on my daughter's backside and wanna talk respect? No, indeed! Not when you've had my daughter somewhere she shouldn't've been."

"Sir, your daughter's a woman of free will."

"But she ain't *free or cheap*! Not to you or any man! I raised her to know her worth. But you obviously don't understand that," Thaddeus stepped towards Roam menacingly, "not after trifling with her like a goddamn piece of something for your pleasure!"

Taffy touched her father's arm. "Daddy, don't."

Refusing to look on his daughter, Thaddeus tossed his voice her way. "You've dishonored yourself and your marriage, but you won't stand here dishonoring me. I've already told you to go indoors, Octavia," Thaddeus scowled at his child, "so go. Let men handle their business."

"Actually, Daddy, this business is mine. I'm a grown woman, not a child, and my choices belong to me."

"You choosing to let some man treat you like you're common?!"

"Roam didn't do a thing I didn't want done."

Roam took advantage of Thaddeus' speechlessness. "Mr. Thaddeus, I wouldn't disrespect you or your family, and I'm not toying with your daughter. I'm marrying her."

"*Fool!* My daughter's already married."

"You might wanna talk to her about that," Roam humbly suggested, genuinely sorry to have offended a man he admired.

"Only thing I'm talking about is you getting your red rusty ass off my property and leaving my daughter the hell alone," Thaddeus countered.

"Sir, I won't be leaving her now or later. Taffy's mine for life."

Thaddeus cocked his shotgun. "Your living ain't long."

"My God, Daddy, what're you doing?!"

Thaddeus ignored his child. "Go home, Ellis."

"Daddy, put the gun away. There's a whole lot you don't know. About me. And Angel."

"That boy has nothing to do with this filth—"

"Daddy, you won't understand unless you listen."

"I'm finished conversing," Thaddeus concluded.

"But I'm not," Taffy replied, "so hear me. Please."

"Ellis, I asked once. Won't ask twice," Thaddeus warned, ignoring Taffy.

"*Daddy!*" Taffy shouted. "Angel and I are leaving tonight, so listen to me now or listen to me never."

"Leave all you want, Taffy, by yourself…but if you go with this here boy, you best not come back."

"Daddy, you're—"

"You have husband and son, and you've offended both!" Thaddeus raged. "That boy woke up crying for you, Taffy! Your Mama called out to Drew's so you could tend your child but you weren't there on account you were too busy laying up…" Thaddeus swallowed hard. "I tell you what, you going in that house and getting your son and taking yourself home to Freeman right here, right now, this night!"

"I can't go back."

"You're going somewhere other than here or with him," Thaddeus hurled, jabbing a finger Roam's way. "What you and Freeman work out is between you, but you won't play the whore in my house."

Taffy recoiled as if struck. "Do you even care to hear truth?"

"Truth is you're gonna fix your family."

"There is no family!"

"Go get your child, Taffy, and take him home to his father—"

"Angel isn't Alfredo's!"

Her words a vise constricting his mind, Thaddeus' heart skipped out-of-sync, but his hearing began to clear. Weeks, months of strangling sounds tumbled from his ears. Still, he was morbidly confused. His words were thick, sluggish. "Whatchu mean he isn't Freeman's?"

Taffy circumvented the unanswerable. "Alfredo entered our lives after Angel was born."

Thaddeus looked on his daughter as if at a foreign, unrecognizable thing. "Good God," Thaddeus groaned, mortally wounded. "You've been with *other* men?" His gaze locked on Roam. Thaddeus exploded. *"Who's the pa?!"*

Roam stepped forward. "Sir—"

Thaddeus took aim.

Taffy gripped the shotgun barrel, pushing it off course. Her unexpected motion had unintended momentum. Teetering into her father, she caused his backward stumble.

The trigger pulled. Roam lunged, snatching Taffy out of harm's way as a blast ripped the night. Silence exploded before settling pregnant and heavy.

Shocked and shaking, Thaddeus lowered the shotgun atop the car and reached for his child. "*Taffy!* Dear God... *Babygirl!* I could've..."

All along 'Bledsoe Boulevard' houselights came on, doors opened, and curious, concerned voices were heard as Taffy stood hot-eyed and wild. Shaken, she stepped backwards into Roam, avoiding her father's reach.

"Jesus, I coulda shot my own child! Forgive me, baby, I'm sorry!" Thaddeus wilted. "Taffy Sweet, I'm listening. Tell what I don't know."

"Taffy?" A rush of lilac powder preceded her mother. "Thaddeus? Honey, what's going on?"

His wife's voice was caught in a void as Thaddeus focused on their child. "Who is Angel's father, Taffy?"

Rachel froze. Motionless, she scanned the gathering of three, unmindful of the voices approaching. "Uncle T.? Aunt Rachel? We heard a shotgun blast. Everybody okay?"

Fixed on Taffy, Rachel perceived the intimate thing. "No, Jesus… Taffy, you promised," Rachel whispered, staggering.

"Mama, some promises can't keep," Taffy wearily replied, "nor should they."

"Taffy…who's Angel's father?" Thaddeus demanded, cognizant of new off-pitch energy.

"I don't know," Taffy answered honestly, thankful for Roam's steadying arm about her.

"Why don't you know?"

"*Taffy!*" It was a strident plea. "*Please*…think of Angel," Rachel begged, voice choked and trembling.

"For the past seven years I've done nothing but," Taffy assured, heart breaking. "I'm tired, Mama." Taffy stepped forward, meeting Rachel where she stood. Facing her mother, Taffy spoke to her father. "Daddy, my intimacy is *my* business but—and forgive any vulgarity—I've *never* been with a man…before…" Taffy watched the desperation marring her mother's cream-and-honey countenance turn to surprise then gratefulness as Rachel unexpectantly whispered God's thanks.

Turning to her father, Taffy inhaled until her lungs ached. "Daddy, I can't outline Angel's paternity because Angel isn't mine. Angel's my brother, not my child."

CHAPTER FORTY-SEVEN

The weight of revelation was quicksand consuming. Realizing struggle would hasten their demise her victims let fate be and faced each other, gray eyes shedding collective tears.

"Taffy, why?" Rachel moaned. "I promised I'd take care of this one day. Eventually. I gave you everything."

"Mama, you took my life and gave me your lies. I can't carry them anymore." Gently, Taffy wiped her mother's tear-stained face. "It's your turn to lift your load."

Thaddeus lost air and breath but he gained light. He saw clearly. Still, he wavered. "Babygirl, Angel's as much Bledsoe as the both of us."

Taffy's heart ached. "That may very well be, Daddy, but not because of me."

Thaddeus looked back and forth between his wife and child, ignoring the concerned voices of family entering the yard. "Rachel, what's happened here?"

Rachel stood mute, sight fastened on her firstborn. Despite the travesty of the moment, something in Taffy glowed. Her daughter's fire would never die. Rachel was proud, pleased. Lacy hadn't won. Taffy had survived.

Rachel surrendered. "You were lost, Honey-Love. Gone to Mississippi without our knowing what became of you," Rachel began, eyes on Taffy, unable to look on her husband. "That organizing of Colored farmers was dangerous, and you disappeared. We didn't know if the Klan got hold of you—"

"I couldn't reach you," Thaddeus needlessly reminded.

Rachel nodded mournfully. "We know that now, but then all I knew was you were missing and I couldn't discover your whereabouts no matter how I tried. And when I failed, I prayed and cried and asked the Lord to bring back my man." Rachel's voice trembled uncontrollably. "But when a year went by and the Lord didn't answer, I knew I couldn't do this alone."

"Do what, Rachel?"

She faced Thaddeus. "Survive. Honey, I didn't know how to without you." Face full of pleading, Rachel stepped towards him. "I'd never been alone. I went from my father's house to yours. Someone always met my needs...it's the way Mother raised me."

"So there's truth in what Taffy says?" Thaddeus queried, eyes darker than night, spirit shifting, posture stretching ominously.

Rachel shed earnest tears. "Honey, you were lost! I swear before heaven, I did my best! Family helped, but things got difficult. Booweevils caused crop failure. I was robbing Peter to pay Paul. Raising a near-grown daughter and running a house not knowing if you were dead or alive. I stayed up many nights drowning...and I stumbled—"

"Who is Angel?" Thaddeus demanded, deaf to the steady influx of family.

"It's as Taffy said—"

"*No*! You tell me, Rachel. Who is he?" Thaddeus bellowed.

"Thaddeus, please, it was once only." Rachel reached for her husband. "*Nothing* justifies my actions, but I floundered without you. I needed comfort, should've refused it when I found it. But it was only once, Honey," Rachel pleaded, dismantling into sobs.

Thaddeus' voice was a hollow pit. "Is he yours?"

"Yes." Choking on tears Rachel nodded. "Angel's my last born."

CHAPTER FORTY-EIGHT

Truths long tucked beneath Rachel Bledsoe's tongue poured forth, sparkling with long awaited liberty. Still, they hurt and destroyed despite the rightness of release.

Honey-Love, I thought Mississippi swallowed you and I'd never see you again. But God sent rainbows. Sometimes word came telling us you were here or there. No matter what, I got on a train and followed every lead. I didn't usually take Taffy for not wanting her pulled from school. But I did that time. Because I knew...

Like with Taffy, my belly didn't bloom until the end. I hid behind loose clothing and regularity. But I could hide only so long. So we left, supposedly following a lead. Customarily, one of your brothers accompanied me for safety's sake, but not that time. I needed freedom to hide.

I took us to a dilapidated town a world away. I told Taffy I wasn't well, and we were seeking a specialist's care. But our daughter saw. Eventually she knew. I begged her for your forgiveness. And she loved me, stayed by me, the "suffering widow" renting the basement of a half-empty boardinghouse where I could hide my shame. I bought the landlady's silence, and other boarders were too consumed eking an existence in that hull-of-a-town to care. Beyond that I didn't know what to do. So we stayed three months at the bottom of the world waiting for a baby to be born.

I made arrangements with an orphanage. I could leave behind the evidence of my great indiscretion, and come home cleansed. But each night I'd watch Taffy asleep beside me. And I'd remember those lost babies that left my body until my heart started turning. Then, a month or so before due, my body *turned on me.*

I couldn't eat. What I managed to swallow, I couldn't keep. My whole self ached and burned like summer lived inside me. When blood started trickling I was terrified. I had Taffy wire Mother. She came and our bottom of the world became the belly of hell with Mother's incessant, rambling grief.

She'd suspected something, but I'd left Bledsoe before she knew. Now she was there, confronted by my degeneracy.

I was a 'disgrace'. An 'infidel unworthy'. Had she known, she would have dragged me down Route 10 to Old Lady Esther, who knew which herbs would set a belly and a baby free. I'd wasted her efforts at raising a child fit for a lady's finery. Mother's reputation and name would be ruined. She was a sharecropper all over again. Common. Low in station and situation, worthy to be ignored.

Mother knew because she'd been left behind before.

Mother saw my grandmother consumed then discarded when of no further use. Mother saw first-hand Negro women never owned our bodies—had watched her own mother give everything, only to be abandoned. Now her own offspring had stepped into ancient, murky water and permitted the temple's misuse. Mother forecast ostracism and ruin. We'd be shunned, the topic of gossip and fast, forked tongues. Mother wailed at her wall of misery. But after drying tears, Mother left, telling me I didn't deserve pity.

Mother broke my heart, still when she returned that night, I was grateful and relieved. She kissed me and told me everything would work out fine before asking the landlady for boiling water to make tea.

Exhausted, I dozed until my belly started cyclone twisting. The pains I had before were nothing now. My body felt split in two, thrown to opposite sides of the room. It was so brutal I asked death to take me. I needed a doctor. Mother saw. She knew. Still, she sat in a bedside chair, unmoved. But Taffy was there. Our girl held my hand—calming my screams, her tears dripping at my agony.

I can still hear Mother's voice, smooth and oily. "You'll be fine, darling. It'll be over soon." Her manner was chilling, her face too serene. I was terrified, screaming, questioning. Mother's answer was, "God's will."

That's when she showed me a small, brown vial. "Your tea wasn't bitter, was it??" Her tone was considerate. "I believe I measured correctly."

Intent on killing the child, my mother poisoned me.

I wanted to hate her, but I could barely breathe for the hot talons raking my insides. I had to get help, but water broke and gushed a foul-smelling, bloody stream full of ugly brown globule-looking things.

Pausing, Rachel looked to Taffy.

You remember, don't you, sweetheart, my asking you to have Miss Malone send one of her boarders for a doctor? But you refused to leave me *even momentarily. Thank God, you were there when your brother tried coming feet-first into the world. We were terrified, but you were bold enough to summon your Gift.*

Rachel touched her daughter's hair, contritely admitting, *That might've been my first time truly honoring and accepting your gifting. Before, she was strangeness, a black magic Mother abhorred. But I needed her. Gracious, she came and guided your way.*

I practically passed out from the pain. Still, Taffy managed. Taffy coaxed and manipulated, turning the baby head-down.

Rachel smiled, remembering.

He didn't waste time meeting the world. He was born too soon, and blue.

He was my last. I was thirty-six—obviously not past childbearing—but I knew conception would never again occur. He'd taken something from me that wouldn't heal, and, as fate dictated, he lay motionless in Taffy's hand. Cruel irony. Like Bathsheba's loss of her firstborn conceived in adultery with the psalmist, Israel's great king.

But Taffy obviously thought differently.

My daughter held my son upside down and hit his backside. Still, he didn't breathe so she laid him carefully on the bed and dug fingers into his mouth. Out came mucous and that same nasty brown mess floating in his birthing stream. Taffy breathed into his mouth before rolling him over in one hand, spanking him again. That child gasped and squalled like he was angry and relieved. And the whole time, Mother stood as if in a trance. When she did try approaching, she couldn't. I like to think Taffy's Gift put a shield about that bed.

Taffy, you remember our swabbing him clean and you insisting on burying the birthing cord? You said NuNu called it an earth offering.

Rachel smiled wide.

You were so concerned. "Mama, his color's not right." I told you he'd be fine. His ears were already tinted chocolate, rich as you. You beamed, and Mother left in search of a doctor, worried, after *the fact. That's when I staked my claim.*

I knew better, but he was so precious and pure. I had to offer him me. That's how Mother found us when she returned alone, the doctor unable to come for tending someone else, my baby at my breast, nursing.

Mother was outraged! She tried taking him, but Taffy waved that blade used to cut the birthing cord like a crazy thing! Rachel laughed. *Lord, what a sight! My daughter was a guardian angel with a knife.*

We stayed that way, wary and distrustful, that first week of the baby's life. Mother said that was all I had, a week to recover before heading to the orphanage. I couldn't come home with another man's child. Still, I couldn't leave him. I loved him! That's why I named him, because he was mine!

Rachel paused, gulping oxygen.

Truthfully, Taffy gave him his first name. We put my father's in the middle. Angel Nathaniel. Taffy called him perfect despite Angel's being born skinny and scrawny. But that first week, he filled out nicely. Even Mother's face lost some of its stoniness. Until Cousin Imogene sent that wire.

Looking on her husband, Rachel couldn't hide her shame.

You were home. After two years that prison set you free. I cried with relief. And fear. I cried for you, for me, for this baby I was supposed to release. But I couldn't *leave my child behind! God would make a way.*

Mother had no patience for what she considered my insufferable, moral weakness. She was relentless and bullying, insisting I see reason. Still, I never gave in, and Angel was with us when we boarded that home-bound train.

The closer we got to Bledsoe, the more I knew it was an impossible situation. I could beg your forgiveness, but Angel would be a living witness. You'd see him and always remember my infidelity, so I entertained Mother's scheme.

"Let him go, Rachel, if not to an orphanage then back to God." I knew Mother still had that brown vial and would use it willingly. "He's a bastard. He can die." I also admitted her dementia, Mother's sharing Grandmother's mental inefficiencies. I tried resisting her whispers, but they settled seductively. "Rachel, have you looked at that child? There's no mistaking he's one of them. Not even you can explain that away."

I couldn't cause the undoing of a family.

"Is a wife's bastard a fitting welcome home gift for a husband gone so long? He might not kill it or you, but Thaddeus most certainly will put you out. What'll you do penniless and disgraced? Don't look to me for help. Can you make your own way?"

I could always teach, but I'd have to leave Bledsoe to do it. And what of Taffy? I couldn't leave her behind, wouldn't choose one child over the other. So I listened.

I sat watching my daughter protectively cradling my son. I tried resisting Mother's mind-bending madness, her reconfiguring Taffy as my ram in the bush.

"He entered the world in her *hands. Essentially, she* gave him his first *breath and his life. She named him. They share blood. Bledsoe genes are so strong, these two already resemble." Mother's face wore an eerie peace when declaring the unthinkable. "He belongs to her."*

I pretended to misunderstand Mother's meaning.

"That's her child," Mother clarified. It was worked out in her mind. "Octavia was sick before you all disappeared, even missed a few days of school." Mother was shrewd. "Look at her, Rachel, she's bursting into womanhood. Heaven's situating this for you."

I was disgusted by Mother's suggestion. I reached across and took my baby back, shielding him from her lunacy.

"There's nothing new about a young girl in trouble. Nothing new about one binding her belly and slinking off like a cat bearing kittens. She comes home empty-armed and survives." The unsettled brightened Mother's eyes. "Every now and then, one of those fools is silly enough to claim her mistake and live in shame." Mother nodded in Taffy's direction. "That one there'll survive."

I refused. "Taffy isn't a sacrificial lamb! And it would be a lie before God."

"Which sin you prefer God see? Your lie or your adultery?" Gripping my hand, Mother told me, "He's coming home, Rachel, but you can't ever call him yours. Octavia…Taffy can. She never need claim him. Folks'll simply see and speak."

Rachel looked at Thaddeus, desperately wanting to touch him, make him understand.

I didn't know it was in me. But when that train pulled into the Richland station and I saw you standing there waiting on us after being gone so long, I did what I've regretted most in life. I wronged us all.

After being in that godforsaken prison, there was a lean hardness about you not there before until you saw us. You smiled! Nothing but bright light until you noticed the bundle in my arms. I couldn't take your joy.

I want to think it wasn't intentional. But it was. I did what Mother schemed. I put Angel in Taffy's arms, lying to us both that it was temporary, just long enough for me to figure a way.

Taffy was terrified. But Mother told her 'he goes to you…or the grave'. That's why our untouched daughter took my sins. I can never repay Taffy for giving my son the chance to live.

CHAPTER FORTY-NINE

Rachel bled a river of tears. But tears weren't enough to blur truth. She had no choice but to see beneath Taffy's strength, to her daughter's vulnerability.

She'd been a monster, not a mother, robbing Taffy of simple, pivotal pleasures. Courtship. Giggling with girlfriends. School dances. Rightful culmination of first love. A mother's protection. She'd been a thief, and she'd slaughtered her daughter's innocence. She couldn't atone. She could barely explain.

"Taffy...baby...I didn't want you with Alfredo, but Mother said you wouldn't hold. You'd talk out of turn and tell your Daddy everything." Lacy didn't trust her, knew Taffy was her daddy's daughter, and without a husband Thaddeus would badger Taffy until she told all. Taffy's sudden marriage and removal were added insurance against discovery. "Alfredo thought Angel was yours and used *my* secret sin against you. And I let him." Rachel shuddered at the depths of her deception. "I let you dangle in my web of lies, let Alfredo and Mother harass and threaten you to keep you gone....married Up North."

"Did you let them take me to Big Baby's?"

Rachel's face crumpled with confusion. "Who took you to Big Baby's, and why?"

Roam's arm about her, Taffy turned her face into his shoulder. Having told Roam what she'd endured at a demented woman's hands, Taffy would tell it never again.

"Taffy...what happened? What did they do to you?!" Rachel shrieked, weeping. "What did they do to my baby?" she cried, stroking Taffy's untamed hair. "Oh, Lord," Rachel moaned. "My sweetheart, if I could do it over again...I'd give it all back. I'd give you your one love." Rachel aimed a stricken look Roam's way. "I'd give everything I took and more. *Lord Jesus! Taffy, forgive me*," fell repeatedly like crushed petals from Rachel's lips.

Her every word had proven a thread of a bizarre, tangled web. When she quieted and silence descended, Thaddeus was left drowning—unsure if life were preferable to death. Murder over mercy?

He hated the way his wife cringed at his approach. He hated her. He thanked heaven for the hands of family gripping him tightly, keeping him from violating commandment six of ten.

"Angel's your son." Thaddeus regurgitated a reality his mind couldn't rightly receive. Yet it made sense—his return from Mississippi and young Taffy's bewildering brokenness and quiet fear. Questions unanswered to his satisfaction. Rachel's initial inability to share his intimacy. Her anxious behavior and even more effusive affection that felt like atonement. Jumping at her shadow and avoiding his eyes. All guilt. All shame. "You dishonored vows *and* made a child!"

Rachel's repentance streamed uselessly. He wouldn't be embroiled by her sorrow, had to hold onto what reason and sound judgment remained. He did so by insisting on legitimacy.

"That boy might not be Taffy's but he's Bledsoe. Whose is he? Who defiled my house and fathered this child?" Thaddeus demanded of his desolate wife and the spattering of family gathered in his yard. There was no reply. Breaking free of binding hands, Thaddeus strode towards his home needing to trace the bloodline. "*Angel!*"

Rachel at her heels, Taffy reached Thaddeus as he mounted the porch. "Daddy, you'll scare him, going in there like this!"

"That I can't help. Your Mama lost her tongue. I'll find my own damn facts!"

"Thaddeus, please, no good can come of knowing," Rachel pleaded, following Thaddeus indoors, past the parlor to the stairwell. She gripped his shirt, preventing his ascent.

Her touch was the emptiness rolling up from his soul, threatening to engulf him whole. Emptiness deadened Thaddeus to everything save the grip he snaked about Rachel's throat.

Voices screamed and hands pulled Thaddeus from murdering. Unleashed, Rachel tumbled to the floor in a ragdoll heap.

Thaddeus glowered at his wife sagging in their daughter's arms. "Let her go, Taffy! You've carried her enough," he raged, voice breaking. "*What did I marry?!* What kind of woman pollutes her union, turns around and assigns that vileness to her child?"

"I'm so sorry," Rachel moaned.

"That you are," Thaddeus agreed, "and you getting your things and taking your sorry ass outta here. You and your ill-conceived son."

"I've nowhere to go," Rachel sobbed.

"Go to your dead mama's house. Live with her crazy memories," Thaddeus spat. "But you going somewhere. *Angel!*"

Springing up, Taffy blocked the stairs, intercepting her father's path. "Daddy, don't take this out on Angel."

"Move, Taffy."

"No, sir! Angel's been mine forever, and I dare *anybody* to hurt him."

"Cleaning house means your mama takes *all* her belongings when she leaves."

"Taffy?" Angel stood atop the landing, eyes wide. "What's wrong?"

Taffy mounted the stairs, unsure how long he'd stood or how much he'd heard. "It's okay, baby. Time for us to leave."

"No!" Rachel pulled herself upright. "Don't touch him." Rachel scrambled towards the stairs but Thaddeus proved an immoveable barricade. "Leave him be, Taffy. He's mine!"

"You can't claim him at your convenience, Mama."

"Taffy!"

Ignoring Rachel's frenzy, Taffy scooped the frightened child into her arms, disappearing towards Angel's room.

"*No!* Thaddeus, Honey, *please*. Let me have my children."

He was a wall, deaf and dead to pleas as Rachel's raw cries competed with crashing sounds overhead.

"Hell," Thaddeus muttered, wounded and exhausted beyond belief. "Dena…Vesta…" He beckoned the women poised on the porch, on the periphery of his family's decline. Intuitively understanding, they entered, escorting Rachel away.

Thaddeus turned his ravaged self towards the stairs.

"Sir? May I?"

Bowed by sounds of wreckage overhead, Thaddeus dropped to the steps. Head in hands, he granted permission to the younger man.

Roam found the room in disarray.

Bureau drawers sagged at odd angles, some about the hardwood floor. Luggage sprawled atop the bed, lids like hungry mouths open and waiting. Angel sat wrapped in a light blanket while Taffy made a fierce mess that passed for packing.

Roam stood silently assessing before entering the room to sit beside the wide-eyed child whose world was forever altered.

"How you doing, Little Man?"

Angel stared, unable to answer.

"You'll be alright," Roam promised, wrapping an arm about Angel's shoulder while digging in his pocket and pulling out a peppermint. "Here. Put a little love on your tongue." He waited as Angel obeyed. "Bet the world's tasting better already." Angel half-smiled. "Think you can go downstairs for a while?"

Taffy whirled. "Stay right there, Angel."

Roam overrode. "Go on, Little Man. Your Papa needs you, and you need him. Here, take your blanket, keep yourself good."

Compliant, Angel left. Taffy rushed for him. Roam obstructed, closing and physically barring the door. "Let him go, Taffy." Roam's words sank in her belly like stones of portent and unmistakable finality.

"I won't…not again," Taffy refused, voice on fire.

"You don't have a choice. You can't take what isn't yours—"

"I did everything but birth that child," Taffy hissed, turning away, ramming Angel's belongings into suitcases, "so stand in my way and watch what happens."

Roam allowed tolerance to be his better part of valor. He approached mindful that Rachel Bledsoe had opened Hades' gates, once and again.

This night was the inevitable outcome of Miss Rachel's transference of sins…as if deeds done in dark couldn't come to light. In her desperation, Miss Rachel had committed selfish and incomprehensible acts, and Roam prayed the worst wasn't yet to come. The paternal piece of Angel's origins remained concealed. Only God knew what calamity would rise if and when revealed. But disturbed by Taffy's frenetic state Roam focused on here and now, on keeping the love of his life from skating too close to crazy.

Roam's baritone was intentionally muted. "Dollbaby, listen, Angel's not going anywhere. Neither are we. Your family needs you here to help ride out this storm—"

"No, Love, *you* listen!" Taffy jerked free of Roam's touch. "*We* might not be leaving, but I sho' 'nuff am."

"Taffy, they need you—"

"*I* need me!" Taffy shouted. "I've given enough, and I'm not riding another nothing for *nobody.* Including you."

Roam knew better than to bite the bait. Yet, he did. "Including me," Roam echoed tightly, jaw pulsing.

Pausing frenzied packing, Taffy glared. "You got what you wanted: me beneath you, legs wide to the wind, so go. Leave if you need!"

Night was twisting, muddying once clear things, and Roam had reached his boundary. "Let me quote you in saying I didn't do a thing you didn't want done. That was mutual greed. *How*-the-hell-*ever,* truth be told…what you gave *wasn't* mine to have. What you gave belonged to our marriage bed—"

"I belong to myself."

It was a certainty Roam couldn't dispute. Still, a steady, rising irritation was spilling over and spouting. "Do you think I would've laid you down had I known? I would've given you my name first."

"I have my own, and be clear about this, I laid myself down," Taffy fired, face liberated and glowing. "But—"

"But nothing, Taffy!" Roam's expression melded annoyance with incredulity. "You lied by omission! I understand that what that crazy-ass Big Baby did left you believing you were fully…opened… but 'opened' and 'engaging in' are night and day. You owed me *that* truth."

"You're right! Roam, I owed you that and more!" Still horrified by her fatal, unthinkable choices, Taffy snatched the baseball in Angel's suitcase, hurling it at a wall. "*Do you know how ignorant I feel?* Like an inch-high fool!" Shame claimed Taffy's face. "I blacked out I don't know how long." She'd never known the extent of Big Baby's doings. Had assumed it great in light that she'd bled for days. "Still, no, I don't excuse myself. I own that I've made damn too many stupid mistakes! And only God knows the price I'll pay." Taffy deeply inhaled. "I'm *ashamed* of all of this! I'm ashamed for my part in my mother's façade, for my denying you *my* whole truth. But I still can't ever regret physically loving you."

Roam's tone was harsh, rattling with remorse for taking something he couldn't return. "Good, Darlin', 'cause I can't rewind time and retrieve your virginity."

Taffy's eyes turned icy. "I'm sorry you chased what you thought was seasoned love, only to be dissatisfied with unlearned me—"

"Dammit, Taffy, I pursued you, not an illusion!" Roam bristled, chest drumming, too annoyed to admit just how utterly satisfied he'd been. "You should've kept yourself."

Voice rippling Taffy spoke to the root of Roam's angst. "Sweetness, you didn't rob, dishonor, or ruin me. I'm still whole and invaluable. I'm still Taffy." Sliding over Roam's attempt to reason—certain Roam had gifted his best—Taffy challenged, "Would your loving have differed had you known?"

"There're other women, certain kinds…"

Slamming a suitcase closed, Taffy flared upright. "Don't you dare label a woman without learning the loving names we call ourselves! What should I call a man rail-riding coast-to-coast, zipper smoking it's pulled down so frequent and furious? Whore? Or hypocrite?"

Dumbstruck and chilled Roam, growled, "That's a man's affair."

"And this is mine," Taffy celebrated, cupping the Eden between her legs. Mute and rooted, Roam watched Taffy fling open the bedroom door. "So don't talk ass-backwards about *my* virginity. It was mine to treasure," her sudden smile was ethereal, "and when I wanted to share it I did. Because I love you and I could. You don't owe me anything, and you sure don't deserve to be saddled with someone else's responsibility. So go where you go, Roam, even if it's hell. I'm woman enough to make my way."

The room swirled in silence as Taffy returned to packing.

My woman is *crazy*, Roam concluded, closing the door. "Dollbaby, this conversation is too off-track and so are we. This night's way wild. We gotta put it to rest," Roam urged, watching Taffy cram luggage beyond capacity. He exhaled heavily. "You can't take him—"

"Watch me."

"Let it go, Taffy. Angel's not yours." Roam reached for her. "Accept that."

Taffy backed away, angrily trying to pry free of Roam's hold—something inside of her cracking, snapping. Pummeled by hopelessness, futility, and unavoidable defeat—emotions convoluted and psyche wounded—despair escalated until Taffy was deaf to reason, hysterically repeating, *"Get off me!"*

"Taffy, stop it!" Roam urged to no avail, Taffy's screams painfully reverberating. At wits end, Roam backed her against a wall, cupping her face. "Baby, my getting off you won't change the fact that I've been *in* you. So let this go!"

Simple rawness of recounted intimacy proved a feather pushing Taffy over the brink.

CHAPTER FIFTY

Drew and Chloe arrived concerned. Their phone calls couldn't be connected. They came intending to inform Uncle T. he was needed at an emergency meeting of church leaders, only to find a somber gathering. But a ruckus above cut the morbid pall, bringing Bledsoe men to their feet, ready to pound upstairs but for Dena blocking entry.

"Sit yourselves down! Ain't nothing upstairs with your names on it."

"Dena, move!"

"I will when I'm ready, Drew."

"Taffy needs—"

"You to mind your business," Dena finished. "She's fine."

"Not with all that going on she's not," Drew contended amid murmured agreement.

"'All that' ain't got nothing to do with you, so back your musty behinds away from these stairs before I cut-the-monkey-and-act-a-fool."

"Babe, Taffy's okay," Chloe assured when men refused to move. "That man loves Taffy better than he loves himself. Roam won't hurt her."

"Better not," Drew fumed, not backing down but not pressing Dena either. "If he does, somebody's mopping blood."

Her fury came from a deep abyss. Roaring. Ripping. She was beyond control, transformed by heartbreak. Her wild thrashing sent them slipping on the mess of clothing at their feet. She crashed to the hardwood floors, inevitably pulling Roam with her. On all fours Taffy scrambled towards the door, only to be snatched back by arms that wouldn't desist. Pinning her back against his chest, Roam wrapped himself about her from behind and held tight until, slowly, fury deflated. Her struggle ceased and Taffy's tears spilled hot, cleansing.

"Let it out, Dollbaby. Cuss. Scream. Do what you need. But *let… it…go!*"

Taffy wailed until her throat ached—until her words trembled like a breeze. "I never did what folks said I did! I promise you I wasn't what they said I was."

"*Shhhh*, Baby, I know," Roam comforted, arms wrapped securely about her from behind, heart sharing her hurt.

"This town called me all kind of unclean things because of my *mother's* sins. I wasn't a 'ruint whore bearing a bastard'. I *wasn't* a disgrace," Taffy sobbed. "I didn't spread my legs for every man wanting a whiff."

Roam flinched. "Come on, Darlin'. I know this."

Taffy shifted in Roam's arms, confronting him. "You believed the worst like everyone else," she accused, pushing his chest, her face streaked with a sea of tears.

"Taffy, I only knew what I lived."

Taffy's voice quieted gradually as she stroked Roam's jaw, soothed by contact. "The moment I stepped off that train with Angel in my arms and saw my daddy, I made up my mind to tell you. My mama could falsify to her husband if she wanted, but I wouldn't lie to you. But you avoided me, wouldn't talk, and went out west, hating my guts. So I gave in. I did what they wanted and married Al, even though folks thought Angel was yours."

"Maybe for a moment I wished he was," Roam quietly confessed, wiping her tears, "and would've done for him even though he wasn't."

"Lord, God," Taffy moaned. "They told me you wouldn't want me." *But they knew!* Roam loved her enough. That's why they'd put her off on Alfredo to prevent discovery, because Roam wouldn't suffer the lie…

"I swore I'd mother Angel and never tell a soul; still they used Alfredo to cart me Up North where I was threat-to-none. I'm no saint. Or martyr. But I cooperated for Angel's sake. But only so far. I swore there'd be icicles in hell before letting that man in my bed!"

Roam couldn't help grinning. "Thank God hell's still hot."

"I wouldn't believe this wreck-of-a-mess but for the fact that I lived it. How do you tell folks 'my child isn't mine, he's my mother's conceived in adultery'?"

Perplexed, Roam shook his head, brushing loose hair from Taffy's brow.

"Lord! So many times I wanted to trade The Gift for Black Magic and snatch 'em all dead! Grandmother Lacy. Alfredo. My mother," Taffy admitted, voice cracking. "I made peace with it best I could, 'cause Angel was my heart and he deserved to be safe. And even though I hated her at times, I let it be done because, right or wrong, Roam, I love my mother. But *I'm* the only mother Angel knows!"

"Let him get to know his own."

"Seven years of my life! *Gone*!" Taffy persisted, weeping. "Angel's all I have to show for my time."

"*You* are what you have, Taffy, and that's plenty sufficient," Roam contradicted.

"I have me." Mulling truth, Taffy stroked Roam's cleft chin. "I kept myself, Sweetness. They tried to take my body and my virtue, but I kept me."

"Sho' 'nuff, you did," Roam acknowledged as Taffy settled into him, dripping crystal tears. "Come on, Dollbaby, let it go and relax for me," Roam coaxed until Taffy softened in his arms. "That's it… kiss it farewell."

"My body is mine and I've done right by it."

"Hell, yes, you have," Roam murmured against Taffy's hair.

"I won't let anyone put a word on me. I call myself something other than 'whore' and 'slut' or 'ruined bitch'. My worth is greater than who has or hasn't been between my legs. *I* own the right to say who and what I am, so I call myself God's daughter, and I'm precious to Him. I'm a good woman, Roam Ellis, and *this* body belongs to *me*."

Roam planted a cloud of a kiss on her brow. "You're a *damn good* woman, Octavia Bledsoe. And you're right." Lovingly, he cradled her, speaking softly. "You own this body, Beautiful, and I thank you for sharing it with me."

That's when armor truly shattered. Curled over Roam's arm, Taffy released the anguish of years until every arduous thing ever borne was drained, out with the wash and gone goodbye.

CHAPTER FIFTY-ONE

The quiet below was almost sinister after the commotion of before. Her mother was gone. Her father sat in the parlor, Angel beneath a light blanket, asleep in his Papa's arms. "Daddy?"

Tired of staring at the emptiness of life, Thaddeus slowly focused on the daughter lowering herself at his feet.

"You didn't deserve this, Daddy." She placed a gentle hand on his knee. "None of it! You had a right to know." Anger and remorse thickened Taffy's speech. "We gave you garbage and lies when you gave us nothing but good. I'm sorry, Daddy. I'm so sorry. You deserved better. I should've told you," Taffy repeatedly breathed, breaking.

A sleeping Angel in one arm, Thaddeus sheltered his daughter in the other, letting her weep on his chest a remnant of tears. "We're gonna be alright," he choked, voice rough, when she'd quieted.

Taffy's words reverberated against Thaddeus' chest. "Now you know why I didn't come home but twice a year. I hated the filthy, godforsaken secret between us, but I couldn't solve it! Not with the blood on her hands."

"*Whose* hands?"

"Grandmother Lacy. I don't know what all she did or to whom, Daddy, but I *saw* that blood! She destroyed before. Many times! So, I didn't doubt her threats, I knew she would again." Taffy shuddered, recounting violent scraps of newspapers and magazines heralding gory stories, sent monthly with Lacy's captioned writing: *Breathe one word and he breathes no more.* "It got so I stopped opening the envelopes and just burned them, but she still sent all those letters and brutal pictures promising Angel harm if I—"

"Babygirl, settle yourself," Thaddeus commanded, but Taffy couldn't hold it all.

"I was scared for Angel, Daddy. He's my brother, but he was my baby! I love this boy," Taffy muttered, stroking Angel's sleeping brow.

Thaddeus touched his child's head. "We all do, Taffy Sweet."

"I refused to let her hurt him, still that won't excuse my keeping this from you. I can't expect your pardon, but Lord *knows* I need it. Daddy, forgive me."

"Hush," Thaddeus murmured, stroking his daughter's bowed head. "Grown folks orchestrated this mess. And grown folks'll stand before God for it. So hush your crying. My disappointment in you is you taking on something that belonged somewhere else. Don't you *ever* again let *nobody* put nothing on you that ain't yours to bear. Roam Ellis!" Thaddeus hailed, halting the young man quietly departing.

"Mr. Thaddeus?"

Thaddeus eyed him shrewdly. "Be clear I would've killed you had I thought you were hurting my child up those stairs. You love my daughter." It was a statement, definitive.

"Always have, always will, sir. Kinda like her, too."

A shadowy smile flickered behind Thaddeus' devastated visage. "Come talk to me man-to-man when it's time."

Roam solemnly nodded before heading out the door. Thaddeus watched his daughter watching Roam and felt the rightness in their bond, despite their improper engagement in the inappropriate...

"I'm not asking you 'bout loving him 'cause I hear it in you," Thaddeus told his child, "but make wiser choices in acting out that love. Do right in the beginning and you're more likely not to have a bitter end." Thaddeus shook his head. "Thought I did right enough by your Mama." Thaddeus gazed at the boy sleeping soundly in the crook of his arm. "Somebody better step up and own this child. He has a right to know who he is."

"Angel's ours, Daddy," Taffy softly inserted, further words stalled by a commotion outdoors. "Lord, what now?" Taffy urged her weary father back onto his chair as he tried to rise. "Rest with Angel. If I need back-up your shotgun's nearby."

Grunting, Thaddeus watched his daughter exit before refocusing on his grandson... "*Hmph*! Not sure what to call you now. But I know we share blood," he concluded, wondering whose life Lacy had spilled, while thankful no one was there to witness an old man's tears.

Stepping onto the porch, Taffy was greeted by Chloe's screams. *"Drew! Roam! Stop it! Please!"*

"I *told* you not to touch her!" Drew yelled, rushing the porch where Dena's Hamp and another Bledsoe had Roam backed against the house, talking him down.

"Be the bigger man, Roam," Hamp urged. "Let it slide."

Roam massaged his jaw, incensed. "Did his black ass just punch me?!"

Taffy whirled. "Drew! You lost what's left of your right mind?"

Blocked by intervening kin, Drew hollered, "I told him to keep his hands off you! You're not his fly-by-night."

"And I never will be. But I *am* grown enough to choose whose bed I climb into!"

Incited by what he considered Taffy's cavalier response, Drew charged towards Roam. Someone grabbed him from behind. Drew shook off her hold, not realizing who it was. Unbalanced, she toppled backward down the steps, landing hard on her back.

"Chloe!" She lay deathly still as Taffy's cry split the night.

ᖚᕽᕽ

Men sat sequestered in the sanctuary. They'd assembled in hopes of resolution and a clear course of action in a world flipped wrong side up. R.J. Tinsley, a threat to none, had murdered a man. Now he waited in the tank. If they left him too long, R.J. was as good as gone.

The tank was where murders belonged...*if* indeed Tinsley's boy did the murdering. Rumor was Thaddeus' wild child had a hand in it. Lord, help if she did.

No one knew the deceased. Perhaps a visitor joining the festivities? Whoever he was, his death could prove a hardship to the town. The Judge and his Richland sheriff would gladly misuse the opportunity to lord themselves over Bledsoe. Worse still, Richland might get it in their white minds that a verdant, Black Bledsoe needed annexing. Or as one of the elders put it, "Next thing you know, Richland be done took over, and we'll be living up under crackers, like most Coloreds in America."

If a murder occurred.

Thus far, there was no corpse—just a missing person and R.J. Tinsley's nonsensical mutterings. The Reverend, elders, and visiting

clergy from Winter Cove and Drexel extended their condolences
to the bereaved (whoever that might be), but they had a way-of-life
worth protecting. The lack of a corpse was a lack of evidence. Some
dared pray that the dead didn't rise.

⌒⌒⌒

In the parlor he dozed, Angel in arms. A soft rapping at the front
door startled him awake. A familiar voice caused alarm. "Vesta?"

His sister-in-law stood at the parlor threshold, unable to enter.

"Everybody alright?" Thaddeus questioned, heart suddenly
thumping. "Rachel…"

Her answering gesture was odd, that of hurling something obscene. "She claims it was only once," Vesta recited, "but ain't once
enough? Once got all of us reaping a harvest can't nobody contain."

"Sit down, Vesta. What's going on?"

She approached, turning on a lamp, bathing the room with light.
She was haggard, intense, staring at the child sleeping against his
Papa's chest. "Just needed to see for myself." Fingers falling on his
forehead, she traced his profile, outlined an ear, laid a hand on his
head and wept. "They went looking for you when you got swallowed
up in Mississippi. All the brothers did. Taking turns escorting Rachel,
making sure she was covered. Wasn't til they found you in that peni-
tentiary that my man took to taking her regularly." Vesta's voice rode
a tidal wave. "He was the lawyer able to fight that foolishness and get
you home. But when that court claimed you were looking at life Rachel got desperate. Says she just needed a little comfort and strength,
that she took the lead and he fell into it," Vesta recounted, shivering.
"All it took was needy lips and hips."

Looking on his brother's wife, Thaddeus' heart turned to dust.
"You telling me Rachel and…*Augustine*…?"

Vesta nodded, sobering, spine straightening. "Do what you see
fit, but I'm saying this only once, and then I'm finished. My husband,
your brother, fathered this child."

CHAPTER FIFTY-TWO

S he tumbled in the center of a stale tomb. Walls wept and floors groaned beneath ostentatious hoarding. In her parents' home, air was scarce amid lavish proof that her mother was delivered from sharecropping.

"Stuff," Rachel muttered, loathing every inch and ounce of Lacy's luxuries. A social climber to the bitter end, "stuff and status" had fed Lacy's mania. Now Lacy was gone, and Rachel was left with lifeless, inanimate trappings. She preferred warmth and breath, husband's arms, and children's love, but Rachel had none.

Monster!

She scoured rooms seeking deliverance from grief. She'd betrayed a love bordering on worship. Fearing disillusionment and loss of pedestal, she'd transferred ugly sins onto her daughter's purity.

Taffy was strong. Taffy was gifted. Taffy was resilient and could absorb Rachel's stain. So Lacy claimed.

"And I capitulated like a fool, choosing one child over the other." *Because*? Angel, an unexpected sweetness in barren years, was the one she could restrain.

From her birth, Lacy harped on Taffy's oddity, questioned Rachel's ability, spoon-feeding ineptitude and insecurity until Rachel felt ill-equipped at mothering the gifted. She couldn't harness the fire of her child—this antithesis of Rachel's stodgy upbringing. Headstrong and bold, where Rachel had been taught to behave, Taffy was Bledsoe to the bone.

"She only has my eyes," Rachel lamented like a non-contributing bystander, finally able to admit her jealousy: of Taffy's bond to NuNu, Thaddeus' stamping their child, of standing on the sidelines while Taffy mothered *her* child.

Marry her off and send her Up North. No need for daily reminders or misery, said Lacy. There was no love lost. Lacy wasn't bound to a granddaughter '*too black, too Bledsoe, and not enough Rachel.*'

Despite the prospect of missing her children, Rachel agreed. But three years later, when Alfredo called lying about Taffy's loose living, Rachel orchestrated her son's return. Rachel welcomed him home, certain a heartbroken Taffy would heal.

She'd used her daughter mercilessly. Now she had no one.

Monster!

Rachel bit the inside of her mouth, suppressing ready screams, fearing she carried *the sickness* of her maternal line. Cousins Imogene and Big Baby. Grandmother's unprovoked rage, peppered with tyrannical ramblings about a white man who loved her only so much. And Lacy's brooding melancholy, and the slaps that came with or without provocation. These women painted disorder across the canvas of Rachel's days. She vowed never to repeat their madness but, stuck there in the middle of Lacy's luxurious clutter, Rachel decided only insanity could account for her defiling a proper alignment of things.

You're one of us. She was clearly next-in-line to bear an unstable crown.

"No…I have free-will. I choose differently," Rachel insisted. Refusing a life of mental incapacity, she pushed aside the clutter atop her father's desk, searched drawers and boxes stacked against the wall. "Where is it?!" she screamed, overturning the desk chair and racing room to room, searching for her father's firearm.

Rachel searched in vain, ransacking, dismantling until collapsing against her mother's bedroom armoire where she wailed and pounded wood as if flesh.

The lock broke. Doors sprang open, spewing treasures. Books, trinkets, fabric scraps, and knickknacks tumbled at Rachel's feet as she angrily rocked the armoire.

A panel dislodged. Rachel wildly tossed it across the room, finding a hidden compartment now revealed. There sat a box. Rachel flung it downward, hoping for closure, only to find history.

She flopped to the floor, depleted, quieting her rough breathing. More curious than calm, Rachel sifted through spilled contents. No gun. Just locks of hair. A leather-bound bible. Newspaper clippings. They lay like puzzle pieces to someone's past.

Golden strands of hair had grown dull with time. The Holy Word held curious births and deaths penned on their proper pages in a steady masculine-like hand. Desperate, Rachel turned the Bible's pages needing perfect peace. Instead, Rachel found mystery.

Worn and aged, the bible's inner lining was frayed. Vellum curled away from its moorings, exposing yellowed glue beneath. Pressing paper back in place, Rachel felt a bulge. Head cocked in curiosity, she pried away lining, finding an envelope underneath.

Her mother's flowery script offered a singular inscription. *Twins.*

Opening envelope, Rachel dumped contents onto her lap. Sepia-toned photographs bore evidence of bygone days.

Two small girls returned Rachel's stare through laughing, funny-colored eyes. One child was considerably fairer, but silken curls, chubby cheeks and cat-like gaze were shared. Obviously adored, they filled print after print, offering no clue of identity other than the *"L. & G., age __"* penned on the back of each. Then a third party appeared.

Rachel gasped, finding a fair-skinned young Colored woman, a twin hugging her on either side. "Grandmother?" Rachel breathed, turning over the photo and finding the name, *Marie.*

The grandmother Rachel recalled was lost to stark melancholy. This timeless woman was beautifully sweet, lively and happier than Rachel ever recalled her grandmother being.

"Then L. is for Lacy," Rachel muttered, reexamining the photographs with new clarity. Yet there was confusion. Lacy's father and only sibling had been lost in Lacy's infancy. Or so she'd been led to believe. This unnamed child with sunshine curls proved otherwise. Her mother's sibling had survived?

"Her *twin*," Rachel emphasized, dumbfounded, examining the remaining photographs showing a progression of years and the fracturing of a family.

Grandmother Marie and Lacy disappeared, leaving the pale-skinned twin to dominate each frame until there was a leap in time and a piece-of-a-man materialized. Time and again, his face was ripped away. Only age-spotted hands and the inscription *"Papa with G."* survived.

Rachel returned to the bible, scouring pages earmarked for family chronology. Amid the marriages she found the joining of Midas and Marie—a date and no surname—and a birth entry coinciding with her mother's, followed by the disconcerting *"L. and G."* Rachel searched, but further clues were missing.

Disturbed, Rachel returned photographs to envelope, reached

into box and retrieved ribbon-bound hair. Silken. Pale. Like those of the photographed girl so fair she could easily be mistaken for something other than Colored.

"Marie and Midas," Rachel voiced, hoping to dislodge neglected memories. Finding none, she smirked at the ridiculousness of pinning such a name on a child. Midas? As in that Greek god of the golden touch...

Hair grew heavy in hands. Golden...flaxen..."G."... Goldie? "Lord, *no*!"

Goldie Hale Thornton was her mother's twin...Rachel's aunt? Memory became a slow-moving reel flickering across Rachel's mind. She recalled Miss Goldie's doting kindness, and peculiar connection to Lacy. Their hush-hush visits. The intimate laughter and obvious affection. Miss Goldie's inconsolable self at Lacy's passing. Two women—one "white", one Colored—tangled, crying, fussing, and genuinely loving.

Closely reexamining the photographs, Rachel found proof in a barely visible surname: Hale. She flipped back to the Bible's beginnings, scanning again the marriage entries, finding atop the page that beautifully penned 'Midas and Marie'. Her grandmother could only print her name and simple words in big, block letters. This entry was elegant, evidence of education and tenderness. Faced with anti-miscegenation laws, had Preacherman Midas Hale written the entry as a tangible tribute to his "wife", Marie?

Her grandfather was a white man. Grandmother Marie was Preacherman Hale's first "wife," the one he'd claimed had died in Goldie's youth?

Grandmother Marie hadn't died young, had lived to nearly eighty; and her 'husband' and child certainly hadn't died in a day. "Pure lies," Rachel mourned, juxtaposing memory with facts now faced. Had they loved each other, these parents of twins who'd split their mixed-heritage in two? Fingering sepia pictures, Rachel concluded Goldie absorbed the father's whiteness while Lacy alone manifested traces of Grandmother Marie's Colored ancestry. Same wide mouths, strange gray eyes, and eccentric behavior. They were different covers of the same book, equal halves of one heart. Bound by 'blackness', Lacy was left behind, her white legitimated twin passing to the other side.

Now Rachel understood Lacy's inherent bitterness, her being

hell-bent about stations in life, skin color, proper this or that. "And I married a dark man." Rachel realized Lacy's taking Angel and putting him on Taffy was punishment as well as race hatred, and not merely abhorrence for bastards in her line.

Grandmother Marie, Lacy, Imogene, Big Baby, poor R.J...now Crazy Miss Goldie? All models of mental inadequacy. And Rachel was one of them. Blood and behavior bore proof.

Rachel threw pictures and hair back into the box as if burned. She refused bitter knowledge, wouldn't add further instability to her ancestry. Yet irresistibly drawn, she peered into the box afraid of what else waited.

There was nothing save morbid newspaper clippings and obit-uaries—three old, one new, marked with her mother's script. An unknown Reverend Odysseus Jenkins *("child defiler")*, some woman named 'Madame' *("slaver")*, Lacy's stepfather *("opportunist")*, and Augustine *("fool")*. Of all the brothers, Lacy preferred Auggie. Even sought his company a year ago. Needed legal advice. Would he mind stopping by and help order her affairs...

Rachel abruptly stood, overturning the box. Out rolled a brown vial, a replica of the one Lacy harbored the night of Angel's birth. Glancing back at Augustine's obituary, Rachel gasped, slow to believe Lacy would harm him only to realize she'd given Lacy cause. Over-come by chills, Rachel backed out the door and away from the room, mind flashing back on the "medicinal" tea her mother insisted she drink during her first pregnancies. Rachel's refusing it when pregnant with Taffy because...

I don't want tar-black grandbabies.

Her mother killed her children? Rachel screamed and screamed, pleading that madness end.

Fire next time.

Her father's missing firearm wasn't her sole solution. Finding a candle, Rachel doused all lights. Flickering candlelight distorted her sobbing features. "No more harming or hurting!" Desperate for freedom, Rachel lit the brocade curtains in her mother's prized parlor. Orange flames warmed her face. Fire spread its wings and ate. When death appeared in the midst of smoke and flames, Rachel smiled and walked into death's sweet embrace.

CHAPTER FIFTY-THREE

F   ire ripped. Pain possessed. Yet, she held on.
    "You're doing fine, Chloe. Just breathe," Dena encouraged,
    beside NuNu at Chloe's feet.

A thin cotton shift plastered against her skin, Chloe lay in her
claw-foot tub, ensconced in water's warm grip, fighting fear. Her
backward fall down Aunt Rachel's front steps had precipitated birth
weeks too soon.

"Please, God, let my baby be alright," she pleaded, tongue salty
with tears.

"*Shhhh*, Little Bird, stop that crying and save your strength,"
NuNu gently admonished.

NuNu came as life's handmaiden. She was escort and ally ushering Bledsoe babies, grand and great. All except Angel, whose birth
had been far removed.

Was always convinced Angel didn't come the right way, yet she
couldn't have imagined the truth of his origins. NuNu grieved. Vexed
in spirit over her daughter-in-law's wrongdoing, and Angel and Taffy's
misconnection, NuNu couldn't welcome this new one. Not like this.
A child deserved to enter an unpolluted space. So, NuNu swept her
spirit, flung Rachel's treachery from her heart, and purified the place
with prayer.

"Gracious Creator, we honor and welcome You. Make us worthy
of Your presence. Grant us Your pure essence and infinite strength as
we receive this child You've kissed. May the ancestors escort her safely
on a pathway of peace. Amen."

"Amen," Taffy softly echoed, perched on a stool and mopping
Chloe's brow. She knew she shouldn't be here. NuNu's handmaidens
needed to have walked this journey themselves before aiding another.
Taffy was childless. But Chloe was adamant, nearly hysterical at the
thought of Taffy's exclusion. NuNu compromised. Taffy would be the

child's godmother, and through Angel had earned motherhood. What NuNu had yet to learn was that Taffy had ushered her own brother to earth. For now, NuNu sniffed the air and deemed it sweet. Life could come.

"Little Bird, I need to check your birthing place to see how far we've come."

Chloe nodded and braced herself for another examination, but before NuNu could move, all pressure shifted downward and Chloe felt the need to release. Breathless with pain, Chloe struggled to push herself upright.

"Girl, where're you going?" Dena demanded, alarmed.

"I can't hold it and I can't do number two in the tub," Chloe panted as Taffy anchored her beneath her arms.

NuNu's laughter was rich. "Little Bird, that urge ain't for the bathroom. That's a prompt to push this baby into her birthday. Ease her back down, Little One, and let's be about this thing. Dena, hand the jar to Taffy. Little One, rub the salve on her temples, soothe Little Bird's mind 'cause this baby's coming fast." *Too fast*, NuNu kept to herself while sanitizing a long-handled razor.

The jar Taffy opened released aromatic perfume. "Rub her temples and help her feel good," NuNu instructed, attempting to distract while praying the ointment recently applied had numbed Chloe good. Chloe was too slight, and this baby too big to come without ripping. NuNu had to aid the birthing place. "Sit there, Warrior Girl, and charm her belly." Dena obeyed, gently massaging, drawing overlapping circles atop Chloe's distended abdomen. "Figure eights for infinity," NuNu reminded, "so our line continues. So we won't know where this child begins and Bledsoes end."

Room filled with soft and orderly motion, NuNu hummed an ancient tune from across the waters, from her mouth to God's ears. "Anchor her good, Little One," NuNu cautioned. "This baby's racing to meet her mama."

Taffy leaned against the tub, bracing Chloe from behind as NuNu launched an ethereal song that swirled about their heads, weaving with Chloe's groans. NuNu's razor sliced. Chloe arched. Her scream tore. Water pulsed with blood and the unborn slid lower, but didn't come.

Taffy whispered counsel received. "Let her go, honey. She's ready."

Chloe's head lolled. She felt delirious watching two wavering figures in the doorway. The dearly departed holding a child's hand?

Mama?

The word slipped from Chloe's mouth, and NuNu's humming ceased.

NuNu smiled. "Ahhh, Corrine, thank you for walking this sweet soul home. Little Bird, can she come?"

Chloe weakly nodded and the vision vanished.

"Warrior Girl," NuNu told Dena, "you're kneading and pushing now, helping this strong baby home. Chloe, if you're ready so are we." Like one living organism, the women named Bledsoe moved in sync. Ragged breaths were shared, every shriek and groan met by loving exhortation. But too long later, when Chloe's body still held on, Taffy slipped into the tub behind Chloe and lent strength—bracing, pushing in tandem until Chloe was vast enough to birth a new universe.

Exhausted Chloe lay back against Taffy loving the first sounds of her child's new song. Unspeakable ecstasy claimed Chloe's soul as her handmaidens tossed hallelujah bouquets.

"Chloe Jean Bledsoe, you have yourself a right fine baby girl and, amazing Lord, I have another little brown naked to love!" NuNu thrilled. "Dena, stop happy dancing and fetch those rags so I can clean this child. What's her name, Little Bird?"

"Corrine Marie," Chloe managed, loving the lusty sounds of her child's cries. "My mother's first, her godmother's second."

"Welcome to the world, Corrine Marie," NuNu whispered, bathing the newest jewel in the Bledsoe crown. "I'm your daddy's grandmother, Octavia, but you can call me 'NuNu' since you're mine," NuNu purred, stroking the slick hair covering the baby's head. Sprinkling water on the baby's skull she prayed, "Walk in wisdom and grow in grace, and fulfill God's purpose for your living always. Amen."

"Amen," the exhausted congregants echoed, basking in the power of a miracle. They watched as NuNu separated the infant from the bonding chord. Reverently, NuNu placed the chord and sac in a bowl as an offering to the earth. When NuNu finished and the child was swaddled, she placed her in Chloe's waiting arms.

"She's amazing," Chloe uttered, the women gathering around, anointing child with awestruck love. Chloe counted fingers and toes, and cherished every raw inch of plumpness, thankful to God and these women, her escorts of life.

⤶⤷

Smoke billowed and rolled—stinging, suffocating. Lungs burned and life ebbed as fire raged about the one gratefully sinking. Cuddling death, she was suddenly deprived.

Strong arms yanked her up, pulled her out into the wide night. Wracking coughs convulsed her frame, shaking her back to consciousness. A starry sky decorated by flames proclaimed her yet among the living.

"I'd be a fool to let you die," the rescuer gasped, maneuvering Rachel's slight weight, depositing her on the grass a safe distance from the blaze. "I pray you live a ripe long while, and every day you do, may you get a taste of what you've done."

In the distance, bells tolled, alerting the town's emergency brigade. Rachel Bledsoe lay on the grass bitterly weeping, angry that even death denied her embrace.

CHAPTER FIFTY-FOUR

He was jarred awake by a sound in the night. Home was a place where locks need not be engaged. But after city dwelling, out of habit, he did. Or so he thought. Padded footsteps testified to the contrary. He reached for the handgun in the bedside table drawer.

"Roam…"

Dog-tired, he was momentarily confused by a bewitching apparition. Light cascading through his open window showered down silver moonbeams that floated uninterrupted through her shift, silhouetting naked splendor underneath.

"Taffy?" Roam's voice slurred with fatigue. "What's wrong? The baby—"

"Chloe and our goddaughter are fine." Hovering close, she kissed him gently. "Mama burned Grandmother Lacy's house near-'bout-to-the-ground."

Roam sat up, amazed he'd slept through the town's latest upheaval. "Is she hurt?"

"Time will heal," Taffy supplied. "It wasn't accidental."

"You don't know that."

"I know my mother," Taffy replied, touching him intimately.

Roam lay back. Even in moonlight she hypnotized. "I swear before God your family tree is twisted at the roots," Roam mumbled about a yawn, distracted by Taffy's fingers skimming his bare abdomen. "Hold up…Dollbaby, now…'," he caught her wrist, "we agreed no more 'til 'I Do'. That's why I left you with Mr. Thaddeus under lock and key. So why're you here?" Roam questioned, the radiating heat of her need making his head swim.

Smiling seductively, Taffy slid covers away from Roam's nakedness, exposing his undeniable readiness. Pulling her garment overhead, Taffy carelessly discarded it and found her place beside him, whispering, "I understand wanting someone like you want your next breath," before bestowing a kiss that unleashed Roam's cravings.

Roam's voice was thick with something other than sleep when managing to speak. "Woman, *you're* out-of-order but your Daddy's liable to kill *me*." Roam reached for her, unable not to. "Hell…'I Do', you do, too."

Not home enough to make it more than a waste, Roam thought the contraption an unnecessary expense on his parents' part and suggested they disconnect the thing. But First Lady Ellis insisted otherwise. It should be there just in case.

Roam fumbled for the ringing contraption, accidentally knocking it from the bedside table. Noisily, it clattered to the ground. She merely turned, snuggling deeper beneath the sheet. Fleetingly, he wondered if Taffy were this deep a sleeper or sleeping deeply *because*. Because they'd been insatiable and uninhibited, desperately capturing all the loving they could keep…

"Yeah," he mumbled into the telephone drowsily.

"We've got crap on our hands." Roam remained quiet. Drew continued. "Imogene Tinsley's on her broom and bringing Sheriff Bailey along for the ride. Taffy's her target." Roam cursed. "Knowing my hot-headed cousin, she's there with you, so don't bother play-acting. We gotta put something on this."

"Drew…brotha—"

"My cousin's grown. What you and Taffy do is between you," Drew grudgingly conceded. "Right now we have bigger problems than your britches breaking. If Sheriff Bailey comes 'round that way—"

"I'll be here."

"So will I," Drew promised. "'Ey, look, I'm sorry about clocking you."

"Punch me again and a Bledsoe's coming up missing." Call disconnected, Roam returned the telephone to the bedside table. Rubbing his brow, Roam groaned before turning towards the sleeping woman in his bed. "You're more trouble than you're worth," he lied.

This woman has me wrapped, tied, and tangled, Roam allowed, knowing he should've refused her and sent Taffy back where she belonged. But where was that except with him?

You didn't want me.

Simply profound, her response nearly broke him when questioning why she'd stayed with Freeman, and prolonged her mother's elaborate deceit. Taffy could've ended seven years of entrapment and lies six months ago when Lacy Marchand died. "It no longer mattered after all that time. You didn't want me, and I loved my brother." Taffy accepted her lot. "He was mine."

Roam's want was unquestionable, unquenchable now. Roam needed Taffy in his life, blood, and bed. Had to roll out on that iron horse the next morning, and wasn't sure what could be solidified in such short time, but Roam vowed to do what he could to ensure he came home to *them*.

He knew porters with 'outside situations'—bigamists with cross-country wives—but Roam was disinterested in a 'set-up'. He preferred Taffy's honor, safety and well-being. With a sudden rush to protect and do right by what they had, Roam renewed a long-ago vow to give Taffy a home, babies, and unquestionable fidelity. Loving only one, he loved hard. This woman was his everything.

Roam's thoughts were diverted by Taffy's incoherent mumbling. Roam was on instant alert, thinking Taffy caught by another Dupre-induced nightmare. But a sleeping Taffy turned towards him smiling softly, bedcovers slipping, treating Roam to the sight of a firm, full breast.

Taffy Mae, Taffy Mae! God knew how to shape a woman right!

Curved, tucked, ripe, lush—Taffy's body was an elaborate minefield of triggers susceptible to Roam's touch. He stroked her gently. Even in sleep Taffy responded, mouth parting, body curving… Roam grinned lustily, remembering.

Thought he'd drown in her honeyed walls that marked him for always—claiming parts, mixing and mingling in places previously out-of-range. She all but owned him, settling inside him, invading, her infinite layers burrowing deep. She left him full. Heart exposed. Cognizant he was first-and-only, Roam struggled to reign himself in, let Taffy set the tempo. Woman proved fire and feast. What she'd stored up and denied was feverishly released, leaving them both weak. Roam readily accepted her lavish offerings. Taffy somehow reduced his past dalliances to simple gratification, taught him that intimacy of body *and* soul produced incomparable completion. Housing wicked wantonness beneath sweet innocence, Taffy was mesmerizing heat and unmatched ecstasy. Their bodies told all and found sweet release as they repeatedly satiated themselves in each other until spent and intertwined with nothing between them, not even the night.

And she was 'unlearned'? Roam muted a laugh. "Lord, have mercy, baby, when you fully come into your own..." Imagining a lifetime of gratifying her every physical need had Roam rising.

Get your mind up and out the bed, Roam self-admonished, calming ready flesh while checking the bedside table drawer. Both were there, his gun and the dead man's.

God knew what Miss Imogene had cooked up or how white law might rise but, additionally, Roam's pearl-handled pistol and double-barrel shotgun were willing and waiting. A momentary thought to take Taffy back to the safety of Mr. Thaddeus' came and went.

That's my *woman.* He'd defend her with his life, was willing to go to jail if not hell.

Kissing the swell of Taffy's breast, Roam rearranged the covers, concealing Taffy from sight not mind. Grabbing an ever-ready cigar and both guns, Roam quietly left the room.

Set. Locked. And loaded.

CHAPTER FIFTY-FIVE

Awaking in an empty bed, massive memories rolled disjointed, far more bizarre beneath the clarity of day. Loving. Revelation. Adultery and maternal claims. Arson. New birth. And at the beginning, death.

Taffy refused 'murder'—a premeditated evil. R.J.'s reaction to the loss of something treasured was horrific and the outcome grisly, yet he was no monster deserving a cage.

He caused all who held them captive to show them mercy.

Inhaling the psalm's gentle comfort, Taffy prayed much mercy before twisting away from the macabre into a warm spot, emanating peppermint, red spice, and tender scents. Her body tingled with memory and loving's sweetest remnants. It was enough to set Taffy squirming, tangling self in cool linen as if Roam's hot embrace.

That man is some kind of good.

Smiling sultrily, Taffy stretched, thinking Roam marvelous, God's handcrafted masterpiece. And Aunt Vesta need not know the measure...

Taffy felt her blood heat.

Had to be sinful, what that man made her feel. In his hands, her body became amazingly animated, supremely sensitive. "Lord, today..."

Wiggling onto her back, limbs dangling over the bed's edge, Taffy labeled Roam more than mere skill, finesse, and prowess. Wickedly delicious, Roam offered his heart wrapped in the body's sensual best. The man was gluttonous, his appetite like a living, all-consuming, bottomless thing. Generous, attentive, his own pleasure ricocheting with hers, Roam gave as good as he got. Persuasive, the man didn't love her by rote. *Show me what you want and need.* Suppressed erotic resurrected, Taffy had—learning her virgin self intimately while shedding a forsaken self like old snake skin.

Taffy sat half-way up against the headboard, thankful for grace. Roam's pardon undeserved but given, Taffy had layered her loving with whispered apologies and soul-deep repentance. Discovering her power to pleasure a man, Taffy wiped Roam's hurts away, forging an exquisite path of atonement, forgiveness, with every tender caress and kiss.

Taffy ran a hand through her untamed hair, marveling at oneness. It was unparalleled, defying description. She couldn't call it any one thing, this night-long loving. It varied, rhythmic, rapacious—brazen but sweet—leaving them both atop a mountain, struggling to breathe. Other times languid enough to satiate, to store and keep. Taffy treasured each, was utterly amazed by the multifaceted means of Roam's giving. Offering herself fully, like a flower stretching towards the sun, Taffy reached for herself, for Roam, and found precious treasures within her femininity. She'd been reckless, devouring, sharing the sacred with the only man she'd ever crave. Now, he was hers. They were one. She prayed not three...

Taffy rubbed her belly involuntarily, chiding self for discarding common sense with her clothing. Neither had been prudent. Not Taffy, or Roam—despite priding himself on self-protection and 'not fertilizing fields'. Having never lain with a woman without his own protective covering, Roam had let down his guard, got lost in loving. Solely with Taffy. Every loving. They shared culpability, yet Taffy placed no blame. Her body was *her* responsibility.

She could head to Trenton in hopes of obtaining that preventative something attainable in an Up North clinic—thanks to Margaret Sanger and her thinly veiled agenda of racial eugenics. Eugenics aside, Taffy agreed with a woman's power to manage her reproductive rights.

"Honey, you didn't manage nothing..."

Caught up in the rapture of Roam, Taffy had left herself vulnerable, unprotected in that maiden, sensual voyage that changed her body and her being. She prayed she hadn't conceived a beautiful possibility.

And if...

She couldn't entertain the idea of forfeiting a life conceived in love. And if she had? What was, was. Still, Taffy carefully protected herself post initial intimacy. She hoped her proactive means proved enough until making it to Trenton. Taffy didn't question NuNu's remedies, rather her own measuring and mixing.

Before returning to Roam, she'd fumbled through NuNu's pharmacopeia, relying on memory, reluctant to expose herself and alert her grandmother to her prophylactic needs. Did the bitter draught take effect immediately, or require time in her system for potency?

Taffy laughed at herself. "A small detail you can't recall."

God be gracious…*if.* If indulgence had led to new life. If the elixir needed time and too soon she'd be required to look Roam in the eye and tell him she carried his child.

I was unprotected only once.

"And?" Taffy challenged herself aloud. Her baby brother was proof positive that once was more than enough.

Taffy shook her head, waved a hand to shoo away anxiety. The morning was too sweet for sour thinking. "And truth be told…" Her lips softened with a smile. Taffy treasured the idea of one day bearing Roam's child. But only when she was Alfredo-free, and 'Mrs. Ellis' was her title.

Slipping from bed with a saturated sigh, Taffy searched for her discarded shift, admitting blurring if not abolishing too many boundaries and lines. Yet, she couldn't apologize to anyone except God.

Even so…

Taffy wanted to lose the world and hide away with Roam in this their oasis of sensuality. But like the sun, reality was rising.

Judging by the warm, golden light sliding between the bedroom curtains, Taffy knew it was too late to slip back into her father's house, absence undetected. She didn't care about sparing herself shame as much as her father further embarrassment. Familial love was certain. Approval? Not necessarily. Walking out the door was walking back into Bledsoe and beneath family's microscopic scrutiny.

Her father was peace-loving, but proud. Learning of his wife's great indiscretion publicly, albeit amid family, could only deepen a mortal wound. Taffy held no grand illusions. Her parents' union was beyond ruined. And she loathed the part she'd played in its demise.

Easing into her cotton shift, exhaling forcefully, Taffy tried reconciling the fact that she was little more than a child when Angel became hers. She'd been threatened, manipulated, lied to, and physically violated. Life had taken liberties. Still, Taffy struggled with allowing the situation so long, couldn't exonerate self from her parents' predicament, or the truths she'd owed Roam and omitted. Yet, she'd been forgiven. Taffy labored to extend herself the same grace.

Moving towards the door, Taffy paused before the dresser mirror to greet her reflection. It was amazingly free of angst—transformed, tender, and testifying.

"Girl…that face'll tell your business," she scolded with a smile. "You just got outta man's bed. And you look a ripe mess!" Miss Marva would pitch a fit at the love-induced birds' nest atop Taffy's head. Such was the price of some *sho' 'nuff* southern comfort in the cookies.

Laughter sparkling, Taffy left the room, pushing back loose hair along with thoughts of Monday. Today was all they had. Tomorrow the iron horse would reclaim her man. Helplessly addicted, Taffy was tempted to find Roam and invite him back to his bed. But overindulgence and excessive discovery left an ache, courtesy of Roam, in Taffy's treasured places. In need of soothing, she headed for a hot bath instead.

"Good Morning, Love."

At the sound of Taffy's approach, Roam entered the house, intent on keeping Taffy from what waited. Planting a possessive grip about her hips, Roam maneuvered Taffy backwards away from day. "My best morning yet."

"First of many," Taffy assured, cupping Roam's face.

"That a promise you plan to keep?"

"Try me," Taffy challenged, melting into Roam's morning kiss so deep and sweet she felt dizzy. Her hands strayed from his face, down chest, lifting shirttail from jeans and across his hard abdomen… southward drifting.

Roam inched back, unwillingly. "Gal, I'mma stop you 'fore you get started." In his arms, Taffy's body dripped heat and promised ecstasy.

"Tired?" Taffy purred, smoky-eyed and sultry.

"I oughta be, messing with all this homegrown honey."

"You'll rest on the rails."

Roam snorted, grinning. "Compared to satisfying you, those rails come easy." Taffy's laughter was supreme. Humor abandoned, Roam turned serious. "Much as I like holding all this extra and seeing you in nearly nothing, get dressed. I'm taking you to Trenton for the Chicago outbound. Your luggage is by the door."

Briefly noting suitcases waiting, Taffy locked sight on the shotgun outside the screen door. Brow arched, she studied Roam's stiff countenance. "What am I *not* running from today?" She stood, arms crossed, absorbing Roam's relayed information: Cousin Imogene was livid at her son's 'wrongful' imprisonment while Taffy remained free.

"She's moved from Sheriff Bailey to The Judge," Roam explained, "and when Judge rises the Klan rolls with him." Roam would protect hearth and home, but he preferred not jeopardizing the lives of others in the process. And what waited on his front porch could result in a bloody Sunday. "So, we're leaving."

"Am I guilty of something?"

"Killing Dupre, according to Miss Imogene's witness. Paris Brown's willing to testify she saw you shoot him."

"She'll testa-*lie*!"

"We both know who killed Dupre and how, Dollbaby."

Taffy's eyes narrowed dangerously. "Then why have me sneaking off like a thief in the night?"

"A witness, false or not, changes the nature of things."

"So just squirrel me outta town and leave R.J. to his fate?"

"The grapevine's circulating word on it," Roam disclosed, referring to that fraternal, interconnected system by which porters moved information rapidly. "We'll find the legal representation R.J. needs. Still, R.J. has a lot riding on his side." Voice fluid as his father's, Roam patiently elucidated the situation, his legal jargon a fusillade of intellectual warfare. Insufficient evidence…absence of premeditation, malice aforethought…R.J.'s inability to stand trial due to mental incapacity and incompetence precluding him from testifying on his own behalf…self-defense and provocation. "Hopefully that's enough to keep him for now. But you're leaving."

Taffy shook her head. "I didn't kill anyone."

"Doesn't matter. Miss Imogene's out for blood."

"I'm not running. Not anymore."

"And I'm not arguing, so get dressed, 'cause you're not stepping on that porch in front a bunch of men, parading your blessings in that piece-of-nothing."

"What men?" Taffy demanded, moving to the front window, shifting curtains aside, gasping and gaping. "What…in the…world is…this?"

"A bunch of Bledsoes."

Bledsoe men—cousins, uncles, Poppy, her father—created an impenetrable wall of flesh. Taffy didn't bother counting. There were twenty if there were two. Enclosed within a human wall of safety, Taffy was overwhelmed, humbled…and annoyed.

Taffy whirled on Roam. "Does *everybody* need a gun or more?"

"Simply exercising our constitutional right to bear arms." Roam grinned smugly, omitting the fact that he had four.

He'd learned from life-on-the-rails that hardworking men played harder still. Consequently, the juke joints, pool halls and Porters' clubs Roam patronized housed hard men, laughing men, soft men who could wax evil at the drop of a dime over a pool shot or card game gone sour. Let the opposite sex be involved and the atmosphere could wax lethal. He'd seen men punched, stomped, and stabbed for messing with the wrong woman. Roam had a *right* woman, and the artillery to protect her.

"This is half-past crazy!" Taffy fumed. She'd known occasions when the men of Bledsoe had rallied, armed, protecting some inno-cent from unlawful harm. But never to this extent. And never on her behalf.

"Might get worse if we don't get to Trenton."

"I don't want anybody discharging not one gun on my account!"

Roam shrugged. "Then put some clothes on and we're gone." Taffy dropped onto the sofa, irritated and uncooperative. "I'm past talking sense into your stubbornness," Roam grumbled, snatching open a suitcase to extract garments.

"And I'm past listening," Taffy volleyed.

Jaw grinding, Roam reached her in two strides. Lifting Taffy from her perch, he began the undressing.

Taffy tried pulling away. "Roam, stop it! Judge Thornton won't step foot in Bledsoe today for the same reason he hasn't in the past six decades. *NuNu!*"

"I appreciate your grandmother's power, but I'm not taking chances."

Taffy's protests were drowned by Drew's voice rolling in from outdoors. "Ellis! Company's coming."

With a curse, Roam freed the pistol hidden at the small of his back, pressing it into Taffy's grasp. "If anybody other than me crosses that threshold shoot 'em."

"Might shoot even if it is you," Taffy mumbled, crossly.

Roam couldn't help chuckling as he left, closing the door firmly behind.

Their coiled energy was palatable. Reverend's boy's most of all. Smoking a stoagie, meticulously checking the mechanisms of multiple firearms, he was a watchdog-at-the-door, wound up tight enough to strike.

Walking up the road, NuNu watched him hard, her mother nature rising. He'd lain with her granddaughter. She saw it, the power and imprint of their intimacy oozing from Roam Ellis like warm oil. Knew it when she played possum, listening to her granddaughter rifle through her sacred pantry in search of herbs to brew and drink.

NuNu bristled. Younguns liked to turn the world backwards, lying together without ceremony, name exchange, or jumping the broom before God. There was a time when Colored folks couldn't marry, and their bodies were divvied out for breeding babies sold from their keep. NuNu fumed, wanting something for her granddaughter other than momentary pleasure, heartbreak, and faded memories.

Pausing in the road, NuNu plumbed that young man's soul, found herself tangled in gossamer strings woven into an eternal, irreversible tapestry. Taffy's claim was great. She found her granddaughter all over that man's heart, knew she'd find him on hers as well. A reluctant smile slowly spread NuNu's strong features. Their claim on each other was indelible. That was ceremony enough for now.

Moving forward, NuNu's gaze shifted to poison in the yard. NuNu watched Imogene and her band of comforters—that loose-legged Paris Brown and a rag-tag crew of dissidents—the taste for evil dripping from their lips. Hurrying her pace, NuNu scanned the gathering but didn't find Taffy. She entered the side yard, walking into Imogene's raging.

"What I care 'bout some porch monkeys with guns? *I want that girl!*" Tears and snot hung from Imogene's face like drapes. "How'd she get to Sheriff Bailey and Judge Thornton, huh?!" Sheriff Bailey was disinterested in 'nigger nonsense'. The Judge claimed his intervening would be an abuse of judicial authority. Deputy Newsome had simply followed protocol by detaining the accused. Monday was soon enough for justice. Tomorrow the courts would rule. "Got them turning deaf ears on me, telling me my boy's bound for the courtroom come morning. Ain't nothing between R.J. and a tree limb 'cept time! How'd she do it? How she turn 'em on her side? She lay down with them white dogs like she did with just 'bout every other damn man 'round here?"

There was the rustling of anger among men. Thaddeus rose to his feet, speaking. "Imogene, we're praying for R.J. and we'll do what we can for him, but its best you take these women and gon' home."

"I will when that bitch leaves with me!"

In the brooding, ensuing silence, NuNu studied Reverend's boy. He'd sat the entire time focused on the pearl-handled pistol he was polishing. Now, he lifted his eyes, talking around the cigar between his teeth, baritone low and gritty.

"Miss Imogene, we're sorry for your suffering, but you won't come here causing any. Right now you're trespassing, and as owner of this property *I'm* asking you to leave."

"*You tryna keep a killer*?! You gonna share the blood on her hands? That girl murdered Dempsey dead! Paris saw her!"

"Shot 'im down like somebody's no-good dog," Paris Brown offered.

Removing cigar, Roam's stare was pointed and unflinching. "My understanding is the deceased died impaled by pitchfork. Takes one man to kill another that way."

"Then maybe you the one did it," Imogene shrilled, approaching.

"Maybe," Roam allowed, calmly assessing his enemy and casually shifting the gun atop his thigh so that it was aimed Miss Imogene's way.

From the sidelines NuNu watched, honoring this young man's battle. But when the front door opened and Taffy stepped into day ready to face Hades' gates, NuNu acted, moving at Imogene's blood-thirsty scream.

Time seemingly slowed as Imogene rushed the steps, raining curses and grappling for Taffy, as if that press of Bledsoe bodies didn't exist. Seeing the upraised blade in Imogene's hands, NuNu approached from the rear, rushing against its downward arc.

NuNu couldn't reach Taffy, thanked all heaven that Roam did.

Thrusting Taffy behind him, Roam aimed pistol, shot sure. NuNu yanked Imogene sideways, sparing her certain death.

Imogene spun on NuNu, steel blade raised. Slapped backwards, Imogene tottered before plummeting to earth. NuNu had finished this fight for now.

"Take your venom outta here, Imogene Tinsley," NuNu seethed. "You, Lacy, and that other one playing pale in Richland—you're finished harming mine! Don't touch her!" NuNu barked as one of her grandsons moved as if to help Imogene to her feet. Paris Brown and her ilk aided instead. They'd already jumped in the pot; let them partake of Imogene's poisons.

"Fools! Every one of you," mewled Imogene, bitterly. "You send my innocent child to slaughter but fight for that *thing* that ain't worth keeping? It ain't over. God ain't through with you, Taffy Bledsoe! Neither am I." Hurled spit punctuated the promise. Cocooned by comrades, Imogene departed, her sin-of-a-wig fallen and forgotten on the ground where she'd been made, like Lucifer, to crawl on her belly and eat the dust of God's good earth.

Stomach rolling with Imogene's hatred, Taffy watched the departure and the green mass, deep as a forest, enveloping Imogene's frame. "NuNu."

"I see it," her grandmother assured, disturbed by the brackish filth waiting to swallow Imogene whole.

Taffy descended the steps. "She should know."

Her father's words stopped her cold. "Tryna save a drowning woman might kill you in the process."

"I won't see what I do and say nothing," Taffy protested, torn between an uncharitable regard for Imogene and obligation towards another human being.

"Listen to your daddy, little girl," her grandfather sternly cautioned, looking at his wife with a peculiar pride, "this here battle's been brewing long before you."

"And that there's a closed heart," NuNu added, exchanging with her husband a tender, loaded look, before focusing on Taffy. "Imogene won't hear a word from anyone, especially you, Octavia. Besides, it's too late." NuNu studied the sun's glint on the fallen knife blade left behind. "It's already done."

CHAPTER FIFTY-SIX

Her actions appeared charitable. She washed the fallen woman, dressed and bound her wounds. She gave bed to sleep, food to eat. Her company alone was grounding. But Rachel's comfort wasn't Vesta's concern. Consequences were.

"My first man treated me like a disease and never suffered a day for it," Vesta recounted, gently brushing Rachel's hair. "Not one court would've made a man, *even a Colored man*, pay for giving his wife 'her due'! I was property, so 'property' walked and left that there, but you better know I ain't letting injustice go unpaid again."

Rachel sat chronically silent, shiny eyes untrained and vacant.

"You and Auggie hurt a lotta people," Vesta grieved. "He ain't excused but my man's dead, so you're the only one can carry this. That's why I pulled you out that fire. You don't get to die. Not 'til God says it's your time."

Parting Rachel's hair into two neat sections, Vesta braided.

"I understand desperation. Been there. But hiding behind your daughter and robbing her life like that," Vesta paused to breathe, "takes a special kind of low-down. You *and* Auggie owe Taffy a whole lot more than you think! You stole her hopes, sent that Roam Ellis riding rails, tryna outrun what he thought *she'd* done. But ain't life funny? Those two're together again." Vesta stepped from behind Rachel's chair to view her head-on. "And I'mma do *whatever* I can to help her get out from under Alfredo. And when they do marry, that Roam Ellis is getting Auggie's law books. Let him fight for justice the white man can't give." Vesta smoothed the front of Rachel's hair. "That Taffy's gonna live *and* love better than you ever did."

Vesta stood eyeing the woman she'd considered confidant, sister and friend. Rachel had given Augustine something Vesta never could; now a piece of her husband lived on in Angel—a precious gift conceived in disgrace. Still, he was a gift, and Vesta had Rachel to thank.

Breathing raggedly, Vesta hauled back and slapped Rachel good.

"*You were my sister!*" Vesta clutched her middle, moaning. "I *never* would've done to you what you did to me." Holding herself, Vesta rocked until in control. "I'm mad as a viper, but Angel's mine now just as good as he's yours. That child won't get nothing but love here. I'm putting his Daddy's war medal on a ribbon for that boy to wear 'round his neck. And when he can handle it, he'll get Augustine's hunting rifle, too."

Slowly, Vesta bent so they were eye-to-eye. "I had a mind to take that rifle and shoot you." Vesta laughed, her tone softening at the fear on Rachel's waxen face. "But you're still God's child, so I can't. Way I see it we're both widows of a sort, so we gonna take care of each other, and I'mma help you do what you can't for yourself," Vesta vowed, straightening the collar of Rachel's dress. "Ain't right for me to punish you when you sitting up here silent and half-dead punishing yourself. I'd rather help you *live*. Bible calls it heaping coals on your enemy's head," Vesta commented, wiping the tear trickling down Rachel's face. "You done divided the family with all this mess. Some for you. Some against. Still, we Bledsoes are protective. But ain't no way we can keep this one to ourselves. You 'bout to be the talk of the town, but I'll be here, sis, 'cause you gonna need help to stand up on the ugly side of life."

❧

Tossing rocks at the face of Lake Florence, Angel said little. Taffy stood beside him, not pressing, but praying his uncommon silence would lift. Her Angel Baby's world had been cruelly stripped.

"Taffy?" He'd been so silent and sullen his voice was startling.

"Yes, sweetie?"

He looked lost and bewildered. "M'Dear's really my mother?"

Despite explaining Angel's genesis it was still much to hold. "Yes, baby, she is."

"I mean M'Dear's *really* for real my mother, just like she's yours? Is that why I'm here instead of living with you?" Squeezing Angel's hand, Taffy nodded. "So you're my sister and not my mother, and Mr. Al's not my pa, and M'Dear is Papa's wife, but Papa's only your father, not mine."

Taffy marveled at the scope of Angel's reasoning, his grasping and

understanding the morass grown folks made and the depth of confusion the whole lot created. She never could have agreed to do what
was done had she foreseen the hurt in Angel's soul. "Everything you
said is correct," Taffy answered, stroking his face.

"Do I have a pa?"

"Everyone has a father, Angel."

"No, I mean do I have a pa here and now? Someone I can *see*?"

Something in Angel's emphasis unlatched Taffy's thinking as if
with a tiny key.

*Papa said I got extra good Bledsoe genes, so that means you gonna be
short one day.*

That cap of black curls so like her father's. The unrest at the mere
mention of her uncles' names, the unsettled sense that rose in their
presence. Proof and intimation all along? "Angel, remember my
giving you that model airplane when I got here last week and you're
saying you'd already seen it?"

I saw it before I got it. I usually do. "Yes."

"Does that 'seeing' happen often?"

"You mean like how it is for you and NuNu?"

Taffy nodded.

Angel cocked his head, thinking. "I'm not sure, 'cause your eyes
are yours and mine are mine...so I guess I see the way I'm supposed
to. But," Angel added, sounding wise, "you can't see *everything*. Some
things the soul just knows."

Amazed by Angel's insight, Taffy agreed that even when sight and
mind were slow to receive truth, your knowing knew.

Now she understood her internal unrest. Her uncles. Angel's
likeness and possible Gift. Angel was Rachel's, but sight was in
NuNu's bloodline. There had been an illegitimate joining of the two.
Taffy had to admit willful ignorance in choosing blindness of Angel's
paternal origins. She'd been broken by the thought of blood betraying
blood, subconsciously perceiving that her father had been betrayed by
a brother. Which? Taffy had refused knowledge. It was easier to love
all than to despise one.

You saw what you refused to see.

Taffy looked about, humbled by the gentle rebuke but grateful for
Knowing, her presence always, and particularly in the barn last night.
Before then it seemed an eternity since Taffy perceived the presence of
her Gift, not since her blatant disobedience the day Roam went away.

Taffy welcomed Knowing's return.

I never went anywhere. Your actions blocked your view.

"So, am I a bastard?" Angel's question cut Taffy's thoughts.

"Angel!"

"I know that word 'cause I saw it in the Bible, but I found out what it meant in Papa's dictionary," Angel quickly explained.

Taffy sighed. "What do you recall of the definition?"

Angel shrugged before picking up more stones to throw. "I don't know... 'inferior'...'dis-kick-able'..."

"You mean 'despicable'?"

"Yeah, that," his voice wobbled, "because I don't have a pa."

Taffy turned Angel towards her. "Honey, listen to me real good. In life, folks will always have a lot to say about another somebody, but don't *you* fix your mouth to label yourself anything other than the Creator's best. Let *your* words and thoughts about yourself be nothing but love and power. You aren't nor will you ever be inferior or despicable. You're beautiful! Understand me?"

Angel nodded before skipping more stones. "Are you still leaving?"

"Not today." She'd postponed departure, agreeing with Roam's wisdom. Taffy needed to stay close to Angel, her father, until the eye of this storm passed. "I'm here another week, maybe two. At least 'til your birthday. After that, we'll see."

"Good, 'cause M'Dear was crying real bad last night and I think she lost her smile. We gotta help her find it. She can't do it by herself."

"That's sweet, Angel, but you can't care-take grown folks—"

"No, but you don't poke 'em when they hurt, either."

"One day that body's gonna catch up with that brain," Taffy praised, hugging Angel tightly as a loud, snuffling came from a stretch of tall grass parted by an old dog built like a miniature mule.

"Hey, Boss!" Angel rushed to meet the ancient canine whose tail wagged excitedly.

Taffy laughed at Boss' pitiful attempts to romp with the child. Barking, Boss pawed a cavorting Angel's backside.

"Be careful, Boss, 'fore you scratch off my birthmarks! A man's gotta keep his necessaries."

Gray eyes flashed and vision wavered, yet Taffy saw clearly. Her cousins— a young Drew, his brothers, and others—screaming, running from their grandparents' cabin long ago, feigning terror at their uncle's injuries. A teenaged Dena had paused an indulgent game of jacks and locked hands on hips, demanding to know what had her younger, irritating cousins 'acting so stupid this time'.

Uncle Auggie had shown the boys his war scars. *"He has three tight wounds…like an upside down triangle…no, a face—two eyes and an ugly mouth!"* Dena had smacked her lips and dismissed their foolishness. But it became fodder for juvenile insults. *"Uncle Auggie's buttface looks better than yours!"*

Uncle Auggie's war hip decorated with three round marks. Like the circular pattern on Angel's left derriere.

The father was found.

"Finished skipping rocks for now?" Taffy strained, wildly reeling and needing to hurry.

"Sure," Angel droned, brightening suddenly. "Can I go see if Willie Ray's finished Sunday supper so we can play?"

"That's fine," Taffy responded, extending a hand to the child who'd once been hers to bear. "I love you, Angel Baby." He would always hold part of her heart.

Smiling, Angel slid his hand in hers. "Taffy?"

"Hmmm?"

"I liked being your son."

∽∾∽

Thaddeus was sunk inside himself. His daughter had been unjustly besmirched. His 'grandson' wasn't his, but belonged to Rachel, because Rachel had known Augustine. His wife had had his brother, and his brother, his wife. Raw betrayal scoured until he felt bloody and exposed as if he existed without skin. But at the very least, Thaddeus understood trouble started where truth began.

Thaddeus berated himself for not digging deeper, for believing his hearing confused…

His head snapped up at the sound of his daughter's voice. He watched her hurry his way, a strangeness about her face. Reaching him, she stood silent, mouth slightly trembling.

Thaddeus touched Taffy's cheek. "You know, don't you?"

She nodded. Thaddeus shook his head and sighed. He remained still a while, merely watching the cloudless sky. Finally, taking Taffy's hand, Thaddeus resumed his slow, meandering journey to nowhere.

"Vesta told me. Last night." His throat felt filled with sand.

"I wonder if Uncle Auggie knew…before he died." Had Uncle Auggie had the chance to work through his own guilt or recrimination? Or had he discovered truth far too late…

Thoughts scratched like alley cats at the back of Taffy's mind.

There'd been a closed coffin because of swift deterioration and Uncle Auggie's discoloring, grayish-green, his odor worse than death. Memory took Taffy to Angel's birth and the brown vial and Grandmother Lacy's poisoning Rachel in an attempt to end the infant's life. *Dear, Lord!* Had they, Lacy and Imogene, killed Uncle Auggie? Because he knew?

Not now. No more unnecessary pain.

"I been wondering the same thing, Taffy Sweet. Truly? I don't think he knew. Augustine wouldn't have let you carry Angel like he was your own. He would've stood up for his."

"He never gave any indication?"

Thaddeus opened his mouth, only to shut it again. Like his father, he grunted. "Lord, today," Thaddeus murmured, memory surfacing. "I got home late one night after handling some business over in Winter Cove. Had to be a year ago or so. Before I could even turn up the drive, I hear shouting. By the time I get out my truck, I see Augustine's car tearing out the back. I get in the house and ask your mama what all the commotion was about. Can't recall what exactly Rachel said, something that obviously made sense enough for me to forget the incident. But within days Auggie was dead and grieving my big brother, I forgot all about it…"

Hindsight. Revelation. Opposite sides of the same coin. Both stared Thaddeus in the eye. Anger internalized. "I've been half-heeding comments as long as Angel's been alive."

"Augustine, if that boy don't look like you did at his age, I don't know my name."

"You'd think he'd be more Thaddeus seeing as how T.'s his grandpa, but that Angel skipped a step and came to you."

"Why didn't I hear what God was telling me? Is that what that shouting match was all about? Did Augustine find out somehow and confront your mama? If he knew, looking at Angel must've been like a reflection in rippling water until the water stilled. When it did, Augustine must've found himself staring back at him."

Tears filled Taffy's eyes at the open pain distorting her father's face. Taffy tightened her grip about her father's hand.

"It explains some things." Thaddeus shook his head, silently concluding that Angel's revelation and Augustine's understanding were linked to his own intimate inabilities, that he'd somehow swallowed the unexamined thing. His body soured and grieved, manhood emasculated. He'd been unable to touch his wife ever since... "Why didn't I listen?"

Suddenly, Thaddeus pitched forward, breathing heavily. Something roared loose before he could contain it. "*Why didn't I hear?!*" His anguish was deafening.

Feeling helpless, Taffy offered human comfort, gingerly rubbing her father's back as agony rolled through him. Gently, she called his name when he quieted.

Voice hollow, Thaddeus raised a hand. "I'm alright...I'm alright..." Slowly, he straightened. Whisking sweat and tears from his face, Thaddeus sighed. "I always idolized Augustine..."

"We're all fallible, Daddy. Even Uncle Auggie."

Thaddeus nodded. "I hate calling Augustine out, but Angel deserves to know his lineage. We'll tell him, together, tonight." Thaddeus turned, looking at Taffy. "Where to go from here?"

"My daddy always told me, 'Taffy Sweet, you gonna break your neck tryna walk forward, still looking back. Tomorrow tastes better when you leave yesterday behind'."

Thaddeus grinned the slightest bit. "I said all that, huh?"

"Yes, sir, many times."

"Well, Babygirl, it's gonna take a heap of tomorrows to get this taste out my mouth. Seems like my whole house is crumbling, chopped down like your old, diseased plum tree. And forgiveness?" Thaddeus snorted. "That notions buried too deep underground for me to even see."

"I know, Daddy." Taffy hugged him tightly. "A sweet tomorrow is too far off to dream. All we can do right now is breathe."

CHAPTER FIFTY-SEVEN

She delighted in the rhythmic sound of his deep, even breathing signifying satisfaction and peace. His head nestled atop Taffy's lap, Taffy toyed with the waves of Roam's hair as he lay stretched out on his cushioned rear porch swing. One foot tucked beneath her Taffy slowly rocked the swing, watching Roam's naked chest rise and fall in sleep. Cherishing his every inhalation, exhalation, Taffy confronted time knowing each passing minute brought them closer to Roam's leaving.

Gently, Taffy smoothed nonexistent lines from Roam's forehead, grateful he'd pulled strings and called in favors enough to stay until evening. But when the sun set and the moon rose, Roam would board a train—for the first time, reluctantly. Countless times he'd come and gone without painful farewells, without absolute synthesis. *Bone of bone. Flesh of flesh.* This here was ripping. Claimed his world would feel lopsided absent of Taffy.

With a soft smile, Taffy recalled Roam's quiet confession.

"I never wanted other women 'til I couldn't have you. But I couldn't taste another woman now with you all over my tongue even if I wanted to." He'd seductively licked Taffy's lips for emphasis. There'd always be willing women along Roam's route casting invitation-kind-of-smiles. Her man was far from dead, but counterfeits wouldn't satisfy. Falsely obliging flesh would be a waste of fidelity and time. She'd curbed his rootlessness: Roam could and would decline. Miscellaneous loving was no longer Roam's way of life. "I'm bringing all this back to you, Dollbaby," he'd vowed before slow-loving her, filling her as if to sustain Taffy these next six weeks.

Quivering with memory of their flesh-shattering goodbyes, Taffy outlined the bridge of Roam's nose, praying this six-week stint on the rails wouldn't feel akin to eternity. She felt incapable of watching Roam leave; still, it was necessary. As long as Roam worked the rails, 'goodbye' would be a part of their lives.

Dollbaby, you'll always be the good thing I come home to.

He'd promised. She believed. They *would* create a home and a family. Like Drew and Chloe?

They'd passed by Drew and Chloe's, allowing Roam time for fond farewells while Taffy snuggled their newborn goddaughter, Corrine Marie, whom Roam refused to hold, as if a breakable thing. Inhaling the baby's sweetness, Taffy experienced intense longing. For purity. Stability. Security. She wanted, but, wouldn't have them fully until Alfredo was no longer an impediment to her living.

"Alfredo won't let go easily. He hasn't yet," Taffy had quietly divulged upon leaving Drew and Chloe's.

Mere mention of the man's name had Roam's jaw clenching. "I gotta gun and a box of bullets that'll help him get."

"Roam Alexander Ellis, I don't do jail visits!" Taffy had reprimanded, laughing. Even so, then and there, Taffy had slowly determined how to do what she had to...

"Hey, Lightweight."

Roam's voice broke Taffy's plotting and planning. Smiling, Taffy traced Roam's eyelids that were closed, weighted with serenity. "Thought you were asleep."

"I was," Roam mumbled, drowsily. "You sitting up here interrupting me with all that thinking. What's got your mind going?"

Outlining his full lips, Taffy liked the sensation of Roam's moustache beneath her fingertips. "I'm missing you already."

"Warned you you would."

Taffy's words trembled. "Just wish I could roll back the years and reclaim every second we lost...and that I forfeited."

"Better to do well here and now than wasting wishes," Roam replied, stretching lazily. "We have what we have in God's time. Dollbaby, what we've been blessed to recover is pretty damn good. You think?"

Taffy took her time answering. "Maybe," she jested.

Opening one eye, Roam looked up at her, grinning. "Gal, 'fess up and tell somebody I'm you're best blessing."

"Amen and indeed," Taffy agreed, praying the Almighty allowed her to wrap herself in this man always. "Thank goodness heaven's smarter than me. I haven't done a thing to deserve you, but the Lord knew we needed us and gave a second chance despite my stupidity."

"Woman, you're a whole lotta things, starting with stubborn, but you ain't never been stupid. I'm proof enough you got good sense. So…really and truly," Roam mumbled about a yawn, "Miss Octavia knew your Grandmother Lacy and Miss Goldie were twins without saying a thing?"

Cloaked in a tranquility that had eluded her so long she'd forgotten its possibility, Taffy gently combed her fingernails through the red strands curled on Roam's chest while voicing, "NuNu says the twins being 'too shamefaced' to claim one another wasn't fit to interrupt her sleep. NuNu scraped Goldie and her whiteness from her tongue after losing her baby brother, Elias, like she did. White folks called her crazy, just lying to prevent her brother's murder by claiming Goldie was Colored." Brutally whipped for her "lies" by that hungry, hanging mob, NuNu flung Goldie out of her mouth to keep from crazy. Taffy shrugged. "NuNu did what she needed to stay sane."

Roam toyed with a stray lock of Taffy's hair, loving the sight of her clad only in her slip and the camellia he'd earlier snapped from a bush to tuck behind her ear. "You never knew, and your mother never hinted at it?"

Twin, mama says you gotta finish dinner, else we can't have dessert…

Softly, Taffy conveyed Knowing's welcoming, waving Taffy forward days ago in the cemetery. The sight of Miss Goldie sharing a meal with the grave had been much for the stomach's sake. Having skipped her grandmother's funeral, and not recognizing the newly acquired headstone Miss Goldie had erected for her twin, Taffy had turned and gone the other way.

"Mama didn't know. Whenever we'd run into Miss Goldie over in Richland she'd stand like a statue staring at my mother and me. Sometimes she'd smile, other times Miss Goldie'd get all misty-eyed. Mama would swat my behind for calling her 'Crazy Oldie Miss Goldie', but Mama still warned me to stay clear of her 'cause she wasn't 'right in the head'." Thinking on the photographs found on her mother's person when delivered from the fire Rachel set—photographs now at the bottom of Taffy's suitcase—Taffy shifted her leg out from beneath her, concluding, "Their pictures tell the tale. Those twins didn't look so alike in old age. But as children? They were two sides of the same coin."

Roam was momentarily silent before grunting. "Gal, you got loony on both sides of your bloodline."

"Begging your pardon?"

"Come on now, Dollbaby, check the evidence. God rest her soul, Miss Lacy. Miss Goldie. Miss Imogene ain't wrapped right. Your Mama, heaven help, is guilty of some *sho' 'nuff* outlandish things. Then there's your Daddy's side!" Roam shuddered. "Dena and the rest of 'em are coo-coo as they come. Loves your grandmother, but Miss Octavia's enough to freeze the Devil's piss."

"Ooo, I'm so through with you!"

Angling towards her, Roam wrapped an arm about her, preventing Taffy's attempt at leaving. Grinning impishly, Roam enjoyed his teasing. "Hold on, woman, I'm not finished! Now you?" Roam whistled. "You're worse than the rest, talking to spirits 'cause you inherited all kinds of loony. But I ain't complaining, Dollbaby. Your kinda crazy makes for have-mercy-Lord good loving."

"Your loving's about to be lonely. Get off me."

"Told you before. Getting off you can't change the fact that I've been all up—"

Taffy kissed Roam hard, interrupting. "Oh, hush, ol' mannish thing."

Roam chuckled deeply. "The moment you sashayed into Drew's kitchen, I knew these high-stepping hips were bad business. I shoulda high-tailed it outta there."

Taffy laughed. "With your pants zipped."

"Touché, Taffy Mae." Head propped in hand, Roam looked up into Taffy's eyes. "When this six-week stint ends, I'll take you to D.C. You need to at least see it first before skipping out on Chicago or Harlem."

They'd dreamt a future, shared sensibilities, agreeing: fidelity and monogamy, no anger sleeping between. Roam was disinterested in "all that hen stuff you and Chloe cackle about," but—after the ill-held silence of the last seven years—secrets weren't sanctioned. Honesty was imperative, as was shared decision making. They'd decided together, and together, Taffy and Roam looked towards D.C.

"I'm not 'skipping' anything," Taffy assured, massaging Roam's shoulder. Savage Studio was a beautiful, but faded dream. "Harlem was my destination when I needed somewhere to hide long enough to find my life." It was a fantastic escape and opportunity. But Taffy was no longer running. "And Cousin Gracie'll understand when I explain I'm not coming to the Windy City."

"I'm not tryna take your dreams, Taffy."

"I prefer our reality," Taffy responded, kissing Roam sweetly. He'd promised her a house with designated space for her craft once Taffy could sign 'Mrs. Ellis' on the dotted line. Having never invested herself in Alfredo's abode, the thought of nesting, settling down with Roam was thrilling. "I can create in any city. I'm fine as long as I have you and my sewing machine. Besides, I've never been, but I like the idea of D.C."

"We'll see. You don't need to be the one doing all the compromising," Roam muttered, mulling over a matter. It could mean less earnings, but he had savings enough to cushion them if need be.

"What?" Taffy questioned, sensing Roam's pondering.

Roam sat up. Leaning forward, arms braced on his thighs, Roam was slow in admitting, "I'm thinking on switching up from six-week coast-to-coast runs to four-days-on-three-days-off, east-coast-only routes when we marry."

"Why?" Taffy demanded. "You love the rails."

"Love you more. *Plus*, all this hot stuff 'll burn a hole in the bed waiting on me six weeks," Roam taunted, running a wide hand up under Taffy's slip and over her thigh, unwilling to constantly be without her for such extended periods of time. "Keep all this honey for me 'til I get in. I don't want nobody else taste-testing my blessings."

Taffy sucked her teeth indignantly. "What in the world would I do with another man when I can't handle you?!"

"I'll come in shooting," Roam threatened, reclaiming his lounging position, head on Taffy's lap.

"Sweetness, you're all the man I need."

Grinning up at her, Roam braced a hand behind Taffy's neck, pulling her forward, muttering, "I better be," before kissing her deeply. "Gal, you taste good from any angle."

"Just like you feel," Taffy purred, running a hand down Roam's naked torso, beneath the unfastened dungarees lying loose on his hips. Roam's treasure in hand, Taffy caressed gently. Roam responded to Taffy's touch instantly.

Eyes closed, Roam moaned. "Lord, woman…we got enough to repent for as it is."

"Best hurry up and make me Mrs. Ellis, then."

"Soon…as we…get you out…that felonious mess-of-a-marriage," Roam rambled as Taffy stroked him tenderly, possessively. "Got you in my bed…now I can't keep you out."

Taffy smiled with soft, sultry delight. Roam was her sweet addiction. She needed this man: to wake beside him, love him, touch, taste, and care for him eternally. "According to Dena, the bed's not the only place for lovemaking."

"That's 'cause your cousin's…" Catching Taffy's sensuous insinuation and invitation, Roam sat up, staring Taffy sideways. A hungry grin claimed his face as Taffy stood, smiling like she held the secret to all his satisfaction. Draping an arm about Taffy's waist, Roam pulled her to him. "You wanna try the wide outside?"

Taffy imagined taking her sweet time lowering herself onto Roam's lap, secured against the powerful press of his body; Taffy lowering one slip strap, letting Roam undo the rest. She could all but feel granting Roam a kiss that only a need for oxygen could end. Purring like a milk-fed kitten as Roam nuzzled the sweet spot below her ear. Her exposed breasts against Roam's naked chest. Their bodies blending, hips rolling, wanton and satisfying. But a flurry of unexpected chills encroached on making reality of Taffy's heated imaginings.

Taffy felt alarm suddenly snaking through her stiffening body as she looked through Roam, deathly afraid.

Taffy pulled away.

Roam's mouth was moving, his words without sound as Taffy's senses were overly saturated with one name, one face and the peril charging his way. Like a gust of wind his name blew from Taffy's lips as her tongue loosened enough to say: "My Angel Baby."

CHAPTER FIFTY-EIGHT

S he sat in catatonic silence, breath erratic, rocking atop a
wooden crate as her son would if free. But R.J. was confined
in a jail cell awaiting a terminal fate.

Swift. Simple. In his chambers, Judge Thornton ruled—*sans* trial
or jury. Taxpayers' money was too precious to waste. And Judge was
king.

But Judge was dead wrong! Her son was nobody's 'murderous,
feeble-minded Negro liable to stray across invisible town divides.'
R.J. wasn't a killer! He couldn't 'encroach upon and jeopardize the
peace and lives of Richland's law-abiding white citizens'. He wasn't
an 'uncontrollable menace', deserving to be 'euthanized.' But Judge
Thornton was too up-his-ass-stupid to see.

High on his whiteness, he impassively allowed Imogene's wild
accusations that her son was bewitched by *that girl,* that R.J.'s deeds
were at *her* command. She'd worked hoodoo on the deceased as well
as her son. They simply need examine the corpse for proof of witch-
ery.

"Rather hard to do without the dead nigger body," Judge Thornton had intoned, tolerating only so much of Imogene's blubbering
and begging, her accusing everyone from Adam to Eve. If that gal was
a communist, registered voter believing in equality, or a subversive
member in that N-double-A-C-P...*that* would be objectionable and
he'd haul her in for questioning. But he needed proof of her deeds
before charging her as murder's accessory.

Yet, Judge would accept Deputy Newsome's pitiful recounting
of what allegedly occurred? And R.J.'s repeated, self-accusatory and
non-sensical ramblings?

But Imogene had a witness! And Judge Thornton didn't entertain
Colored recounting.

Embarrassed by Imogene's bloodcurdling pleas, Judge Thornton cued his deputy to escort the Tinsleys from his chambers, softly advising, "Y'all gon' and visit your boy and say your farewells. Tomorrow's his last sunrise."

Defeated and barely on this side of life, Imogene rocked a vicious rhythm. She wished them dead. Judge Thornton. Sheriff Bailey. Even Goldie.

Aunt Marie would be disgusted! Aunt Marie, a woman kept by a white man in infamy. Tired of her shame, she'd left Preacherman Hale for a Colored sharecropper, and Preacherman Hale retaliated by taking Goldie. Sure, he wrote Lacy and Goldie equal in his will, but Lacy couldn't pass. Only Goldie sat in the lap of white luxury. They were twins divided by the color line.

Shameful—Goldie's extremes and Judge choosing to be ignorant—shipping off Colored midwives instead of seeing Goldie's blackness. And, when Goldie took to visiting Bledsoe's graveyard, folks swore NuNu's roots twisted up her mind.

"Bitch was Colored all the time," Imogene seethed at Goldie's turning her back on her kind. Protecting self and siding with whiteness, she sat over in Richland refusing to make The Judge recognize the error of his ways. Goldie disconnected the call on Imogene's threat to help her or she'd reveal Goldie's born identity, Goldie uttering one silencing word only.

Augustine.

His death was necessary after Rachel came crying when confronted by an irate Augustine bent on redeeming Taffy and telling Vesta everything. So they made it natural, Lacy and Imogene with Goldie knowing.

He was a lawyer. Lacy was a widow, needing advice in affairs long ignored since her husband's death. Augustine complied and stopped by. Lacy refreshed. Dainty sandwiches were washed down by strong coffee, hiding every trace. Business concluded, Augustine went home and died at Vesta's feet.

At all costs. Such was the vow. But Imogene had failed, letting the kingdom crumble beneath Rachel's girl. Always was trouble on heels. Looking. Seeing. Smelling blood on their hands. Questioning. Crying that she couldn't lie to her Daddy. So they'd tamed her, using Alfredo as whip.

Nothing but a husband-for-hire, they'd uncovered Alfredo's past buried deep in Mississippi after he showed up in Bledsoe, looking.

Sentence served in Greenville for nigger blood in a white boss' car, he'd come to town, a messenger with missives. Housed in different quarters, he'd never met this particular letter-sender, but Thaddeus Bledsoe sent desperate letters, claiming false imprisonment. Did the ladies sitting, chatting behind the counter of Tinsley's know where to find the family?

Destroying Thaddeus' letters, they deemed Alfredo ideal. They'd wash his past and give him opportunity. If he'd take the gal and child Up North, they'd keep him living comfortably.

His conscience held him off, initially. But Alfredo returned, needing what Lacy had. Angel was weeks old, and Thaddeus had been released by then. Still, Alfredo was salvation and solution. They forged Taffy's marriage certificate, dating it before Angel's birth in case Thaddeus got to snooping. They crafted lies about Alfredo's going home to finalize affairs before coming to claim his family. It worked ideally. But Alfredo proved disappointing, sniveling when craving his conjugal due. Lacy took Taffy to Big Baby to break virginity before Alfredo did and discovered Rachel's untruths. But it was out and over now.

Imogene stilled, frozen by vile sorrow. She'd done all she could. Still, tomorrow, her child would die alone and confused. No one to hold his hand and walk him through.

No one but me, Imogene decided, resuming her rocking. She'd lived a full life, was too old to refashion reality this time. Blindly fingering the brown vial, Imogene admitted being too tired to do anything but die.

"Imogene? Join me in prayer?"

Slipping vial beneath apron, she ignored her husband's slow, limping approach. Would God who'd sacrificed His only begotten for the sins of the world spare her son the repercussions of his own? "I'm finished talking to God."

Rayford stalled at her sacrilege. "He ain't through talking to you, but you too busy hating that girl to hear. Taffy ain't done none of this and you know it, 'Gene. R.J. woulda killed *you* over that cat. Let it go and come pray a miracle."

"You heard what I said, nigglet. *I'm finished!*" Imogene screeched before swimming down deep into a silence where Rayford couldn't reach her. Resigned, Rayford left his wife to her own brooding company.

He's right. Imogene hated that girl with every fiber in her being. She hated her inexorable resilience, Taffy's wearing purity like Sunday morning finery, when at that age Imogene had been handled by innumerable men.

She hated her thriving, not merely surviving. She hated Taffy for broadcasting Rachel's stepping out on marriage. Imogene had done the same. However, Imogene faulted *Rachel's need.* Need for comfort wrapped in a man's pleasuring, and the need to keep that man's seed. Had they known they would've given Rachel drink at first sign just like Imogene…

She shivered, glad for that failed termination. R.J. survived despite ingested toxins unsettling his mind. "I loved him just the same," Imogene sobbed, devastated he was marked to die. He wouldn't go alone. She'd greet her child on the other side.

The sudden rapping on the door of Tinsley's General proved distracting.

"Mr. Rayford? Miss Imogene?"

Imogene tried ignoring the caller, but the rhythmic rapping was so like R.J.'s rocking—metronomic and steady. Clutching the vial, Imogene stumbled from her dark perch. Approaching the door, she found two burr-heads peeping in.

"Hi, Miss Imogene." Willie Ray Williams III sounded like he was underwater, speaking through her polished glass.

"Hi, Cousin Imogene," called the other, looking like Augustine.

Imogene stood, silently staring, barely deciphering Willie Ray's prattling.

"Grandmama says she knows you're closed and not in best spirit, and she's sorry to disturb, but it's an emergency. She needs stomach seltzer. Bad!" The boys giggled, privy to private humor. "Oh, and some headache powder and a couple cans of sardines. Grandmama says charge it to her account if you don't mind."

Thick blackness swirled inside Imogene. Was she to bother with Olivette's eating herself into yet another intestinal predicament on the eve of her son's demise? Took all Imogene had not to smash her fist through that glass separating her from Augustine's child.

She watched him long and hard, ignoring traces of Rachel and focusing on Augustine, Bledsoe blood, and Taffy. Seeing his sister in him, Imogene's mind whirled with bitter memory of NuNu's assault leaving her on her belly.

That's why Judge wouldn't bother, doing little more than stopping by that Ellis yard with Sheriff Bailey in tow, talking up porch monkeys, asking disinterested and obligatory questions, waddling his fat ass back to Sheriff's cruiser, too fast for justice, too ready to leave. Because he still feared NuNu! Imogene didn't. Her final act would bear proof.

"Get what you need," she snapped, unlocking the door and moving aside, woodenly.

The boys stood shocked at Miss Imogene's relaxing her 'no-lil-niglets-running-amuck-in-my-store' policy. Willie Ray could gather his own damn necessaries. Feeling quite grown, he did, best friend at his side.

Somebody better wire Big Baby and tell her her boy's gone, thought Imogene, eyeing the two nuisances shopping. Would Dempsey's death surprise? Not likely. Those that lived by the sword were liable to die by pitchfork. Imogene snorted with demented mirth.

The boys looked her way.

"Hurry up and get what you getting and gon' out of here!" she commanded.

"Yes, ma'am," answered Augustine's boy.

Imogene studied him. Like his sister, he'd been consumed by Bledsoe blood. Unlike his sister, he hadn't the decency to take his mother's eyes. Mother? Funny, calling Angel Rachel's when he'd been Taffy's. Still was in Imogene's mind.

Taffy's son. Free. Imogene's doomed. *Too unjust!* Imogene steamed, her hatred twisting towards Angel, her mind brightening. Was this God's final gift? "You boys want a cool drink for the road?" Thrilled affirmations annoyed Imogene. Ambling to the cooler behind the front counter, she queried their preference. Orange for one, root beer for the other. It was confirmation enough.

Uncapping soda bottles, Imogene told the boys to help themselves to a licorice whip. It was final kindness and distraction as she opened vial and dispensed poison into dark root beer, better able to hide death's sting.

Indifferent to their thanks, Imogene watched the two depart before returning to her dark perch where she upended the vial's remains. She'd step into eternity first, would be there waiting when R.J. was executed and arrived. She didn't gloat at her victory. Rather, relaxing her hatred for all things Bledsoe, Imogene deigned to keep watch over Taffy's seed. Swallowing the brown vial's bitter dredges, Imogene knew Taffy was bright enough to understand.

An eye for an eye. A tooth for a tooth. A son for a son. Amen.

CHAPTER FIFTY-NINE

She came for Cousin Tinsley.

She came in celebration that her Angel Baby was still amongst the living.

She stood in hopes that her mother would regain reality's footing, and find courage to face a fragile future. And that her own private path would be cleared of obstructions and somehow paved with peace.

One of many assembled on that paved road in front of Tinsley's General Store, Taffy attended the vigil for many reasons, least of all Imogene.

Head bowed, Taffy breathed deeply, letting air fill her being as she stood thankful that, once again, grace had spared Angel's being.

She meant to kill him.

Taffy shook her head in disbelief, grateful for God and four-legged guardians.

He'd tagged along, that old canine well past prime. Patiently, Boss had waited outside Tinsley's General until two friends exited, mouths sweet with licorice. Nose twitching and sniffing, Boss' ears lay low. A vicious growl rumbled in his chest. Scared by memories of a bit bottom, Billy Ray's orange soda plummeted to the ground untasted. But it was Angel Boss targeted. Advancing on the child ready to chase candy with cold root beer, a snarling Boss plowed into the boy, knocking him flat, and pinning him beneath massive paws. Jarred from his hand, Angel's soda bottle rolled across the wooden walkway, crashing to the ground below. Whining apologetic relief, Boss bathed Angel's face with sloppy, dog kisses. Hopping up, Angel had stomped off, fussing up a storm, not knowing he'd bypassed the grave.

This was the foreboding that snatched Taffy from passion on Roam's porch. Dressing quickly, they'd called around looking for Angel. Learning he'd gone to town with Willie Ray, they'd raced that way. They found Angel marching up the road hot as a hornet. Wiping tears of praise, Taffy let Angel fuss over his lost root beer while removing his shirt stained brown and smelling like death. In private, Taffy savagely ripped that shirt to pieces before burning it. Angel didn't know. Taffy wouldn't tell. Imogene could go to eternal rest, Angel's soul unmarked by wicked intent.

Now, leaning the wick of her candle into Roam's flame, Taffy watched light catch and burn.

He's safe.

Out back, Angel was busy making ready for all the fun a sleepover with Cousin Dena's boys and tomorrow's granting their first day of summer, school-free, could bring. Taffy wanted to hover, to watch over Angel, doggedly. But death had passed, and her brother was amazingly resilient. Her near-comatose mother's story, however, was decidedly different.

I didn't mean to hurt you, Mama. I just needed to breathe.

Glassy-eyed and chronically silent, propped stiff as wood in Aunt Vesta's front porch chair, Taffy's words had felt unheard as Rachel sat lost in a world governed by guilt.

"Little One, Rachel'll fix herself when she's ready to be fixed. With Auggie's passing your Mama's bearing both their sins. Ain't nothing wrong with her other than shame," NuNu had vigorously stated. "And you ain't wasting your days sitting up here worrying after her. Gon' to the vigil for Imogene so you can close that chapter on the evil-intending. Leave us old ladies to ourselves. Me and Vesta'll help your mama through this. Rachel's borrowed enough of your living."

Surrendering a deep need to fix things, Taffy kissed Rachel's cheek and left her in NuNu's and Aunt Vesta's care conceding that transgression was demanding, the floodgates of revelation once opened were difficult if impossible to close, and consequence was beyond human control.

Now, Taffy offered her candle to the person beside her, passing light to the next link in a somber chain. No matter how odious in character or the manner of her self-demise, Imogene Tinsley deserved a vigil of candlelight. Perhaps it would purify and consume any darkness Imogene left behind.

Taffy bowed her head, letting the dredges of her anger reduce to a syrupy pity as Reverend Ellis' prayer showered over the gathering like sweet, spring rain.

Praying comfort for Cousin Tinsley and a miracle on R.J.'s behalf, the Reverend's voice bathed Taffy's soul, allowing Taffy's thoughts to settle and soften enough for her to realize Imogene's passing fulfilled NuNu's prophecy. A chapter of prolonged torment had ended. Life's path was clearer. The hand of the divine had knit Taffy's loose ends back together again.

Taffy knew not to rejoice at Imogene's death. Rather, Taffy added her prayers to the Reverend's, wishing Imogene—and finally, Lacy—eternal peace and rest.

The pillow-soft cloud of "amen's" floating above Taffy's head as Reverend Ellis concluded his prayer, gently faded beneath the pure voice of some sweet songstress.

When peace like a river attendeth my way...

Having learned the song's history in grade school, Taffy marveled that the writer—who'd lost his wealth to the great Chicago fire, and four precious daughters to a horrendous accident resulting in an unfortunate, aquatic grave in the Atlantic—could yet pen the words, "It is well with my soul."

Heart full, Taffy could only listen as others sang.

She'd endured much these past seven years; weathered a lifetime in recent days. Yet, whatever her lot, Taffy knew to say it was, and would be, well with her soul.

Hand-in-hand, Taffy and Roam made their way through the solemn gathering to get to Cousin Tinsley. The matter and the moment kept folks from eyeballing them too openly. But come morning, Taffy Bledsoe would—yet again—land front and center on the gossip mill.

Taffy could only imagine the names she'd acquire this time, shamelessly parading herself on the arm of a man other than her mister. And a minister's son no less! By midday tomorrow, she'd no doubt be Satan's sister. Taffy lost her amusement as she and Roam approached the raised sidewalk where Cousin Tinsley sat receiving condolences.

"Sister Freeman!"

His mellifluous ocean-of-a-voice caught Taffy where she stood. Taffy and Roam watched the caller approach, an inscrutable expression on his face.

"Son...may I?"

Nodding, Roam stepped away, and Taffy allowed herself to be

navigated to a quiet edge of the assembly. Once there, she stood watching Reverend Ellis struggle with the unspoken.

"Sir…was there something you wanted to discuss?"

Hat in hand, eyes lowered, the Reverend experienced an unusual loss for words. Clearing his throat, he lifted his head, but still found himself unable to address Taffy.

Taffy touched his arm gently, letting him recover his way.

Reverend Ellis reclaimed his tongue and let words fall as they may. "I don't know how the Lord'll work things out for you and my boy, but I believe He will. 'Til then, I can only hope you won't—or *haven't*—done anything to compromise yourselves…" The Reverend stopped, shook his head, as if what he'd said wasn't what he'd intended. "I can't condone wrong…still, I've been judging too long, and it's not for me to do. My heart is right in simply wanting the best for my son…and for you." Reverend Ellis paused, looked Taffy directly in the eye. "Young lady…should the Lord deliver you from your…current situation…First Lady and I'll be waiting to welcome you back where you belong. Truth be told, you're already there."

"And where is that, sir?"

With a warm smile, Reverend Ellis tapped his heart. "Right here, daughter." Opening his arms, he offered Taffy a penitent and loving hug. "Forgive this old fool for faulting you."

With so many consolers, it took a moment to gain a private audience with Cousin Tinsley. Surrounded by supporters, Rayford Tinsley's face was a mask of tragic disbelief. His son was imprisoned, his wife deceased. This new aloneness was foreign, perhaps frightening.

"You have our prayers for comfort, Mr. Rayford," Roam offered.

Rayford Tinsley thanked the younger man who respectfully stepped aside, allowing Taffy to place a flower at Rayford's feet.

Gripping the consoling hand she placed on his shoulder, a red-eyed Cousin Tinsley begged Taffy's mercy. "Forgive Imogene. *Everything!* Don't let all that mess Imogene or Lacy did keep control of you." His voice caught. "You gotta whole lotta life left they can't contaminate."

Taffy's thoughts flashed on the night she arrived, a ritual cleansing and the blessings NuNu prayed over her while in that tin tub.

I'm asking for love. Wisdom. Protection. Patience. Fire for life. Joy so big it can't be contained. Let all things lost be restored, and the good wait-

ing outweigh sorrows gone. Kissing her granddaughter's face, NuNu had ended the anointing, releasing Taffy to her future with, *When you leave here this time, Little One, you'll find heaven's purest blessings waiting on you 'bout the bend.*

Glancing back at Roam, Taffy was humbled. She'd already received heaven's gift.

"Pretty Gal, this is all I have left," Rayford mourned, opening his hand to reveal a lock of his wife's hair, a precious keepsake for when all else was consumed.

Imogene wouldn't rest in Bledsoe's cemetery. Murderers-of-self could contaminate eternal resting places. No one wanted souls rising to collect dust and bones, spirits wailing on the midnight wind like an anguished sea. For now, Imogene waited in cool mortuary confines. Tonight, in the midst of comforters, Rayford would gather strength for tomorrow when he'd be required to say fare-thee-well before committing his wife to the crematory's fire. So he held that lock of hair with a loving tenderness Imogene never allowed in life.

Hugging him soundly, Taffy whispered in Cousin Rayford's ear. "Your heart holds a whole lot more." She squeezed Rayford's hand before moving aside so that others could comfort him and ease his grief.

Taffy looked about, in search of love. She found him on the opposite side of the paved road amid a cluster of quietly conversing men. Dressed in full uniform, Roam stood head-above many. Taffy took her time openly admiring him.

She treasured her Sweetness, his solid presence and unwavering stability that grounded her in grace throughout recent, cyclonic events. She loved his carriage and stride, Roam's unapologetic consumption of space as if whatever he possessed was God-made for him. Taffy studied his burnished copper face, the lift of sensuous lips. She recounted their taste, the sinfully wicked loving those lips lavished on her body. Taffy's whole self flushed with satisfaction. Peace. Lust. And heat.

Lord, help me love and cherish that rock-solid-mountain-of-a-man for eternity and a day, Taffy silently prayed as she weaved her way through the crowd, intent on joining Roam across the way. Instead, Taffy was detained, arrested by an unexpected flash of white light.

Curious, Taffy headed towards the end of the raised walkway, leaned against the railing, scouring the distance in search of the unseen.

There was nothing. Just long abandoned, unfinished railroad tracks that headed to nowhere, and giant age-old trees. Concluding it little more than a figment of her imagination, Taffy started to leave but a soft swish of white caught her eye.

Intrigued, Taffy watched as the semblance of a woman appeared.

She moved with a dancer's grace, snow white skirt billowing about brown legs, railroad gravel like silk beneath her bare feet. She generated a cool summer breeze. She felt like ocean air, flowed like a calm sea. Young. Ancient. Endless. She was an expansive reflection of God's limitless being.

"Knowing?"

Her voice reached Taffy on the evening breeze. *You looking mighty fine, Miss Lady. Whatchu celebrating?*

"Life. And love."

I'll say! Must be mighty good, indeed. You on your way somewhere?

Taffy smiled at Knowing being in the center of a secret. "Just for a day or two. Long enough to find somebody who recalls." Earlier on Roam's back porch Taffy had decided to do what she had to to resolve a marriage of misery, no matter how extreme. Come morning, Taffy would board a train to Greenville where Alfredo's skeletons dwelled. She need not tell Knowing how Alfredo's face had collapsed in fear the night Taffy returned to Bledsoe, all because of a word spoken softly. *Greenville.*

"Knowing, small towns have long memories. Whatever Alfredo's skeletons, they're only buried seven years' deep. Someone there remembers *something*." Whatever she unearthed, Taffy prayed it was leverage enough to force Alfredo's hand and guarantee her liberty. If not? She'd buy her freedom...do *whatever* Taffy had to. "I *mean* to marry my blessing. Those divorce papers are getting signed this time." Taffy smiled broadly. "Watch and see."

Knowing's voice floated with an odd mix of sorrow and peace. *Won't be a need.*

Taffy frowned, not understanding. But Knowing continued, not allowing for questioning. *When you gonna tell that "blessing" 'bout you're going to Greenville?*

"Tonight. Once his train's rolling too fast for him to do a thing."

Knowing's laughter was the kiss of hummingbird wings.

I see, now, the two of you gonna keep me busy.

"Watch over him for me, please," Taffy quietly petitioned. "And, please, Knowing...forgive me my disobedience...my repeatedly failing to regard your leading."

Knowing merely nodded. *You're human, child. You ain't exempt from foolery.* Knowing shimmered at Taffy's laughing. *Truth be told, you're my pleasure even when you're contrary.*

Hand over her heart, Taffy offered, "I'm obliged to you always."

Likewise. With a smile soft as moonlight, Taffy's Gift turned and walked away. The farther she walked, the less transparent Knowing became.

"Hey..."

Glancing over her shoulder, Taffy found Roam mounting the walkway steps and heading her way—a lit candle moored to the bottom of a small tin can in hand. "Hey yourself," Taffy responded peering back at the tracks only to find them empty, absent of Knowing. Grateful for The Gift and all of God's goodness, Taffy sighed, contentedly. "You just about ready?" she asked, cradling Roam's jaw when he neared.

Without answering, Roam gripped Taffy's hand, pulled her along that railed walkway to the rear of the buildings, beyond nosey eyes. Placing the candle-in-can on the walkway, Roam wrapped Taffy in an ever-ready embrace and took his time conveying with a kiss his reluctance to leave the only woman he'd ever love, pressed like a sweet-smelling blanket against him.

Leaning away enough to lock eyes, Roam slowly trailed a thumb across Taffy's bottom lip. "Ready or not, I gotta work to keep grits on these hips."

Taffy's laughter was buoyant, free. "You forgetting I'm a working woman who can buy grits enough for us both?"

"Get it straight, woman. I provide for you. You don't take care of me."

"Chauvinist."

"Proud to be."

"So silly." Smoothing Roam's lapel, fingering the buttons of Roam's uniform gleaming in candlelight, Taffy looked up at him, smiling. "I didn't think this man could get more handsome, but you obviously can. Bring this all back to me."

"Dollbaby, I can't take it nowhere but. You have the map?"

"Yes, sir," Taffy answered, recalling Roam's marking out his route, hoping distance proved more palatable on paper.

"I'll call when I can. You know how to reach me if you need."

Taffy nodded. Roam had provided points of contact on that fra-ternal Grapevine—a swift conduit in keeping them connected.

"So...what did my Daddy say to you earlier?"

Taffy smiled impishly. "That was a private conversation to which you weren't privy."

"Woman, I done licked all over your privy so ain't nothing pri-vate."

Taffy's laugh came out like a screech. "Jesus, why'd You give me this heathen?"

"He knows what you need."

"Amen," Taffy murmured, suddenly sobering. In a matter of min-utes Taffy would join Reverend and First Lady Ellis in seeing Roam off at Richland's station where Roam would depart for too long for Taffy's taste. *Child, you've been without this man seven years. You can't tolerate six weeks?*

She blinked back an avalanche of tears.

"Come on now, Dollbaby..." Roam wrapped her in comfort, kissed her forehead, choosing not to divulge his west coast run would include a trip to San Francisco's diamond district. *His* wife was worthy of a ring. It was but a first gift of many that Roam intended to shower his wife with. San Francisco was a secret. How to be rid of Freeman was the mystery. Could a non-consummated marriage be annulled after a near-decade? Had to be a legal loophole somewhere. If not? Despite Taffy's objections that heaven didn't need Roam's help, he hadn't relinquished the idea of a little 'pearl-handled persuasion' that had become increasingly enticing. Especially now. If Taffy was...

"Roam..." Taffy eased back, looking up at him shrewdly, intui-tively. "What're you scheming?"

Roam grinned. "Taffy Mae, you have your methods. I have mine. You looked real natural holding our goddaughter this afternoon." Roam splayed a hand across Taffy's abdomen, his grin fading beneath probability. "*Real* natural. And nice. The moment you know, I know if you're missing your next monthly."

She'd struggled with silence and needing to see *if* before admitting her unprotected state in first intimacy. In the end, Roam's disgust for secretive things had Taffy disclosing.

Woman, you saying you might've gone and caught yourself something?!

If I did, you threw it.

Yeah, but, come on now, you didn't think to protective yourself, Doll-baby?

Roam Ellis, that street called 'Stupid' runs both ways!

Taffy could laugh now at their exchange. Initial disbelief and expletives exhausted, Roam owned up to being a relentless aggressor, consummating at his insistence, without thinking, consensually, sans his own protective covering. *He'd* let his guard down, been unprotected the first and *every* subsequent loving, only with Taffy. Accepting fate, Roam had wrapped Taffy in an embrace, offering, "If it's done we had some sho' 'nuff pleasure in the planting'." Whether or not Taffy was in a family way, Roam reaffirmed a lifelong commitment to them.

"Just so you know, I went and asked Mr. Thaddeus for your hand in marriage."

Taffy eased her arms about Roam's waist, relaxing against him. "What did Daddy say?"

"'Good luck and good riddance'."

Taffy laughed. "I'm sure he did."

"Just so we're clear, I'm only marrying you 'cause you mighta gone and got yourself a baby in your belly," Roam teased, hands sliding over Taffy's hips, "*and* for a lifetime supply of the sweetest home-grown honey this side of heaven."

"Truth be told, I'm marrying you 'cause I love the way you handle my honey."

Roam's chuckle was belly-deep. "Lord knows I wish I was handling it right here, right now." Heat easily surfaced between them as Roam planted his lips firmly against Taffy's, exchanging passion and unspoken promises while drawing out here-and-now and defying goodbye. Reluctantly ending their kiss, Roam pulled back enough to devour her visually—gaze consuming every detail, from Taffy's fancy hat to the butter-yellow Sunday-Go-Meeting dress caressing the body he craved. "You don't make 'goodbye' easy," Roam murmured, loving the rise and fall of Taffy's breasts against his chest.

"You're not leaving much if it is."

"Love me like I love you?"

A love she'd thought forever lost had been reclaimed, cast off its fragility and put on strength. She would nurture their love with her life. Nurturing necessitated relinquishing guilt for her part in their painful past; loving freely was more fulfilling than being a flagellant. "*Absolutely*! Only. And always," Taffy vowed, punctuating each word with a gentle kiss.

"I know so well," Roam stated, doing the unexpected. Taffy stood stunned as Roam clasped her hands and bowed a knee in prayer. Her eyes filled as Roam thanked heaven for unending goodness and grace, asked the Lord's guidance and His pardon for premature, intimate indulgence—dedicated their lives, their forthcoming union to God always. Their 'amen's took flight and floated upward at the closing of a tender, poignant prayer.

Moments passed before Taffy managed, "That was lovely, Sweetness."

"As are you, Taffy Marie Ellis-to-be," Roam stated, standing. "My parents are most likely looking for us. You ready?" Roam questioned.

"No." Anchoring her hat, Taffy stood on tip-toe long enough to return Roam's love with the slowest, sweetest, deepest kiss she could. "Now I am."

"You wrong, woman, kissing me 'til I can't walk right," Roam complained, readjusting the front of his pants.

Her laughter fresh and pure as country air, Taffy squeezed Roam's hand. Together, they moved off. Taffy stopped suddenly. "The candle…"

Carefully Taffy retrieved the still lit taper, its glow illuminating her face. She stared into the incandescent flame, glimpsing there the life she'd lived these past several days since being awakened by a crimson dream that sent her running for a train.

Taffy saw a path littered with missteps and mistakes, yet covered by God's goodness and grace that had miraculously restored her to a wealthy place of closure, completion, and sweet beginnings.

Dreaming a divine path to pleasure and purpose, deep and wide as the ocean and equally without end, Taffy gripped Roam's proffered hand and gently blew, extinguishing the candle's flame, grateful for love given and love gained.

Down Home

AND

Up North Again

EPILOGUE

Miracles didn't fail to find the zip code of a small town called Bledsoe.

The morning after Roam Ellis left town leaving love behind, miracles came bearing gifts and grace even white law couldn't override. The hangman was hung-over, and Richland's General was short on rope supply. With insufficient evidence, Dempsey Dupre's silent next-of-kin, the lack of a corpse, and a questionable witness, Judge Thornton overturned a death sentence. With erratic manner-isms and mental deficits, R.J. Tinsley—a dolt and dunce and threat to none—was comical at best. Assuaging a modicum of guilt over Imogene's fatal end, Judge Thornton showed uncommon mercy and released R.J. to his father so that the widower rejoiced, receiving his son again.

Confused by his mother's absence, R.J. Tinsley sat in Tinsley's General, empty-handed, rock-rock-rocking until someone with pres-ence of mind put a puppy in his arms and helped him—despite his grief—to stabilize.

Once a bit steady, his father asked R.J. about the whereabouts of his dead kin, Dempsey. Preoccupied with his new puppy, R.J. couldn't clear his mind enough to tell. So a cursory search was con-ducted, but proved futile, leaving the location of Dempsey Dupre a mystery and fodder for terrifying stories children tell.

Weeks later, the well out back of the Turners' decrepit, abandoned barn would begin to crumble in on itself, creating a natural grave. He'd only meant to wash the bloodied man that carnival night, help him get clean again. Hands red and slick, R.J. lost his hold and dead Dempsey slipped. That well water would never be drinkable again.

⌒⌒⌒

The day after Taffy Bledsoe waved love goodbye, Up North, people of The Flats gathered around the perimeter of Truly Earl's front
yard, careful to leave room for the authorities bustling with officious
energy. Authorities cordoned off Truly Earl's plot-of-a-yard, yet the
little brown-buttered neighbor girl with freshly plait hair who carted
laundry for a living managed to slip past the crowd and around to
Miss Truly's backdoor.

A slip-of-a-whip, she went unnoticed, stretching her ears with
grown folks' business. What she saw made her eyes bulge and her
body quake.

He laid sprawled face-down, half on, half off the bed, an ice pick
buried in the back of his dead neck.

Blood dripped-dropped onto Miss Truly's dirt floor, pooling
about the deceased's discarded britches to create a muddy, rusty-red
mess.

"Get him out of here! I don't want him here. Get him gone!" Truly Earl screamed, smothered by clinging, crying daughters, five out
of six. Only one sat calmly beside the bed, the center of investigative
attention.

Jonnie Mae sat without legal representation, incriminating self,
long before Miranda had Rights. "Yes, sir, I stuck him."

"Anybody see you do it?"

"Mama and the girls were all gone…'cept my baby sis."

"Which one?" the officer inquired, lowering himself until eye-to-
eye with a young murderess.

Jonnie Mae pointed out the girl eleven months her junior, clinging to their mother, and crying worse than all.

"Care to tell me why?"

"Why what, sir?"

"Why'd you stab and kill this man?"

Jonnie Mae eyed her scuffed shoes her big sister had outgrown.
"'Cause he didn't listen. I told him not to, but he did it anyway. He
bothered my baby sis."

"Bothered her how?"

Jonnie Mae's answer was a dark, meaningful look that drifted
from the officer to the bed, the dead man's discarded britches, and
back to the blue eyes boring into her.

"That's how," she said. "But he didn't get far before that ice pick."

With a defeated sigh the officer stood. A firm grasp about the girl's arm, he pulled Jonnie Mae to her feet. "Find a wallet so we can notify the next of kin," the officious man instructed an obviously junior officer.

"He ain't from 'round here. From somewhere down south and I don't know nothing 'bout no kin," Truly Earl sniveled, rubbing a belly swollen with the seed of the man bleeding his blood on her floor. "And his wife's too uptown to care."

"Maybe his neighbors or a boss can be helpful. Was he employed?"

"Yeah, as a whoremonger at that Hughes Street brothel!" Truly Earl cracked in her distress. The officer's look was corrective. "He has his own business, owns that funeral parlor over on Maple." Truly Earl eked out a tear. "Try his neighbors if you want. He lives…*lived* in that funeral parlor of his. The name's Alfredo Freeman."

Serenaded by her family's screams, Jonnie Mae was led away, smiling. She *was* a good girl, not a promise-breaker. God *had* heard and answered a most repeated prayer. An ice pick was the something nice she could do for baby sis *and* Miss Taffy. Glad at God's goodness, Jonnie Mae left home with the law, finally feeling better than.

ACKNOWLEDGEMENTS

Time and again, while writing *Taffy*, a recurring theme of "birth" surfaced. Priceless friends encouraged me with: "Keep pushing! You're birthing a story." When I, like Chloe, was weak and weary with the birthing process, these, my beloved, midwives jumped in the pool and pushed with me.

Christine D. Lovely: Sis, I've said it before, but it bears saying again *and* again: THANK YOU! You were there, at the ready, letting me lean on you. You endured my sniveling, and—despite my countless requests and intrusions—you loved me through. You read *Taffy* when I thought she was ready, but she had a tad more developing to do. Still, you urged us on. Your feedback, legalese, and encouragement were priceless. We made it, with great thanks to you.

Ellie Townsend-Hough: E., your silence alone told me the "baby wasn't ready." So, I let her gestate. Hope you like her now.

Janera J. Miller: J., you're my steadfast encourager who makes me feel I can climb mountains. Sometimes I wonder what you see, but thanks for believing in me!

Jeline L. Gulley: My Ditter, the original midwife. Remember when *Taffy* was first born, way back when? She was gorgeous, but rough, and way too long! You read her and loved her like she was your own. I'm honored to share "our baby" with you.

June R. Powells-Mays: My Dear, you let me pick your legal eagle genius a long time ago, just so Roam could "talk intelligent" instead of out the side of his neck when unleashing his legal fusillade. Thank you!

Kimberly D. Davis, PhD: Kimmy-Kim, you have the ministry of "cheerleading!" Your endless enthusiasm and optimism are heaven-sent. You can lasso a storm and ride it to the rainbow. I *so* appreciate you!

FURTHER APPRECIATION

My Family: Mama, Briana, Jeline, Janaik, Aaron, & Niyah-Boo—my life is so rich because of you. Love you!

My Harrisons & Them: Mom, 'Vette, Patrick, Liz, Auntie Eva, Auntie Deborah, Missy, Katie, & all y'all—I appreciate & love you!

My Dinky: Stacey L. Knox (& Thomas)—you already know I love you, but it's sure nice putting it in print.

My Book Club: Literary Ladies Alliance (Camille, Christine, Debra, Fanita, & Ellie)—life & reading are enriched because of you.

My Editor: Michelle Browning of Magpie Editing—Thanks, Michelle, you trimmed the fat!

My Cover Artist: Sanura Jayashan—You are simply marvelous & a master in patience.

My Center & Circle, my husband and children: I feel a bit speechless, thinking about you, my most precious jewels! I'm elevated by your constant support. You're priceless and beyond compare. My husband of nearly 30 years, *Taffy's* beautiful face wouldn't have materialized on the cover without you. My babies, your light is magnificent. I shine because of *you*!

My Father, God, Master, Creator, Savior, & Everything: I saved the best for last, because You're never that! You are first and foremost. Who am I that You were and are mindful of me? You created, anointed, appointed and endowed me with Your gifts. That's incredible to me. Without You I'd have nothing to write and no skill to do it. I'm humbled in Your presence, and forever grateful. I bless, praise, worship, serve and adore You. I can never thank You enough for choosing me.

SUGGESTED QUESTIONS FOR READING GROUPS

1. The novel opens with Taffy's "blood-soaked dream." How does this dream filter throughout the book, or impact Taffy's decisions?

2. Upon her return downhome to Bledsoe, Taffy removes her shoes to run a race with Angel. She leaves those shoes behind and is found barefoot in several subsequent scenes. What is the significance of this barefoot state of being?

3. During a symbolic cleansing ritual, followed by the embroidering of the first Octavia's cotton sheath, NuNu tells Taffy after Taffy admits she can see the gift, Knowing: "God's gifts are in His image. So are you. When you know yourself, you've already glimpsed His gifting." Elaborate on what this means to you. (See page 45).

4. Describe the relationship between Taffy and Angel.

5. How does Rachel's upbringing impact her life and influence the horrific choices she made?

6. Should Taffy have revealed Rachel's wrongs to Thaddeus when her father first returned from prison? Do you fault Taffy for keeping Rachel's lie?

7. Before the reveal, did you at any time suspect that Angel was Rachel's child? If so, why?

8. *Taffy* deals with female powerlessness—or as the book says—the "unjust burdens of the female and weak." Outright examples can be seen in Jonnie Mae and the little "browned-butter girl" who carts laundry for her grandmother near the story's opening. In what ways is a lack of autonomy or power seen in the **adult** women in the story (Taffy included)?

9. Taffy's relationship with her mother, Rachel, is severely strained. Yet, Taffy is blessed with positive relationships with other mother-like figures and sister-peers. Discuss the impact of these relationships on Taffy's life.

10. Were you surprised by Jonnie Mae's reappearance at the end of the book, and her proving to be Taffy's "salvation"?

11. Both Taffy and Roam have "special calling" and rich, lengthy legacies. While Roam departs from his (i.e. preaching), Taffy upholds her gifting. How do said choices impact their individual lives?

12. In what ways do Taffy and Roam's personalities or ideals clash, and what ways do they complement one another, or keep each other in check and on track?

13. How would you define "Black manhood" as embodied by Roam Ellis? How does that embodiment reinforce or overturn notions of Black manhood today?

14. Did you, at any point of the story, think Angel was Roam's child? If so, why?

15. Which villain did you detest the most: Imogene, Alfredo, or Dempsey? Did their backstories enable you to sympathize with them in any way?

16. Discuss the instances where Taffy is required to exert and stand up for her rights with the men she loves. And in what ways does Taffy challenge the patriarchy of her times?

17. How does Taffy define herself? How does she exert her liberty?

18. In what ways does Taffy's life parallel NuNu's?

19. Did Taffy "owe" Roam knowledge of her virginity prior to intimacy? Why or why not?

20. Would you live in an all-Black town if given the chance?

21. *Taffy* is full of true historic events and personas. What new history or personages did *Taffy* expose you to?

22. Do you think Roam will be able to "quit the rails" and settle his travel shoes?

23. Were you able to suspend your contemporary sensibilities in order to understand or appreciate Taffy's predicament(s)?

PREQUEL TEASER

Taffy's grandfather, Matthias "Poppy" Bledsoe, isn't a pivotal character in the story. Yet, he founded the town of Bledsoe with his "blood and tears." In an impassioned conversation with Taffy, NuNu states: "Blood requires blood, and every drop your Poppy shed, I took it back by the pound!" What do you think happened to Poppy in his younger years?

SEQUEL PLEASER

Yes, God willing and with God's blessing, there will be a sequel! Who do you think the villain(s) will be?

ABOUT THE AUTHOR

Suzette D. Harrison, a native Californian and the middle of three daughters, grew up in a home where learning and literature were highly prized. Her literary "career" began when her poetry appeared in a volume of creative writing published by her junior high school. While Mrs. Harrison pays homage to Dr. Maya Angelou, Alice Walker, and Toni Morrison for initially inspiring her spirit and creativity, it was Alex Haley's *Roots* (which she read at the age of fourteen) that unveiled the tremendous power and importance of African American literary voices. In addition to being the wife of a university professor and mother of the most gorgeous children God ever made, Suzette is a cupcake proprietor who loves singing gospel-with-a-hint-of-jazz. She's currently working on her next novel…in between batches of cupcakes.

BOOK CLUBS & AVID READERS

Thank you for being the backbone of support for the literary community. Book Clubs, I would *love* meeting with you via Skype or Facetime for a discussion of *Taffy*. Please feel free to connect with me via one of the methods below.

WEB: www.sdhbooks.com
EMAIL: suzette@sdhbooks.com
FACEBOOK: SDH Books
TWITTER: SDH Books@Ariasu62

Blessings,
Suzette